Praise for Jason Guriel's *Forgotten Work,* the precursor to *The Full-Moon Whaling Chronicles*

"A futuristic dystopian rock novel in rhymed couplets,
this rollicking book is as unlikely, audacious
and ingenious as the premise suggests."
—*New York Times*

"A wondrous novel written entirely in heroic couplets."
—Ron Charles, *Washington Post*

"Strange and affectionate, like *Almost Famous* penned by
Shakespeare. A love letter to music in all its myriad iterations."
—*Kirkus Reviews*

"Guriel's bountiful celebration of connections
between art finds an inspiring, infectious groove."
—*Publishers Weekly*

"*Forgotten Work* could be the most singular
novel-in-verse since Vikram Seth's *The Golden Gate*.
Thanks to Jason Guriel's dexterity in metaphor-making,
I found myself stopping and rereading every
five lines or so, to affirm my surprise and delight."
—Stephen Metcalf

"This book has no business being as good as it is.
Heroic couplets in the twenty-first century? It's not a
promising idea, but *Forgotten Work* is intelligent, fluent,
funny, and wholly original. I can't believe it exists."
—Christian Wiman

"Jason Guriel's *Forgotten Work* is a sci-fi thriller
written in heroic couplets, and it is amazing."
—Micah Mattix, *Spectator World*

"Like the bumblebee that flies even though it shouldn't
be able to, *Forgotten Work*'s amalgam of epic poem,
sci-fi novel, and deep dive into rock-fandom gets improbably
airborne, a feat attributable not only to its author's large
and multifaceted talent, but also to his winning infatuation
with the diverse realms his story inhabits. I can't think
of a book that's more patently a labor of love."
—Daniel Brown, *Literary Matters*

"This is no novel for fans of 20th-century CanLit's plodding
linear plots of settling the land and alcoholism. This one is for
the boundary pushers and bohos, jazz snobs with their
fanatical attention to minutiae that allows them to feel
superior to those who do not know about what Bukowski calls
'the thing!' ... In an ironic and meta turn of the screw,

Forgotten Work has the potential to become the
object of the very kind of micro-fan obsession it explores."
—Micheline Maylor, *Quill & Quire*

"*Forgotten Work*'s biggest pyrotechnic is its form...
Guriel shifts comfortably between his formal constraint and
the more prosaic needs of the narrative. Guriel's formal
choice reflects his characters' obsessions with the past...
Through this playful postmodern fictionalizing,
Guriel signals the way that our approaches to past works
and traditions form flags to rally around..."
—Ryan Fitzpatrick, *Canadian Literature*

"It's an SF epic poem, an excellent ekphrastic entertainment
for English majors, a figment of imagination made real,
and the perfect discovery to make for yourself
in the hidden corner of your favourite bookstore."
—James Crossley, Madison Books

"In a class by itself, *Forgotten Work* is also
one of the best books of the year."
—Nicholas Bradley, *University of Toronto Quarterly*

"The heroic couplets of Jason Guriel's *Forgotten Work*
present complex and nuanced visions—
lightened by wit—of a dystopian future..."
—A.M. Juster, *Claremont Review of Books*

"Here's a verse-novel that is a sustained,
dazzlingly crafted, adventure into the 21st century."
—Molly Peacock

OTHER BOOKS BY JASON GURIEL

Technicolored

Pure Product

The Pigheaded Soul:
Essays and Reviews on Poetry and Culture

Satisfying Clicking Sound

Forgotten Work

On Browsing

The Full-Moon Whaling Chronicles

A Novel

Jason Guriel

BIBLIOASIS

Windsor, Ontario

FIRST EDITION
10 9 8 7 6 5 4 3 2 1

Library and Archives Canada Cataloguing in Publication

Title: The full-moon whaling chronicles / Jason Guriel.
Names: Guriel, Jason, 1978– author.
Identifiers: Canadiana (print) 20220474281 | Canadiana (ebook) 2022047429X
     ISBN 9781771965514 (softcover) | ISBN 9781771965521 (EPUB)
Subjects: LCGFT: Novels.
Classification: LCC PS8613.U74 F85 2023 | DDC C813/.6—dc23

Edited by Luke Hathaway
Copyedited by Emily Donaldson
Designed and typeset by Ingrid Paulson

Published with the generous assistance of the Canada Council for the Arts,
which last year invested $153 million to bring the arts to Canadians throughout
the country, and the financial support of the Government of Canada.
Biblioasis also acknowledges the support of the Ontario Arts Council (OAC),
an agency of the Government of Ontario, which last year funded 1,709
individual artists and 1,078 organizations in 204 communities across Ontario,
for a total of $52.1 million, and the contribution of the Government of
Ontario through the Ontario Book Publishing Tax Credit and Ontario Creates.

PRINTED AND BOUND IN CANADA

For my mother,
Shirley Guriel

and my daughter,
Annie

... I began to be sensible of strange feelings.
I felt a melting in me. No more my
splintered heart and maddened hand
were turned against the wolfish world.
—*Moby-Dick*

Scroll One

1.

Above the wharf, a moon had clarified
Itself: the third full moon since Thom had died.
("Wolf overboard!," they'd cried on deck, *en masse.*
"Beloved wolf," the priest had sighed at mass.)

The wharf was on a bay hemmed in by hills.
On one hill, near the top, a papermill's
Discarded water wheel observed the business
Of the bay. (The townsfolk wound white Christmas
Lights around its spokes in wintertime.)
The houses on the hills were painted lime
Green, fire-wagon red, and other vocal
Colours meant to indicate a hopeful,
Hearty people. Each house was a box;
From out at sea, the town resembled blocks
Set down by children's paws. It also twinkled;
Hanging orbs suggested sprites had sprinkled
Stars about the town. The hills gave way
To beachgrass, rocks, and gritty sand too grey
To call a beach. Waves crashed against the shore's
Indifferent turf, where stunted tuckamores
Were stooping, horizontal bodies tending
Landward. Wind had forced their limbs to bend

Toward, and tendril over, rocky ground.
But wind was not the only howling sound ...

A full moon meant a full wharf: werewolves queued
Up for a whaling ship. The wolves had crewed
Since they were cubs; they knew no other lives.
They stood on two paws, upright, blubber knives
In scabbards at their waists, and wore short slacks
With cable sweaters. Shoeless, they left tracks
When crossing sand or mud; when crossing decks,
Their lower claws would sing in clacks and clicks.
Their paws had nubs no wolf would ever label
"Fingers"; these could hurl harpoons, rig cable.
Finer work, like knitting scarves or scratching
On a scroll, required claws. (Crosshatching
Was the novice werewolf-artist's go-to
Move.) Wolf tailors used their claws to sew
Or cut strategic slits that let out tails.
(A sure paw could turn linen into sails.)
A paw's nubs worked like sheaths; a wolf's claws stayed
Concealed, though tavern wolves in need of blade
Were apt to whip them out.

                      The ship had docked
And dropped a shaky gangplank. Down it walked
A werewolf with a notescroll. "Shut your gobs,"
He said. His job was to disperse the jobs—
Two dozen in his charge—to strong and able-
Bodied whalers who could set a table,
Wolf the main deck, tie a sailor's knot,
Or be alone for hours with a thought
Up in the crow's nest.

                Cap pressed to his chest—
That studied sign intended to suggest

A sad sack's eagerness—the first in line
Approached the notescroll wolf.

                        "Um, Roddy Hine,"
The whaler said.

                The notescroll wolf made note
And waved the whaler onward to the boat.
The whaler donned his cap and shuffled
Up the creaky gangplank.

                    Breezes ruffled
Necks. Two seagulls, overhead, had lifted
Several heads in howl. Whalers shifted
On their haunches, huffing into paws.
One whaler's paw, his right, was wrapped in gauze:
A flophouse injury. The whaler tried
To play it down—"It's working fine," he lied—
But notescroll wolf said, "Sorry, b'y," and sent
The whaler home.

                The winding lineup went
Around a heap of tangled nets. It clambered
Up a hill and passed through several clapboard
Shacks, the siding muffling the surf.
A saying scored in pine—A Wulf's True Turf
Is Wat'r—hung above the entrance to
The first shack that the whaler line snaked through.
Inside, a nun, claws out, was tweezing ticks
From disrobed pelts. A chunky crucifix
Swayed as she worked. A white coif framed her furry
Muzzle. Often, sternly, she'd refer
More raucous wolves—the ones inclined to curse
The Moon or cuss each other—to a verse
Of John or Luke.

                The line passed through another
Clapboard shack. A wolf, addressed as "Mother"

By the whalers, served each one a plate
Of fried bologna, cod from Rabbit Strait,
And pickled beets. They licked their plates clean while
They queued. An older wolf who didn't smile—
Missing half an ear, its tip mauled off—
Received the plates and stacked them in a trough.
He wore a pair of ragged purple pants
And drank most nights. (He spurned the whaler's lance.)

The wolfish world was waking up from sleep.
For moonless days—or weeks—their souls would steep
In dreams. They'd come to when a full moon sidled
From its clouds. According to the Bible,
Which the whalers tended to believe,
No wolf had seen the sun since reckless Eve,
Her pelt exposed but for a leaf, had eaten
Cod she'd netted from the Pool of Eden,
Thus condemning wolves to lives at night:
From first glimpse of the full moon to first light.

But nighttime suited whaling; sperm whales kept
Their heads below the surface while they slept
For spells from dusk til midnight. Werewolf eyes
Could sift the night like netting—analyzing
Waves for sperm whales floating vertically—
Which made the wolf a natural enemy.

The whalers gored whatever they could get.
The schoolhouse rang its bell at nine and let
Its charges loose at midnight. (That would be
The Normal School, which covered poetry,
Seafaring, math, and ancient lupine thought;
The Other School, for Wayward Teens, could not

Afford a bell. The orphanage outside
Of town, a grim Victorian, supplied
The wayward students.) Shorewolves, "drypaws," hustled
Hard til two, harpooning shrubs that rustled
And extracting rabbits, lanced and twitching.
These wolves worked in happy darkness, stitching
Hems or hauling wagons. Six-ish hours—
Not much time to stop and nuzzle flowers
With one's muzzle—is about what Rabbit
Strait's wolves gave to work. They made a habit
Of avoiding small talk, worked their tails
Off, and, at most, might pause to watch for sails,
For cheering wolves returning to the shore,
Their dark pelts spiky-stiff with breeze-dried gore.

Of course, such cheering would be softer now,
Since Thom, who'd been hot-dogging on the bow-
Sprit, had gone overboard and smacked his skull
Three moons ago: a thump against the hull . . .

* * *

They'd found him easily. An oddly pleasant
Glow marked where he'd fallen: phosphorescent
Light that seemed to pulse within the ocean.
When they hauled him back aboard—commotion
Giving way to silence as they tried
To pump his chest—the phosphorescence died,
The glow's circumference shrinking.
                                        "Angels," whispered
One wolf. "Angels made that light." His whiskered
Muzzle, moonslick with a mix of tears
And sea spray, snuffled noisily. His ears
Were flat, his tail between his legs.

❧

                                        "What angel?"
Said another wolf, his voice disdainful,
Ears up. "Thom is *dead*." He spat on deck.
They gazed on Thom, a locket round his neck.
He'd never worn the thing before. "A trinket,"
Thom had said. His pa, who'd worked a frigate,
Bought it off a pire overseas
Some years ago. The locket bore a frieze
In gold: a ship afloat on abstract waves,
The waves as high and regular as graves.
That evening, Thom had worn it on a whim.
The whalers touched their paws and sang a hymn.

* * *

Sharp claws were pickling lyres in a tavern
By the shore: The Full-Moon Whaler's Cavern.
Some nights there were full bands like The La's,
The local troubadours whose gifted paws
Would bang out "Thar She Blows," a brilliant tune
The La's had stolen from their muse, the Moon.
Less gifted paws were swabbing tabletops,
Unlocking doors, unshuttering their shops.
A group of fisherwolves in waders cast
Off from the shore. A pair of pirates, glassed
In by a tavern window, eyed the harbour.
One possessed a pawhook, used to barber
Crewmates, while the other wore an eyepatch.
Plundering had lately hit a dry patch.

Soon, the ship had gobbled up its line.
The whalers with the know-how and the spine
Would work the sails. The wolves with twenty-twenty
Vision held harpoons. The cognoscenti,

Puffing pipes belowdecks, held the store
Of tall tales. (These wolves, bards, saw little gore.
They mostly sat and sang.) The "windward fang,"
The phrase a curio of whaling slang,
Consisted of a couple wolves with tough,
Elastic lungs. They'd mount raised platforms, huff
And puff, and blow out all the wind required
To propel the ship where they desired.

2.

The first time Mandy Fiction's novel bayed
At Cat, its spine had taken on the shade
And feel of fur: a wolf's coat. Cat ignored
It, walking on. The book fell quiet. Snored.

She wandered round the store and took a second
Pass. As she drew near, the softback beckoned
Once again—but this time with a howl.

"Christ's sake," Poe said, sighing. With a scowl,
He put down his MOJO, sidled round
His counter, grabbed the book (the howling sound
Increasing to a frantic keening), shook
It once emphatically, re-shelved the book,
And went back to his counter.

                                     Cat leaned in.
The coat the spine displayed suggested wind
Was running over it and ruffling
The follicles. The book, self-muffling,
Was mewing softly now. She tipped her head.
The title, sideways on the spine's fur, read,
THE FULL-MOON WHALING CHRONICLES. CHURN.
A hand-drawn windmill's blades began to turn:
The logo of the press. The animated

Spine stood out against the more sedate
And botless volumes all around it. (Poe's
Shop stocked a novel product: static prose.)

The fur and blades went still—then stirred again,
The wind on loop. The snobby sort of men
Who frequented Poe's shop did not abide
Their books on pixiepaper. Poe had died
A little when he'd bought the *Full-Moon*—part
Of someone's basement purge. He dealt in art,
He liked to say. *A Time of Gifts*. *The Old
Man and the Sea*. But shit like *Full-Moon* sold.

* * *

The next time *Full-Moon* made an overture,
It started barking blurbs designed to lure
A teenager: "'Eclipses *Twilight*,' *Slate*.
'An instant YA classic. I can't wait
To wolf it down again,' the *New York Times*.
'It grips you with its claws—and fang-sharp rhymes,'
Library Journal."
                                Cat was sitting on
The floor, against a shelf, a *Breaking Dawn*
Above faced out to signal "YA shit"
(Poe's words). This was the one wall he'd permit
Cat to obscure; his customers were after
Other, grownup matter: Peter Laughner,
Paula Fox, George Johnston, Slint, The Slits—
Great artists who had failed to have great hits.
Poe's customers dropped names that made Cat frown,
Cult poets she'd not heard of: Daniel Brown,
Bruce Taylor, A.E. Stallings, Christian Wiman,
David Yezzi, Vikram Seth, Kay Ryan.

She didn't know the artists on the hi-fi
Either; she was there to poach Poe's WiFi.
Laptop on her lap, Cat blocked a vital
Traffic artery. You had to sidle
Round the vinyl bin that occupied
Most of the floor, the bin a box inside
A slightly larger box: the disused freight
Container Poe had claimed and christened "Crater
Books and Discs." At one end of the box
Sat Poe, and at the other end, in talks
With someone hawking Something Something's *Greatest*
Hits, was Graham, Poe's part-time salesclerk, daised
At the buying counter. Dumbprint lined
The freight container. Someone with a mind
To circumnavigate the bin would have
To pause at Cat and, with a frown or laugh,
Step over her.

            "'A monsterpiece!'" declared
The *Full-Moon* shelved above her head. She stared
Hard at her screen and tried to focus on her
Work. A passing customer's red Converse
Stepped across her.

            Now, the shelf began
To buzz. Cat frowned. Kept editing. Her plan—
To post her latest zlog to ZuckTube—was
Beginning to disintegrate. Buzz buzz,
Buzz buzz, buzz buzz. She sighed, clicked save, and tipped
Her screen down. Faded denim legs, with ripped
Knees, stepped across her. Then, the howls started.

Cat looked up. The softback had outsmarted
Poe. Its pixiepaper, made of bots

Too small to see, had rudimentary thoughts
Like PLEAD or SHIMMY OUT. The bots could vibrate
Willfully and make their softback migrate
Inches. Thus, the book had edged itself
A shade beyond its neighbours on the shelf.
Much like a simple lifeform hatched on land—
Whose first test is to scrabble over sand
Toward the safety of the sea—the novel
Had a storeward thrust: part-crawl, part-grovel.

Cat put down her stickered laptop, stood,
And looked around. A cloaked man with a hood
Was rifling through the bin. A slightly seedy
Dude—the denim legs—lurked by the CD
Wall. Poe often told her, "Leave the books
Alone." (She'd creased the spines of Plath, bell hooks,
Kurt Vonnegut, and many more.) "It's not
A lending library." (She'd never bought
A book.) But Poe and Graham were busy at
Their counters, sorting media. So Cat
Tipped out *The Full-Moon Whaling Chronicles*.

The coat was gone. A crust of barnacles
Had climbed the cover, which resembled rusted
Hull. The wolf voice growled, "'*The* most trusted
Voice in YA.'" Cat, who'd read her share
Of smartbooks, shook the wolf voice silent. There.
She heard the slosh of waves now. Seagull cries.

"Put down the book."

　　　　　　　　　She looked at Poe. His eyes
Were on the CDs he was stickering.

Cat thumbed the thing, its pages flickering,
Then held it up. "I think I'm gonna borrow
This."

       "'Put down the book,' he said with sorrow."
Poe, mock sad, kept stickering. "He tried,
But no one paid him any mind." He sighed,
Then aimed the barrel of the pricing gun
At Cat. "Okay, a week. But when you're done,
There better not be creases in the spine.
And tell your mom I'm picking up some wine."

* * *

They'd been a couple, Poe and Cat's mom, Anne,
For several months. It hadn't been Cat's plan
To bring the two together. But: Cat's need
For Wi-Fi had, like Cupid, interceded,
Bringing Anne to Crater to collect
Her daughter.

       That first night, he'd somehow checked
His impulse to chew out the lovely, long-
Haired woman running fingertips along
The spines that rippled outward from his walls,
Their titles still, the woman's eyes a doll's:
A manga heroine's. The frown he'd been
Rehearsing for The Mom became a grin,
His anger fading as he followed her
Around the store and showed his customer
His shelves, the two of them in sync and stepping
Over Cat, the girl immersed in prepping
Some new zlog thing.

       Poe would later learn
Cat's mother's eyes (so blue they seemed to burn
Like welding flames or sea-refracted rays

Of light) were smarteyes loading text. Her gaze
Of wonder, then, was actually addressed
To eyemail: ads and postcards. Anne confessed
This over first-date drinks at Coffee Hack.
(Her choice: a Pumpkin Something. His: Large Black.)
The eyes, she told Poe, were installed before
She'd ever moved to Montréal. The store
Of built-up mail that filled her gaze whenever
Anne, ascending, left the Crater never
Failed to take Cat's mother by surprise.
(She should've known the zuck would find her eyes.)

Those with the means had taken out their fleshtech;
Pitizens preferred to live a rustic
Life. "But Cat has real eyes, naturally,"
She added—this bit rather hastily,
She realized later. "And a phone. For days when
Cat's upslope." Anne talked to flirty patrons
At the diner daily; she served tables
Jutting from the Crater's walls, fine cables
Sprouting from her uniform and swinging
Her across sheer rock, the cables singing
In the Crater's wind. So why was she
So nervous?
                Thankfully, Poe said that *he*
Still had a smartphone, even though his home
Was downslope, too, where phones could only roam
In vain to find their signals. "Never got
The smarteyes," Poe laughed. Still, he said he thought
That Anne's were lucky to be housed in such
A face. She thought that line a little much—
Looked down—but thanked him for it all the same,
Annoyed the eyes had made her feel, well, shame.

* * *

He'd parked his store, the salvaged freight container,
At the edge of Montréal's great Crater,
Near some stairs. As deep and vast abysses
Went, the Crater, rimmed with businesses,
Was busy. All along its upper edge
Assorted stairwells corkscrewed to a ledge
Ten metres down and several metres wide:
An unpaved ridge that ran around the inside
Of the chasm. Stores were cut from rock
And paned with pixieglass. A kid could walk
This ridge for many hours or descend
Another flight of steps (there was no end
To these) to reach the so-called "Second Ring"—
And so on. Thus, it seemed to drone and sing,
The Crater, as its people bid their farewells
To the upslope world and filled the stairwells,
Iron steps resounding with a din
The chasm's echo tripled.
                                        Cat lived in
A Fourth Ring pod her mother leased. It clung
To rock, and far away, the rock looked strung
With Christmas bulbs. Cat slid down to the iron
Ramp the Crater's founders had named "Byron
Avenue." (She tended to avoid
Stairs, prompting Anne to mutter, "Omivoid,"
The Crater variant of "omigod.")
She crossed the ramp and stood below her pod.
A ladder led up to its underside.
She started climbing rungs. A round door eyed
Her from above: a knobless wooden hatch
The ladder seemed to pierce. An optic latch,
Approving of Cat's face, went beep: all good.

Cat climbed up through the solid door, its wood
Grain rippling around the girl, her soles
Last in.
         Interiors of pods were bowls,
The furniture in frozen promenade
Across the floors and up the walls. Walls shaded
Into curving ceilings chandeliered
With chairs and lamps that righted as you neared.
Cat threw her knapsack up. It flipped to crouch—
A horror-movie movement—on a couch
Above, beside an unmade slab of bed:
Her patch of sphere.
            She walked, the space a treadmill,
Kitchen counters rolling down toward
Her. Soon, she'd reached her roughed-in bedroom. "Gourd,"
She said. Four planes resolved around her, fading
In and gaining mass, their atoms braiding,
Walling in the bed, the couch, and other
Stuff. (With gourd mode on, her prying mother
Had to knock.) The walls were pocked, shot through
With holes, the lacy kind that insects chew
In leaves. The pod was old, its mason bots
Forgetful; sketching gourd in, they'd leave spots.
But then most of Cat's stuff was worn and old.
The wiseweave blankets on the bed could fold
Themselves, but all the books and discs had come
From Poe's shop.
        Yawning, she began to hum
A pop song, "There She Goes," which Poe had played
For her last week. "A work of brilliance, made
By human beings in the 1980s,"
Poe had said. "Pre-zuck. Before this Hades.
Band was called The La's. From Liverpool.

They did one album. *This* song is the jewel."
He'd often turn to Cat and analyze
Some "great" forgotten work. He'd demonize
Pop music made by pixies, Cat his captive.

Cat kicked off her Converse, which, adaptive
To their turf, could grip and morph with it.
For fun, she flung one down—and hard. It hit
The floor and flattened slightly, as if slapped
Down by a spatula. The pink shoe mapped
Its structure on a length of floorboard, drawing
Streaks of wood grain up, the smartsole gnawing—
And becoming—flooring. Cat had hacked
The pink shoes' safeties; Kaye, her friend, had cracked
The code that kept the soles from fusing to
Just any surface. You could thrust a shoe
At someone's face, and if the kick was hard
Enough, you'd leave your target's kisser scarred.

While Cat's shoe snuffled at her bedroom's flooring,
Cat jumped on the bed and heard faint snoring:
Knapsack. Cat unzipped it. Dumped her laptop
And the borrowed novel, now in nap
Mode. There it stayed til evening, when Cat said,
"Please make yourself." The blankets on the bed,
Self-darning dunes, began to smooth, which caused
The book (its cover now a pair of paws
Armed with a long harpoon) to fall behind
The bed (where more books lay) and out of mind.

* * *

The next time *Full-Moon* howled, Cat and Kaye
Were bleating back and forth.

They'd bleat all day.
The active threads of Crater teens enlisted
Adolescent labour, which consisted
Of small children running notes from pod
To pod. These "Kids," a play on young goats, trod
The Crater's ramps—and sometimes caused collisions.
Like a flock of vintage, well-trained pigeons
Loosed from roofs, they'd started as a postal
Service, but then morphed into a social
Media utility that linked
The zuckless chasm. It was fun to think
In bursts of text, the Crater's teens had found.
They scrawled their notes on scraps of dumbprint, wound
Them into scrolls, and sealed them with a slug
Of wisewax. Small but scrappy Kids would lug
The scrolls, the so-called "bleats," in canvas sacks
Around the Crater's rings. The rigid wax
Would soften when it read the fingerprint
Belonging to the bleat's recipient.

You'd get some bleats you didn't want, like spam
From Crater shops or scrolls that were a scam.
Some bleats tagged others; once you read them, they
Were re-rolled by the Kid and borne away.
You could, though, "like" a bleat—or note dissent.
A small "b" meant thumbs up, a small "p" meant
Thumbs down.
The bleat loop Cat and Kaye had made
That night was closed; a single boy, arrayed
In wiseweave, moved between their pods, one bleat
In hand. A pair of Basecamps on his feet,
Two orange blurs that glowed, enabled him
To run along a narrow, crumbly rim

Of rock and even leap up on the walls
To pass pedestrians. A couple falls
A year were normal. Tolerated. Wiseweave,
Though, could amplify your desperate cries
For help or even airbag all around
You, to absorb the impact of the ground—
Provided that you landed squarely *on*
A ring (and didn't bounce into the yawning
Void the Crater's curving wall enclosed).

The book began to bark as Cat composed
A short bleat, standing underneath her pod,
The boy in wiseweave waiting.
                                        "OMG,"
She wrote. "That fucking book is howling
Again!" She drew a small face scowling
And rolled the bleat. The boy took off with it,
Along the iron ramp.

* * *

                              Above the pit,
The sky was dark; within, a galaxy
Of lights was winking on. What alchemy,
Cat thought, had turned the Crater's sloping rock
To firmament, the pods like stars? The shock
The missile had inflicted, when it struck,
Had mostly faded.
                            It'd been bad luck.
The missile (meant to terraform some land
In Nunavut) had swerved and plunged, disbanding
All the molecules that meshed to form
The city and its occupants—a storm
Of molecules the missile teleported

Into space, the very ground deported,
Bedrock banished to the exosphere in
Seconds. Montréal, now incoherent,
Came to mingle with the preexisting
Mass of exogarbage slowly listing
Round the planet. Z-Chute tech had shifted
So much global trash to space, the drifting
Waste had coalesced to form a shroud
That walled away the sun: the so-called "Cloud."
The stars were now the farfetched stuff of dreams,
The sky a slate.

                  A few years later, streams
Of immigrants began rappelling down,
Belongings on their backs. Some fell—to drown
In darkness or be swallowed by the horrors
Minds fill darkness with. These first explorers,
Though, had nothing much to lose. A ragtag
Group, they reached the First Ring, placed a flag, and
Set up camp. (The missile had left rings
For miners to traverse.) They lowered slings,
These pitizens, with animals and food.
They set up pods, made love, and birthed a brood
That learned to climb with ease.

                  The Crater's walls
Were strangely smooth at first, like rigid shawls;
The missile's tech had teleported out
A cone of earth and left a perfect spout
That tapered into darkness. Over time—
And as more fortune hunters tried to climb
The slopes—the walls assumed the look of rock,
Of flinty shelves.

                  The Crater seemed to balk
At Wi-Fi; smarteyes stopped receiving mail

And downslope dwellers learned they had to scale
The walls or climb the stairs to reconnect.
The Crater's founders lost the urge to check
Their mail or surf the zuck. Their offspring, though,
Were less romantically inclined. They'd go
Upslope to post on ZuckTube, say, or stream
A show. They didn't share their parents' dream
To live offzuck: an analog existence.
Cat herself had pressed, with great persistence,
For a pair of Apple eyes.
                                        The Crater
Could look nice, though. Citizens of Greater
Montréal would wander to its lip
At night, lean on a railing, watch each blip
Of light—which signified a life inside
A pod—blink on and shine. (She'd quickly dried
Her eyes the time Poe caught her on the ramp
Below her pod, her cheeks a little damp,
The swirl of stars below them.)

* * *

                                        Soon, two feet
Came clanging back along the ramp: Kaye's bleat.
Cat took it from the Kid and thumbed the wisewax.
Wax-bound pixies quickly analyzed
Her fingerprint. The wisewax seemed to glow,
Then soften. She unrolled the scroll.
                                        "So throw

It in the Crater!" was her friend's reply.
Cat laughed.
                        The Kids who carried bleats were spry
And patient. Cat's had turned around to offer
Up his back, encouraging his Author

(Kid slang for the bleater) to extend
The thread.
                  She wrote, then rolled the bleat up. "Send,"
She said.
              He hurried off across the ramps,
Toward the pod where Kaye lived with her "Gramps"
And mom.
               Cat turned and climbed back in her sphere.
The howling increased as she drew near
Her bed. She found the book where it'd fallen;
Howling had given way to bawling.
Cat retrieved it, shook it til it stopped,
And slid it underneath her bed. She flopped
Down on the mattress. Lay there for a beat.
Then stood and went outside to read Kaye's bleat.

* * *

A few days later, Cat and Poe were sitting
On a catwalk's edge. Small flies were flitting
By. The flies, in fact, were bonsai bats
Some hobbyist had zubered into gnats.

"I still don't get why we can't clear the sky
Of—omivoid!" She batted at a fly-
Cum-bat up in her face. "If we can fill
The sky with garbage, can't we find the will
To beam the stuff away?"
                    Poe raised a cup
Of coffee to his lips and, looking up,
Said, "They've politicized it. People on
The far right—old enough to've seen the dawn,
To've watched a fucking sunrise—actually
Believe the sun's a myth. It's factually

Impossible, but people spread all kinds
Of stuff onzuck. It's hard to break through minds
When they've been brainwashed, right?" He looked at Cat
And dropped his voice. "Don't tell your mother that
I said that."

        "Said what?"

                "'Fucking.'"

                        Catwalk rattled

As a Kid with bleats ran past.

                "I've battled

Assholes in my shop," said Poe, "who say
The sky—the Cloud—gets brighter in the day
Because of *ozone*. Dudes who say that climate
Change is bullshit. Or they'll say those violent
Storms you see onzuck are CGI.
Those vanished coasts? They claim it's all a lie.
These dummies get their facts from Russian bots."
He shook his head.

                A few more bleated thoughts
Ran past them, borne by Kids.

                    "What did it look

Like?" Cat said.

        "Mmm?"

                "The sun, I mean."

                        He took

A sip of coffee. "Well, you couldn't stare
At it directly, right?" He squinted. "Glare
Was crazy. But the moon was beautiful."
He drew a circle on the air. "A full
Moon was the best. This disc of icy light.
The thing was like a hole punched into night
Itself, you know. It looked so pure and clear."

He trailed off, gazing pitward.

> "That a tear?"

Said Cat.

> "Shut up."

> The pit was growing colder.

Cat edged closer, leaned against his shoulder.

* * *

Three days passed before the algorithm
Judged it safe to speak again, the rhythm
Of its bark iambically inclined—
A-ruff, a-ruff—as if a poet's line
Sang through its muzzle. Cat was lying on
Her bed, her gourd up. It was nearly dawn;
Her mom and Poe had argued through the night.

A-ruff.

> She noticed on the floor red light,

Which seemed, like pooling plasma, to be spreading
Out from underneath her bed and heading
For her piled clothing and the pair
Of Converse, chewing on the flooring where
She'd flung them. So, she felt beneath the bed
And pulled the book out. Wolf eyes, glowing red,
Were floating on the cover, which had turned
A solid black. The eyes, though, burned and burned.

The bark sped up. The book began to plead.
Cat thumbed it open and began to read.

3.

A lone wolf watched the whalers take their spots.

She'd climbed up to the water wheel with thoughts
Of scratching out a poem; Dorothy Stead,
Or "Dot," was sitting with a notescroll spread
Across her lap, her back against a spoke.
With one claw, she'd been etching words, each stroke
Removing ink, revealing white. (Her brief
And fluent flicks left writing in relief.)
But Dot had paused, claw poised. The moving boat
Below had caught her nose . . .
                                                    She spread the note-
Scroll further open, which revealed a fresh
And untouched stretch of ink-rolled scratching flesh.
Abandoning a roughhewn haiku on
The darkness in a werewolf's heart at dawn,
Dot started scratching couplets, pausing every
Line to brush away the "ticks," her reverie
Interspersed with automatic flicks
Of paw. (The tavern bards called ink-flecks "ticks.")
She scratched a title: "Scroll One: Whalers' Hearts."

The hilltop where she sat was cold, but Art's
Not comforting; it ought to make you suffer,

Claimed the tavern bards. "They comes from rougher
Stock," Dot's mom had warned her. "You're not going
To no tavern, Dorothy Stead." But flowing
Words—sung by the elder wolves with awe,
Delight, and reverence—never failed to draw
Her to the tavern's door. She'd lurk there, ears
Erect, absorbing lines and drunken cheers.

Dot leaned her head against the weathered spoke
And sighed. She wore a bright red hooded cloak.
Her sidesack held a spyglass and a scroll
Called *Ariel* (last howl of the soul
Of Wulvia Plath). Dot always kept some tangled
Cordage on her left wrist. Makeshift bangle.
Poet-wear.
            She looked to sea. The ship
Had dwindled in the darkness to a blip
Of light, the only whaler on the ocean—
Still as starlight but, in fact, in motion.
But a single blip of light was wrong;
A line of "buoys"—orbs—was tacked along
The hull. The ship resembled constellated
Stars, as if the heavens, relocated,
Were afloat.
           The teenage troubadour
Exposed more scratching flesh and scratched some more.
"The sea," wrote Dot, "was like the River Styx,
Where life meets death." She brushed away the ticks.

She sat beneath a buoy; wolves had strung
The hillside's trees with orbs. They'd also hung
An orb on every home. Each ball-sized moon
In miniature began to glow as soon

As moonlight touched it—but would start to dim
At dawn. The buoys offered wolves a slim
But helpful window to get home before
The sun rose. Whaling ships too far from shore
Dropped anchors when the light began to leave
Their buoys. (Cautious ships preferred to cleave
To shallows.) Several young wolves in the town's
Employ maintained the orbs. They'd take them down
As needed.

            Dot had always found the word
Confusing. "Buoy," as she heard it, blurred
The bright orbs with those things that floated on
The sea. "They helps us steer away from dawn,"
A teacher told her once. "That's probably why
They're called that." Buoys warned against the sky—
The sunlight.

            Someone was approaching, coming
Up the slope: a black-cloaked werewolf humming
"Thar She Blows." They stopped in front of Dot.
Dot looked up. Paige. The wolf seemed lost in thought.

"I thinks I'm gonna be a nun," Paige said.
"I rather likes the thought of being wed
To Jesus. Plus, no talking." Paige's prow-
Like muzzle faced the sea.

            Dot frowned. "A vow
Of silence? That's what *monks* take."

                   "Right, I thinks
I'll be a monk, then. Monks still get to drink."

Dot rolled her scroll up, slipped it in her sack,
And stood.

Paige turned to Dot. "I likes that black
Thing, though, that nuns are always wearing."
                                        "Habit?"

"Habit, yes!"
            They heard a rustle—rabbit?—
To the right, behind a shrub-shaped shadow.
Both wolves jumped, claws out, as if they had no
Choice but to attack the faceless scruff
And shake it still.

* * *

                    They headed down the rough
Slope. Not far from the wharf, they stumbled on
Another werewolf: Del, the late Thom's son.
The wolf was walking on his own, his paws
Behind his back. The paws were wrapped in gauze,
They'd heard. Some said that Del had punched a pane
Of glass in wordless anger. Others claimed
He'd clawed his wrists in anguish.
                                "Paige, let's walk
The other way," said Dot. She hated awkward
Moments.
            Paige, though, bounded up and said,
"It's Del!"
            Del waved. (No gauze.) He'd draped his red
Pelt in a mourning cloak, a heavy, shapeless
Bolt of fabric, which encouraged weightless
Spirits moonward.
                    "Paige." He brightened slightly.
Rumour was the werewolf wandered nightly
To a dock and contemplated leaping.

"You okay?" said Paige.

                      "Me mum's been weeping.
Otherwise, it's like he hasn't left."
The werewolf sounded numb, his voice bereft
Of feeling. "He was never home much any-
Way. He kept me mum up waiting many,
Many nights, b'y."

                  Paige was nodding; Paige's
Dad had had his share of drink-fuelled rages
Since her mom had died. He bussed plates at
The wharf, no longer stepped on ships, and sat
The night out on a stool. He'd wander off
For moons, then wake, his muzzle in a trough.

"I'm sorry, b'y." Paige wrapped her arms round Del—
Who looked surprised, as far as Dot could tell.
"I'm here, okay? You ever wants to talk."

He tried to smile, then resumed his walk,
Paige staring after him.

                      Dot sidled up.
"Poor thing," she said.

                "But such a lovely pup,"
Sighed Paige.

            "Let's go." Dot's voice had grown an edge.

"Ahem," said Paige. Her paw held out a wedge
Of moonlight, pooled in chain. A ship on waves,
The waves as high and regular as graves.

"Please tell me, Paige, you didn't fish his pockets."

Paige said, "Shhh," and tried to pop the locket
Open. "Rust," she muttered, frowning at it.
Both paws bearing down. "Great bloody rabbit!"
Giving up. "The thing is pretty, though.
And warm."

        A nearby buoy made it glow.

* * *

They'd reached the beach beside the whalers' wharf
When Paige first saw the mound at sea. It dwarfed
The ship, its moon-white surface bright and wet.
The mound had made the ship a silhouette.

"The moon is that?" said Paige. She looked at Dot.

Dot took her spyglass out. She stretched the squat
Tube—telescoping with a brassy click—
And raised the spyglass, squinting through its thick
Glass lens. It took a steady paw to frame
The frantic whalers. (Cubs would play a game
In school to master scopes: they'd try to track
A moving gull.)

        They passed Dot's spyglass back
And forth. The distant wolves were running round
The deck. (Their open muzzles had no sound.)
Beyond the ship, the mound—or island—loomed.
Up near its peak, a jet of something plumed.

"Volcano?" Paige said, passing Dot the scope.

Dot squinted. "No, that's water. Plus, the slope,
It's way too smooth." Waves broke against their feet.
"It's flesh."

They heard a distant horn—a bleat
Of SOS—and howls on the wharf.
They saw old Dickie Lush, the polymorph,
Come scuttling down the pier that jutted from
The wharf, his head a wolf's, his waist a drum
With half a dozen haunches. (Dickie's speed
Was that of something like a millipede.)
He almost never changed his shape these days.
He didn't like to draw the wolfish gaze.

They turned back to the sea. A horizontal
Line now spanned the mound, the ship (a model
Made of matchsticks from this distance) slowly
Turning as the line grew thicker.
                                        "Holy
Moon, b'y," whispered Paige.
                                        The line was soon
The top half of an oval: half a moon
Of black. A maw. The mound, now following
The ship toward the shore, was swallowing
Moon knows how many tons of sea, its maw
An arch above the ship, its lower jaw
Presumably a molared reef beneath
The ship and studded with a row of teeth.
The ship, in silhouette, dissolved against
The backdrop of the maw. The maw commenced
To close, became a line, and then was gone,
The mound descending as if being drawn
Back into depths, its edges foaming with
The water it displaced, the mound a myth
Already, drawing names from shorewolves in
A state of shock—The Thing, Leviathan—

And where the mound had been, the ocean bubbled
Briefly—rudely—then went still, untroubled
As a mirror, not a single sail
In sight, and that's when Paige said one word: "Whale."

4.

She had to drag Kaye to their first convention
In New Ottawa, an intervention
To expose Kaye to the world of *Full-Moon*;
Kaye had yet to give in to the pull
Of Fiction's book.
                    The girl at registration
(T-shirt crawling with an animation:
Werewolves in white kit and playing cricket)
Aimed a scanner-thing and beeped the ticket
In Cat's paw, a fake paw Cat had found
Onzuck. The registration girl had frowned—
Or so it seemed to Cat, who felt a touch
Self-conscious. After all, the paw, not much
More than a furry glove, a pouch of felt,
Was nothing like the custom silver pelt
The registration girl had teased out of
Her skin, a labour of obsessive love
That must've taken months. The pelt was bulging
From her sleeves, the cricket tee divulging
Fur, a silver fringe along its edges.

"Jesus, it'd be like pruning hedges,"
Kaye said, as the girls approached an arch.

"Shhh," hissed Cat.
                              It was a sluggish march
Inside. The arch scanned ticketholders for
A range of fleas and ticks. A homemade spore-
Bot had been smuggled into last year's Con,
A pixiepest that soon began to spawn
And spread from pelt to pelt, inciting rampant,
Itchy hives: a campaign of harassment
Perpetrated by the Ivory Troop,
Some Nazi thing. (They'd also spliced a loop
Of snuff film—several men dressed up as whalers,
Whipping shackled wolf cubs—into trailers
Screened at three of last year's fan conventions.)

Someone pushed past, sporting twig extensions
Braided into what appeared to be
A pelt of leaves.
                              Kaye whispered, "Hedges, see?"

Cat shook her head. "That one's 3-W."

Kaye stared at Cat. "My Catarang, you *do*
Know you sound crazy, right?"
                                          Cat sighed. "It's short
For 'Weeping Willow Wulf.'" She'd tried to sort
Out all the convoluted strands of fanfic
For Kaye's benefit. *The Green Organic
Wolves*, an onzuck novel, was about
A world where Fiction's wolves have come to sprout
A shock of shoots, transforming into trees.
("Their leafy pelts were ruffled by the breeze.")

They passed a booth for Amazon, which sold

Assorted *Full-Moon* stuff, and Young & Scrolled,
A press that printed *Full-Moon* books on rolls
Of pixiepaper that resembled scrolls.
They passed a kiosk for Wolfpack Salon,
A site where Moonheads tested theories on
Where Fiction was (she'd disappeared ten years
Ago), uploaded fanfic, shared their fears,
And talked about their hopes for *Full-Moon*'s rumoured,
Long-lost sequel.
                              "Right, I think I've humoured
You enough. Let's make a break for it."

Cat grabbed Kaye's shoulder. "Oh, you *will* submit,
Me cub."
                    The conference room—high-ceilinged, vast—
Spread out before them. Someone's homemade mast
(With crow's nest!) rose above the maze of stalls.
Above the din of white noise, wolfish calls
Ah-ooohed at will, composing dialogues.
The stalls sold posters; t-shirts; wooden clogs
Carved into claws by super fans from Holland;
Several types of milk derived from almond
Elements and popular with those
Who'd gone full pelt; in cardboard boxes, rows
Of resin statues, some of which presented
Full-Moon's wolves as manga types; fermented
"Shark," which mimicked what the residents
Fished out of Rabbit Strait (which evidence
Suggested was a reference to one "Cabot
Strait," a name some still used out of habit,
But which Zuck Maps didn't feature any-
More); assorted action figures, many
Loose and scuffed, but many Mint in Box;

A line of necklaces whose pendants, rocks
Of no distinction, were purported to
Have been recovered from the Reef (in lieu
Of Newfoundland), which scubabots had plumbed;
And several upright lyrebots that strummed
Themselves, each string dissolving into blurri-
Ness, as if plucked by a ghostly, furry
Paw and not the AI housed within
The bot, sea shanties mixing with the din
The Moonheads, thousands of them, made as they
Perused the booths.
                              A popup maid café—
Based on a fanfic titled *Full-Moon Coffee*,
From Japan—served omurice and frothy
Drinks, the maids in uniform, their fur
Tamped down by netting. (Netting helped deter
Stray hairs in food and seemed to be intended
To resemble fishnet, which offended
Some of *Full-Moon*'s more progressive fans.)
The café's walls were made, of course, of cans
Of Fussell's Thick Cream, stacked by steady paws.

* * *

The girls passed rooms erupting in applause.
They sat in one (behind a wolf whose flannel
Work shirt quoted grunge) and watched a panel
Manned by warring camps: the Classicists,
Who prized the source text, and the Fan-Tasists,
Who cherished works of fanfic that "disfigured"
Mandy Fiction's work. The latter—triggered
By what they believed to be a right-wing
Way of reading—felt that "texts, like light
Approaching prisms, are refracted through

Our selves. Moreover, selves themselves lack true
And stable structure." Fan-Tasists were apt
To implant pelts and cop to feeling trapped
In human "fleshsacks." Classicists eschewed
Implanted fur—they called this "going nude"—
And, comfortable as humanoids, wore bow
Ties, lauded figures like Jean-Jacques Rousseau,
Deplored the state of culture in defeated
Tones, read *National Review*, and treated
Full-Moon's first edition as if etched
In stone. They felt the Fan-Tasists had stretched
And mangled Mandy Fiction's true intentions.

"Fan-Tasists have marred the pure inventions
Of Ms. Fiction," said one panelist,
X. Goldberg, representing Classicist
Positions. "And with none of Fiction's style."
Something green—a tiny crocodile?—
Crossed his red Lacoste shirt's pixieweave
And snapped its jaws. "It's ego to believe
That anyone can write a work of art.
It's left-wing nonsense." Seemingly by heart,
He reeled off "Dover Beach" by Matthew Arnold.

The Fan-Tasist (they/them, in blue fur) snarled
Back, describing Goldberg as a "Nazi."

Goldberg, arms crossed, countered with "Ben Gauzy,"
"Locker Up," and other ancient curses,
Which, like certain quotes or Bible verses,
Carried meaning even if their contexts
Weren't well known.
                          "It's just a pissing contest,"

Cat said.

> As they stood, Kaye made a cup
> Of hands and hollered, "Werewolves are made up!"

* * *

Cat read the titles of some other panels:
"Queering Dot: Rethinking *Full-Moon*," "Flannel
Pelts: Grunge Fanfic Fantasies," "Commercial
Compromise: Exploring Controversial
Wolfwashed Dialect in *Full-Moon*," "Tricky
Dickie: Politics in *Full-Moon*'s Wiki-
Wars," "A Dire Strait: Decolonizing
Fiction's Landscapes," "Ancient Scrolls: Revising
Fiction's Early Couplets," "Shedding Selves:
The Palimpsests of Dickie Lush's Shelves."

They sat in on a panel on the meaning
Of the moon, which people had been dreaming
Of, and hadn't seen, for thirty years.
(The panel's title: "Hashtag *Full-Moon* Tears.")
Cat bought a t-shirt with the line "I was
A teenage werewolf," letters raised in fuzz
Implying fur. (The line was from a rock
Song by The Cramps, who'd dealt in B-film schlock.)
Cat bought a resin statuette: a hard-
To-find-ish Dickie Lush, his paw a shard
Of sharpened bone, drawn back as if to run
A body through. (Kaye looked at it. "That's fun,"
She said.) Kaye waited while Cat posed with bots
Whose fluid faces swirled to look like Dot's
And Paige's. ("Who are they again?" said Kaye.
The cosplay bots were made of pixieclay.
Cat groaned and turned away.) They looked at prints

Designed by *Full-Moon* fans (which made Kaye wince
In pain). They passed a six-foot, musclebound
And bearded fan who had a bonsai hound
Inside a purse. (Their red cloak was like Dot's
But long.) Cat learned to tie some werewolf knots
(E.g., wolf hitch) and stood in line to get
An autograph from someone who had set
The first edition's type. ("Wolf Medium!"
Said Cat, who gripped Kaye's shoulder. Kaye said, "Um . . .")
They stepped around the bonsai wolves fans led
Along the conference floor. (These house pets—bred
To be as small as squirrels, the space between
Their molecules compressed—would pause to preen.)
They saw some macros, too, but these were solely
Rabbits, relegated to the lowly
Parking lot, where conference rules were lax
And where the off-book, unofficial acts
Of fandom were permitted or at least
Ignored. (The rabbits—large as cows, each beast
Inside a trailer—seemed to quote the whale-sized
Rabbits from the fanfic *Dickie's Tail*.)
They looked at someone's model of the ship
Described in Chapter Two. A bo'sun's whip,
A tiny spool of rope the hobbyist
Had spun by hand, hung from a micro twist
Of iron on the vessel's mainmast. Chapter
Two was rarely reread, but still captured
Certain minds—the minds of kids who loved
To fuss with handmade models, soft hands gloved
In latex. (Cat leaned in and scrutinized
The ship. Its hobbyist had improvised
A hull from reclaimed driftwood, cut the sails
From vintage cotton, and used pixienails

Instead of glue.) They also walked through life-size
Dioramas. One young girl with bright eyes
Had constructed, based on Chapter Four,
The bedroom where Paige sleeps, her wolfish snoring
On a loop. The room gave off the smells
A wolf's den might—and had the jar of shells
In which Paige hides the locket. It was faithful
To the text, said Cat, but for a bagel,
Half-consumed, on Paige's floor of clawed
And wolf-worn tiles. ("It's a little nod
To Montréal," the bright-eyed girl explained.
"We're from there, too!" squealed Cat. Kaye's face looked pained.)
They waited thirty minutes for a screening
Of a documentary on the meaning
Of the "coast" and "Newfoundland" in works
Like Fiction's book. ("The submerged island lurks
In many texts," a voice said over shots
Of St. John's sunken buildings, filmed by bots
Presumably. "The choice to set a novel
On a coast—or picture Dickie's hovel
By the Wulvish Sea—is basically
A radical attempt at memory
And elegy.")

       Cat zlogged the Con. A tiny
Sphere—its surface covered with a spiny
Fuzz of microphones—flew out ahead
Of her as both girls walked. "It's cool," Cat said,
"To see so many Moonheads in one place."
Kaye's hand was up as if to mask her face
In protest while the sphere, a Rebel, eyed
The girls. Cat thumbed a phone-shaped thing to guide
The Rebel's shots.

       Her favourite sidesack—modelled

After Dot's, its wiseweave aping mottled,
Weathered twill—began to buzz. She tapped
Her left ear's silver stud, its surface capped
With pixies. "Hey," said Cat. "I'll let you know.
Two hours, tops." She tapped the earring. "Poe,"
She said to Kaye.

He'd dropped the girls off at

The Con. "Be careful," Poe had said, and Cat
Had rolled her eyes (though Kaye knew Cat was pleased
He'd made up with Cat's mom). He'd slowly eased
The scow, a rental, off the landing pad
And waved—and now was waiting (in the sad
Way of all chauffeur fathers) in a nearby
Coffee Hack.

* * *

"Last Walk: A Myth to Steer By"

Was the final lecture of the day.
An older prof—his beard an unwashed grey—
Climbed up on stage. His glasses seemed to dim
As people, Cat included, clapped. His grim
Expression, though, remained unmoved. He raised
A thermos, silencing the crowd, and praised
The previous presenter in a hurried
Monotone. His t-shirt's Dickie scurried
Briefly, then appeared to freeze and flicker.
(Buggy print?)

"Apparently that's liquor

In his thermos," Cat explained to Kaye.

Kaye squinted at the prof, who seemed to sway.

"He's brilliant, though," said Cat. "A rock star prof.
His zlog is gonna be a book with Knopf."

He'd barely started when he stopped, peered stage
Left, and (his face scrunched up in sudden rage)
Tapped on the mic. No sound. He made a sign
Like what the fuck. A voice cried, "Should be fine
Now!" So, he started in again—and shot
Stage left a thumbs up.
                                        Emmett Lux was not
A clotheshorse. In addition to the sloppy
T-shirt, he wore khakis and a poppy
That presumably was meant to mark
Remembrance Day, though it was June. The dark
Shades hid his eyes. His unkempt, springy beard
Was like the fluffy stuffing that appeared
To bloom from razored slits in sofas. Reading
From a sheaf of notes, he blended pleading
With annoyance—like he had a truth
To share but also, in his jaw, a tooth
That needed pulling.
                                        Kaye leaned forward, chin
On hands.
                        "I first met Mandy Fiction in"—
He searched the hotel's ceiling for the answer—
"2050? They'd just found my cancer,
Month before. That's when I read her master-
Piece. I've never read a novel faster.
Wolfed it down in two days."
                                        Scattered laughter,
Which he paused to frown at.
                                        "Shortly after
That, I wrote her. I was sick, beleaguered,

Really, by the chemo. But I figured
I should try her. Back then, no one thought
The book was gonna be a classic bought
By millions. She was private, but she'd talk
To fans. She'd even do a puppet walk,
I'd heard. And so, I sent this fawning postcard,
Never thinking she'd write back. The Coast Guard,
Off the shores of what was left of P-
EI, had puppets you could rent to see
The Reef. I'd asked her in the postcard if
She'd take a walk with me. A rental skiff
Would taxi puppets to St. John's. We'd log in—
Me from Tokyo, and Mandy, Hogtown,
Slang for New Toronto—while the puppets
Scuba'ed down.

          "She wrote me back in couplets—
I've still got the postcard. She was game.
She'd do the interview. 'The Whale of Fame,'
As Mandy later called it, hadn't yet
Consumed her. Turns out I was gonna get
The final interview she'd ever give.
The only thing I had to do was live."

* * *

They walked a stretch of silt a popup labelled
"Water Street." They walked northeast to "fabled
Signal Hill." Beyond the buildings on
Their right, the seabed's silt dropped off. The yawning
Pit was St. John's Harbour. Pincered strips
Of sloping land curved round this pit; their tips,
Just out of reach, defined a gap that vessels
Once passed through. The slope ahead had levels,
Houses on each one, their vibrant coats

Of paint now muted. Once, they'd gazed on boats
Below them, vessels hauling goods and cod.
But then the harbour rose as if some god
Had summoned it, the hillside's roofs now under-
Water, insulated from the thunder,
Rain, and other thrashings of the sky.
The windows of the homes watched fish fly by.

"This neighbourhood was called 'the Battery,'
Said Lux. "A bit like Dot's hill. Chapter Three."

The puppets, galvanized by human thoughts,
Took slo-mo steps. They passed unruly plots
Of seaweed that had swallowed up assorted
Homes. The conversation was distorted,
Laggy. He would leave a lengthy pause
Each time he spoke to her. One of the laws
Of puppet talk was letting awkward silence
Hang a little, to avoid a violence—
Cutting someone off.
                                    "It seemed like time
Had slowed," Lux told the room.
                                                    They came to climb
A hill, their heavy steps like steps in dreams,
The trudge of astronauts. Two pairs of beams,
Extending from the shoulders of the puppets,
Swept the seabed. Grubby orange doublets
Swelled their chests and made the puppet's heads
Seem tiny. Trailing tubes suggested dreads.
The heads were balls, their faces inset panes,
Glass screens that flattened features into planes.
Their economic limbs were afterthoughts
Of fleshless plastic.

Only in those spots
With upright, algae-shaggy street signs was
It obvious the ground was road. A fuzz-
Filmed hump defined the odd abandoned car.

"'It's outer space without a single star,'
She told me through the crunchy intercom."

They climbed and climbed. There was a winter's calm
About the place. A coat of snowy stuff
Furred everything. The ground released a puff
Of it with every slo-mo step they took:
Suspended silt in bloom. They paused to look
Back at the city they had trudged up out of.

"Mandy said her novel was *about* love—
Love of home. The home she'd had to leave.
'I wrote the book to find a way to grieve,'
She said."
                    They gazed upon the sunken city.
For a zuckcoin, you could play a ditty—
Something maritime-ish, with a fiddle
Adding local flavour—said the little
Text box that had popped up in the corner
Of their puppets' eyes.
                              "Not what a mourner
Wants to see," said Lux. "A tacky detail."

Lights were flickering in homes and retail
Shops below: the beams of other puppets
And assorted scavengers with buckets,
Scooping up forgotten treasure from
The Reef. ("A bottle of the local rum,

Called 'Screech,' might still be good—if you can find
One!" said a cheerful popup.) Tourists mined
The city daily. Treasure, though, was tough
To turn up; puppets had removed most stuff
Of worth.
        "She singled out a distant box,
One of those houses she described as blocks
Set down by children's paws. 'See that one there?'
She said. She turned to me. The dreadlock hair,
The floating tubes, were in her face. 'My life
Was in that house. My little boy. My wife.'"

He looked up, briefly, from his sheaf of notes
And said, voice softer, "They were late, the boats."

She turned and started trudging through the snow
That wasn't snow, toward the peak. 'Let's go,'
She said."
        They wound up on the parapet,
On Signal Hill. He had prepared ahead
Of time a set of questions. Someone's sub,
A limbless puppet writhing like a grub,
Swam past them, snapping tintypes.
                "What a thrill,
To pick her brain. I asked her if the hill
Where Dot writes"—here he pointed at the stage—
"Was *this* hill. Signal Hill." He flipped a page.

Cat looked at Kaye; her friend was staring straight
Ahead, engrossed.
        "But Mandy said, 'I'd hate
For you to think the book's that black and white.
Of course, the details sometimes bear a slight

Resemblance to the world I lived in years
Ago.'"
                She blinked out pixelated tears,
Low-res, as rendered by her puppet's face,
The screen set like a porthole in the space
That more expensive makes reserved for 3-D
Features: noses, lips.
                        "The thing was seedy.
Scratched-up plastic gave her tears and words
A poignancy."
                Quite suddenly, like birds
Possessed, they lifted off the hill and found
Themselves in flight. The rental puppets, bound
By policy, had been recalled toward
The surface.
                "But the Coast Guard hadn't stored
The audio or video." He sighed
And flipped a page. A storage disc had died
Before the interview had even started.
Fiction had already left—departed
From her puppet—when he figured out
Their walk had failed to tape. What's more, a drought
Was coming; this would be the very last
Talk Mandy Fiction, soon to be harassed
By countless rabid fans, would ever give.

"And yet," he said, "it was transformative,
That afternoon we walked beneath the ocean,
Just the once, our puppets in slow motion."

Lux stopped there. Stared at the lectern. Paws
And hands began to clap until applause
Filled up the room. He seemed annoyed and raised

A hand to still the crowd. The cheering, crazed
By this point, failed to stop. And Kaye, who'd balked
At *Full-Moon* mania, was slightly shocked
To find her own hands clapping as the prof—
Who took a swig of thermos—seemed to scoff
At all of this and, clearly irritated,
Left the stage.

* * *

           The floating scow was waiting
By the entrance. Domed with glass in which
A gap had opened, it looked kind of kitschy,
Like a flying saucer. As the rental
Pulled up, Poe said, through the gap, "Parental
Protocol suggests I ask you how
It was, I guess." Cat climbed in first, the scow
Adjusting to new weight, her bag's haul heavy.
Kaye had barely entered when the Chevy,
Revving, started rising off the ground,
Its glass still irising, a sucking sound
Suggesting liquid going down a drain.
The glass sealed with a pop. Poe found his lane
And merged with other scows. They looked like '60s-
Style bubble cars, designed for cities
Of forgotten futures.

                 "Great," said Cat.
She noted that the dome was like the hat
A sleuth will wear, the ceiling dipping down
The way fedoras do; the slumping crown
Of glass just grazed their heads. "But please don't kill
Us, 'kay?"

           "We'll see."

                The Chevy made a shrill

Whine as it flew through spaced-out rings of light.
These floated in the air as if the night
Were fabric, and the light rings, gleaming grommets.
Zipping past, the rings resembled comets
But in fact were still—and stayed that way,
Afloat, defining traffic lanes all day.

"I will confess"—Poe reading floating print—
"I might yet crash us into Parliament."
He found the skyway out of Ottawa
And back to Montréal.
                            Cat pulled her paw
Off. She began to rifle through her bag.
Kaye watched her curve of windshield, like a flag,
Begin to ripple as the scow got up
To top speed.
                    Poe felt for a coffee cup
And half-turned. "What's the deal, Kaye? You a convert?"
Far below, a bowl contained a concert:
Strobing stadium.
                        "I haven't gone
Full pelt," she said, and raised a hand to yawn.
She looked down at her phone.
                                        "You wanna stay
For dinner?" Poe asked. "Weekend ramen…"
                                                        Kaye,
Transfixed by phone, "My dad is coming. Next
Time."
            Poe caught Cat's eyes in the mirror. Vexed.
"Your dad's in town tonight?" said Poe. He knew
Kaye's father rarely showed.
                                    The Chevy blew
Past billboards: holographic panes announcing

Rest stops. One sign seemed to be denouncing
Immigrants. It could've been a prank
By hackers—or the platform of some rank
New right-wing party.
                              "Yup," said Kaye, her eyes
Still phoneward.
                         Nearing home, Cat said, "Surprise,"
And thrust a book between Kaye and her phone.
A *Full-Moon* paperback. "Your very own
Edition. And"—Cat reached to flip the cover
Open—"it's the classic text." ("Discover
Rabbit Strait as it was meant to be
Explored, with Mandy Fiction's artistry
Intact.")
            Kaye took it in her non-phone hand.
The cover showed a pawprint stamped in sand.

"It's dumbprint," Cat said, "which I know you're not
A fan of. But it's nice to read a bot-
Free book."
                    Kaye looked at Cat through narrow eyes,
Then turned back to the book. A decent size.
Not thick. "I'll think about it." She tried shaking
It; the thing stayed quiet.
                              Kaye would fake
Indifference til they dropped her off; she knew
Her father wasn't coming. But she drew
A little comfort knowing she had something
She could read that night—if only dumbprint.

5.

"Come in, come in," he said, already turning
 Round, as if the polymorph were spurning
 Both girls even as he let them in.
"Make sure you close the door." A dorsal fin
 Was jutting from between his shoulder blades,
 Emerging from a sodden pelt. "The maid's
 Day off," he said, "so mind your fur."
                                        The two
 Wolves stepped inside the stone-built hut. They knew,
 Of course, no maid had ever set a paw
 In Dickie's dusty home. A crosscut saw—
 A Cheshire grin with fangs—was hanging on
 One wall, above a fireplace. A pawn
 Sans chessboard stood upon a window ledge.
 Green moss expressed itself along the edge
 Of every stone in spurts. They noted shards,
 Which looked like shark teeth; scattered playing cards;
 Small bits of glass, which roiled in the glow
 The fireplace gave off; a domino
 (Just one, though) standing on the mantelpiece
 (A micro-obelisk); a centrepiece
 Shaped like a whale (and beached beside the fire-
 Place), which saw few feasts. A soft quagmire
 Of assorted quilts, which made a mound

For sleeping on. In short: a lost and found
That treated every trinket as a jewel
Worth preservation.

                       Dickie dragged a stool
Toward the fire, where a chair already
Stood. The stool looked weathered and unsteady,
Made by paws whose owner was long dead.

"One of you girls will have to stand," he said,
  Collapsing in the good chair. Frowning, Dickie
Turned as if he'd sat in something sticky.
"Bloody Moon." He'd left the dorsal fin
Protruding from his back. It drew back in,
Retracting into fur as if a great
White shark were slowly sinking in the strait
Of Dickie's pelt.

                Dot took the stool, afraid
To irritate the polymorph. Paige stayed
Beside the door, in awe of Dickie's store
Of junk and treasure.

                  "Close the bloody door,"
Said Dickie. He had slumped and spread a bit
Across his chair. His flesh appeared to fit
Itself to anything he pressed himself
Against. (But if he leaned against a shelf,
Paige wondered, would a stave of horizontal
Lines imprint his pelt?) He grabbed a bottle
On the table by his chair and watched
Paige scan the door, a slab of blue wood notched
With clustered, crossed-out nicks. Had Dickie cut
Each nick to mark a day? A moon? She shut
The door and Dickie grunted ("thanks," she'd come
To understand). He took a draught of rum.

"We saw you see the whale," said Dot.

                              Mid-swig,
He eyed her. They could hear a distant jig
Of fiddle from the tavern, fast and grave.

"It ate that ship, right? Like a living cave?"

He put the bottle down. "I did," he said,
And taking in the pair of them, "It did."
He turned to contemplate the fireplace.

Paige took a step inside the cluttered space.
The room was brighter than her eyes were used
To; he'd hung several buoys. Paige deduced
The shifter used them mainly for their light.
He didn't have a werewolf's night-proof sight.

A hutch sat in one corner of the hut,
A box for rabbits, darkly empty. "What"—
Paige searching—"*happened* to your rabbits?"

                              Dickie
Grimaced at the flames. She'd touched a tricky
Topic.
          "Were you swimming, Sir, to try
To find surviving wolves?" asked Dot.

                              An eye
Appeared to swivel round his furry head,
His snout still facing fireplace. It read
Dot's face, then ploughed its way back to its spot
Below the brow—and stopped.

                              "Perhaps I thought
A wolf or two might surface." Watching flames,
His wet coat gleaming. "Called and called their names.

64

Your teachers know you're here?"

                              "They cancelled school."
Paige took another step. She marked a pool
Cue, mothballed scrollsacks, whittled figurines.

He laughed. "I trust the School for Wayward Teens
Will soon resume its fine curriculum."

"Dot doesn't go there, Dickie. I'm the dumb
Delinquent." Then, Paige frowned. "So, *is* it true
You never fall asleep at dawn? That you
Can stand the daytime?"

                              "Yes, me skin absorbs
The sunlight, love."

                              She noted that the orbs
That hung around the hovel had begun
To dim—but only slightly. Soon, the sun
Would climb the sky.

                              Dot broke in. "Look, I heard
Me father. He said this was like the third
Time this'd happened, but the first time in
His lifetime. Said the 'shifter' might've been
Around the last time. Figured he meant you."

The whole head turned now. Looked at Dot. "And who,
Me love, are you? A wolf who likes to gawk at
Monsters, whale or otherwise? That locket,
Paige"—his voice now louder—"please restore
It to its shelf." He looked toward the door
Where Paige was standing with a paw inside
Her black cloak's pocket.

                              Turning round, Dot sighed.
"For moon's sake."

Paige set down the locket where
She'd found it. Pressed her paws together, prayer-
Like.

      "Paige, you said you'd check your paws," said Dot.
She turned. "I'm sorry Mr. Lush. She's got
A problem."

        Dickie snorted, "I'd say *you're*
The one who has the problem."

          "Look, Sir, more
Attacks are coming, right?"

          The shifter rose;
The girls stepped back. His wet pelt turned to clothes.
Pyjamas. As his fur changed, it expelled
A cloud of mist; the water he had held.

"I don't feel much like analyzing whale
Attacks with thieves. In any case, you'll fail
To earn the town's esteem if someone sees
You talking to the outcast—who's got fleas
Or so I've heard the town's cubs chant at playtime."

"Mr. Lush—"

      "Go *home*, girls. Nearly daytime."

* * *

They walked along the shore. A wind had drawn
Their cloaks toward the sea as if the dawn
Were tugging at them. They would have to hurry;
Wolves caught out of doors at dawn turned slurry,
Sleepy. Once the sun was overhead,
They'd topple where they stood as if struck dead
And sleep where they had fallen til the next
Moon. This would leave their helpless, shaggy necks

Exposed to passing predators—and worse.
Dot's parents used to say a horse-drawn hearse,
Steered by a furless ghoul, would pause to gather
Fallen wolves, the ghoul's mouth white with lather,
Dripping drool.

But Dot was full of rage
Right now, not fear. She'd walked ahead of Paige
For several minutes when, at last, she felt
A flying object—pinecone—strike her pelt.
She turned to find her friend's paws raised as if
To soothe the air.

"Dot, wait." She paused. A whiff
Of something in the air. Fresh meat? She shook
It off. "I didn't—"

"Paige, I wish..." Dot took
A breath. "I wish you'd think."

"That locket, it
Was like the one I took from Del—a bit
Warm, too." She looked up at the dark blue sky.
The sun would surface soon.

They heard a cry
From further down the shore. A gull was wheeling
Over someone. He was crouching, feeling
Something with what seemed to be a stick.
The figure turned—still crouching—and was sick
Upon the sand.

The girls drew near. Paige focused
On the heap beside the wolf and noticed
It had arms, but no legs left, its pelt
Encrusted with damp sand. A leather belt
Still cinched its waist, which ended in a tattered
Fringe of fur. The belt still had its scabbard,
Minus knife.

Paige turned, saw Dot had doubled
Over, paws on knees. The sea, untroubled
By the torso it had coughed up, broke
Against the shoreline mildly.
                                        He spoke
At last, the retching wolf who'd found the body,
Paw still gripping stick.
                                        "I think it's Roddy
Hine," he managed. "He was on the ship."

Paige gazed across the waves. A warming strip
Had lit the limit of the sea—a line
Of crimson light. She knew him, Roddy Hine.
One of the town's more introverted souls,
He'd liked to sit on piers, a bulging scrollsack
By his side. Such sacks filled Paige with dread.
One time, she watched him fish a scroll out, spread
The chapter on his lap. The scroll was thick.
The title on the sack was *Moby-Dick*.

* * *

"Scrollworm Roddy Hine," his brother called him
Several full moons later, in a solemn
Voice. No ships had shoved off on a search
For whales to spear; the town had filled the church.
The brother, in a mourning cloak, was standing
At a lectern near the front, expanding
On his sibling's life.
                                        "He loved to read,"
The brother told the pews. "A constant need.
He'd be at family gatherings, his muzzle
In a scrollsack. Roddy loved to puzzle
Over novels, stories, ancient myth,

And even poems."
                                    Paige was sitting with
Dot's family. Dot had stuck her whiskered snout
In Paige's window earlier. "Get out
Of bed. It's time." She'd dragged Paige to the service
For the whalers. Dot was feeling nervous.
She'd been asked to write a poem for
The funeral. ("Short," the priest had said. "No gore.")

"He sometimes wished he could've written tales,"
The brother said. "Instead of hunting whales."

A wooden werewolf on a crucifix—
Its muzzle ringed with thorns, its paws affixed
To wood with nails—presided overhead.
(Some paw had daubed on blood: two drops of red.)
A banner ran below from post to post:
"And Jesus howl'd, giving up the Ghost."

The whaler's brother stepped down from the pulpit.
Father Byrne, the priest, stepped up, consulted
Notes, and, squinting, peered across the pews.

"Dorothy Stead, who's heard her Moonlit Muse,
Will read a poem. Dot?"
                                    She stood and made
Her way up to the pulpit. "Flayed, I prayed,"
She read. "Prayed for the sunken whalers' hearts
Lost to the endless night, the sea's dark arts."
Her voice was shaky, but she read on to
The end, which noted that the sea was blue
Because its waves were sad about "the deaths
Of whaler wolves who'd drawn their final breaths."

When Dot returned, she found Paige growing restless.
"Bloody moon, the service is relentless,"
Paige hissed.

          Dot's face dropped. "You didn't like
Me poem?"

          "It was great. I loved the 'dyke
Of tears is bursting' part. It's just I've had
Enough"—Paige waved a paw—"of all these sad
Snouts. Thinks I'm gonna leave."

               "You can't leave now,"
Hissed Dot. "We haven't said the Wulvish vow."
Dot's mother glared at them.

             Paige pulled her hood
Up, clasped her cloak. She looked around, then stood
And sidled out. A cub had started reading
Goodnight Moon.

          The Big Bad Pire, pleading
For the mercy of the Lumberjack—
Who towered over, axe raised in attack—
Was featured on one window in stained glass.
Behind this tableau, wearing red, the Lass
Observed the two, her paws raised up in fright,
Her crimson, stained-glass cloak aflame with light.
Another window showed a sheep dressed in
Wolf's clothes: a false and woollen prophet: sin
Personified. Yet *more* glass: Luke 10:3,
Where lambs hunt wolves, a sign of devilry.

Paige walked toward the entrance, wolf heads turning
In their pews. The sea's waves, crashing, churning,
Reasserted as she pushed the door
Aside. The white church faced the foaming shore,
Its spire's cross like spume above a spout.

Behind it, to the north, the wood spread out.
A young wolf—maybe seven?—stood outside.
He held a long pole, hook-tipped; he was guiding
It toward an orb that hung above
A window. Hooking it with care—with love—
He bore the orb away, presumably
For maintenance. He headed to the quay.

A plan was formulating: find her father,
Toss the shifter's hut. They wouldn't bother
With his scrolls and junk; they'd get the locket,
Where she'd left it—see if they could hawk it.
Maybe, though, she wouldn't mention Del's,
Back in her room, inside the jar of shells.

Most nights, her father bussed plates by the water.
Now, though, he'd be drinking; sperm whale slaughter
Had been cancelled.
                              "Paige!"
                                        She turned to find
Del in the church's doorway. Just behind
Him, wolves were singing now, their howls rising.

"Where's me locket?" He was clearly sizing
Up the situation and, Paige guessed,
His own resolve. She conjured up her best
Look of confusion.
                              "Locket?"
                                        "Paige, I know
You took it." Del stepped forward, moving slowly.
"Give it back."
                    "I didn't take whatever
Thing you're rabbiting about. I'd never

Steal it, 'specially now, Del." Working up
A show of outrage.

                    Del, though, made a cup
Of one paw, tipped with claws, and thrust it out.

"I know you're hurting, but you're off your spout,"
Said Paige. A wave exploded through the silence:
Breaking on the rocks with frothy violence.

Del drew back the paw and frowned. "That thing
Was *his*." A soloist began to sing.
"They took it, Paige, right off his body when
He drowned. I'll never see me dad again."

"You hardly saw him when he was around."
She couldn't count how many times she'd found
Her own dad at the tavern; Thom was often
With him.

            Del's face fell. She tried to soften
Up her voice. "Look, Del, I'm sorry"—reaching
Out a paw.

               They heard a distant screeching.
Both wolves looked toward the wood, a thought
Between them: pires. Then, Del said, "I thought
I liked you, Paige." He turned toward the wood,
Unbothered by the screech.

                  She pulled her hood
So tightly that its black cloth made a cavern.
"Bloody moon." She turned toward the tavern.

6.

Kaye'd crossed the quad toward her bonsai dorm
Room when she saw a see-through, jerking form:
The day-use puppet Emmett Lux had used
For class. Its plastic carapace was bruised,
Graffitied. Untold pilots—often students,
Undergraduates not known for prudence
In their post-pub states—had steered the bot
Toward collisions. Lux, though, always taught
In grubby skin as if it were a nuisance,
Dressing up. The day-use bot's translucence—
Inner guts and gearwork on opaque
Display—was further proof Lux couldn't fake
An interest in appealing avatars.

The bot was meant to step between two bars:
A bear trap that secured the other rentals,
Still as statues. Each bot wore a dental
Guard: protection from the poachers who
Would sometimes pry the precious teeth from blue-
Chip models, those that looked more human than
The scratched-up, bulb-faced puppets frugal men
Like Lux preferred. But Lux was having trouble
Locking up the bot. It seemed to stumble
As he tried to stand it in the bear trap.

Kaye approached. "Professor Lux? You there?"

The prof's face turned within the bulb to face
Her. "Kim," it said. The face appeared to chase
Itself, a phantom trail of pixels lagging.

"Kaye," she said.
                          A macro dane with wagging
Tail loped past, a prefect in full gown
Astride the saddle. Prefects rode to town
In academic dress, an old tradition,
Dating back to when the stated mission
Of the school was educating sons
Of wealthy bot lords. (Silver arms with guns
For hands crisscrossed beneath a shield to make
The crest.)
                    Lux waved at dust the prefect's wake
Had stirred up. "Bloody fool," he said. He stared
At Kaye. "A little help, please?" He had snared
A foot inside the bot rack's workings somehow.

Kaye bent down to help. "I think it's dumb how
Prefects ride around, for what it's worth."
She got the foot reset.
                                  "The U of Perth
Makes decent zuckcoin charging assholes for
Their foolish dogs." He frowned at Kaye. "And your
Name's…"
                  "Kaye. I'm in your third-year seminar."

The pixelated face's owner, far
Away—and drunk?—was nodding. "Kaye," he said.
"Okay." A ding. The face inside the head

Dissolved. The head drooped slightly, bot bereft
Of animating spirit. Lux had left.

* * *

The sun was shining overhead, a fact
She wasn't used to yet. The Cloud had cracked
About a year before, and for the first
Time in her life she'd felt real warmth, her thirst
For light a thing. She'd seen the moon as well,
In all its phases. It would cast a spell
On people out for walks when it appeared.
They'd stop, look up, and point. Some even cheered.

Most governments had given up on solving
"Cloud Disintegration" (trash dissolving
On its own inside the exosphere)
And scientists were stumped; there was no clear
Cause for the sudden, stunning dissolution
Of the Cloud. The far right cried, "Illusion!,"
Claiming that the Cloud was still in place
And that projected stills of outer space
Were being cast by "globalists and Jews."
But there were many onzuck lies to choose
From. Some believed the reemergence of
The stars was proof of concept for God's love;
At last, the Second Coming had begun.
Still others, skeptics, argued that the sun
Was just a massive, flaming ball of gas.
New Marxists viewed the Miracle through class.

For Kaye, it was a thrill to see the moon.
She'd bought a long, commemorative harpoon,
Moon-stamped, to mark the moment. *Full-Moon* fans,

In general, were giddy. Nightly scans
Of moon-flush skies were written up and shared
On fan sites. Moonhead get-togethers flared
Up all across the globe when nights were clear.
Obsessive fans would meet #beneaththesphere.

* * *

Turning off the central quad, Kaye passed
A long wall, several metres high, of glassed-
In boxes: dioramas stacked like cinder-
Blocks. A waist-high moat—designed to hinder
Those who might feel tempted to tap on
The dioramas' windows—ran along
The bottom of the wall. Some panes were clear,
While others were opaque. Kaye paused to peer
Across the moat at one specific pane.
Without her body's presence to explain
The scale, the stacked-up boxes would've looked
Like normal condos, and the moat that hooked
Around the far end of the wall, a pliant
River. Kaye, though, loomed above: a giant.

Someone had appeared now at the pane.
Kaye knew that he'd be smiling (in vain).
His name was Owen. They'd hooked up, though only
One time. Frosh week. His dorm. She'd been lonely;
He'd been simply there, a boy who meant
Well. But he'd struggled. Floating near, consent
Bots (issued by the university's
Directorate for Dorm Diversities)
Had tracked the groping couple's every move.
At last, he'd stopped; he couldn't find a groove,

He'd said. She'd guessed that meant he wasn't hard.
A poster on his wall said "Avant-Bard."

She waved back, weakly. Then, she turned her head
(Kaye passed his window every day with dread)
And hustled to the far end of the wall,
Adidas crunching leaves. She loved the fall.
A flyer on a post displayed an ad
For Nick Drake's music, which was leafy. Sad.
Perhaps the pixiepaper had explored
Her mind to source an artist she adored?

The sky above was filled with pigeons; they
Were streaming from the campus coop, a grey
And looming turret in the centre of
The quad. (It made Kaye think of courtly love.)
The pigeons carried mail. Each one was made
Of pixiepaper, beak a 2-D blade.

She reached a booth: a tube of frosted glass.
The glass yawned open. (It had scanned the pass
Admissions had installed: a makeshift mole
On Kaye's left cheek.) A floating holo scroll
Began unfurling. Terms of Use. "Accept,"
She said. Unread, the scroll re-rolled. She stepped
Inside the booth.
            The hole the glass had made
Began to shrink, its curving edge a blade.
She knew that if she stuck a hand inside
The quickly shrinking iris—if she tried
To fuck with it—the glass would pause and *not*
Chop off her hand. But stupid kids had caught

Their limbs in glass before; she kept her hands
On knapsack straps.
                            The booth performed its scans.
The glass turned green: OKAY. She closed her eyes
And felt her body dematerialize
In seconds. When she opened them, she found
Herself indoors, the street's noise—background sound
She'd barely noticed—now abruptly muted.
It was as if her ears had been rebooted
At a lower volume.
                            Skin still forming,
Kaye stood on the doorpad in her dorm.
A beige and beat-up couch, its squat legs castered,
Rolled toward her. *Full-Moon* posters plastered
Several walls. A single sock, a widow,
Languished on the floor. One wall, a window,
Faced the lane she'd only just walked down.
She felt deep thumps; the prefect in his gown,
Still mounted on his dane, rode past her pane
Of glass. The whole room shook as if a train
Were rattling by.
                            The booth had scanned Kaye's "chasms"—
Basically, the gulfs between her atoms—
Then collapsed the gulfs a bit so she
Could fit inside her dorm. She'd read of flea-
Sized families, thousands to a tenement
In less-developed countries. Negligent
(Or fascist) governments were shrinking people
To a scale that had been deemed illegal.
Several global treaties had decreed
That bonsai hives designed for those in need
Could only shrink a person to a size

A healthy human eye could scrutinize.

And yet, as coastlines crumbled, countries shrank
And space became more precious. So-called "tank
Life" had become a low-cost option for
Communities retreating from the shore.
On campus, those in need of student aid
Were placed in tanks. More well-heeled students stayed
In full-sized antique dorms with pedigrees:
Old turrets, ivy, doors demanding keys.
(Those status-anxious types, who liked to dangle
Wealth, would wear their keys on belts; the jangle
Was a sign of class, while left-cheek moles,
Which bonsai dwellers bore, suggested proles:
A downcast, orphan folk.)
                                        Kaye shrugged her knapsack
Off, slumped on the couch—a quickish nap
In mind—then said, "Call Cat." The room's ring harkened
Back to vintage phones. The window darkened;
Cat's face filled it.
                        "Hey," said Cat, distracted,
Eyes on something else. (Her stream.) Foot traffic,
Pounding by the dark pane, passed behind
Cat. "I'm on Joyce."
                              The site, which dragged her mind
And streamed Cat's thoughts to several million fans,
Was always open. Cat had scrapped her plans
To be a ZuckTube star when Joyce first broke.
She'd moved to New Toronto, where she spoke
Her mind all day and made a living off
Of ads. (They'd try to blend into her slough
Of thoughts, but often stuck out awkwardly,

As Sponsored Content does. A memory
Of Phil—Cat's absent, bearded, shitheel dad—
Was often followed by some ill-judged ad
For razorblades.)

           "What's in your stream today?"
Asked Kaye.

         "This song Poe used to play. And Kaye"—
Now squinting—"you've shown up. Which happens when
We talk. There's sex stuff, too. Like, faceless men.
Stone torsos."

        "Well, that's creepy. Hope I'm not
Adjacent to the torsos. What's the thought
Of me?"

      "A nice one. 'Member when you helped
Me move and dropped my mirror?"

            Kaye's watch yelped:
Bespoke alert. She stilled it with a finger.
"Ah, the mirror..."

        "Yes, Joyce likes to linger
On one's grievous wrongs. It's pulled a tintype:
Heirloom mirror slipping from your thin white
Chicken arms, and then you're looking at
Me, pale and horrified. You say—"

          "'Um, splat?'"
Kaye finished. "I remember. What's the song
Poe used to play?"

       "This jangly thing from long
Ago. Called 'There She Goes.'" Cat's brow had furrowed;
She was reading comments.

        Kaye had burrowed
Into cushions. "So, we talked today."

It took a moment for her friend to say,
"Who's 'we?'" Cat's eyes met Kaye's—then widened. "You
Don't mean..."

Kaye nodded. Grinned. "He'd caught his shoe,
His bot's. I helped him out. And Cat, we *talked*.
He never talks to us. First class, he mocked
Some girl who'd introduced herself. Then started
Reading *Full-Moon*. Half the class departed."

"Yeah, yeah, I remember." Cat was doing
Something. Typing. "Sorry, chaos brewing
In my comments. Kaye, I don't think I
Can come tonight." She sighed. "Some fucking guy
Is making trouble. Posting Nazi shit."
Her eyes met Kaye's.

Cat never could commit
To plans. Still, Kaye forced out a grin. "No prob.
Tomorrow?"

"Yes! And Kaye, you met your prof—
Amazing. Not that many Moonheads get
To talk to Lux."

Kaye yawned. "I know." She'd let
A hint of sleepiness inside her voice—
To hide her disappointment. "Back to Joyce."

"Tomorrow, Kaye. Okay?"

"You bet."

Cat's face
Went out. The window brightened. Rolling bass
Approaching, steady. Not a macro's hooves,
Though. This was wheeled—and bumping sidewalk grooves.
A giant torso slid by, likely on
A skateboard.

Kaye stood up. "Wolfpack Salon,"
She said. The window dimmed again, displaying
Full-Moon's social site. Two werewolves (baying
At a full moon) flanked the banner, while
Several streams of posts began to pile
Up below. The site drew massive traffic—
Ninety million fans, who posted fanfic
Mostly. Mandy Fiction had controlling
Interest in Wolfpack Salon, where trolling
Was policed, bots booted right-wing jerks,
And amateurs could upload homemade works
Of fantasy.
           Kaye tidied as her room
Read posts. A wall-bound blue whale, edged in spume,
Began to spout: a cherished pixieposter
Cat had given her. A moon-white coaster—
Which had been Cat's coaster long ago
Before her fandom waned—began to glow.

* * *

The next day, Kaye walked into class and found
A new prof writing on the board. Kaye frowned.
The board said, "Sable, she/her," in a looping,
Leaning hand. Kaye watched her jot a coop
ID. A bobbing blond bun held assorted
Needles. Sable wore a rubber corset,
Ripped jeans, classic Docs, a necklace strung
With vintage anal beads (a trend the young
Had largely given up), and thick-framed specs.
The look, Kaye felt, said, "I have edgy sex,"
A little too insistently.
                  Kaye took
A seat, unzipped her bag, removed a book

(The dumbprint *Full-Moon* Cat had given her)
And, turning to a girl with cosplay fur,
Said, "Where's Professor Lux?"

                                        "He's gone on leave,"
The Moonhead whispered. "Someone lodged a grievance.
Public drunkenness. Or maybe reckless
Use of rental."

                        Kaye recalled the feckless
Prefect.

                Corset woman now arranged
Herself cross-legged on a desk. (He'd ranged
Among the rows, Professor Lux, unable
To stay still when teaching.) "My name's Sable.
Pronouns she/her. I'll be filling in
The next few weeks." She tried her warmest grin,
As if remembering a teacher needs
To smile.

                Kaye frowned at the anal beads:
Gap knockoffs. Clearly, Sable meant to come
Across as younger. But the look was dumb
And weirdly dated.

                        Sable raised a brand-new
Full-Moon, spine uncracked. "Your prof had planned to
Cover several things today. Let's start
With Chapter Six, page seventy-three, the part
Where"—checking notes beside her—"Paige is in
The wood."

                Kaye loved this scene. The werewolf's been
Rejected by her father, having sought
Him out inside the tavern. Paige had thought
He'd like her scheme: they'd steal the locket Lush
Kept in his hut. But Paige's father, flush
From Screech, had called her dumb, a mewling cur.

So Paige has run toward the wood, the fur
Beneath her eyes accumulating tears.
She goes the way she thinks Del went, her fears
Be mooned. She wants to tell him that she took
His locket; she can feel a harpoon's hook
Inside her conscience.

                    Soon, she can't hear waves.
Above, the trees have woven leafy caves.
She's deeper than she'd venture normally.
The orbs strung through the trees in orderly
Procession have thinned out. She starts to tire,
Slows her pace. That's when a cloud of pire
Bats—who occupy the deepest region
Of the wood—descends, a flapping legion.
Paige is startled by the cloud and screams.
The bats are in her face; the forest teems
With beating wings. The werewolf flails and starts
To run. The cloud is all around, then parts,
A flying something soaring through the hole
The bats have made: harpoon! It flattens, bowl-
Nosed, as it strikes the ground. (Kaye loved the awesome
Simile that Fiction used: "it blossomed
Like a small blast crater, viscous matter
Petalled out.") The bats begin to scatter
As the cratered bowl now tendrils up,
Tornado-ing in place to make a cup,
A torso, tendrils splitting off to form
Two legs, two arms. And where there'd been a swarm
Of motion stands a wolf-shaped . . . *thing* (Kaye'd struggled,
Though, to love this lazy noun), a muzzle
Pointed at the bats. It's Lush, still nude
Because there hasn't been time to extrude
A pelt. He draws an arm back like he means

To hurl a spear—then whips it forward, streams
Of arm now forking off like javelins
Which stay attached but pierce the abdomens
Of several bats above. He draws the pitchfork
In, the tines retracting, three bats twitching
On the tips. The pitchfork's mostly paw
Now, so he flicks the bats away. They claw
And scrabble in the grass a beat or two
Before expiring.

              "So what do *you*
Take from this passage?" Sable asks the room.

The class is silent.
              "I think I'd assume"—
Consulting notes—"the conflict stands in for
A larger conflict. It's a metaphor—
Vampire versus werewolf—for competing
Ideologies in YA." Beating
Bat wings broke the silence: someone's smart-
Book copy.
            Kaye said, "What about the art?
It's brilliant." Lux, an aesthete, mostly read
At them. He'd sometimes pause and hold his head:
Mock-awe at Mandy Fiction's artistry.

The woman's face turned stern. "The poetry
Is nice. But rhyme and meter re-inscribe
A bourgeois voice." She went on to describe
The book's accomplished, virtuoso style
As "conservative." She tried a smile,
But she looked concerned for Kaye.
                    Kaye smiled
Back. She raised a hand, and in a mild,

Even voice said, "When's Professor Lux
Returning?" Sable didn't give two fucks
About their prof, Kaye guessed.

                    The woman peered
At Kaye through narrow eyes. (You could've speared
A writhing fruit bat with that look, Kaye thought.)
"Real soon, I hope," the woman said.

                          She taught
Around Kaye for the rest of class, then handed
Back their first assignments. Lux's candid,
Snarky comments filled up every page
Of Kaye's brief essay, fussiness and rage
Suggested by the hand her prof had used
(A tiny one) and red ink. Kaye felt bruised,
Especially when she looked around and noticed
That her classmates' work was blank. He'd focused
All his wrath on Kaye.

                      "Your grades will come
Tomorrow," Sable said. A student's dumb-
Print essay never bore a letter; grades
Were sent by pigeon, in well-vetted shades
Of forest green, a safe and soothing palette.
This, thought Kaye, was wrapping up a mallet
In a leaf. Protecting profs from students'
First reactions was best practice: prudence
At a time when young minds might be triggered
By a D or even C, Kaye figured.
Kaye, for her part, was just happy to be
There, in school, discussing truth and beauty,
Grades be mooned. She didn't like to say,
Though, where she lived. When talk began to stray
To housing, dorm décor, what have you, she
Would gently steer her friends to poetry

Or politics.
                    Kaye headed to her dorm.
She'd pass on pub night, which she loathed. She'd warm
A thing of ramen, log on to the chat
Salon, then go and have that drink with Cat.

But when she beamed into her dorm, she found
A lamp was down, a pigeon flying round
The room. Official stationery.
                              "Roost,"
She said.
                It paused midair. The bird produced
Unfolding planes—its lower half a sheet
Of paper—while its wings continued beating.
On the sheet, the U-Perth crest began
To fade in, then was swapped out for a man:
The dean out on a run. He gasped, "Van Bree,
I'd like to meet with you tomorrow, three
O'clock. My rooms." The tintype shuddered. Started
Over.
         "Flock," said Kaye. The pigeon darted
To a distant corner of her dorm
Room. It refolded, landed, joined a swarm
Of milling pigeons Kaye would fireplace
At some point. Pigeons ate up living space.

They'd overtaken postcards as the main
Way campuses connected. ("Far less strain
On mental wellness," research had concluded.)
Sure, the pigeons constantly intruded.
Postcards, though, left smarteyed users facing
Stress alone. (Kaye's eyes, in any case,
Were real.) The campus sieve, a firewall

                    ∵

Enclosing U-Perth grounds, converted all
Incoming mail to pigeons, turning words
And tintype content into paper birds.

Her father's unread pigeons formed their own
Small congregation. (I want to atone,
Is what she guessed the missives said. To chat
About my errors.)
                          "Couch," she said, and sat.
The fuck the dean want?
                                    Sudden steps. A thump—
Room-shaking kick of bass drum—made her jump.
A massive blob had struck (and duly dimmed)
Her windowpane: a single circle rimmed
With brownish flesh, surrounded by a wider
Ring of lighter flesh. The glass divider
Of the window made the blob seem flat
And flush: the suction-cup-tipped tendril that
Some monster (risen from the sea) will whip
Out, press against the hull of someone's ship,
And suck with.
                        "Christ," said Kaye, who edged around
Her couch and backed away. She heard a sound:
A small group's laughter. Then, the sucker thing
Slid off her windowpane, unflattening.
Kaye watched as giant fingers pulled a kind
Of mesh across the sucker, now confined
In what—Kaye realized, angry—was a bra.
The sucker was a breast. She saw hands draw
A t-shirt down. The torso lurched away
And out of sight. The sophomores were at play
Or drunk—or both. They would've placed a plank
To span the moat, she guessed. A pub-night prank.

* * *

"You're gonna kill me." Cat's face, in the pane
Again, now frowned. "What happened?"

Kaye was straining,
Tiptoes, to retape her poster's corner.
It was blank, the whale beyond the border,
Out of sight. (The thing returned when Kaye
Backed off; she often heard the jet of spray
While in the kitchen.) "Monster Z-cup tit's
What happened."

"What?"

Kaye stepped back. "Little shits
Who snowglobe dorms." At last, she turned toward
The window, trying to seem laid-back: bored
But bracing for the bad news. "So, I'm gonna
Kill you?"

"Thing's come up. A gig. A *ton* of
Coin."

"Uh huh." Cat's life was never simple.

Grave, Cat touched a finger to each temple.
"Motivational thinking. I'm supposed
To think these thoughts, right? Way I'd do a post.
They're aimed at someone's workers."

"Whose?"

"Can't say."

She made a scribble motion. "NDA."
Then winced, teeth gritted. "I'm a shitty friend."

"You are." Kaye went to sit, the couch extending
Its upholstery. "Do they *know* they're being
Fucked with?"

79

"Well..."
                    "My Catarang, I'm seeing
Lawsuits here."
                    "They've still got agency,
I'm sure! They just can't wander aimlessly.
It's free will lite is all." Again, she placed
A finger on each temple. "'You won't waste
The company's time. You'll make your goals this quarter...'"

"You owe me drinks."
                            "'...you'll crush those slides,' that sorta
Thing. Just motivation. They're not bots."

Kaye scrunched her brow. "I'm sending grumpy thoughts."

* * *

The dean in mind, Kaye wore her one good coat,
A denim thing she'd cinched. She walked the moat
And saw Irene, a girl in SF Classic
Novels II, Kaye's second-favourite class.
Irene would sneer at works Kaye loved—e.g.,
Forgotten Work. ("The book's technology
Makes *no* sense," she'd say with a knowing smirk.
"It's set too close to now. It doesn't work.")

Irene wore sweats. Her left hand held a Rebel.
Reaching back, she flung a clutch of pebbles
Clear across the moat, towards the dorm,
The fistful spreading like a factious swarm.
Kaye guessed the Rebel, held aloft, was streaming
To the zuck. The students would be screaming;
Flying, full-size pebbles surely sounded
Boulder-loud.

Irene looked to the ground
For more grenades.
                    "That's quite an arm," said Kaye.

The girl looked up. Her smile fell away.
"The fuck you want?"
                    Kaye saw the right hand curl
To make a fist. She stepped toward the girl
And kicked her in the chest the way her father
Taught her years ago. Kaye didn't bother
Looking back; she heard the heavy splash
As she walked on, and then the body thrashing
In the waist-high moat beneath the lower
Windows of the dorm.
                    A smooth lawnmower,
Nosing through some tall grass on its own
(But slowly, like a sluggish curling stone)
Passed Kaye, then calmly passed the moat as well,
The sophomore's curses glancing off its shell.

* * *

The office of the dean was in an old
Victorian, its ivy like green mould.
(It wasn't bonsai; deans lived life to scale.)
She passed a bookcase. One book, with a sail
Across its cover—Lux's classic text,
*A Sloop on Choppy Waters: One Man's Vexed
Quest for his Fiction*—occupied the middle
Of the case.
                    She reached a door. A little
Nameplate on the wall said, "Keating-Wyatt
Chair in Content." Just beyond: a quiet
Waiting room. A steno sat behind

An empty desk. The thing worked in its mind,
Arms hanging creepily. It beamed at Kaye.
Kaye wished there was a prop to give its grey
Hands business—laptop, say.

                      "You're Kaye Van Bree?"
It asked, the question-tone a courtesy;
Its eyeballs—cameras—had already swept
Kaye's face, comparing it to thousands kept
Inside its massive database of faces,
Which stored info on the genders, races,
And identities of U-Perth's student
Body. Had Kaye spoken French, the fluent
AI would've switched its language.

                              "Present."

With a grin, it raised a hand, a pleasant
Gesture, flat palm up as if it bore
A plate. "Just to the right."

                      Another door,
And Kaye was in a messy, book-lined room.
The dean, behind a broad desk, had a plume
Of white hair and a short-sleeved button-up
With tie. The desk was chaos: lidless cup
From Coffee Hack, a holo of some kid,
Steep cliffs of paperwork, the cup's white lid,
And other strata'ed clutter. He was frowning
At an open laptop.

                "Please sit down,"
He said. He hadn't paused to look at Kaye.

She took a seat and scanned his bookshelves. Gay
Talese, Tom Wolfe, Clive James—the names of Dead
White Dudes.

"Your RA needs to change," he said,
And turned to her.

"RA?"

"Research Assistant-
Ship. The prof you're moving to's insistent
It be you. We had you slated for
The archive. Shelving dumbprint. This is more"—
He paused to ponder adjectives—"well, let's
Say fun." He slid a sheet toward her. "LUX,"
It read. The static letters of the name
Began to split and morph. The sheet became
A detailed CV—one Kaye knew by heart.

She looked up. "*He* wants *me?*"

"You'll need to start
Tomorrow. Tokyo. You swim?"

She shook
Her head.

"It's fine. The average road's a brook.
And gills are cheap now. But you'll want a pair
Of smarteyes." Clucking tongue, the dean was glaring
At his screen. He sighed. "It seems to say
You've got none."

"It?"

"Your file. We can pay
To put them in."

"I'm getting eyes?" she said,
The dean now typing something.

"They'll be red.
Our U-Perth red."

"What happens to my old
Ones?" Kaye looked worried.

Deadpan: "They'll be sold.

Celebrities like getting eyes as swag."
He looked at her. "You'll get a doggy bag,
I'm sure." He typed some more.
                            "I thought you guys
Were into wellness. Aren't you phasing eyes
Out campus wide?"
                        "You'll need to zuber twice
A week. We pay your travel. Emmett's . . . nice."
He'd added that perhaps to reassure
Himself.
            "But wait, you're absolutely sure
Professor Lux meant me? He massacred
My first assignment. Circled every word.
Wrote epic comments."
                        Eyebrows up. "I'd say
That likely means he rather likes you, Kaye.
Our Emmett never marks up student papers."
Squinting at her now. "You're from the Crater,
Yes? Your file indicates you came
Here on a scholarship."
                        She heard the name
And stiffened in her seat. "That's right." She never
Spoke of home.
                    He nodded. "You're a clever
Bugger, something tells me. With a spine."
He paused. Doubt crossed his face. "No, you'll be fine."
He shook it off and stood up. Kaye stood, too.

"One other thing," he said. "I'm guessing you
Know Emmett's on a little teaching break?"

She nodded carefully.
                        "He can't quite shake

A habit. Emmett drinks. He isn't well.
But he's our star, Kaye. Marquee name. You'll tell
Us how it's going? Keep us in the loop?"

"Of course. I'll send you pigeons. What's the coop
ID?"
      "We'd best use eyemail. I can give
You my address. Goes round the campus sieve—
Straight here." He tapped a temple. Something slightly
Different in his voice.
                    She grinned politely.
"Postcards. Sure."
                He beamed, then came around
The desk. Stopped at his door. "I hope you've found
Your res has met your needs? The dorms in my
Day were to scale." A small face on his tie
Was slowly morphing: Jekyll into Hyde.
"The rooms I had were rather large inside.
Of course, you're likely used to smaller spaces,
Being from the Crater. Hearty races
Live within, I'm told. Hardworking folk."

She forced a laugh as if he'd made a joke—
Then kicked herself for trying to appease him.

Suddenly, he frowned. "You're not Van Bree's
Girl, are you? Zach Van Bree?"
                    The name was like
A lance. (The bot had surely sensed a spike
In Kaye's heartrate.) "Yes, Zachary's my father."

"Ah, I thought so! He's my favourite author."
Puzzled. "Didn't know he lived inside

The Crater, though."

               "He doesn't," she replied.

The dean said nothing. Smiled.

                    Outside, walking
To her dorm, she noticed pigeons flocking
Overhead. Her irritation with
Herself was fading; Emmett Lux, more myth
Than man (and Mandy Fiction's greatest critic)
Maybe liked her work?

                 The parasitic
Pigeons up above were green, translucent,
Flush with light, each searching for its student,
Even as it helped maintain its squad.
One bird broke off and plunged toward the quad.
It came to hover just in front of Kaye.
The paper bird became the letter "A."

He sat her on the good chair by the fire.
Then, he rummaged through the soft quagmire
Of old quilts he pooled on every night
And draped a blanket over Paige's slight
And black-cloaked shoulders. Next, he boiled water
For some tea. He served it on a blotter,
Reimagined as a tea tray (Dickie
Had no friends to write). The cup was sticky,
Rinsed sporadically, but Paige said, "Thank
You," looking up. She sipped it, pulled the blanket
Snugly round herself. He took the wobbly
Stool and swore beneath his breath. A knobbly
Limb, a spider's leg, grew from his flank
And steadied Dickie.

             "There's no need to thank
Me," Dickie said. He raised a paw and coughed;
To hurl his body skyward—get aloft,
Then harpoon downward—clearly wore him out.
The breathless shifter made his mouth a spout
To draw in air, and frowned. "But love, what *were*
You doing in the wood?" He'd grown his fur
Back; fuzz had started forming as they'd walked
Toward his hut. The two wolves hadn't talked
The whole way there.

                    "I got into a fight,"
She said at last. "Me dad." She felt a slight
Twinge—guilt—remembering the reason for
The quarrel. Outside, waves crashed on the shore.
She stopped herself from glancing at the locket,
Worried that the shifter might pickpocket
Paige's thought. She focused on the flames
And sipped her tea. Her ears, erect, heard strains
Of someone's fiddle, distant, in The Full-
Moon Whaler's Cavern. Dickie's blanket—wool,
Dark blue, and threadbare—felt profoundly soft.
"I ran toward the wood. I goes there often."

"Bloody foolish thing to do," he said,
Annoyed. He crossed his paws. "They could've bled
You dry." His furrowed brow looked at the fire.
"Long ago, I crewed with one—a pire,
Name of Gaddis. This was when the ships
Would give the pires work. We took some trips
Together. Last one—*that's* the one our friend,
Well, interrupted." Dickie seemed to bend
The word.
             "Our friend?" said Paige.
                                He laughed. "The whale,
Me love." His smile dimmed. His coat went pale,
As if the shifter's body could assume
The colour of his feelings. Maybe gloom,
His default mood, explained his normal hue,
A storm cloud's. Maybe sadness travelled to
The outer tip of every follicle.
It struck Paige as a diabolical
Condition to be stuck with. She'd be blue
Most days, she guessed; her father, like the flue

That fumed above their shack, a charcoal black.

"Dot's dad said you survived the last attack."

He met her gaze. "I did." He stooped to reach
An object by his feet, a jar of Screech.
His forepaw lengthened slightly—spooky witchcraft,
Paige decided. Still, the furthest itch
Demanding paw would be accessible.
(Forget about the more incredible
Display: the forepaw forking up to skewer
Three retreating bats, a cool maneuver
Paige had yet to process.)
                                        Jar retrieved,
He said, "When I made shore, no wolf believed
Me. They assumed some foul play. Perhaps
I'd killed the crew. Perhaps I'd had a lapse
Of reason. Some wolves—those who'd never trusted
Me, who'd always felt deep down there must've
Been some wickedness, some devilry
Inside me—formed a mob. The 'cavalry,'
They called themselves. They took up whaling spears
And"—lifting up his jar—"submerged their fears
In drink. Then made their way to this, me modest
Dwelling." Dickie took a drink. "The hottest
Of the lot, well, we had words, let's say."

Paige put the cup down. "Tell me 'bout the day
You saw the whale." She drew the blanket in
Around herself.
                        As if lit from within
By incandescent memories, his coat
Began to glow a bit. His story, boat-

Like, started slowly, then began to pull
Away and pick up speed. The moon was full,
Of course, or else there would've been no tale
To tell; it's always full when wolves set sail.
Regardless, Dickie started, "Once upon
A full moon," talking all the way til dawn.

* * *

He'd been in demolition, blowing down
Old clapboard cabins, honest work the town
Approved because it could be done alone.
He'd hike up to some site, a lunch, bologna,
In a sack. (He'd make one paw a hook
And hang a buoy, so that he could look
Where he was going.) Then, he'd huff and puff
And blow ferocious blasts. Wolf lungs were tough,
But given Dickie was a polymorph,
His stretchy chest could swell and almost dwarf
His body. He'd release a breath and flatten
Everything in range—from grass to cabin.

Soon, the captain of a whaling vessel,
Anson Pike, caught wind of what this devil
Who changed shapes could do. He summoned Dickie
To the wharf.
                "I'll say right now, I'm picky
'Bout the help I brings aboard," he said.
The pair stood by the shore. The Lucy Dread,
Pike's ship, loomed over them. Pike wore a sweater,
Brown and frayed. An eyepatch, humpback leather,
Sealed one socket. "B'y, it's tough to find
Good wolves to fill the fang. They've got a mind
For drink. For mating. Most of 'em can barely

Blow out candles." Pike looked Dickie squarely
In the snout. "But you, you're never at
The tavern, are you, Lush? You're never sat
There with some young thing."

       Dickie shook his head
And looked away. He stayed at home and read
In bed most nights. He knew he'd only turn
Snouts at the tavern.

     "Wolves who likes to learn
Are wolves I wants aboard," said Pike. "Let's see
What you can do."

     So Dickie went to sea.
The *Lucy Dread* had three masts, staved with yards
And trailing line for paws to yank on. Shards
Of moonlight tipped the implements that stood
In racks on deck—in reaching distance should
A whale present—from toggling harpoons
To blubber forks. The ship was strung with moons.
From far away, the whalers' shore-bound wives
Could just make out the moonlit mincing knives
Of wolves bent over blubber, blinking like
Morse code. Not that they needed light, said Pike.
His paw-picked crew of wolves had eyes like owls.

That same crew met Dickie with hard scowls.
But the sidelined whalers, who comprised
Pike's three-lung windward fang, were mesmerized
When Dickie climbed the set of stairs up to
The platform (where the three wolves stood) and drew
A breath that seemed to comb their pelts. His chest,
A furry frog's, ballooned—and then compressed,
The bulge collapsing even as his muzzle
Opened outward like a blowgun's funnel.

Suddenly, the *Dread* jerked underfoot
And picked up speed. The polymorph's output
Had filled three sails—and lost three wolves their jobs.

"Yes, b'y," said Pike that night, "you *see* their gobs?"
He'd asked the polymorph to join him in
The captain's cabin for a nip of gin.
They sat on facing stools. The polymorph
Sniffed at his tumbler.

                   "Once we reach the wharf,
We'll draw a contract up," said Pike. He drained
His glass and beamed at Dickie. Dickie feigned
A cheery mood. He hadn't thought that Pike
Would *fire* wolves.

              The crew proved not to like
The polymorph. Perhaps, he thought, they feared
Him, or were angry. Anyway, they steered
Clear of the "shifter" as they came to call
Him, even as he saved them from a wall
Of fog, his lungs providing wind the sky
Had failed to muster. No one met his eye,
Including those who worked the very sails
His exhalations, hurricane-grade gales,
Filled up. Pike noticed this. He singled out
A werewolf who'd been rude—a tall and stout
Wolf called McGrath—and hauled him by the scruff
Toward the on-deck pillory, a "rough
Comeuppance," as the other whalers called
It. Clapped inside, paws cuffed, the werewolf bawled
All night.

          And when the sun began to creep
Across the waves, the shifter didn't sleep—
At least not automatically. She'd lift her

Rays above the sea's edge, but the shifter,
Though he needed *some* rest, had a stronger
Will than werewolves. Thus, it stayed out longer,
Pike's ship, than all other boats. Its special
Sun-proof asset could ensure the vessel
Made it back to harbour, even when
Its werewolves were asleep, their bodies zen
On whalebone cots.

* * *

          One night, stars overhead,
The crew arrived to find a figure bled
Of colour, pale and pelt-free, up inside
The crow's nest of the vessel. "Furless!" cried
One whaler, pointing. Dickie watched a deck
Hand rush about, his paws clamped on his neck,
As if protecting it. The figure gazed
Down on them, mute and curious, then raised
A *hand*. The gesture only sparked more cries,
Which drew Pike topside.
                  "Don't antagonize
The lad," he said, his paws massaging air
As if to soothe it. Pike peered up. "You'll scare him."
Cupping paws, he cried, "Apologies,
Me son."
        The furless man was on his knees
Now, arms across the crow's nest's rim, his chin
Propped on the arms. He'd waited out the din
His mere existence triggered many times
Before, sensed Dickie. Pires, stuff of rhymes
And bedtime stories, rarely left the wood.

Pike faced his crew, paws on his hips. "I shoulda

Mentioned he'd be joining us tonight.
He goes by 'Gaddis.' Says he doesn't bite."
He laughed and winked at Gaddis, who blinked back,
Unmoved. The pire's hair was long and black.
His placid, chalky face appeared to gleam—
But that was moonlight. Gaddis didn't seem
To get Pike's joke, or maybe he had heard
It many times before.
            "He'll be our bird—
Or bat, I s'pose—and fly ahead to see
What he can see. A ship, the *Friendly Flea*,
Near Cuddy's Cove, has got a pire now—
This funny little thing perched on the bow-
Sprit." Pike spoke like the pire wasn't there.

They drew the anchor up. Pike said the prayer
He liked to say. "No more me splintered heart
And maddened hand"—the captain left this part
As is; most would've swapped "hand" for a word
Like "paw"—"were turned against the wolfish world."
The prayer was from the scrollsack *Moby-Dick*,
Which Dickie'd read once via candlestick.
(He'd left about a hundred melted stumps
Of spent wax in his wake.) They gave him bumps,
The scrolls. His gooseflesh wasn't pointillist,
Though; Dickie's skin would gasp, its cry a cyst,
And during scary parts, his hide would bubble
Up or spring out of itself like stubble.

As Pike prayed, his whalers touched their paws.
When Pike declared "Amen!," they heard applause
And looked up: Gaddis, in the crow's nest, clapping
Earnestly.

The *Dread* set off, waves slapping
Hull. The wind was strong, so Dickie, hanging
Back, leaned on a mast. The werewolves sang
A rousing shanty, flogged on by the whip
The bo'sun cracked against the deck: a strip
Of leather. Dickie raised a paw to shade
His eyes and looked up. Gaddis, calm, surveyed
The sea, his long pale fingers on the crow's
Nest's rim. Some said that pires had no toes,
But Dickie couldn't tell; the pire's bottom
Was obscured.

            He'd read that pires common-
Ly were nude, as this one clearly was.
His skin was white and glowing, free of fuzz.
The groin, though out of sight, was very likely
Smooth and memberless. A fibrous, spiky
Husk eclipsed a werewolf's genitals
(According to the townhall's chronicles)
When he endured a pire's bite. His fur
Would fall in clumps. His features would defer
To furless ones, his paws, to hands. (The toes
Would fuse, however; each foot would disclose
A talon, which would split the skin.) The husk,
In time, would start to crumble. Soon, a musk
Was present, which the pire couldn't help.
It drew in suitors; nearby wolves would yelp
With longing when their muzzles caught a whiff.
But nothing could be consummated. If
The suitor came too close, the pire's pangs
Of thirst produced a pair of curving fangs,
Much like a cobra's. Pires saw well in the
Darkness, but the sunlight would disinte-
Grate them, leaving ashes.) Anyway

That's what the *chronicles* said.

"Head this way,"
Cooed Gaddis, in a voice both soft and high.
The pire seemed to vanish from the sky—
Then Dickie saw it: just beyond the ship,
The outline of a bat. He heard the flip-
Flap of its wings, a paper flutter that
Grew fainter as it flew ahead, the bat
Dissolving into darkness.

For a beat
Or two, the crew stood frozen. Then, a bleat
Of horn, the one the bo'sun wore around
His neck, woke up the wolves. One wolf unwound
A rope and crossed the deck. He cried out, "Hard-
A-lee!" His own chest twinkled with a shard
Of something whitish. Whalers liked to soothe
Themselves with bobbles. This one was a tooth,
A whale's, he'd strung himself. It swung with every
Step. He frowned at Dickie, lost in reverie.
"Hard-a-lee!"

The shifter said, "Aye, aye!"
Then climbed up to his platform in the sky,
Which faced the mainmast's sails. The water churned
Below the tacking ship.

The bat returned
Some minutes later. Then, quite suddenly,
The pire was above them—utterly
Inert, as if he'd never left. He pointed
Languidly, his long hand multi-jointed,
But the werewolves could already smell
The sperm whales sleeping just below the swell.

Two wolf harpooners leaned across the railing

Of the ship. Three shadows for impaling
Floated vertically beneath the surface.
Each wolf crossed himself to ward off curses.
Pike, emerging from his cabin, crossed
The deck. He joined them at the rail and tossed
His head back in mock-howl; no one made
A peep, of course.
                          The first harpooner weighed
His weapon in his paw. He seemed to heft
It knowing he held more than just a shaft;
A whaler knew his toggling harpoon
Condensed his soul. It glinted in the moon-
Light like a spear of lunar ice, its tip
A fat, inverted "V," designed to rip
Through skin and blubber. They would lower whaleboats
Next, the better to approach—impale.
The fat, inverted "V" would end up buried
In the sleeping whale, the line it carried
Basically invisible, the spool
Back on the whaleboat paying out, a jewel
Of sea spray indicating line existed.
One half of the "V"-tip, having twisted,
Would remain secure, but not forever;
Lanced, the whale would thrash and try to sever
Its connection. Several wolves would plant
Their paws and grip the line. The bo'sun's chant—
"Hang on!"—would focus effort.
                                        Dickie turned
Away. He'd seen the way the ocean churned
When werewolves hurled harpoons too many times
To count. The poems, songs, and children's rhymes
He'd grown up with left out the grisly details:
Blubber bleeding out; the way the sea wails

In the frantic, frothing key of foam;
The meaty slap of tail. He thought of home,
The hut awaiting him, a scroll, his fire.
Dickie looked up at the nest. The pire,
Too, had turned away. Their eyes met briefly,
Sharing something like a feeling—chiefly,
Horror. (Also: just how hard the world
Can be for monsters.)

                        Dickie heard the hurled
Harpoon impale the waves, the slightest splash—
And then more noise, as life began to thrash.

* * *

"Weeks passed," said Dickie, reaching for a poker.
"Pike's crew often played a drunken poker
Game belowdecks. Course, the table had no
Room for us"—the polymorph stirred shadows
Round the hut as he adjusted embers
In the fireplace—"the *only* members
Of the crew they'd leave out of the game.
I'd sit off to the side. Pike's wolves would shame
Each other"—putting down the poker—"slap
Down cards. The pire liked to take a nap
Outside in bat form. Hanging, he'd attach
To yardarms."

                Dickie stopped to strike a match;
He lit a whalebone pipe. "One day, I went
Above deck while the others played. A scent
Had nipped me snout. I found the pire smoking,
Staring at the waves. The noisy joking
Down below—as foolish whalers shuffled
Cards and guzzled Screech—was distant, muffled
Now.

"I joined him. Gaddis looked at me,
Then calmly turned his gaze back to the sea.
There was a clicking coming from the deck:
The pire's idle right foot, tapping—pecking—
At the wooden boards. The foot disgorged
A single curving nail, inferno-forged."

* * *

"Not one for cards?" said Dickie.

                              Gaddis, chin set
Slightly skyward, said, "I saw an inlet"—
Here, he panned his pipe, a bat prop—"scouting
Yesternight." His murmur seemed like shouting
To the polymorph; the pire rarely
Spoke.

          "An inlet?"

                              Gaddis nodded. "Barely
Even that. I've never noticed it
Before. By Kelly's Bay." He took a hit
Of pipe and blew a ring, a stylish wave
Of smoke, into the air. "Inside's a cave.
Quite vast." The pire's eyes were careful not
To meet the polymorph's, as if a thought
Might fly between them. "So, I flew inside.
Flew to the very end. I nearly died"—
His lips betrayed the flicker of a smile—
"Nearly died *again*. There was a pile
Of large rocks. An island. It was glowing."

Dickie listened, quiet. Time was slowing
Down, or so it seemed, the pire's words
Becoming thicker. "Something's nest—some bird's,
I thought, at first. There was a tiny star

Of light on every rock. Like caviar
But brilliant." Gaddis paused, exhaled another
Claw-tipped wave of smoke. "No sign of mother—
That is, if the little stars are what
I think they are."

                    ("What were they?" Paige, in hut,
Her wide eyes large and liquid in the flicker
Of the flames.)

                  The pire's voice grew thicker,
Deeper. "You and I should go and take
A look," said Gaddis, smiling. The snake
Fangs could be glimpsed.

                      "We all should go, me son!"
A voice declared behind them.

                  Dickie spun
Around and saw him. Pike.

                "We've had a dry patch,
B'y," the captain said. His leather eyepatch
Had been flipped up, socket like a cave.

The pire seemed unmoved. He blew a wave.

"It's been a while since we've had a treasure
Hunt," said Pike, voice menacing. "A *pleasure*
Jaunt."

* * *

      "We had no choice," said Dickie, stirring
Embers, fur retreating, then re-furring,
Mossing down his forepaw as he drew
Back from the fire.

               Paige, confused, said, "You
And Gaddis could've thrown Pike overboard

Or made your arm"—she stabbed the air—"a sword."

"I wanted the approval of the town"—
Voice lower—"and the crew." He paused to frown,
Annoyed now. "Plus, he would've cried 'sedition'
If we hadn't done the bloody mission."

"'Kay, okay," said Paige.
                                            The *Dread* set sail
For Kelly's Bay next full moon. Every tail
Was limp. The town's ships tended to avoid
The area; most maps displayed a void.
The scuttlebutt was that the furless had
Bewitched poor Captain Pike, who'd since gone mad.
Some whalers thought the trip a lark to find,
Well, moon knows what—perhaps their captain's mind.
In any case, the whalers traded fearful
Looks as Pike clapped paws, his voice both cheerful
And a little crazed. They left the wharf
And soon were flying as the polymorph
Filled up three sails.
                                            There were no other ships.
They passed a single cay; apocalypse
Had swept across this modest patch of rock
Some years before and left a slumping dock
(A ramp into the ocean) and a leaning
Shack (its narrow door a wolf's mouth screaming
Out the wind). The polymorph observed
An upright, uncrossed A: one bone that curved
To form a pointy apex. He was shocked
The arch was standing (how had wind not knocked
It down?). A pair of werewolves could've passed
Beneath the arch quite easily. At last,

He realized what it was: a bowhead jaw.
Pike took up next to him, in silent awe,
As if the jaw, erected years before,
Proposed a portal or a sign: a door
To somewhere else.
                              The waves were choppy, sheets
Of sea spray lashing pelts, the bo'sun's bleats
The only noise that pierced the seething surf.
In time, they reached a wall of rock. No turf
Surrounded Kelly Bay; its looming cliffs
Rose from the foam like paw-proof obelisks.

On Gaddis' advice, they found what seemed
To be a vertical incision seamed
With darkness: basically, the slit the pire'd
Called an "inlet"—so thin it required
Several wolves to lower, creak by creak,
A narrow whaleboat. No snout dared to speak.

Pike squinted up at Gaddis in the crow's
Nest. "Let's go, Dracula. Get on your toes—
Or toe, I s'pose." He laughed, then turned to Dickie.
"You, too, me old cock. It might get sticky.
We could use a paw, case of attack."
He turned; he wore a scrollsack on his back,
His arms in loops. The sack looked empty. Old.
(Moon knows where Pike'd dumped its scrolls.) A fold
Had warped the title. Dickie, though, could make
Out *Yelps of Innocence*, by William Blake.

* * *

He'd made his paw a lengthy oar, to steer
Them through the passage like a gondolier.

The pire's pale back faced the polymorph.
Pike sat towards the front. The sound of surf
Grew fainter. Cliffs reared up around them: walls
Of rock that would've howled back their calls
If they had dared to speak. Above, between
The cliffs, a strip of stars could still be seen.
The polymorph's left paw had curled to form
A single hook, a carbonated swarm
Of moths around a hanging buoy. (He'd
Removed the bright orb from a mast. "We'll need
This to keep track of dawn," he'd said, but Pike
Had snorted, turned to Gaddis. "Lad's not like
Us. Barely sees." The pire'd let this fact
Go by, untouched. He'd looked at Dickie, tactful.
"Orb makes sense.") The makeshift lantern swayed
Now, while the shifter's stretched-out right paw stayed
Submerged, its movements slight. It looked like he
Was petting something underneath the sea.

Fur parted on the back of Dickie's head;
An eye appeared and peered back at the *Dread*.
The vessel vanished as the passage swerved,
The orbs snuffed out.
               Ahead, the cliff's walls curved
Away. The narrow, winding passage widened,
Opened on a cove. The water brightened
Slightly as the whaleboat slid out under-
Neath the moon again. They looked in wonder
All around: the cove was vast but hemmed
By cliffs, as if a lake had been condemned
And walled away.
            "How does she get her eggs
In here?" said Pike. The bobbing of his legs

Vibrated through the boat. He looked back at
The way they'd come. "How could she squeeze through that?"

"I wonder," cooed the pire.
                                        Dickie let
Pike's question pass. He didn't want to get
Entangled further by engaging in
(And validating) chitchat with the gin-
Soused captain.
                                Gaddis raised his pallid, jointed
Anti-paw. Uncurled a finger. Pointed.

It was dead ahead, the cave a sneer
Of toothy rock. The polymorph felt fear,
A feeling Dickie hadn't known in years,
Not since his mother, leaving, pawed his tears
Away when he was fourteen, saying she'd
Be back, though Dickie knew his mom had freed
Herself the moment she'd resolved to go.

He stilled his oar. The boat began to slow.
The cavern, half-submerged, proposed a gaping
Mouth, the surface of the water aping
Perfectly the arch above to make
A lower jaw that floated on the lake.

"I'll scout ahead," said Gaddis.
                                        "No," said Pike,
Removing what appeared to be a spike
Of silver from the scrollsack, "you'll remain
With us for now, me son. And let's refrain
From flying off or trying something foolish."
Pike's snout, in the buoy's light, looked ghoulish.

Gaddis clasped his long hands: as you like,
The gesture seemed to say. He'd had a spike
Waved in his face before, thought Dickie, who
Himself had faced an angry wolf or two
At times. He moved the oar again, the boat
Now gliding through the cave.

                               "We're in its throat,"
Pike whispered.

                    Dickie panned his moth-furred lantern,
Lighting pitch-black patches of the cavern
As the boat edged on. The cavern's maw
Had disappeared behind them. Soon, they saw
A glow ahead.

               "That way," said Gaddis, who,
Again, allowed a languid finger to
Unwind, a wand with which he tapped the air.

Pike mumbled something to himself—a prayer?—
Then made a scooting gesture with his paw—
Let's go, let's go—his one eye wide with awe,
For even Pike, for all his madness, knew
That gods were near.

                  The island came in view:
A heap of rocks that lit the cavern's ceiling,
Strewn with tiny stars as if for stealing.
Just beyond, the walls began to bend
And meet. The island was the cavern's end.

Its rocks had room for several sets of legs
To roam. The boat drew close. The starbright eggs
Were evenly distributed across
The island: one per rock. A dark green moss
Had climbed the rocks and snugly covered them

As if each lambent egg, a precious gem,
Had summoned up the sort of jeweller's felt
A diamond lounges on. The werewolves' pelts—
And Gaddis' pale skin—had taken on
The spectral gleam the constellated spawn
Projected.

        Pike untied his sack, removed
A pawful of cheap lockets, crudely grooved
With etchings. Dime-store stuff. He passed them out.

His paws were busy, so a third arm sprouted
From the shifter's chest and quickly sleeved
Itself in fur. This extra paw received
The locket.

        "Put the mother's eggs in these,"
Pike whispered.

        Dickie's locket had a frieze
Engraved in gold. Two lovers were depicted,
Muzzles fused together. Dickie flipped it
Open. Empty.

        Gaddis', engraved
Like Dickie's, showed a ship on abstract waves.
The polymorph made note of Pike's, which featured
Something like a tentacled sea creature
Underwater.

        Gaddis had already
Stepped out. Pike had gripped a rock to steady
Them. The polymorph reeled in his arm,
Put down the buoy.

        Gaddis frowned. "It's warm."
He'd tweezered one egg with his fingertips
And brought the brilliant bead up to his lips:
"There, there." He placed it on his locket, clam-shelled

Open. Hand a platter, Gaddis clambered
Up the heap of rocks that was the island.
As he went, he plucked each waiting diamond.
Something—two things—clacked as Gaddis moved
About: the talons with which he was hooved.
A naked pire was as white as shark flesh,
Shoulder blades like fins. A slit of darkness
Split his gleaming buttocks into moons,
And as he scaled the rocks, two tiny prunes
(A sign of shrivelled genitals, of dregs?)
Revealed themselves between the pire's legs.

Pike started climbing, too, his locket lying
On his palm. He filled it quickly, flying
Rock to rock and breathing wheezily.

The shifter could've scuttled easily
Across the island, on the legs he sometimes,
Facing rough ground, millipeded from
His torso. But he thought it might be best
Presenting as a wolf to Pike. (His chest
Had drawn the extra limb inside; his standard
Arms had claimed the locket.) He meandered
Slowly, stooping for his stars, while keeping
One eye on the others. Was it sleeping?
Dickie wondered, thinking of the thing
That must've laid the eggs.

                              The pire, singing
Softly, skipped across his stones and stopped
In front of Captain Pike. He kneeled and propped
His locket open, lighting up his face.
His mannered gestures, mockeries of grace,
Were meant to be satiric. He was fooling,

Dickie realized. Offering faux jewelry
To a mad king.

        "Good!" hissed Pike. "Now close
It!" Pike had put his locket on. "How goes
It, shifter?"

        "Getting there," said Dickie, bending
For his eggs. They seemed to be expending
Way more light than even gems could hope
To throw off.

        Pike produced a brassy scope.
He eyed the way they'd come, then panned it all
Around the cavern.

        Mindful of his haul,
The pire snapped his locket shut. His face
Went out, the glowing eggs cut off, encased
In dime-store gold. He pinched the locket by
Its chain and held it out.

        Pike flipped his eye-
Patch up, exposing hole, and plugged the socket
With the scope. He reached out for the locket
Dangling from the pire's hand—but grabbed
The pire's wrist instead and, lunging, jabbed
A paw into the pire's gut. He said,
"I'm sorry, Gaddis. Even if you're dead
Already." Pike embraced the thrashing form
And looked at Dickie. "He's not even warm,
Me son."

        The polymorph stood frozen.

        "Like
You're gutting, Christ, a ghost." Pike pulled the spike
Out, and then stepped away, the locket in
His paw. The pire crumpled. "It's no sin,"
Said Pike. It seemed like he was talking to

Himself. "No sin." He gazed on Gaddis. "You
Can trust me, Dickie. On me life you can.
The pire's death"—he nodded—"that's God's plan."
The spyglass was still jutting from Pike's brow,
As if his mind had burst and formed a bow-
Sprit. Buoy light had washed his fur to ash.
He tossed the spike into the darkness. Splash.

"I trust you," said the polymorph. A claw,
A modest shiv, was forming in his paw
Reflexively, occurring to him like
A thought. He'd bring it to the surface, strike
Down Pike if need be. "Gaddis was a monster,
Cap. No court would call that werewolfslaughter."

Pike seemed lost in thought, his good eye dazed.

"You hear me, Captain? Captain?" Dickie raised
His voice. "Hey, Pike!"
                          Pike shook the fog away.
He looked at Dickie. "We should leave. It's day-
Time soon." He motioned with a paw. "Your eggs."

Dickie, wary, stepped toward Pike, legs
Extending, splaying root-like on the rock.
He stretched his arm and handed Pike the locket.

Pike received it. Held it for a beat.
"Well, these'll buy a wolf a whaling fleet."
He bowed his head and drew the lockets round
His neck. The cave was dark. They'd stripped the mound
Of every star. The junk-store lockets floated
Chainless on Pike's chest; the shifter noted

That the lockets' chains had vanished in
The captain's mane. The chains were cheap and thin
And breakable.
                        They got back in the boat
And Dickie grew an oar again. They floated
Back the winding way they'd come and passed
Below the rocky fangs that lined the vast
And yawning entrance to the cave. They glided
Through the cove, then through the slit provided
By the cliffs. Sea-level stars were dead
Ahead: the buoys on the *Lucy Dread*.

"Ahoy!" cried Pike, a sea breeze ruffling
His fur.
                        A flip-flap—someone shuffling
Some cards—approached them from behind. A whistle,
High-pitched, pricked their ears. The two wolves swivelled
Round to see a pair of bat wings bearing
Down on them.
                        The bo'sun's horn was blaring
Now—a warning maybe? But the bat
Was on them, flapping madly, flying at
The face of Captain Pike, who tried to shoo
It off. It seemed to strike his chest, then flew
Away, with moonlight in its mouth, a broken
Chain in tow. The polymorph was frozen
For a moment. Mesmerized. He gazed
On Pike, still waving at his muzzle, crazed.
The captain, less a locket, stepped back, tripping.

Dickie dropped the buoy he'd been gripping.
In a flash, he flung a long, unfurred,
Elastic arm at Pike. The paw secured

A locket of its own and yanked it free
As Pike fell backward, swallowed by the sea.

The fur on Dickie's chest appeared to split.
He stuffed the locket in the gaping slit.
Withdrew his paw. The edges seemed to melt
And fuse, the slit resealing, Dickie's pelt
Erasing any hint there'd been a rip.
He figured that the whalers on the ship
Were too far to have scrutinized the business
With the locket. Plus, the shifter's swiftness
Often baffled eyeballs.
                              Dickie noticed,
Then, a light below the boat. The locus
Seemed to be where Pike had fallen in.
He contemplated diving, as a fin
Grew on his back instinctively, protracting
Blade-like from his pelt—and then retracting
As he changed his mind. Perhaps the glowing
Was an omen. Dickie started rowing.

* * *

"Even then, I knew the glow meant trouble,"
Dickie said to Paige. "I had to scuttle
Up the ship. Pike's wolves refused to throw
A ladder. So, I climbed. 'We've got to go,'
I said." He leaned back in his chair, looked at
The fireplace.
                              "But what about the bat?"

"He vanished. Never to be seen again.
The locket, that's another story. When
They fished out Thom, he had one round his neck.

I gather, as he lay there on the deck,
No bugger thought to open it. Why would
They, though?"
                        He gripped his chair and, grunting, stood.
He squeezed past Paige. "I watched them carry Thom's
Corpse off the boat, some fool reciting Psalms.
Thom's wife and cubs were there. I saw this whaler
Place his paws on Thom the way a tailor
Might. He took the locket off and carried
It to Thom's boy, Del. The wife looked harried,
Off her spout. The whaler placed it in
Del's paw, then bopped the boy beneath the chin.
I had to squint a little, but I have
No doubt: Thom's locket represents one half
Of what's now left. The third went under with
Me captain. That one's basically a myth.
Perhaps Mum found it."
                        Dickie paused beside
The shelf where last time, lurking, Paige had tried
Her luck. He raised the locket by its chain
And walked back, grimacing as if in pain.
"The *other* half." He placed it on her paw.

She studied it. The wolves still shared one maw,
Their kiss intact. The locket throbbed.
                                        "It still—"

"Feels warm." He looked away. "Try not to spill
'Em."
                Paige gave him a look, then flipped the locket
Lid—and lit her muzzle.
                        "*And* don't drop it."
Dickie sat back down. He couldn't bring

Himself to look toward her, at the thing
He'd yanked off Pike so many years before.

Outside, a wave exploded on the shore.

The locket's bottom half contained a mound
Of caviar-sized stars, each star a round
And glowing bead. She looked at Dickie. "What
Do they become?" The lone sound in the hut,
The fire's crackle.
                        "Mobies," Dickie said,
And turned to Paige. "Their mother chased the *Dread*
Back to the shore. I think she senses when
They're in the sea. It happened once again,
When Thom fell overboard. The water makes
'Em glow—and call out. Nothing ever slakes
Mum's need to find her eggs."
                                    "What happened to
The *Lucy Dread*?"
                        He sighed. "The Moby grew
These tentacles. It plucked wolves from the deck.
The *Dread*'s below the sea now. Sunken wreck.
But that's a bloody story for another
Moon." He leaned to tip the locket's cover
Down, which dimmed the werewolf's glowing face.

She stood, returned the locket to its place,
And turned.
                "So, thanks for saving me."
                                    He waved
A paw. "I'd rather not see wolves enslaved
By bats." He noticed something in her eyes.
A warm look. "Please don't overanalyze

The gesture, dear. You've stolen quite enough
Of this brief moon." He'd shifted to a gruff
And slightly deeper voice—and pushed away
All thoughts of Paige's father. Soon, the day
Would start, the sunlight driving every creep
Who's had too much to drink (thank Moon) to sleep.
He'd seen her father stagger through the night.
The wolf had lost his left ear in a fight.

Paige turned to leave, then said, "What makes you think
I won't tell others?"
                        Dickie took a drink
Of Screech and shrugged. "I'd like to try to trust
A thieving wolf whose life's been less than just."

She thought about that. "Where did your mom go?"

"Wherever yours went, b'y. The Moon would know."

She nodded. Turned.
                        "We'll have to get that other
Locket," he said suddenly. "The mother
Will be back again."
                        This gave Paige pause.
She looked back at him. "I can get me paws
On it, I think." She pictured it inside
Her jar of shells.
                        "I'll bet." His smile wide
As if he knew.
                        Paige lingered for a moment
Longer. Then she left. Her pause was potent,
Dickie noted, pleased. His liquid form
Arced over to the good chair. It was warm.

8.

Kaye stood and waited, trying not to look
Toward the wall lined with her dad's new book.
She worried that the Japanese edition's
Smartspam would invade her field of vision,
Peer into her soul, and peg her as
The kin of Zach Van Bree, whose latest, jazzy,
On-the-Road-esque novel was the talk
Of literary zlogs. The book had clocked
Big numbers, leaving ZikZok critics rapt.

Kaye tried to focus on the "maids," who wrapped
Their wares with care. The maids employed brown paper
(Pricey dumbprint stock) and strips of tape,
Whose cherry blossoms—still, unanimated—
Popped against the old-school wrap. Kaye waited
As her tiny maid, back turned, worked on it:
Cutting, taping. Book Maid's staff wore bonnets,
Skirts, and lacy aprons—and stayed silent.

Kaye knew that she'd wince at Lux's violent
Shredding of the wrap when Kaye presented
Lux's find to him. Her prof resented
Wastes of time and chafed at flourishes
Like packaging. But style nourishes,

She felt, and anyway, Lux was the one
Who hated zuber booths and made her run
Out several times a week to pick up books
He'd bought. "Those booths," he'd say, "they get their hooks
Into the paper grain and change the smell."
He often likened Amazon to Hell.

The tiny clerk in French-maid getup held
A package out. Kaye took it, felt compelled
To bow low—"Arigato!"—turned, and hurried
Out the door.
                    Some bonsai hippos scurried
Close. They liked to congregate outside
The bookstore, humped like cobbles on the sidewalk
Or submerged within the river just
Beyond the sidewalk's edge. She'd built some trust
With them; when Kaye stopped by the store, she shared
Conbini chicken, hippo nostrils flared
Defensively, the grey beasts jostling
To claim the best spot.
                    She'd been hustling
All morning. Lux's coffee had to be
Procured from one specific stall, which she
Would have to visit last; Kaye's list of tasks
Was long.
           But as pedestrians in masks
Streamed past, a swarm descended: ads for giftwrap,
Vintage books. The algorithms, swift and
Ruthless, had dispatched their wasp-like spam.
No Zach Van Bree ads, though...
                        "Go on now, scram!"
She said, and waved the package at the swarm,
Which briefly scattered, only to reform

And hang back several metres. Smarteyes took
Some getting used to. She was loath to look
Too long at any object lest her pupils
Get ideas. (Smartspam had no scruples.)
Plus, she'd been so swamped she kept forgetting
She could mute invasive shit in SETTINGS.

As if tossing it, she shoved the book
Behind her shoulder and, without a look,
Fed Lux's rare find to her wiseweave knapsack.
Next, she threw a leg across the Humpback—
Floating where she'd left it, several feet
Above the ground. (It sank a shade to meet
Her weight, then nosed back to its standard height
For idling.) Its hull was milky white
And tapered like a whale, the front end wide.
She gripped the pebbled handlebars, applied
Some pressure (making contact with the bots
Housed in the Humpback, who now skimmed her thoughts),
And felt the hull thrum through her navy tights,
Her shoes in stirrups. Kaye set mental sights
On Lux's newsstand, where a dumbprint *New
York Times* was held for him. Her jacket grew
A sheen of fuzz as if anticipating
Headwind chill. A small screen, calculating
Several routes, displayed an hourglass;
The screen stood on a stalk. The Humpback's ass
Tipped up, encouraging its passenger
To focus. Then, as if she'd stuck a spur
Into its flank, the Humpback took off down
The sidewalk—screen abob on stalk—weaved round
Pedestrians, and, edging over, veered
Onto the river.

                    Mostly pixie-steered,
The Humpback zoomed ahead above the water,
Which went concave like the spot a potter
Presses on, the water smoothing out
Once she'd gone by. She passed a Tesla Trout
And Kia Prawn, and headed up a ramp,
Above which floated spheres, each sphere a lamp.
The ramp went up and up. It briefly split
In two around a high-rise, then reknit
Itself, the speed-smeared lamps above suggesting
Steady hyphens.
                    Soon, she came to crest
The onramp, Tokyo before her, endless
Towers ringed with water as if Venice
Had exploded skyward, buildings taking
Leave of what our eyes can take in, making
Their canals seem modest, more like moats.
Street-level Tokyo required boats,
But elevated roadways were amassed
Around the buildings' waists: spaghetti cast
In concrete. Gauzy tendrils grew between
The buildings, forming bridges. Giant screens
With roiling tintypes spanned the faces of
Some towers, pocked by static glass. Above
The towers, lights implied a grid of linked
And sliding stars. The stars were scows and blinked
As sunlight dinged them. Glare had taken getting
Used to—how the bubbled, sun-abetting
Scows would twinkle! They could take your breath
Away, if you forgot about the death
Toll: untold numbers snuffed out as the ocean
Had spread through the city in slow motion
Over several years, displacing lives

And driving millions into bonsai hives.
The Cloud was gone, the sun and moon were back,
But carbon had rebooted its attack.

* * *

The manse, where Lux lived, was a large, three-storey
Building owned by Ichiro Hatori.
Ichiro—a wealthy businessman
By day; by night, a *Full-Moon* super fan—
Had loaned the manse to Lux. It was a base
For research; when not teaching, Lux was tracing
Fiction (for his next book, *Lost and Found*,
He liked to joke).
                    The manse sat on a mound,
Roppongi Hills, which loomed above the city.
It was like the mound—a mountain—pitied
Tokyo, though distantly; it rose
Like something that's shrugged off a set of clothes
It has no use for. Water swerved around
Its base as if in deference to the mound.
Indeed, the inching ocean hadn't climbed
Roppongi Hills; an outer smartwall, slimed
With algae, had held off the rising tide.
The pixies in the smartwall's concrete eyed
Approaching shapes and sifted out the threats.
(The wall could bristle into bayonets.)
The wall enclosed exotic personhoods
And precious plant life. Several bamboo woods
Had been transplanted to Roppongi Hills,
Where people lived without implanted gills
Because they could; the wealthy had retreated
As the city's firm ground had receded.
Many called Roppongi Hills the "Wood."

The city's most exclusive neighbourhood,
It hosted several hundred homes and shops,
And boasted private airspace, pixiecops,
And parks that scanned your pupils for a toll.

The Humpback slowed down, mindful of its goal,
And settled on a lily pad the wall
Around the Wood provided. (Protocol
Prevented "outside" rides from entering.)
The girl dismounted, pixies rendering
The Humpback's hull invisible: a subtle,
Heatwave shimmer that appeared to ruffle
Tintypes on the wall behind, looped ads
For Prada and Hermès. The other pads
That jutted from the wall were occupied
By heatwave shimmer, too, but one flash ride,
A Maserati Swordfish, had been left
Unshrouded. Showing off. (Its anti-theft
Response, Kaye figured, would be detrimental
To one's health.) The pads bobbed on a gentle
Current.
          Kaye approached the wall, which seemed
To yawn: a door. The pixieconcrete teemed
With Burberry tartan, the black and red
Lines warping slightly as the doorway spread,
Like brickwork bending in a funhouse mirror.
Kaye stepped through—deep breath—and as she cleared her
Door, it quickly shrank, the ad reforming.
On its other side, the wall, performing
Permanence, looked made of stones, a soothing,
Rough-hewn sight. (A hand would find it smooth
As glass, though.)
                    Kaye walked up a path, a grove

Of bamboo trees on either side. A stove
Approached her: black, Victorian, and squat.
It scuttled quickly, fluent as a bot,
Though residents preferred the term "enchanted
Object." Its oven was its brainpan, canted
Forward slightly on four bulbous thighs,
Which tapered to fine points. Large manga eyes,
The left one monocled, were set above
The oven's door. Its short arms wore white gloves,
And as it waddled near, it cried, the door
Aflap, "My Kaye, have we discussed the Boer
War yet?"

        "I think so, Stephen." Kaye walked past
The stove, not looking back. (She kept a fast
Pace to discourage him.) He pivoted
To follow her.

          "I haven't given it
Much thought in recent years," he said, his arms,
Like penguin flippers, flapping. "Many harms
Were visited upon my nerves by thoughts
Of what I'd glimpsed. One night, the boys drew lots—
We had to amputate our surgeon's leg,
You see. Gangrene." He paused. "Poor Will. Good egg."

The bot was based on Stephen Stove, from *Beauty
And the Man*, a *Full-Moon* fanfic. Snooty
Fans, though, viewed the book as more than merely
Fanfic. Ichiro adored it dearly,
Going so far as to have commissioned
Real enchanted objects. He'd envisioned
Them as vaguely sentient residents:
They'd roam the Wood at will. A decadence,
Thought Kaye, but then she'd never cared for *Beauty*,

With its old-school take on love and duty.
(Plus, she found the mannered speech a hassle.)
Beauty took place mostly in the castle
Of a prince, the cursed "Man" of the title.
He was once a noblewolf: entitled,
Smug. A slighted witch, though, turned his minders
Into objects: bureaus, coffee grinders,
And spittoons. The wolf himself became
A man—or rather "*The* Man," lack of name
A sign of monstrousness. The castle stood
On grassy veldt.

                              A werewolf in a hood,
Named Paige, walked to the gate one rainy night.
The storm had spooked her pony into flight:
He'd galloped off and forced the wolf to wander
To the castle. Soon, she'd come to ponder
Matters of the heart: if wolves and men
Can mate, say. Paige, the "Beauty," would befriend
The Man's chum, Stephen Stove, a military
Hero drawn to opium and wary
Of loud noises. Stephen was The Fool:
A trove of comedy, each joke a jewel
Of wisdom.

                      Ichiro's team hadn't quite
Perfected him, thought Kaye. He lacked some byte
Of brilliance. Mostly, Stephen mooned about.
He'd wag an iron haunch, complain of gout,
And call to mind his Matthew Arnold, verse
Dissolving into sighs. He'd seen the worst
Of wolves, he'd say; he'd whispered lines from "Dover
Beach" while watching as a Boer picked over
Stephen's fallen comrades, pelts in blood-
Red regimental tunics, snouts in mud.

He'd lain still, Stephen, mimicking the dead.
He'd watched the Boer bend down and yank a head
Up, making sure the wolf was dead, then drop
The head. The Boer then drew a sword to lop
The tail off. Trophy. Stephen seemed to heat
Up in the telling. Fume. "They'd suck a teat,
Some ravished lady's. Make the husband watch.
Marauding savages." A rusted splotch,
A liver spot he claimed, had spread below
His door. In wintertime, a square of snow
Would settle on his head: a frigid cap.

* * *

Kaye climbed the gently graded path. No map
Explained Roppongi Hills, though towers loomed
Beyond its trees where city life resumed.
The towers could be used to navigate;
The SEGA building, neon concentrate,
Burned blue all evening.
                                    Long before the Wood,
Before the tide crashed in, the neighbourhood
Had been a maze of shops, a controversial
Real estate development, commercial
Spaces all around the base of Mori
Tower. Subterranean shops, the story
Went, had once been linked by passageways
Designed to be confusing, drawing praise
For mimicking an unplanned city's harried
Feel. But worried city planners buried
Mori to rebuff the rising tide,
Resulting in a mountain; trees supplied
A canopy.
                    Kaye found it hard to find

Her way. The Wood had clearly been designed
To baffle minds. She passed a Tokyu Hands store
She'd not seen before. A box-shaped sandstorm
Would've whirled and hardened overnight,
Its fizzing glow, a shaken snow globe's, lighting
Up the bamboo trees. Indeed, the shops
All moved at midnight; planners had placed drops
Throughout the wood, foundations that would grip
A structure, then relinquish it and ship
It off, the shop appearing to dissolve
As if the neighbourhood had no resolve
To be itself. You'd wake to find a Gucci
Standing gleaming where there'd been a Muji
Yesterday, the Muji having shifted
Elsewhere in the wood. Small sprites had lifted
It, the residents would say. An act
Of impish mischief. Trickster charm.

                                        In fact,
A zuber feed had merely moved the structures
Randomly, producing tiny ruptures
In the mental maps a mind will often
Try to draw. Your sense of space would soften
In the Wood. You'd feel what residents
Once felt inside the buried maze, a sense
Of bafflement procured at no small cost.
A luxury to feel so safely lost,
Kaye thought, as Stephen's cries began to fade
Behind her.

* * *

                Soon, she'd reached a quiet glade
Where several homes sat, turreted, their gables
So engorged they should've been in fables,

Homes that swelled and bulged like mushroom caps.
A jogger was approaching, running laps
Around the glade. A popup word balloon
Bloomed over them, a brilliant text-filled moon.
(The crisp blurb was so high fidelity
It clashed with analog reality.)
It read: "She/her, Roppongi Hills, likes cats,
DMs are closed"—a modest set of stats
The jogger had allowed her eyes to share
With any other co-located pair
Of pupils set to roam. Kaye loved the under-
Stated bio. (*Her* blurb was a blunder.
She'd filled in too many fields, though she'd
Seen worse, blurbs listing every sexual need
And semi-legal kink.) Kaye waved away
The text, resolved to fix her own that day.

She thought the jogger out of place among
The turrets. Then, she saw the tail that swung
With every jounce—the tail fed through a slit
The tracksuit made available—and it
Was clear the jogger was enjoying *her*
Own fantasy. Transplanted blue-black fur,
A panther's, climbed the jogger's neck and shaded
Into hair a bot had likely braided,
Plastic hands so quick they would've blurred.

But "fantasy" was wrong; Kaye knew the Furred
And Fauna Indeterminate—the FAFI—
Weren't just dreaming, stretching selves like taffy.
They were truly what they meant to be:
A panther, wolf, or walking manatee.
"Okay, admit you want a tail," Kaye joked

To Cat once, as a FAFI couple stroked
Each other's pelts at Starbucks. Yet, Kaye found
The tail transfixing, as she did the sound
The jogger made, her heavy breathing—panting,
Really.

   *   *   *

      Bots in prairie skirts were planting
Tulips at the base of something like
A cottage made of gingerbread, its spike-
Tipped fence embellished with the heads of witches.
Bots in overalls were digging ditches.
There was one plantation (problematic)
And a home with madness in the attic.
Some things never moved: the homes, for one,
And several temples, each a static sun
Round which the pricey shops arranged themselves
As if borne on the backs of stealthy elves.

It was a place of play, of make believe,
A space where people with the means took leave
Of lives they'd tired of and took up skins
Their souls demanded. Eight-eyed artisans
Astride their multi-headed antelopes
Might congregate upon the southern slopes
For coffee. Girls with manga eyes might walk
By, twirling parasols, while men with rock
For flesh might hoot at them in revelry.
The Wood permitted cosplay devilry:
You'd eyeball men whose lower halves had hooves
Or fourteen-legged girls with B-boy moves.
The Wood was basically a non-stop masque.

A strain of tumbleweed—self-rolling cask,
Specific to the Wood—would rumble up
The mountain's slopes in search of needy cup.
But when casks rolled back down the slopes to be
Refilled, they seemed to spurn the tendency
Of rolling things to pick up speed: they kept
An eerie pace or paused, mid-slope, and slept.

Kaye stopped and closed her eyes, the sunlight on
Her face. The ground shook: someone's macro swan
Was stomping by, with smaller ones in tow,
Their feathers luminescent, bred to glow.

* * *

Strange spectral breezes blew by: people shrouded,
Wanting privacy. Some tourists, crowded
Round a store, were shrouded. But their blurbs,
Left on, betrayed them. Rookies from the burbs.

A postcard flew into her line of sight.
It started playing something black and white:
A looped scene from *The Third Man*, where the hero,
Holly, shoots his best friend. Kaye had zero
Interest in old tintypes. Cat, though, loved
The ones with Orson Welles. She often shoved
Them on her friend. They swooped in every day.
Kaye watched them once, then waved the cards away.

She passed beyond the glade and took a path
That forked off to the left. She marked the bathtub,
Foaming with assorted macro flowers,
Heads so big they bowed. A nearby tower's
Shadow striped this section of the Wood,

But Ichiro's repurposed building stood
Unscathed in sunlight, on a plot of grass
The Wood encircled perfectly, a glass
Sphere hanging on each tree (alluding to
The brilliant, moon-shaped buoys threaded through
The wood in *Full-Moon*). From above, the spheres
Helped pilots touch down; Ichiro's worst fears
Were manifold, but chief among them was
His fear of zuber booths. A gentle buzz
Announced the gondola he often took
To reach the manse. He didn't like the look
Of wealthy men on foot, she'd heard him say.

The manse was not a spectacle the way
Most structures in the Wood were. Modest by
Roppongi standards, meant to bore the eye,
The manse looked like a small apartment made
Two centuries ago, its brick arrayed
In ivy, windows narrow like the ooo-
Shaped mouths of ghosts.

                                        She made her way up to
The door, which opened inward, hinges creaking
Harshly. Ichiro was standing, speaking
To the foyer's wall, his shirtsleeves rolled,
His navy Windsor loosened. Something scrolled
Before his face, invisible; he tapped
The air a couple times and, sighing, slapped
The unseen thing away. No blurb had sprouted
Over him. She figured he had muted
Blurbs—or blocked her eyes. He looked at Kaye,
Then turned around. She thought she heard him say,
"It needs revisions," but her Japanese
Was shaky still.

She passed the foyer's frieze
(A pack of werewolf whalers in relief,
One corner carved to indicate a leaf
Of paper being turned) and pushing through
French doors, she bounded up a stairwell to
The second floor.
                        The whole floor was a single
Room: once-sectioned units forced to mingle.
It was like a room you roam in dreams,
Tall windows gaping, rustic cedar beams
At well-spaced intervals, and from its bowels,
Something like a voice reduced to vowels.

With her right shoe's toe, she nudged the floor
En pointe-ishly. Two wheels per smartsole (four
In total) formed, the pixie-lined Adidas
Lifting her a notch.
                        "The rumours lead us
Further into fog," the voice was saying
As she rolled toward its owner, swaying
On her shoes. The four wheels rumbled like
A copper cask rolled over wood, a mic
Inside the cask.
                        "The daylight's slowly dimming…"
Lux was standing by a glassed-in, swimming-
Pool-sized tank, dictating to a bald
And milk-white steno.
                        "Got your stuff," Kaye called.

Lux raised a finger. "…dimming, Mandy's where-
Abouts unknown. But still we search, we stare
At screens, the Wave of Data, dreaming of
The vanished author of the book we love."

He stopped. "Let's print."

                                    The steno, sitting primly
On a woven lounger, nodded dimly,
Offering her milky hands, which grasped
Themselves, their fingers laced. She then unclasped
The hands, a sudden paper fluttering
Exploding upward: holographic wings,
A dove's wings, disappearing as they struck
The ceiling, bound for orbit—for the zuck—
And then eventually Wolfpack Salon,
Where Emmett Lux (@dontgivetwolux) had drawn
Two million Moonheads. (@psychedelicurs,
Kaye's handle, had two hundred followers.)
The steno placed her hands back on her thighs.
She wore a grey blouse and distressed Levi's.

The dove thing was annoying. Kaye had shown
Lux how to switch the bot to STATIC PHONE,
Ensuring that the steno sat still, only
Moving when her user said, "I'm lonely,
Jane," or when said user had to go
Somewhere. (Some owners kept their bots in tow.)
But Lux, like, *never* changed a default setting.
Kaye had watched him strip the steno's netting
(Fishnet that had kept her limbs in check
In crate) and pull a toggle on her neck
(Deflating what appeared to be an orb
Around the steno's head, which helped absorb
Stray impacts). He'd said, "I agree," as soon
As she began explaining (to the tune
Of Weller's "Start!") the Terms of Use: the thoughts
That lurk inside the heads of brand-new bots.

As Kaye came rolling to a stop, a postcard
Flew before her, trailing pixels: ghost shards
Due to laggy eyes. Wolfpack Salon
Sent postcards ("howls," in the lexicon)
To Lux's followers, alerting them
When he so much as sneezed or said "ahem"
On matters wolf or moon.
                              "You're live," she said.

The floating postcard filled with words. She read
Them as her body lowered slightly, wheels
Retracting into soles. She heard low peals,
A nearby temple's bell, which sounded sombre
In the wake of her Adidas thunder.

She could sense that Lux was staring at
Her. Wanting a response. She said, "The chat
Is filling up."
                    "It always does."
                                        She gave
Her prof a look. "The zlog is good. The 'Wave
Of Data' bit is great."
                          He shrugged, pretending
Not to care. His ego needed tending,
Kaye had found.
                    She slowly walked around
The tank: an oblong bubble's top half, round
At both ends like a pill. The hardwood floor
Gave way to checkered squares, a tiled shore
That ran around the tank. She marked her double
As it slid along the chin-high bubble,
Funhouse tall. Her in-eye postcard, though,
Gave no reflection, prompting vertigo

Or something like it. After all, her brain
Was being fed a lie, her eyes maintaining
That a postcard hung before her face.

The bubble's contents looked like land from space,
Obscured by clouds. In cloudless mode, you'd see
Clean through the glass. A coast beside a sea
Lay at the bottom of the tank, a settle-
Ment along the shore. The sea was metal
From the vantage point of Kaye, but down
Below, real water crashed against the town:
A flawless bonsai replica of Rabbit
Strait, designed (and fine-tuned) with a rabid
Eye for detail.
                    From where Kaye was standing—
Just outside the tank, a god's commanding
Perch above a world—a set of human
Eyes could make out little else. A zoom-in
Iris could be summoned, though, by double-
Tapping any point upon the bubble.
This would dim the glass and bring the plate-
Sized iris up: a view of Rabbit Strait
From any angle, thanks to bots on wings
Or paws. The iris offered gripping things
To watch. Thrill-seeking visitors could pull
A lounger up and stream the shots a gull
Was shooting as it wheeled above, or through,
The town. The iris accessed any view.

She turned. "Which chapter—"
                              "Eight," a little crabby.
Lux's hands were doing something, jabbing
At the air. "Can't seem to fucking log

In..." He was clearly checking on his zlog.

She closed the postcard, tapped the tank, and brought
The iris up. Defaulting to the plot,
The iris showed a ship made tiny by
A bird's-eye view: a soaring gannet's eye.
It was the *Lucy Dread*, white stuffing foaming
In its wake, the Moby likely roaming
Near. But no one on the ship could see
Kaye. From their in-tank, worm's-eye POV,
The bubble was a night sky—not a dome
Of glass that turned the sea's far edge to foam.

The tank was pressure-sealed. Kaye couldn't merely
Thrust her full-sized arm in cavalierly
If she wanted to adjust some part
Of it; the contents, which rebuked the art
Of jewellers, were too small. You had to shrink
To enter: through an octagon-shaped sink
Embedded in the floor and boothed in glass
Beside the tank. The glass booth squeezed your mass,
Collapsing space between your molecules.
Your skin would sparkle as if set with jewels,
Then turn to strands, which swirled around a drain.
They'd reconvene inside the tank, no grain
That formed your body unaccounted for.

You'd wind up on a hill above the shore,
Beside a water wheel that eyed the bay.
The ground had give; the turf was pixieclay,
Which could reorganize itself at will.
A flying junk would settle on the hill,
Collecting visitors. The atmosphere

Itself had been compressed, so scuba gear
Was not required.
                    As she viewed the iris,
Kaye began to think about the crisis
In Ukraine, where POWs
Were being herded into bonsai flues—
Which sent the soldiers to erasure hives
To spend the final minutes of their lives.
The shrunken POWs were given
Only full-sized air to breathe, their shriven
Lungs exploding as the men expired,
Fists on glass. The oven-hives were fired
Up, the dissidents incinerated.
(Thus, their Russian captors had translated
Lives to dust.)
                    Kaye also thought about
The surge in so-called "shooters" who would scout
A preschool hive (located in some town
In Idaho or Maine) and slowly drown
A class of little kids in nitric acid.
Bonsai hives could cultivate a rancid
Attitude to living things, in brains
That churned with chatroom-driven hurricanes.
(A hive could pose a Nietzschean abyss
To troubled boys in camo gear.)
                                  But *this*
Tank had no legal lifeforms—just a troupe
Of bots, which looked like werewolves, in a loop
Defined by Fiction's novel.

* * *

                    Just behind
The ship, the mound-like Moby, with a mind

To overtake the *Dread*, now tugged its own
White wake. The bonsai Dickie, who had blown
The *Dread* this far, was far too small to see,
Though.

           Kaye said, "This part's where he tries to flee
The Moby, right?"

                 "He's telling Paige the tale,"
Said Lux, "of how he got to shore." The whale
Kept inching closer, trailing foam. Lux sat
Down by the steno, whose expression, flat,
Suggested something like a blinking cursor.
"Got my items?"

            Kaye unslung the purse her
Knapsack had contracted to while Kaye'd
Been speeding to the manse. No longer splayed
Against her, it puffed up. She stuck a hand in,
Pulled a *New York Times* out, which expanded
Slightly; Kaye's sack leveraged bonsai tech,
Compressing what she fed it. Next: a Czech-
To-Wulvish dictionary Lux had ordered;
Coffee in a paper can; assorted
Katsu sandos from a Family Mart;
And finally, the find!—in Book Maid's artful
Wrap. She crossed to where Lux sat and placed
The items on a treated trunk that faced
The loungers. Lux seized on the package. Tore
The paper off.

           Kaye craned her head and swore,
"Fuck me. A *Full-Moon Whaling Odyssey*."

Lux turned it in his hands, an oddity—
A rarity. He thumbed one corner. Scuffed.
He didn't understand why readers roughed

Such precious books up.

                        Kaye was at a loss
For words. The cover's title was embossed
And silver. Wolf and pire, paw in hand,
Stood on a starsloop's deck. Each figure manned
A harpoon ray gun, bulbous as a ham.
Behind the pair, a school of starcod swam.

The Full-Moon Whaling Odyssey was fanfic
Few had read. Its author held romantic
Views on authenticity—and balked
At pixiepaper. Worse, they'd somehow "locked"
The text. The ink resisted scans. The words
Themselves had been arranged in careful herds
Designed to trigger onzuck bots that wiped
The book from zucksites. (So, if someone typed
It out—and posted it—its DNA
Would mark its onzuck form as chum-like prey.)
Plus only several hundred copies, handsewn,
Had been made. The stubborn books would stand their
Ground when zubered. (Kaye had wondered why
The package hadn't swelled a bit: the sly
Book had defied compression! Book Maid's wrap
Had merely tightened like a finger trap
Inside the sack, the brown wrap splitting at
The corners.) So, to make a photostat
You'd need a fucking monk; the thing resisted
Reproduction. Someone had insisted
That originals be held and read.

The author was unknown, but many said
That Fiction was the culprit. After all,
The book (according to the very small

Cult following that had, in fact, enjoyed
Its words) had stuck to Fiction's plot, employed
A style that was strangely similar
To hers, and all but bore her signature.
Of course, no one had seen the author in
Awhile; she had zubered into thin
Air sometime back in 2052.
Lux thought the fanfic held a hidden clue
About her whereabouts.

* * *

He put the book
Down. Stood. He'd gone in for his standard look:
Impassive shades, a grey tee, and a pair
Of cargo shorts. He grabbed a woven chair
And dragged it to the tank. Kaye followed him.

He sat back down. His face seemed tired. Grim.
"The good part's next." He gestured at the bubble.
"Zoom in."
Kaye approached the tank and double-
Tapped the iris. Then, she spread her thumb and
Index finger several times, which summoned
Up a closer view, the iris fringed
With frothing pixels. Kaye had often binged
On Lux's model, which he had her Windex.
(She'd put down her rag and bring the index
Up to toggle to her favourite scenes.)

She couldn't hear the whalers' desperate screams—
The sound was off—but watched the werewolves running
Round the deck, the *Lucy Dread* still gunning
For the wharf. The Pike had washed ashore

Some distance back; the beach had reabsorbed
The captain's corpse. (When Lux rewound the plot,
The tank would generate a brand-new bot
To play Pike's part.) The pixieplastic bots
Weren't sentient. They had single-minded thoughts.
So if you tried to block one, it would frown
And, focused on its plotline, step around
You. If you tried conversing, it would smile
And decline your overtures. The style
Of the models (vaguely anime
That morning) could be altered day to day
As one desired. They were amiable.
The pixieplastic made them malleable.

Kaye touched the tank and dragged the iris back;
The Moby was now moving to attack.
But as the mound eclipsed the ship, a figure
Leaped into the bonsai sea. Kaye's finger
Double-tapped the glass, which bloomed, revealing
Dickie swimming hard, his arms pinwheeling
Like the paddle wheels on steamboats. Lux
Leaned forward, elbows on his knees, soft clucks
Of tongue suggesting thinking. Then, he nodded
At the swimming Dickie. It was spotted
Like a cheetah. "Dickie's looking funny."

"Let me guess. The model needs more money."

Kaye and her professor turned to find
That Ichiro had crossed the room. Resigned.

Lux pointed. Ichiro, now sighing, hunkered
Down beside them. "Spots? Let's send the junk."

Kaye piped up. "Hey, can *I* come?"
                                    Both men, blank,
Looked at her. Then, they turned back to the tank.

"You sure we need to?" Lux said. He preferred
To leave the tank alone—and leave its furred
Constituents to hoist and carry off
The buggy bodies to an unmarked trough
In town. The problematic bots would lose
Their shape and whirlpool round a drain, the ooze
Pumped out through flues into a holding pen
Inside the manse, first floor, where quiet men
In scrubs would analyze the plastic's code,
The bonsai ooze expanding as it flowed.

"I'm sure—" He straightened suddenly, his gaze
Far off, the businessman now in a daze.
His eyes were moving, though. "Apologies,"
He said—to Lux, Kaye guessed. An unseen breeze
Had brought some urgent matter to his eyes.
He wandered off, dictating his replies.

The businessman believed in purity.
He felt that in the name of accuracy
Lux shouldn't task the bots with extra-novel
Business: Dickie shouldn't clean his hovel,
Say, or make his paw an android's fist.
The businessman's approach was Classicist:
Let wolves be wolves. He didn't like to see
The bots break character and haul debris.

What's more, he'd financed Lux's pricey model.
It was like a ship inside a bottle,

Something Ichiro preferred to fuss
With in a hands-on way. He liked to putz
Around inside the tank on board a junk,
A vessel studded with a single punk-
Rock mohawk, which paid homage to the fan-
Creased sails of Chinese boats. He liked to man
The junk with modellers, who lived to fly
In spaces that rebuffed the human eye,
Though they created macros, too: terrific
Gundam models, pummelled by Pacific
Waves. You'd see these giants standing in
The ocean, tiny figures on their skin.
(The tiny figures were the modellers.
They scaled a netting fine as gossamer.)
The coast of Okinawa was a hot
Spot for the hobby. There you'd find some bot,
Erected over waves too rough to surf,
At war with its Godzilla over turf.

For Lux, the tank supplied a visual
Dimension, supplementing textual
Analysis. Examining the model,
Which laid out the landscape of the novel
With precision, Lux had turned up hidden
Meanings. (Rabbit Strait described a bitten
Wolf neck where its borders met the pire
Wood!) Lux hoped that Ichiro's desire
To maintain the model would support
More work on symbolism in the port—
Or in the village layout—in addition
To the work of finding Mandy Fiction.

Kaye said, "Look, I'm coming with you guys."

She waved at spam afloat before her eyes.

Lux fixed her with his dark shades. "No, no, no.
It's not a theme park."
                              "Well, I need to go."
She didn't want to say she lived in student
Housing and was used to hives.
                              "Not prudent,
Kaye. The dean would have my head. We can't."

"We'll log it as a field trip." Then, she planted
One hand on the tank. "We'll analyze
Some shit."
                    Lux took his shades off. Rubbed his eyes.

A flicker caught her gaze. She saw the iris
Start to move—to leave the spotted, virus-
Ridden Dickie swimming in the past.
It slid three feet along the pixieglass,
Then stopped and zoomed in smoothly on *another*
Dickie, who'd been saying how the mother
Of the eggs had smashed the *Dread* in rage.
This polymorph was walking with its Paige
Along a stretch of beach. The tank collapsed
The novel's timelines: scenes set in the past
Unfolded on the same terrain as scenes
Set in the present. Hasty quarantines
Ensured a flashback's set of bots receded
When the present moment's bots were needed.

Paige and Dickie Lush were walking west,
Away from town. The bots were on a quest
And soon would clamber over rocks, a hoop

Of boulders in their way, to find the sloop
That someone had abandoned years before,
Its sand-steeped hull half swallowed by the shore.
It was the sloop that Paige would use to bring
The eggs back to their cave. A gentle ding
Would signal Chapter Eight had reached its end.
The pair of bots would stop dead in the sand.

Scroll Two

9.

The School for Wayward Teens was domed with glass
That showed the stars. A werewolf couldn't pass
Beyond the dome without their suit and bubble
Helmet. Craters pocked the landscape. Rubble.
Gravity was low, the surface barren
But for domes. Long tunnels formed a warren
Deep within the arid asteroid,
Connecting homes. Still, many wolves enjoyed
The surface—and the single moon above,
Which looped the asteroid as if in love.
These werewolves had a slow and springy gait.
They gently trampolined through Rabbit Strait.

If you walked east, however, you would reach
A row of booths that marked the so-called "Beach."
And if you stepped inside one, you could port
Up to the port, where vessels would depart.
The port looked like a kid's sketch of the sun:
A ring with ray-like prongs. It slowly spun
Above the asteroid. The prongs that spined
The ring were whaling ships; each ship's behind
Had slowly backed against the ring and mated
With an airlock. Docked, the ship then waited
For its crew, its prow set on a star.

Each ship possessed a single, yard-ruled spar.
Once hoisted, solar sails—flat panes of foil—
Drew in light and charged the lightspeed coil.
Ships detaching from the floating ring
Would stretch toward a distant point, then slingshot
Out of sight.
     But from the glassed-in deck—
Where whalers oversaw the touchscroll tech,
The werewolves at their lecterns, scratching out
Commands—it looked like space had formed a spout
Through which the ship was moving. Stars were streaks,
And hours on the deck were really weeks
Back on the "Rock," the name the asteroid
Was known by. Ships returning from the Void,
With blubber in their holds, would find an older
Rabbit Strait. Some wives gave vacuum shoulder
To the husbands they had grown apart
From. (Thick fur slowly pelts a broken heart.)
The children, too, were distant. They'd been left
Behind for months—or years—and felt bereft.
Their fathers, whaling on the other side
Of far-flung galaxies, had all but died.

The School sat at the base of Good Wolf Hill.
It tried but failed to teach a single skill—
Avoiding trouble—to its troubled charges.
Recess found them outside, watching barges
Hauling mounds of rainbow-coloured yield
Mined from the Reef, the asteroid-strewn field
The Rock was part of. (Wolves had mined the Rock
Itself some years before.) Some teens would balk,
But most would one day whale or work the Reef.
They'd smoke their cigarettes, glass tubes that briefly

Melded with their helmets and allowed
The wolves to take a drag. A smoky shroud
Would briefly fill the helmets, curling all
Along the glass. The murky crystal ball
Each wolf now wore would purge the smoke by way
Of glass bots, programmed carefully to prey
On "output."
                              Every helmet's set of bots
Comprised a colony—and shared its thoughts
With other colonies. They worked together,
Different helmets, to determine whether
Noises their respective owners made
Were meant for others' ears and should be played
Within specific helmets. Bots would open
Channels when they felt their wolves had spoken.
That said, protocol suggested airing
Any gasps: the Rule of Oversharing.
(Helmets *used* to edit coughs and breath-
Like noise—until a young wolf choked to death.)

The glass bots were too small to spot by eye.
They *were* the glass and kept the air supply.
Beneath a pixiescope, they looked like grapes,
Which scaled to form assorted real-world shapes—
Like helmets. Nearly all their mass was given
To the air they held. The bots looked shriven
When depleted. Helmets, by extension,
Softened up and lost their rigid tension.
Helmets looked like squash: a smaller bubble,
Bulging from the main one, held the muzzle.

* * *

At the top of Good Wolf Hill, the Normal

School was domed as well. It lacked a formal
Name. Presumably its students were
Less wayward: kept their claws clipped and their fur
In line. Paige couldn't quite remember, though;
The Normal School had chucked her moons ago.

As Paige and Dot approached the steep and cratered
Hill, the dome that capped the School for Wayward
Teens produced an iris. Glass bots local
To the dome had quickly scanned the vocal
Patterns of the two wolves (data that
The helmets' bots had offered via chat).
The dome's bots matched the raspy wolf to Paige,
Thus triggering the iris.
                                    "Well, me cage
Awaits," Paige said.
                                    Their suits were white and quilted,
Sleeves accordioned. The backs had built-in
Scrollsacks. Paige's sack was lined with crumpled
Touchscrolls (several strata deep) and rumpled
Gym cloaks. She'd been staying at Dot's dome
For several moons, and only ventured home
To pick up scrolls and clothing when she knew
Her father would be out. (She'd said, "I'm through
With him," and then for emphasis had thrown
A rock from Dot's front yard. The thing had flown
For one kilometre before it bent
Toward the ground. A distant dust plume meant
A landing.)
                    "Howl *only* when you're howled
To, okay?" said Dot. A plea.
                                    Paige scowled,
Stepped inside the dome, and turned to Dot.

The iris dwindled to a point. She brought
Her paws up to the glass and pounded in
Mock desperation. Then, she stopped to grin.
Dot sighed and turned. She started up her slope.

Paige stood inside an inner bubble, soap-
Like in its shimmer. It was vaguely red,
But as the bubble's glass bots slowly fed
The bubble air and ran Paige through their screening
Protocols, the bubble switched to green.
A second iris bloomed: the entrance to
The schoolhouse proper. As the wolf passed through,
Emerging into class, the airlock sealed
Behind her.
              Paige removed her helmet, kneeled
To put it down, kicked off her boots, and zipped
The space suit's fabric to the groin. She slipped
It off. She wore black leggings and an old
Shirt of her dad's. A locker sphere then rolled
Across her scattered things, which wound up stranded
In the sphere, afloat as if enchanted.
(Each wolf had a sphere.)
                 The School for Wayward
Teens was sparse in its appointments, tailored
To the learning style of a pack
Of "problem" students who'd been deemed to lack
The skill to do much more than sit in rows
Or reproduce, by claw, a line of prose
Until the scratchboards, floating in the room
Like monoliths, were filled up. Idle grooming
Was discouraged. Basic whaling skills
Were covered: how to deftly carve up kills
Or handle blubber forks. They sat with touchscrolls

Such as *Lupine Farm* and *Hamlet*, much-loved
Wulvish texts. Their desks were oval planks
That sprouted from their chairs, arranged in ranks
Beneath the dome. The teacher walked around
The dome's edge, shushing wolves who made a sound.
A double of the classroom curved along
The glass above, its stretched-out students long
And thin like funhouse figures. (As he cruised
The quiet rows, the teacher often used
The room's reflection to identify
Illicit acts. The dome became his eye.)

Paige passed a holo of Virginia Woolf
And took a seat behind a hulking wolf.
He wore a hoodie, head propped on a paw,
Each claw clipped off. A cage enclosed his maw.

"What happened now?" hissed Paige.

                                    The wolf leaned back
And, over shoulder, whispered, "Brute attack
On werewolf civil liberties."

                                    "For what?"

He raised his claw-less paws. "Beats me. I cut
This ghoul—by *accident*. He shoves me, so
I shoves the fellow back." He sighed. "Yes, Moe,
You have a thought to share?"

                                    A second, smaller
Wolf, beside him, leaning in. "Was baller,
Paige." She wore a black tee and a plaid
Skirt. "We're just hanging out, right, when this vlad
Crawls from his cave to pick a fight—and Campbell
Rips his furless face off. Fucker gambled.

Fucker lost." She leaned back in her chair,
Her eyebrows raised as if to say: and there
You go.

        Paige faked a grin. She hadn't shared
Her own attack with anyone, how scared
She'd been until the shifter had appeared.
Low gravity had slowed him. Still, he'd speared
Three bats ...

            The muzzled werewolf, Campbell, shook
His head and fixed Paige with a deadpan look.
"That's pure exaggeration, Paige. You know
I'd never hurt a fly." He looked at Moe
And winked. "Well, not too many."

                    Moe grinned broadly—
Then turned grave. "Of course, they're not 'ungodly.'"
Thoughtful now. "They're not 'monstrosities.'
I've heard that *wolves* have harmed their colonies.
The G-word, too, can harm them."

                     Campbell frowned.
"The G-word?"

        Ghoul, mouthed Moe, avoiding sound.
"You shouldn't even really say, like, 'G-word.'"

"Says who?"
        "Alice."
           "Figures."
               "That's what *she* heard."
Moe's friend Alice often shook her muzzle
At injustice, war, and pire struggle.
Still, Moe couldn't help enjoy the fearless-
Ness of Campbell facing down the furless
Entities who carpeted the ceilings
In the tunnels. Thought to be unfeeling,

Pires lived an upside-down existence.
They would prey on werewolves for subsistence,
Sometimes crawling from a crater's lip.
A janitor had once described the flip-
Flap of a pire's wings when one, assuming
Bat form, had snuck in the School's main room.
The bat had settled on a glowing sheet:
A touchscroll *Moby-Dick*. (Scroll Six: "The Street.")
The wolves believed all tunnel bats were feral;
This one, though, had made itself a carrel
With its folded wings: a reading teepee
Inching over words. And when the sleepy
Thing had fallen still, the janitor
Approached the pire with a canister
And scrollsack, capturing both scroll and bat.
The sack expanded, grew so heavy that
It slipped free of the janitor and spilled
A child. Fearing that he might be killed,
The old wolf ran.

                    They lived exposed to Void,
The pallid pires, tending to avoid
The suits worn by the "Furred." Their genitals
Were hard to grok, their groins illegible.
But Moe claimed she'd seen pires wearing boots—
The kind that werewolves use—and even suits,
As if the pires, in appropriating
Wulvish forms of dress, were indicating
They'd been wolves once, vulnerable to vacuum.

As the teacher strolling through the classroom
Walked past Paige and Campbell, both wolves focused
On one scratchboard's Bible passage: locusts
Crawling over Egypt's moon at God's

Command. These clawed-out passages were rods
Presumably intended to leave marks
On misfit minds. (The LORD's resounding barks,
They read, produced a wind, a roaring storm
That lifted up the locusts, swept the swarm
Into the Red Sun.) Once the teacher had
Moved past them, ruler drumming on the pad
His upturned paw had made, Paige nudged the hoodie.

Campbell half turned, brow raised.

                                     "Let's play hooky
After lunch," said Paige. "I wants to show
You something."

                      Campbell turned some more, aglow.

She frowned. "Not that." Then added: "Or whatever
Filth you're thinking."

                          Wounded look. "I'd never
Think such thoughts. Me love is true, not fleeting."

"So," said Moe, who'd leaned in, "where we meeting?"

* * *

Paige and Dot stood on the hill. "Come on!"
Cried Paige. Above the wolves, the brittle spawn
Of starcod—razored facets from a jewel—
Turned quickly as a single-minded school.

As Campbell clambered up the rocky hill,
His glass bots aired low clicks; his cage's grille
Kept clinking on the snout part of his helmet.
At the top, he paused, bent double. "Well met,
Girls." He placed his gloved paws on his space

Suit's knees and looked back.

                           Moe was at the base
Still, peering up the crumbly incline, wary.
Her bots had relayed her grating, merry
Humming all the way as if on loop—
But now they'd stopped.

                     He turned and saw a sloop—
Or, technically, the burnt-out chassis of
A sloop—below them.

                 "It could use some love,"
Said Paige. "And you know sloops."

                           "You're serious."

She nodded, one brow raised, mysterious,
As if to sell the sense that he was in
The midst of something thrilling. "It's a win-
Win. You restore a vintage Cub and help
A friend in need."

               A crackle of a yelp—
From Moe, now struggling up the slope—came through
Their helmets. They ignored it.

                   "I can *do*
It," Campbell said, "but why don't I just steal
A starsloop? So much easier. An Eel
Or Finn is all you need. I knows this lot
They leave unlocked."

                "We can't risk being caught,"
Said Dot, who added hastily, "Hey, Campbell,
Wicked cage." She raised a gloved paw, bangle
Winking. Dot wore jewelry on the outside
Of her gloves. The chunky fingers flouted
Rings.

        "And anyway," said Paige, "we'll all be

Heroes, right?"

      They turned to see Moe crawling
Into sight—and gasping. "Could've used
A paw there."

     Campbell squinted. Looked confused.
"Wait, what d'you mean, 'we'll *all*?'"

* * *

       The sloop seemed draped
In hardened cellophane. The same stuff caped
The stern—a flowing, scalloped mantle, thin
And clear, as if a waterfall had been
Arrested. Basically, the dome had lost
Its shape and fallen, settling across
The sloop.

    The owner had been sent to debtors
Prison, Paige explained. The hull bore letters,
"*H.O.W.*," and then a spot
Of glaring space, as if the author's thought
Had stalled. Apparently, he'd never had
The chance to paint the final "L."—a sad
Fact, though it hadn't dampened Paige's spirit.

"Needs a bit of paint," she said.

       "I fear it
Needs a grave," said Campbell.

       It was twenty
Metres long with room for cognoscenti
Down below. It lay at one end of
A trench that it'd clearly ploughed, rocks shoved
Aside presumably when it'd had
To make a hasty landing on this bad
And bumpy runway. Ploughed rocks ran around

The sloop's perimeter and made a mound
The wolves could climb. The rock-mound only took
Them halfway up the side, but they could hook
Their gloved paws round a hoop, which rimmed one port-
Hole, for a boost.
                        The deck was like a court
For bushel ball. Contrasted with the pock-
Marked asteroid's uneven, cratered rock,
The shrink-wrapped sloop seemed starkly smooth. On deck,
A touchscroll rested on a narrow neck;
It looked as if the deck had grown a lectern.
(Wolves who knew the nautically correct term
Called this thing "the wheel.") The wheel was draped,
As well; the shrink wrap lent a phallus-shaped
And condomed bent. The sloop could move from star
To star still. It possessed its lightspeed spar,
A cross behind the fallen dome, toward
The stern.
                        The werewolves slowly climbed aboard.
The shrink-wrapped deck was slippery. The slack
Dome, having settled into every crack
And hole, had briefly formed a gland that spanned
Some stairs, a dark companionway. This gland,
Distending down, had bulged and split, its dead
Fringe curling back in fronds. The stairwell led
Belowdecks to a hold.
                            "Our Dot will wrest
An epic poem," Paige said, "from our quest.
All ships need poets, right? A bard in space?"

Moe looked at Campbell. Frowned.
                                "In any case,
She'll work down here," said Paige. Paige had no clue

Why ships required poets, but she knew
Her quest required Dot. She knew she'd need
Her friend.

     "The whaler bards would often read
Out ancient verse," said Dot. "They'd strum a lyre.
Sing. The cognoscenti would inspire
All the wolves on board with poetry."
She knit her brow. "Of course, their stuff could be
A little dated. Love of brotherhood.
The Void as silent mistress. Womanhood
As mystery. That's why me whaling epic's
Gonna have a feminist aesthetics."

"Dot, I'd like to be described as 'Moe
The Resolute,'" Moe noted. "'She of Snow-
White Pelt.'"

    Ignoring Moe—the wolf would ramble
Til the end of Void—Paige turned to Campbell.
"So, we've figured Dot's part out. How soon
Can we get going? Blessed Holy Moon
Permitting obviously."

      He looked at her.
"I thinks all sense has left your bloody fur.
What if we get out where you wants to go
And something fails on us. I mean, I know
Enough to get a dome back on the deck
And thrusters working. But, well, it's a wreck."
The hold was heaped with boxes, wires, sprockets,
Coiled tubes—the unkempt guts of rockets.
Campbell turned to Paige and frowned. "Where *are*
We going?"

    Nodding ceilingward. "A star.
Not far from here. Where Dickie thinks the whale

Came from."
                    "What whale?"
                                        Paige spread her arms for scale.

He laughed, but Paige was deadpan. "Wait, you mean—"

"The one that ate that ship like whale cuisine?"
Asked Moe. She seemed delighted.
                                        "Yes, we're going
To its nest," said Paige.
                              "Okay, let's slow
Down, everyone," said Campbell, lifting paws
To pat the air. "Let's take a breath and pause."

"What's wrong?" said Paige, now wide-eyed, playing dumb.

"You said, 'where *Dickie* thinks the whale came from.'
The polymorph?"
                         "Yes, b'y," a voice behind
Them said. "I'm coming, too, if you don't mind."
(Their helmets did their best to represent
Where sound was coming from; the bots that spent
Their lives along the non-snout hemispheres
Of helmets aired all rearward noise to ears.)

They turned. Beside the hold's companionway,
They saw the wolf-cum-squid. "I knows the way,"
It said—a wolf's head in its squash-shaped glass
And balanced on a writhing, pinkish mass
Of tentacles unfurling from the bottom
Of the helmet. "Hope that's not a problem,"
Said the head. It moved the way a tank-
Bound lifeform might: its helmet briefly sank

Into its limbs, and these, in turn, compressed—
Then straightened. Thus, the wolf-cum-squid progressed
Through low-grade gravity, its body springing
Forward, tentacles like tassels bringing
Up the rear. The glassed-in head did not
Require air; the helmet merely brought
Its voice into the helmets of the others.

* * *

"I don't gets why we can't destroy the mother's
Eggs," said Campbell.
                              "Tried that many times,"
Said Dickie. "Lasers. Flames. Acidic slimes.
Once tried to boil 'em. They live for years.
They're kept alive, the scrolls say, by our fears."

They'd sat down on the hold's cold tiles, in
A circle. Campbell had called up a thin
And bulbous backup dome to cap the deck,
Restoring gravity inside the wreck.
Their helmets lay about like toys in some
Cub's messy room. Moe held hers like a drum.
The wolf head, holding forth, now sat atop
Its mass of tentacles, a splayed-out mop,
Each smooth appendage like a pinkish dreadlock
Shading furrier toward the head.

He'd turned some lights on, Campbell. Paige had noted,
In a whisper, that the shifter floated
Round by touch; his eyes weren't great ("they damn well
Do just fine," he'd claimed, annoyed). So Campbell
Had plugged in some buoys, which now streamed
Their chilly light. The chamber's panels gleamed

The way a blubber freezer's innards do.

"So Dickie, it's been decades, right, since *you*
  First got your locket." Campbell turned to Paige.
"And yours is just as old. How come—"
                                    "An age,
  As understood by wolves, is like an hour
  To a Moby," Dickie said. "They flower
  Slowly. Hatching takes a century.
  Each egg's"—he paused—"a penitentiary."

"But why the Moon would anyone return
  The eggs?" said Moe. "Like, won't they only churn
  Out Mobies?"
                  Dickie, pooled within his limbs,
  Regarded her. "I've read the ancient hymns
  Our people have forgotten. Mobies never
  Bother wolves—unless, of course, they're severed
  From their little ones. That's been the case
  In me experience. It first gave chase
  Because me captain took its eggs. And then
  It showed again last month, but only when
  The eggs fell into space by accident."
  The shifter crossed two tendrils, adamant.

Paige pictured Thom, gambolling on the deck,
  No helmet, paw around a bottle's neck.
  He'd tripped and stumbled through a faulty patch
  Of dome. The ship's AI was quick to catch
  Him with a tractor beam. ("Wolf overboard,"
  Its voice had noted over PA—bored
  And treble, as all robot voices seem
  To be.) But Thom was dead before the beam

Could reel him in. His locket was afloat,
Connected to the chain around his throat.
The locket's eggs had somehow found their voice
In frigid space—and called across the Void.

Both lockets, now, were in a jar of moon
Rocks; Paige had moved it to the extra room
In Dot's dome.
               "Wait, I'm not quite following,"
Said Dot. "The Moby risked, like, *swallowing*
Her eggs. She didn't know the things weren't on
That ship she gobbled." Dot could see the yawning
Moby's mouth still.
             "Mobies don't digest
Ships," Dickie said. "Their bodies will divest
Themselves of vessels. Rubbish gets expelled.
I thinks their stomachs know to push out shelled
Stuff, scraps, debris"—he grimaced—"werewolf legs.
Her stomach would've sifted for the eggs."

"So let's just throw 'em into outer space,"
Said Campbell. "Why not let the monster chase
Her eggs around?"
            "That won't endear us to
The Moby," Dickie said. "She'll rampage through
The stars, destroying every dome in sight."
He seemed resolved. "We have to set things right."

"In other words," said Paige, "we needs to bring
Her eggs back to their nest. That way they'll sing
Across the galaxy—and draw her back
To them. That's how we'll stop the next attack."

The wolf head took them all in. "You must vow
To keep this to yourselves, at least for now."
He looked at Moe. "You hear me?"

                      Campbell prodded
Her. She shoved back. Looked at Dickie. Nodded.

Dickie raised a limb. "Now I'm too old
To do this on me own. Me flesh"—he rolled
The twitching limb into a scroll—"is spastic
Sometimes. Slowly losing its elastic."
Dickie let the limb unroll. It lay
Flat on the floor. "To get to Kelly Bay
Takes work, and this old ship"—he looked around—
"Will need a crew." He seemed to hear a sound
And cocked his head.

                  Paige heard it, too: a cough
Within the helmets they had taken off
And left about. All made the same complaint,
Enrobed in feedback. Still, the cough was faint.

The limbs that bore the wolf head rose and scuttled
To the centre of the werewolves' huddle.
Four of them unfurled: one limb per paw.

Paige took one. Dot and Campbell, too. In awe,
Moe grabbed a limb and held it to her chest.
"I loves pacts. By the way, I keeps me best
Knife with me at all times. We'll cut our paws."
Her free paw searched her suit. "We'll need some gauze…"

"I thought I took her knives away," said Campbell,
Looking at the shifter. "It's a gamble
Letting Moe have access to harpoons,

Just so you know. It's been a dozen moons
Since Mr. Peddle let her hold that pair
Of blubber forks."

                Moe fixed him with a stare,
Then turned to Dickie. "Mr. Lush, I've got
Some fireworks that we can use. I brought
'Em in me scrollsack—"

                  "You are now a crew,"
Said Dickie to the larger group, "and you
Will keep our quest a secret." Dickie squeezed
The paw attached to Moe. "They won't be pleased,
Your parents, if they hear you're sailing off
To Moby nests."

              The helmets marked a cough.
But there was no point swearing not to spout
To parents—Moe and Campbell were without.
Paige knew they slept inside the orphanage,
A small dome on a nearby rock, a bridge
Between the asteroids. And Dot, well, she
Was happy to be scratching poetry.

"While we're still holding, um"—Dot eyeballed Dickie's
Tentacle, which seemed to ooze an icky
Texture—"*paws*, I'd like to share a passage
By Lord Byron. It's a hopeful message:

"'As little as the moon stops for the baying
  Of wolves, will the bright Muse withdraw one ray
  From out her skies. Then howl your idle wrath,
  While she still silvers o'er your gloomy path!'"

Dot looked around like: wasn't that the best?

"Thus marks," said Moe, "the launching of our quest!"
She raised her paw and, with it, Dickie's limb.
The polymorph endured this with a grim
Face.

      Campbell turned to him. "I'll fix the fang
Next?"

        "Fang?" said Dot.

                "It's old-school whaler slang,"
He said. "Means 'hyperdrive.'"

                    The shifter shook
His head. "Not me. Your captain's *there*." He looked
At Paige.

      Paige blinked. "Excuse me?"

                    Dickie broke
His grips and, turning, said, "By moonlit stroke
Of luck, we've found our lookout, too."

                        He crawled
Toward a heap of junk and, reaching, hauled
Out someone in a helmet and a suit,
The shifter's tendril wound around a boot.
The snout part of the squash-shaped helmet, though,
Was empty. Paige saw soot-black hair and snow-
White skin within the helmet's larger bubble:
Soft skin that'd never known rough stubble.

Paige backed up a little, heart a hammer.
"Dickie, it's a . . ." She could only stammer.

The space suit (which the skin did not require,
Given that the skin enclosed a pire)
Was a child's size. One shoulder bore
The image of a cartoon dinosaur,
A red triceratops, its face all smiles.

Underneath this patch, in stitching: "MILES."

But it thrashed half-heartedly, Paige thought.
Perhaps the thing had wanted to be caught.
(Why would a pire need to clear its throat?
They didn't breathe.) She took a breath and noted
That the swaying pire's pale hands held a
Glowing touchscroll: *Moby-Dick* by Melville.

10.

Kaye barely dodged the tree-wolf ("they/them") bearing
Down on her, the redwood turning, glaring
Back. The Wood was dark so she'd been using
Blurbs to sort the Flora who were cruising—
Or just hanging out—from static trees.
She flinched as something grazed her arm: a breeze
Or shroud?

          A pop-up masque had spread across
The Wood. She'd spotted Floras filmed with moss
And ivy. Forking branches topped some heads
Like antlers. Thick vines fell in ropey dreads
Across bark-roughened backs. The leaves of leeks
Stood stiff on pallid scalps. One "he/him's" cheeks
Had broken into baby's breath, the girl
Beside him ballerina-ed with a twirl
Of large, translucent petals at her tiny
Waist: a tutu. Heavies went for spiny
Implants: cactus shit.

                Still, most of what
Kaye saw was surface: seeded in the rut
A scalpel draws. A deeper, all-year branch,
Commitment-wise, would make most people blanch.
Plus Kaye had read of poor fools turning in
Their sleep and snapping off the leafy, thin,

And long-term branches they had grown out of
Their cells: the labour of a gardener's love.

A postcard flew into her line of sight
And paused. The pixelated card was bright
And crisp against the dark. She blinked it open.
Dean L. Avary, Chair of Blah Blah, hoping
For an update on your prof—she blinked
It shut. The postcard left a white, distinct
Square floating on the Wood—then slowly faded
From her eyes.
                    She hurried up the graded
Path and saw some nods to M.L. Clarke's
The Green Organic Wolves. She'd heard loud barks
And turned to find a pair of tree-wolves, coats
Like shaggy willows, bearing shoulder totes.
(The totes were clinking and presumably
Contained some bottled stuff for revelry.)
At dawn, in honour of Clarke's novel, they
Would pause, as tree-wolves always did in daylight.
Stretching arms up, they'd pretend to freeze
As if the sun had turned them back to trees.

The Green Organic Wolves—a horror romp
And paean to Alan Moore's great comic *Swamp
Thing*—wasn't quite Kaye's favourite *Full-Moon* fanfic.
Right-wing critics, sowing social panic,
Liked to link it to a recent spate
Of Floras. Kaye, appalled at hedgelord hate,
Had duly bought the novel. But the frothy
Fanfic Kaye loved most was *Full-Moon Coffee*,
Words and pictures by a virtuoso
Artist, Riko Haida, from Kyoto.

It took place inside a boat-café
Whose maids served furless patrons in the day
But, when the moon was out, grew fur and served
A werewolf clientele. (The café swerved
To seek out ships in need of caffeination.)
Kaye had read the fanfic in translation.

Clarke's book also paid homage to sci-fi
Classic *Involution Ocean*, by
Bruce Sterling. In the latter, fine dust stands
In for an ocean. (Clarke's book uses sand,
Though.)
              Over Tokyo, the moon was full.
A *Full-Moon* fan could scarce resist its pull.
In fact, one subset—fierce and absolutist—
Spurned all moonless nights. They'd howl "Judas!"
At those fans who congregated under
Partial moons: a sacrilegious blunder.

Still, most Floras, here, were unrelated
To the *Full-Moon* franchise. These ones mated
When they gathered, pressing fingertips
In plots of soft earth. This was how their lips
Enjoyed a kiss, by sexy proxy of
The soil. This was how their roots made love.

* * *

She sidestepped Floras, dodging more collisions.
Kaye had left the Wood to buy provisions:
Extra clothes and toothbrush. She'd resolved
To stay the night, she'd told Lux; she'd dissolved
Enough that week, her molecules in flux
And flensed by customs sieves.

                    "Alright," said Lux
A little later, out of nowhere. Kaye'd
Been sitting with him, by the model. They'd
Been watching Chapter Ten.
                    "Alright?" She knew
What Lux's outburst was referring to,
But made a point of frowning.
                    "You can come,"
He said, his shades reflecting tank. The dumbprint,
Witchy *Full-Moon Odyssey* was resting
On his lap.
            The iris showed Paige fessing
Up to Del. She says, I did indeed
(Claw quotes) *obtain* your locket. But I needs
To bring it to this cave, see. Paige is standing
On a dock. Del's on a raft; he's sanding
Something like a prow. She'd followed him
Down to the sea, and now recalls the grim
Talk going round: that Del's been contemplating
Leaping to his death. She frowns. So wait,
You're working on a boat? They said that you
Were down here screwing up the guts to do,
Well, something stupid.
                    It's a raft me father
Started, Del says, eyes down. Please don't bother
Me, okay? I'm leaving on a quest.

Paige crosses paws. So where you going?
                                    West,
His eyes still down.
                    She steps onto the raft.
You're joining *my* quest, Del. She grabs a shaft
Of wood for balance. Makeshift mast.

                                         He looks
At her. I'm leaving, Paige. He stoops, unhooks
A thickly braided rope lashed to the dock,
And holds it up. The raft begins to rock
And drift.
                    But Paige sits down and grips a log.
She stares him down . . .
                                    A paint-by-numbers slog,
Felt Kaye officially; this battle of
Two wills, two hearts, will culminate in love.
And yet: she'd found she had to linger while
Lux watched the chapter, holding back the smile
Forming on her lips. (He'd turned the sound
On; voices, done by actors Kaye had found
Annoying, traded quips.)
                                    The Dickie bot
Had gone back to its hovel. When the plot
Was done with someone, they would hurry home
And wait there, charging up. (They couldn't roam
The tank at will.) So Dickie sat inside
His hovel, cheetah spots across his hide,
While Del and Paige's bots explored their snouts—
A kiss the novel hammers when two spouts
Conveniently "spurt water out at sea,"
A much-loved stretch of purple poetry.
Kaye's essay (A!) critiqued the scene at length.
She felt that romance wasn't Fiction's strength.

* * *

Now Kaye was heading manse-ward, items in
Her knapsack. Nearby, someone's mandolin
Was issuing a mournful melody.
She turned to see a six-foot willow tree

Was sitting on a stump, the instrument
Against his chest. A box-shaped ornament—
A birdhouse?—dangled from one ear. More trees
Sat round him, still, like figures in a frieze.
They sat so close their branches seemed to mingle.

Just beyond this audience, a single
Figure watched the willow. Ichiro.
He'd lost the shirt and tie, the Savile Row
Vibe. He now wore a golf shirt and a pair
Of jeans. His shoes—a shock—were Chucks. His hair
Seemed slightly shaggier, attractively
Unkempt. She guessed that pixies actively
Adjusted random follicles, ensuring
Ichiro gave off a cool, alluring
Look. (A pricey dandruff, though she'd read
That low-cost versions for grade-schoolers' heads
Were being used in schools to root out lice.)
His eyes, reflecting hanging orbs, were ice.

The man was only thirty, Lux had told her,
Even though when working he seemed older.
He'd inherited a family business,
Which had carved on him a constant grimace.
(Steady eyemail—postcards, DMs—tried
To claim his eyes.) His mom and dad had died
When he was twelve. Assorted lawyers kept
The business going, while the young man slept
Or read, avoiding endless nanny bots
Or therapists entrusted with his thoughts.
He'd shown no aptitude for numbers, math.
He felt his life should take an artist's path.

At twenty, as a dropout and a dandy
Drinking heavily, he'd first read Mandy
Fiction's book. It "howled" through the strife
Inside him (Lux's verb). Capsized his life.
He seized the family business, which employed
Four thousand staff, and soon, he'd redeployed
A portion of its vast resources to
The hunt for Fiction, tracking every clue
And rumour since she'd vanished back in 20-
52. He found the cognoscenti
He required: Emmett Lux would help
Him flush out clues by scanning every yelp
And howl in the novel, just in case
The author's text had left the slightest trace.
An unseen team of scrappy data shepherds
Handled harder stuff: financial records.

Kaye walked up to Ichiro. His arms
Were folded. "Ichiro."

                         "Their grafts get worms,"
He said, not looking at her. "Something that
I read somewhere." His voice was even. Flat.
"Why would a person stitch on bark?" He turned
At last and looked at Kaye.

                         She shrugged. "I've learned
That *Full-Moon* fandom is a giant tent."

He slapped the air. (Her blurb?) Some trees had bent
Their torso-trunks and linked their arms to make
A huddle. Tourists paused to watch them shake
Their leafy heads, their foliage entwined,
The tourists taking tintypes. "I don't mind
Them, though. These Rebels, on the other hand—

A pestilence. They really should be banned."

"Agreed," said Kaye. The Wood's cosplayers drew too
Many gawking eyes—as Harajuku
Once did. Tourists overran its slopes,
Their Rebels out or smarteyes on, in hopes
Of snapping content they could post for likes.
A succulent walked by adorned with spikes,
A green-skinned woman with a punk-rock vibe,
A comrade of the local cactus tribe.
They watched her for a moment.

                      "Lux says you'll
Be staying overnight."

               "That's right."

                    "Your school
Approves?"

        "Well, it's a university,"
She said and faced him. "Not a nursery."

"I didn't mean—" He paused. "You'll find a couple
Suites up on the third floor. Bachelor bubbles.
If they let you in, that means they're yours
To access freely. Nothing here has doors.
But once you're in, you'll have full privacy.
And Stephen keeps an eye on piracy."

"Piracy?"

        He smiled. "Corporate. I've
Been kidnapped several times. For bonsai hive
IP." His face turned stern: "We don't, of course,
Negotiate. My Stephen will use force."

"Who's Stephen?"

"Stove. You've met. A very rare
Collectible, you know."
                                 She had to stare.
"That thing from *Beauty and the Man*?"
                                           He nodded.
"Stephen's quantum CPU's been lauded
By a four-star general. His instincts
Are superb—and ruthless. Stephen's in sync
With the manse's grid." He frowned. "He's not
Without some bugs—he's stubborn for a bot—
But he's reliable."
                          She thought about
That. "How do *you* know I'm not here to out
Your secrets? Maybe I'm a spy."
                                          He laughed—
"We've vetted you"—and raised a hand. A craft
Descended: gondola, with scarfed bot standing
At the stern in striped shirt. It was landing.
"Let me take you up."
                              She waved a hand.
"It's fine, I'll—"
                          "Nonsense." Brushing at a strand
Of hair, which had detached to mar his brow
Or lend some character. A charmer's bough.

The slowing gondola, which worked this stretch
Of Wood, had paused above the turf. He stretched
To take Kaye's hand, his other on the fèrro—
Basically, a heart lanced by an arrow.
"Come."
               She took the hand and stepped inside.
(She noticed how his careful grip applied
Firm pressure.) There were several facing seats.

She sat, her knees an inch from his. Vast fleets
Of scows and bikes were flying overhead,
Long perforated lines of brake lights, red
And blinking. Blue lights signaled Tesla Eels,
Her father's favourite scows.
                              She pressed her heels
Down—to be safe. They sank a little, merging
With the gondola, the soles submerged
An inch. She glanced across her shoulder at
The gondolier, the bot's expression flat,
Remote. She'd hacked the safeties on her shoes—
A Crater tic—though footwear that could fuse
With turf was contraband, illegal in
The Wood. Such tech was basically akin
To smuggled firearms. How weird, then, thought
Kaye: *no* one, not a single sieve or bot,
Had stopped her.
                    As the craft began to rise,
She looked down. Blurbs were blinking out, her eyes
Too far. The Floras, from this height, were fables
Set afoot. Kaye thought she noticed Sable's
Ball of harpooned hair, the needles gleaming
Just below, but figured she was dreaming;
What the fuck would *she* be doing here
In Tokyo? (Kaye'd often heard Lux sneer
The fill-in's name. He hadn't liked that he'd
Been forced to take a leave.)
                              The vessel's speed
Increased. It flew above the canopy.
The businessman, implying gallantry,
Sat primly, arms refolded, towers all
Around—the towers' waists, that is—a wall
Of them. The traffic was much louder here,

The skyway's scows and aerocoaches veering
Overhead; the treetops formed a net
That dampened noise.

                              "So what's it mean to vet
An undergrad in English?" Kaye asked, noting
With surprise her voice's edge. The floating
Boat had slowed, the copper bot now dipping
Something like an oar through air, wind slipping
Over it—a prop, she guessed. The craft
Began to turn. The hands that held the shaft
Raced with reflected light. She wondered if
The copper stood for darker skin—a whiff
Of racist thinking that implied Italians?
Certainly, the moustache was a stallion's
Mane. Cartoonish.
                              "Someone on my team
Creates a dossier. I have them screen
For what they can—for criminal convictions,
Legal issues, worrisome addictions,
Economic status, debts, parental
Situation, history of mental
Illness"—trailing off; he'd noticed Kaye,
Her eyes far off. He said, "Are you okay?"

"What do you do with all that information?"
Kaye said, feeling now a dull vibration
As the gondola, its prow the right
Way, started moving.
                              "It's secure." A slight
Warmth in his voice. "And I don't read it any-
Way."
          She tried to focus on the many
Holograms the skyline had arranged.

"I read your essay, though," he said. "It changed
My view of Chapter Ten."
                              She turned to face
Him. Ichiro looked serious, no trace
Of humour. "Wait, you've read my work?"
                                          "Of course."

She looked alarmed. Below, a macro, horse-
Themed, jutted from the canopy giraffe-
Ishly. At last, she loosed a snorted laugh.

"Of course, he did. Of course, he shared it with
You."
        "'Wolves and Hearts Afloat: Constructing Myth
In Fiction's *Full-Moon Whaling Chronicles*.'
I liked the title."
                    Men with monocles
And top hats, in another gondola,
Passed by, a swelling, vintage Victrola
On one man's lap, its broad cone like a bloom.
The men were blue; the SEGA tower loomed
Behind them, SEGA's logo lucid as
A laser. Brassy blasts of big-band jazz
Were coming from the cone.
                            "Your work's impressive,"
Said the businessman. "You bring obsessive
Focus to Ms. Fiction's poetry.
You spot small details of topography
And theme most readers miss. I *do* think, though,
The Paige-Del love scene works." A passing, glowing
Buoy briefly lit him.
                      "Sure," she said,
"Aesthetically. But every book I've read

Insists some clueless heroine has gotta
Fall in love."
            A sudden, white regatta
Broke around them: bonsai yachts, a flock,
Like seagulls.
             "Stephen," Ichiro said, talking
In the strained but calm tone that a parent
Uses for a four-year-old, "apparent-
Ly we have a street race—ah, of course
You *would* be on it. Please, though: gentle force."
He lost his far-off look and looked at Kaye.

"Where were we? Ah, yes, I had *meant* to say
I liked the way your essay was in couplets."

Kaye felt patter on her jacket. Droplets.
"Think it's gonna rain," she said, ignoring
What he'd said, the nice thing. They were soaring
Under stars, but over them as well,
The treetops flush with orbs, each orb a cell.
She leaned and said, "I love those lights that draw
Their power from the moon." She caught her awe—
And straightened. Serious. She was embarrassed
That she'd brought the sky up.
               Condos terraced
With what looked like lily pads of stiff,
Chartreuse, and sumptuous velour—as if
A moneyed class of frog lounged on them—were
Below now.
          "Yes, a truly wondrous blur,"
He said, "this last year. Galas underneath
The full moon. Daylight brunches on the heath
Behind the manse." He frowned. "I think we'll soon

Forget what it was like *before* the moon
And sun. The Miracle." He turned to Kaye.
"Do you remember it?" he asked. "The day
You saw the moon? The first time?"

                                     "No," she lied.
Of course she did, though; she had even cried.
She tried to change the subject. "How's the search
For Fiction going—hey!" The small craft, lurching,
Dodged a lagging yacht.

                           "We have some sense
Of capital. Her fortune was immense.
We're hoping Emmett's model helps us find
Ms. Fiction—helps us get inside her mind."

His arms were folded still; the wealthy, those
Who rarely zubered, shared a certain pose
Acquired from the act of being driven
By their bots. When wealthy dudes were given
Sudden swerves, they leaned in easily,
While Kaye held on for dear life, queasily.

"She cared about the climate. Poverty.
Ms. Fiction owned a lot of property,
Small islands not yet swallowed by the tide."

It felt as if the gondola were gliding
On real water now; its thrusters gave
The sense of being buoyed by a wave.

"And there were other, let's say 'odd,' investments.
We've conducted several deep assessments
Of her wealth."

                   The craft began to slow

And drop. The landing pad was just below
Them, brilliant buoys marking where the Wood
Had paused. Its ring of well-spaced bamboo stood
Like spears in Spartans' hands. The craft touched down.
He helped Kaye out, then climbed out, too. A frown
Had crossed his face.

              "I don't think Paige is 'clueless,'
Though."

        "I'm sorry?"

                "That was your word. Foolish,
Sure." He craned his head in thought. "But Paige
Is in control, at least. She soothes Del's rage.
I like it when they're kissing and they fall
Right off the raft. And how she has to haul
Him to the shore and give him snout-to-snout.
'She pumped his chest. He sputtered like a spout.'"
He smiled to himself, then turned away.

"You really didn't read the dossier?"

He stopped. And then: "I don't need intimate
Reports. I'm really only interested
In knowing if a person might be dangerous.
If she will"—he turned around—"betray us.
Plus, I do know what it feels like when
The world's obsessed with what you did back then."

"Back when?"

           "Whenever you were someone else."
He smiled, turned, and looked up at his house.
"That said, my shepherds might still poach your thoughts."
He looked back. Winked. "Come on." The walk showed spots
Of rain.

"One thing," said Kaye. "I don't mind romance
If the author earns it." But there's *no* chance,
She assured herself, this guy has any
Interest, so whatever. Plus, how many
Gullible and wide-eyed *Full-Moon* fans
Had Ichiro escorted to the manse.
She tried to swat her thoughts away—in vain—
In case his shepherds *were* inside her brain.

But either Ichiro had not quite heard
Her—or felt Kaye should have the final word.
He walked toward his building. Kaye approached
It, too.
       And sensing someone had encroached
Upon the manse, assorted bots—small bats
Affixed to bamboo trees; a pair of rats
That ran along the manse's eves; and even
Smaller creatures, all controlled by Stephen
Stove, out strolling on the grounds—ran silent,
Sweeping scans to gauge if Kaye had violent
Thoughts. A silver snail that trailed no ooze,
Its shell a sonar pack, okayed the shoes
She wore. A camera-mounted caterpillar
Made the final call—and didn't kill her.

11.

As he stood upon the deck, one paw
Around a clewvine, Campbell scratched his jaw.
It wanted pruning, being pronged with twigs.
A shiver ran across his body's sprigs;
Above, the moon seemed stamped from light, so full
He felt it in his flowers, how its pull
Had summoned every petal on his pelt
To full attention. He could swear he felt
A few stalks stretching, straining to drink up
The moonlight, each bulb on his body cup-
Like in its attitude—but surely this
Was his imagination? Still, the bliss
Of standing under moonlight couldn't be
Ignored.
      "Ahoy!"
           He turned to see a tree-
Wolf coming, trundling on a clutch of roots
Across the dock. She seemed to froth with shoots:
An outward sign of something like affection.
Dot. In bloom.
          He sighed. He'd tried deflection,
But she hadn't taken Campbell's hint.
As she approached, he saw the trademark glint
Of gold amid the foliage that lined

Her left wrist. Moonstruck bangle. Vines entwined
The tree-wolf's body.
                              "Dot." He figured he
Should try a tone that wouldn't tease the tree-
Wolf. Flat, say. Unenthusiastic. But:
Not *too* unfriendly. It was cruel to cut
Down young love (Campbell being several years
The poet's senior). Careless words were shears.

"Hey Cam!" She reached the hull and gripped its ladder's
Dark-green rungs, which throbbed like braided adders.
Dot climbed up, then threw a root around
A vine-wound railing, feeling for the ground.
He grabbed her paw and helped the tree-wolf stand.

The ship was hovering above the sand,
A sea of dunes no tree-wolf crossed without
A craft. A plume of sand—a sign of spout,
Of whale life—geysered up at times across
The dunes. The dunes themselves spilled onto moss-
Edged shore, which duly faded into forest,
Where the tree-wolves made their home, a chorus—
Birdsong—in their heads. (Indeed, small flocks
Of lovebirds were now nesting in Dot's locks.)

The masts exploded into petals at
Their peaks. The petals served as panels, flat
And angled moonward, drinking in the light
And drawing energy throughout the night.
The mast that bore the crow's nest trembled like
A bulb-topped tulip (or a head-tipped spike).
The main mast's petals—larger than the other
Ones and spinning—helped the vessel hover.

They were basically propellers made
Of fronds: each petal was a floppy blade.
Three blades behind the ship, a tasselled tail
That dangled, stiffened when the ship set sail—
And started spinning.
       "Think I might've dreamed
About you yesterday," said Dot. She teemed
With noise, a rustling within her pelt.
(The lovebirds maybe? Feeling what she felt
And duly fluttering?) He saw the blue strap
Of a scrollsack running through a few gaps
In her leaves.
     He gazed up at the mast
That bore the crow's nest, hoping to move past
Dot's comment—and avoid the earnest glow
Her leaf-rimmed eyes gave off. "It looks like Moe
Has taken to the venus." Campbell pointed.

The crow's nest really *was* a bulb, appointed
With a tulip's peaks and swaying slightly
On its mast. Moe climbed the tall spar nightly.
She would stand beside the venus, peering
At the sea, and talk, the tree-wolf sneering
As she listed schoolyard enemies,
Or softening as she described the trees
She had a crush on. Miles mostly listened,
Nodding here and there; his flat head glistened
As it caught the moon. He wore a cloak.
His mouth split like a clamshell when he spoke.
It seemed that Moe was now the venus'
Accomplice. ("We're the T.R.O.W.L.'s geniuses,"
She'd said at one point; Miles, though, had glanced
At Campbell worryingly.)

                              "Our Moe's entranced,"
Said Campbell, "by our little visitor."

Dot crossed her arms. "I think he's sinister.
A flytrap that becomes a bat? Un*holy*."
Dot was still quite angry. It had only
Been two months since Paige had been assailed
By several venuses. The things had failed,
Of course. The polymorph had fought them off
And sent three to the sky's Great Compost Trough.

"I think he's good," said Campbell. "Moe does, too.
She says"—his paws made quotes—"we've got to do
The work." The tree-wolf shrugged.
                                        Moe loved to love
"The Other." She would wear a venus glove;
She'd snipped the fingertips to show her shiv-
Sharp thorns, the glove a sign for how to live—
An edgy, anti-bourgeois signifier.
Moe claimed tree-wolves were the occupier.
They had stolen Partridgeberry Strait
And steeped their hairy roots in racist hate.
A few had even draped their leaves in hoods
And driven venuses into the woods.
But Moe felt venuses were plants as well,
And didn't think the things were bound for hell.
It didn't bother her that Miles snapped
At passing flies and held them buzzing, trapped
Inside his beartrap mouth. He'd even shown
An interest in the fireworks she'd blown
Up shit with. Plus, he'd listened to her thoughts
On politics, religion, war, the plots
Of earth best suited for a tree-wolf's roots,

The awkward spring she started bearing fruits,
And so on.
        "Anyway," said Dot, "I guess
I'm glad Moe's found a second buddy.
                    "Yes,"
Laughed Campbell.
           "Think it's love?" Dot grinned at him.

He tried to pivot. "Tell me 'bout your hymn."

Her face changed. "It's an epic in heroic
Couplets, not a hymn." Her tone was stoic,
Grave.
      "Hey Campbell!"
                Campbell looked past Dot.
Two tree-wolves, Paige and Del, approached on taut,
Arachnid roots that made a pitter-patter
On the dock. The couple climbed the ladder:
Del went first, then offered Paige his paw
And hoisted her aboard. She gazed in awe
Upon the sloop's main deck, though Del looked less
Enthused: a tougher tree-wolf to impress.

The toughness, Campbell guessed, was masking grief—
Though Campbell didn't really give a leaf
About Del's feelings; Campbell couldn't help
But stare at Paige, whose leaves were green as kelp.
He guessed that lovestruck Dot was watching him,
But hoped her eyes had not begun to brim.
(It sounded like her leaves had ceased to trill.
The lovebirds in her pelt had grown quite still.)

"I can't believe it, Cam." Paige walked across

The deck, snout tilted up. "I'm at a loss
For words." A shard of moonlight gleamed from deep
Within her chest.

                They'd made the call to keep
The lockets round her neck—the "Howlship,"
That is, which meant the tree-wolves on the ship
("And Miles," Moe had added). Dot had chosen
"Howlship." ("It's cool, right? Comes from Tolkien!")
Dot adored *The Tree-Wolf of the Rings*.
She liked to think they'd been dispatched by kings
Or Ganwulf, say—that they had had a brush
With Noble Tree-Wolves (not just Dickie Lush).

As Paige gazed up, her head's vines seemed to water-
Fall behind her. Straightening, she brought her
Shag up, rummaged in its mass, and took
Her paws away, the locks erect. The look—
A topknot, bound by errant vine—had started
In the School for Wayward Trees, then darted,
Tree to tree, as if the trend were roaming
On a pair of wings. The upright, foaming
Foliage—arrested spouting—seemed
To Campbell proof the Moon approved. It deemed
Their coming voyage to be true and good.

* * *

Paige placed her green paw on a mast: the wood
Was thrumming faintly. Paige knew if she went
Belowdecks, paw out—feeling bulkheads, bent
On pinning down the pulsing—she would spot
A bulging patch of wall, a whipped-up knot
Of wood that shared the palette of a mussel,
Grey and salmon. There she'd find the muscle

Through which Campbell's living, throbbing ship—
For surely it was *his* now—pumped its sap.
She shook her plume of foliage. "Amazing."

Campbell shrugged, though Paige could tell that praising
Him had brought a blush up through his bark.
"We're all shipshape and ready for your lark,"
He joked, deflecting from the blush, then added,
"Captain."
          Del stepped up beside Paige, placid.
"Yeah, it looks alright," he said. He hooked
A vine round Paige's paw and coolly looked
At Campbell.
          Paige, who'd noticed Del's maneuver,
Slipped away. "Where's Moe at?"
                  "Tryna prove her
Point," said Dot. "A tree-wolf can befriend
A venus. Well, I thinks I shall descend"—
She flexed a thorn-tipped paw—"and scratch some verse."

Paige watched her go belowdecks. Dot was nursing
Something. Seemed annoyed.
               Above, the night
Was starflush. Paige looked up, saw Moe and Miles,
Elbows on the crow's nest's rim, their smiles
Moonbuffed. His was flytrap-wide and lined
With fine white needles. He'd been on her mind
Since Dickie had discovered him inside
A cask and, holding up the thrashing wide-
Eyed thing, appointed him the lookout of
The sloop. The creature's presence, just above,
Gave Paige the creeps. His leafless skin was snow.
His scalp grew tar-black stems.

* * *

A moon ago,
While light winds raked the sea, she'd cornered Dickie
On the deck. "Can we be *some*what picky
'Bout the crew we brings on? 'Member when
Those venuses attacked? Explain again
Just why we needs one on the ship?"

He merely
Said, "It's fate, me love. The Moon. I fear we
Have no choice. It was a venus who
First led us to the Moby's cave, then flew
Away when Pike betrayed him. We can make
Things right."

A bulging line of sand, the wake
Of something underneath the sea, had crossed
Below the sloop. The sea's dunes were embossed
With many similar trajectories.
Some viewed these as the short-term memories
Of dune seas. Whalers often chased these paths.
They'd lance the raised lines, which would end in baths
Of dark sap. Wind would rub the dark away;
A hunt's signs rarely lasted til the day.

"The venus," Dickie added, "also seems
To be an orphan. Many venus queens
Will cast the runts out of their colonies.
But small ones have attractive qualities.
They're quick, resourceful. They can fly a loop
Around a bay in minutes. Plus, the sloop
Had been his home. If it's to sail again,
Then he should come." His shag disclosed a wren
As if to stress his point. It flew away
Toward the shoreline's trees. "And anyway,

It wouldn't hurt to have a deeper bench."

"But he's a *venus*. You don't think he'll quench
His thirst for tree-wolf sap?"

He shrugged. "I'm not
Too worried." Frowning. "I'm not sure I've got
What you'd consider sap."

"But what about
The rest of us?"

They heard a distant spout,
And then they turned their muzzles seaward, where
They saw a hissing jet of fine sand flare
And fall, a whale now surfacing, the dunes
Dividing, sliding from its back, the moon's
Reflection like a doily on the shelf
Of whale skin.

Later, Paige was by herself,
Belowdecks in the hold, attempting to
Tack up a fallen vine. She'd placed a few
Thorns in her mouth, extracting them when needed
As she inched along a bulkhead beaded
With the caps of mushrooms. She would stop,
Pluck out a thorn, position it, and bop
It with a mallet.

"Hi."

She jumped and whirled.
A feeling, like her foliage had curled,
Ran down her branches, shivering toward
Her roots.

The venus, cloaked, sat on a gourd,
One of a couple seats the room had furnished
For its tree-wolf crew: a patch of burnished
Globes that pumpkinned from the floor. He sat

Cross-legged, hands on knees, his cloak a mat
Beneath his naked bottom. Venuses
Wore nothing usually, their penises,
Vaginas, and attendant fur long gone.
But Paige had noted dark cloaks lying on
The deck throughout the ship, which Miles flew
Between like docks. And yet he'd crept up to
The gourd in total silence, neither talon
Clacking on the floor. He had a talent,
Clearly, for clandestine creeping.

                                                  "Esus,"
Paige said, round her mouth of thorns.

                                                 The venus
Looked confused. "Who's 'Esus?'"

                                             "Ake ome oise."

"What's that?"
                            She took the thorns out. "Make some noise.
Like, flap your wings." She put the thorns back in.

"I like your fangs," said Miles with a grin.

She looked at him, then turned back to her vine.

"You need a hand?" He raised one. "One of mine?
I'll hold your nails."
                       "O anks," she said, and smacked
Another thorn. Since Paige had been attacked,
She'd thought of carrying a stake around.
She smacked a few more thorns, a meaty sound,
And tried to focus on her hammering
Until she heard a fading fluttering
Of wings.

She turned. The shed cloak was a pool
That draped the gourd. She said the G-word: "Ghoul."

* * *

Del turned to Campbell. "What about me raft?"
There'd been some talk of taking it.
                                        "It's aft,"
Said Campbell.
                "Aft?"
                                "Behind the sloop. We've lashed
It to the stern."
                        Del looked. "It's getting splashed."
He turned to Campbell. "Can we put a sheath
Around the prow?"
                        "That weird part with the teeth?"

Del blinked. "That part's supposed to be a head—
Me father's."
                "Del, I'm sorry—"
                                        But the red-
Leafed wolf stormed off, as Campbell turned to Paige,
Teeth gritted: oops. She brought a leafy cage
Of paws up. Masked a smile.
                                Dot, below,
Was scratching couplets. Wind began to blow,
A storm advancing. Paige approached the railing.
Ships afloat above the sea were trailing
Nets and dragging depths, the fine sand slipping
Through as cod collected. Hulking shipping
Vessels—each expressed in dotted lines
Of light, each dot a buoy—made their signs
Against the distant darkness: language on
The ocean's edge. She felt it coming, dawn,

Then quickly turned to Campbell.

"Where is—"

"Dickie?

Climbing on the hull. His paws are sticky.
Doing spiderwolf."

She turned, leaned over.

Since the sloop was idling in hover
Mode, there were a couple feet between
Its belly and the sand: a gap a lean
And crawling shifter on all eights could slip
Through.

"Dickie!"

As he crawled around the ship—

Around the curving lower hull and into
View—she heard a peeling sound. More wind blew,
Ruffling her leaves; the storm was coming
Closer. Paige watched Dickie, who was humming,
Slap one paw against the hull (a seal
Established) and remove (with bandage-peeling
Suck) another—then slap that one down
As well. His muzzle (frozen on a frown,
His default face) was stubbled with white moss.

He reached the top and flung a limb across
The railing, Dickie's pliant forepaw landing
On the deck and puddling—expanding.
But the limb remained connected to
His shoulder as the forepaw pooled like glue.
The limb was now a stream, the puddle spreading
Further. Soon, the stream bulged as his head
And chest passed through its length and fed the pool,
Which grew and grew. A waterfalling jewel
Came down the stream, and then its mate: each one

A tardy eye. The pool rose like a bun
In timelapse til the polymorph was standing
On the deck, his skin expelling (strand
By strand) the willow fur it sometimes kept.

* * *

The moon before, she'd asked him how he slept
At night. Like, did he use a cot? Or did
He can himself? How did he turn the lid?
She'd finished hammering her thorns and climbed
The tight companionway, its railing thymed
With sprigs. She'd found the shifter standing oak-
Still on the deck—and hit him with the joke.

He eyed her coolly. "Humour is your crutch,
Me love. I did, though, sleep inside a hutch
Once..."
            It was made of tin, he said, a hole
Drilled in the back for air. There was a bowl
Of water for the rabbits, and a glass
Face you could watch them through. He'd often pass
The hutch and smile.
                    One night, Dickie's mother
Locked him in it. (She had meant to smother
Bad behaviour; Dickie had reshaped
In public.) Dickie cried out as she draped
A brocade tablecloth across the box.
She went outside to gather heavy rocks,
Then placed these on the hutch's top: thump, thump.
He clawed the ceiling's tin, the rabbits jumping
Clear of Dickie, crouching near their bowl
In darkness. In a calm state, he could roll
Himself into a ball and blow his matter

Outward like a cannonball—and shatter
Glass. Or he could pause, his mind condensed
To make a point, and bunch himself against
A small hole, pushing through, his body spilling
Out the aperture like rubber filling
Up with air. But Dickie loathed tight spaces.
He would dream of being trapped in cases.
(Dickie's mum had liked to say that rich
And idle tree-wulves—with a morbid itch
To paw at—would've killed to have him under
Glass.) So little Dickie—left to thunder
In the hutch, his heartbeat hammering
Inside his head, his muzzle stammering
Two syllables, "Ma*ma*!"—passed out and fell
Among the rabbits. Woke up to a bell.
The church's.

        "Well, I'd better find a trough
To pool in for the day." He wandered off
Then, leaving Paige alone on deck and feeling
Herbsmall, picturing poor Dickie reeling
In the darkness.

        He still had the hutch,
Though, she remembered. It was in his hut.
Why *had* he kept it round?

* * *

        Del had returned.
Paige took his paw and tried to look concerned.
(This couple thing was new.) They watched as Dickie
Walked around the sloop's deck. He'd been picky
As they'd fixed the ship up.

        "How's it look?"
Asked Campbell, looping vine around one hook,

A branch that jutted from a mast.
                                        The shifter
Took a breath. "I don't suppose we'll lift her
Higher." Then he let a long sigh out.
"I guess she'll do, though."
                                Campbell quashed a shout
Of joy, while Paige and Del swapped glances of
Relief.
            Del turned to Dickie. "So, we shoves
Off when?"
                    The shifter looked at Paige. "We leaves
At Captain *Paige's* leisure."
                                        Del was grieving,
Paige knew. Still, she felt a bit annoyed.
Since kissing on the raft, they'd both enjoyed
This—what to call it? Courtship? Twining of
Their roots? Relationship? Not (surely) love?
But Del had looked to *Dickie* several times
For supervision. Not an awful crime,
And yet . . .
                She shook the thought away. "We'll sail
Next moon." She looked at Del. "We'll bring the whale
Her brats." She pawed the lockets. Nearly smiled.

Distant thunder rumbled. Clouds had piled
Up out on the sea, their bottoms dark
As dirt. The storm was moving in, a stark,
Fast-moving front.
                        "The Moon's about to weep,"
She said, a Wulvish saying. "Time to steep."
They'd soon disband, returning to their plots
Of fenced-in soil. Paige would head to Dot's.

She noticed Dickie wander off and, touching
Del's arm, said, "Hold on."
                                    She found him clutching
What she'd learned was called a "clewvine," dangling
From above. It helped control the angling
Of the mainmast's petals.
                              "Dickie?"
                                            No
Response.
              She stepped toward him.
                                          "Long ago,"
He said, "me mother"—frowning at the vine—
"She used to say that. You could smell the wine,
But"—Dickie let the vine go—"she was sweet
Then. She would lean across and pull the sheet
Across me roots. I'd change shapes in me sleep
And kick it off. 'The Moon's about to weep,'
She'd say." He smiled. "They weren't really roots,
Of course. I'd grow all kinds of leaves and shoots
To fit in. Anyway, she knew I couldn't
Stand all night in soil. So, she wouldn't
Let me steep outside. She'd build a mound
Of blankets up. A bed. She'd say, 'The ground
Is not for shifters.'"
                          Paige felt wind comb through
Her foliage. "I thinks me mum had blue
Eyes, but I don't remember."
                                  Dickie nodded.
"Mine—she wasn't mine. I was adopted.
When she left, she left the sloop."
                                        "You said—"

"The owner was in prison, maybe dead?

His sloop abandoned?" Dickie laughed. "I know.
I lied. Me mother told me I should go
To sea someday. To find me parents maybe.
Mother found me when I was a baby."

* * *

Paige approached him. Placed a green paw on
His arm. They turned to face encroaching dawn.
—So Dot described the scene much later, thorn
At work. She worried that the lines were corny,
Though. Her goal: well-rooted characters
Designed to please her future connoisseurs,
The picky, half-soused bards inside The Full-
Moon Whaler's Garden, who would one day pull
Their stools (small pots of soil) to the fire,
Listening as Dot took up a lyre
And declaimed her couplets on the quest
To bring the seeds back to the Moby's nest.

But here, though, in the present, she was focused
On the sloop: describing it. The locusts
That had left the hull half-chewed were long
Gone; Campbell had worked wonders. Thus, her song,
If worth a howl, surely had to sing
Its praise of Campbell's work: the thorny thing
Now jutting from the front (a "figurehead"
Which he'd refurbished) or the "timberheads"
(Which he'd pruned back to life). She'd had to look
Up proper names on clayscrolls, in a nook
Behind the whaling office at the port.
She'd learned the meaning of the word "athwart!"

But she'd been struggling to scratch out Paige

And Del's dumb fling, to get it on the page.
The brooding bard now sat belowdecks on
A stump the sloop itself had stumped up. Lawn-
Lush fuzz had crossed the floor like living carpet.
She was starting to feel like an artist.

As she listened for the Moon's dictation—
And as Dot's friends made their preparations
Just above her, rigging vines and working—
No one saw the one-eared figure lurking
On the shore: a tuckamore with brittle
Limbs. The hunched thing's leaves had gone a little
Brown. It looked as if he'd lanced his eye and
Held the shaft in place. It was a spyglass,
Actually; his shaggy brow leaves seemed
To swallow up the brassy shaft, which gleamed.
Glen Budgell, Paige's father, eyed his daughter
On the sloop's deck. Rain was falling, water
Beading on his lens.
                              Paige probed her chest,
Pulled something from its leaves, her care suggesting
Consequence. Her father wore a ragged
Pair of pants, which let him keep a jagged
Shiv of whittled whalebone in a pocket.

Through the spyglass, raindrops struck a locket.

12.

Kaye stood beside the water wheel that gazed
On Rabbit Strait, the bonsai ocean glazed
With sunlight. Lux had kept the model running,
But he'd left the sky's sun up, a stunning
Cosmic shift the model's wolves had failed
To notice.
         Ichiro, beside her, hailed
The junk, a tiny point above the harbour,
Moving quickly—basically, a shard her
Smarteyes couldn't parse. They'd analyze
Incoming targets, popups in her eyes
Explaining shit, but always lagged a little
After zubering, her vision stippled
With stray pixels. Ichiro had clapped her
Back, though, pointing out the white junk.
                           Chapter
Twelve, unfolding down below, returned
The plot to town. The heroes had adjourned
And headed home. Next moon, they'd sail to Kelly
Bay. But in the tavern, Machiavelli-
Like, a one-eared, livid wolf was plotting
With a pair who specialized in robbing
Boats. The pirates planned to intercept
His daughter's sloop.

They'd all donned "pelts," except
For Kaye. "The tank's cold," Ichiro had warned.

"I'm good." She'd gone with wiseweave sweats, adorned
With Nike's swoosh. The rest—two modellers,
The businessman, and Lux wore cosplay furs.
A grumpy Scottish tailor in the Wood
Had cut the jackets. Mink supplied each hood
Its collar. Kaye knew no one who could buy
Such clothing.
                    Lux had had to draw an eyelid
Down. The booth had made a ding, its glass
Relaxing. One by one, the party passed
Inside and vanished, swirling down the drain
And out the water wheel. The whirling grains,
Which seconds earlier had lost their grip,
Became their bodies—smaller ones. (The drip
Of wonky teleporters could take hours,
Though, two shoes disgorging legs like flowers.
Topline teleporting built a body
From the ground up, feet first. But a shoddy
Booth placed hapless patrons' atom swarms
An inch above the surface, fully formed.
You always knew your bonsai booth was shit
When you re-formed—and fell a little bit.)

The junk was starting its descent: an ivory,
Mohawked ship the modellers had wisely
Left unpainted, thus alluding to
Some Universal Build—pre-paint, post-glue.

She'd never been inside a bonsai model.
Bouncing, Kaye tried out the springy, novel

Pixieclay. The ground was filmed with green
Shreds—grass, in theory—with a glossy sheen
That looked a little off. She gazed up at
The sky: the underside of Lux's vat,
Inside a rich man's compound. Clouds were drifting,
Wind produced by hidden fanblades lifting
Brittle leaves (which never had been soft
To start with) into scarlet schools, aloft
And turning, of one mind. You had no clue
That staff of Ichiro's were staring through
The ozone's curving shell to monitor
The jaunt and also give the modellers
A hand if shit went down (or Ichiro
Required drinks).

               Kaye turned to Lux. "But so,
Like, *how* exactly does a hardwood floor
Hold up this tank?"

               "It doesn't. There's a core
Of dense titanium below the Wood,
A couple miles deep." He coughed. "They stood
The manse on top of it. The core"—he motioned—
"Comes up *through* the manse, right? So, the ocean,
Town, it all sits on the core. The story
Is they piped titanium through Mori
Tower. Filled it in."

               The junk had "landed"—
Floating overhead. Its hull was branded
With a claw that Kaye thought pretty swish,
Hatori's corporate logo. Ivory fish
Fins, creased like folded fans, were jutting from
The lower hull. As if a see-through thumb
Had pressed the hull, a patch went concave, popped,
And yawned to form a mouth. A white tongue dropped.

"The bus is here," said Lux. "You better hold
Your buddy's hand."
                         The tongue began to fold
Itself, suggesting stairs. Posts sprouted, swerved
Like snakes, and joined up. "Railings," Lux observed,
The junk reflected in his shades.
                                    "Professor,"
Kaye said, "you know you can check off 'yes or
No' in SETTINGS if you want to bring
Up sunglass mode."
                    He said, "I like my things."

They climbed the airstair, straight up through the hull,
The passage like the inside of a skull.
Kaye reached the deck, which seemed made of the same
Material: a polished, ivory plain.
The modellers were last, and once they'd cleared
The stairs, the topside entrance disappeared
As if there'd never been a set of stairs.

The deck was bare but for a ring of chairs
Arranged around a sheer infinity
Perimeter. A smart divinity
Around the ship, a pixie-governed trough,
Would grow and catch those klutzes who fell off.
A see-through force field also formed a fence:
A cushion made of nothing. Air grown dense.

The modellers were deep in conversation,
Geeking out about some incarnation
Of *The Full-Moon Whaling Chronicles*
She'd never read: *The Aeronautical
Were-Mechs*. The characters were human teens

Who mostly sat in cockpits lined with screens.
They piloted gigantic were-mechs powered
By full moons. (The sleeping were-mechs flowered
In the evening, muzzles lifting, claws
Extending: drill bits siloed in their paws.)
The modellers receded to the stern.
The junk began to rise and slowly turn.

"Let's take a tour," said Ichiro, his hands
    Clasped like a waiter's. "Maybe see the lands
Of *Full-Moon*?" Brow raised.

                              Lux said, "Waste of time."

"Oh, come now." As the junk began to climb,
    He turned the brow on Kaye.

                              She looked between
    The two men. It was up to her. "I mean,
    I'd love to see the Moby . . ."

                              Ichiro
    Tried not to grin and, turning, said to no
    One in particular, "Roppongi Ocean!"

Seemingly on polished rails, its motion
    Liquid smooth, the junk began to head
    Toward the water. Ichiro now led
    Them to recliners situated near
    The bowsprit. Wind had brought a single tear
    To Kaye's eye, which she dabbed at with her sleeve.
    Cloud-cliffs swept past. She couldn't quite believe
    That they were flying out to see a whale—
    A bot, but still.

                              The ocean at this scale
    Looked finely wrinkled. Hidden fanblades raked

The water into waves. Small vessels, waked
With peacock tails of fanned-out foam, were hauling
Netted fish. Their bo'suns would be calling
Orders, Kaye assumed. She knew their voices
Could be piped at will, that minor noises—
Like the grunts of shorewolf extras loading
Vessels—could be heard. The waves exploding
Shoreward were recorded by small mics
That bristled everywhere, a down of spikes.

The cunning modellers had siphoned several
Million tons of water, which was stressful
Work. They'd had bots carry traps (about
The size of trumpet cases, pronged with spouts
For intake) to the shores of Okinawa.
Bonsai seas took work. A trap could draw a
Lake's worth in, compacting molecules.
The traps were not quite legal; clumsy fools,
She'd read somewhere, had somehow fumbled small,
Handcrafted traps, which smashed and loosed a squall
In Ginza.
          Kaye sat on a blue recliner's
Edge. Its pillow, made by French designers,
Felt extremely firm. (Her buttocks might've
Been the lounger's maiden ass.) The height of
Fashion had been bonsaied down to fill
The deck—or artisans with arcane skill
Had sat *outside* the tank and built the model
Lounger as one might a ship in bottle,
Using tweezer drones.
                She crossed her arms
And looked around. Perhaps the upscale charms
The junk had been outfitted with were meant

For Moonheads Ichiro had met and spent
(Or was *about* to spend) the night with: tourists
From the Wood. His motives weren't the purist,
Surely, even if the tank, as Lux
Insisted, was for research, not deluxe
Seductions over Rabbit Strait. The random
Fucks the junk had likely hosted—fandom
Preyed on by a wealthy player—made
Her mad, though who cared, really, if he'd played
Some Moonheads?

                  Ichiro and Lux had gotten
Into something heated. "She'd forgotten
All her early writing," Lux said. "Mandy
Hated it."

          "Her name, back then, was candy
For the scholars," Ichiro replied.
"'Man(fiction)' meant the self *itself* had died,
A death reflected typographically.
Now 'Mandy Fiction' was, commercially,
A better option. *Both* names, though, suggest
A person who's decided to divest
Herself of something like a stable self.
Her early characters—a cyborg elf,
A teen vampire—are in constant flux,
Right? Always changing?"

                   "Meaning what?" said Lux,
Now picking at a thread his chair's designer
Pillow had produced. The lush recliner,
Made of pixieweave, had sensed Lux leaning
And contrived a flatter angle.

                      "Meaning
She became another person—or
Another something. *Full-Moon* was the door

Into that other self."
                    "So what, she grew
A pelt—big deal."
                    "My shepherds have gone through
Her various investments. Quite exotic
Stuff. Genetic engineering. Optic
Implants. Protein-culture pollination.
Sub-molecular design translation.
Embryonic tissue seeds and sutures.
Lupine replication stocks and futures.
Geodesic nano architecture.
Artificial atmospheric pressure.
Why, though, would a brilliant YA author—
With a multibillion fortune—bother
With such things?" He gazed across the ocean.
"Every word she wrote expressed devotion
To rebirth, renewal, and arrival.
Anyway, I'm worried that a rival
In the cloning space—the Chinese, maybe,
Or the oligarchs—will get to Mandy
First."
          "Community."
                    The two men turned.

"Community," said Kaye. "That's what she burned
For most. That's what her characters seek out—
Discover at the end. Her book's about
Community. That's why she launched the site,
Wolfpack Salon. To link her readers, right?"
She blinked.
                    Lux laughed. "That's it, I'm bumping you
To A+."
          Ichiro said, "That's a new

Interpretation." Eyeing her. "Perhaps
The themes of ecological collapse
And transformation are too obvious."
He smiled. "Well, I'm just a hobbyist."
He turned back to the ocean. "We're arriving."

Kaye fell back, the bonsai junk now diving.
They had reached a nondescript expanse
Of waves. She had to tell herself the manse
Was just behind the sky, and just beyond
It, Tokyo. The ocean was a pond,
Glassed in. And yet the waves the tank compressed
Looked right. You couldn't tell they sloshed against
A distant, curving wall.
                              The junk had levelled
Out. A plinth was rising, one edge bevelled,
From the deck. The bevel was a glassy,
Touchscreen plane, the growing plinth in classy
Wood grain.
                    Ichiro stood up, approached
The plinth, and tapped its screen. The plinth, reproached,
Stopped growing as his hands keyed in some code.

The modellers had reappeared. One showed
Him something on the screen, then, leaning over,
Tapped its face. The junk had come to hover
Several hundred feet above a patch
Of ocean that was bubbling.
                                      "Our catch,"
Said Lux.
              Kaye stood and walked toward the edge.
She reached a hand out; she could feel a hedge
Of spongey air, the see-through barricade.

(A sprinting body, hands clasped like a blade,
Could puncture it.) Kaye didn't mind the sheer
Edge, though; the Crater had dissolved all fear
Of dangerous heights.

                "We house it here," said Lux
To Kaye.

        "We like to call this stretch the 'Crux,'"
Said Ichiro.

        The Moby rose, a round
And sunlit island fringed with foam. Its ground
Was off-white, veined with subtle traceries.

"This stretch made sense because of vagaries
  Of plot and such. It's equidistant to
  Both nest and shore."

            The Moby grew and grew.
Arms crossed and leaning forward, Kaye was silent.
It was scary, sure, but not as violent
As the animated version from
The latest tintype, which spewed half-chewed chum
And cried out skyward with a bird-like shriek,
Expressed through several nested beaks, each beak
Concealing yet another, smaller, gaping
Beak. (Some fanboys pegged this as a "rape"
Of Fiction's classic text.)

              The one below
Was less baroque. It split like soundless dough
To form a yawning rent that faced the sky,
Resembling the heavy-lidded eye
That slowly opens in so many horror
Tintypes, just behind some cave explorer,
Who will shortly turn and raise her lantern . . .

"Not bad," Kaye said, peering down the cavern
Of the mouth.
                "The plastic's quite responsive,"
Ichiro said, typing out some missive
With a flourish. Down below, the chasm
Closed, the dough went smooth. A subtle spasm
Rippled through the surface of the Moby.
Then, a line formed. Curved. Two dots. Emoji.

Lux had turned away to shake his head.
"Let's get the fucking Dickie bot," he said.

The Moby's smiley face collapsed in frown.

* * *

They flew to Rabbit Strait. The junk set down
Beside the wharf. It stayed afloat and dropped
Its airstair. All was silent. Nothing clopped
Along the cobblestones—and no one barked.

With Kaye in tow, the party disembarked.
The sacrilegious sun, still up, was gauzed
With threadbare clouds. The modellers had paused
The model. Werewolves stood like statues. Through
A windowpane, Kaye noted white shampoo,
Landsliding in slow motion down a small
Cub's muzzle. In an alleyway, a ball
Sat still between two wolves, their paws extended.
Seagulls lay about; all birds descended
When a chapter froze. The werewolves' eyes
Were giant, pupilled pools of white, the size
In manga.
              Carefully, Kaye looked inside

A one-eyed busker's mouth. Its gape implied
A deep and heartfelt moment in the song
It had been singing. Small fangs ran along
The mouth's edge, but the pinkish throat was dry,
As was the busker's single open eye.
Kaye raised the eyepatch, finding only fur.

"My team's still polishing each character,"
Said Ichiro. He reached out, flipped the patch
Back down, his fingers grazing Kaye's. "A batch
Of wolves takes work. The setting, though, is perfect.
You will find we've indexed every object—
Mentioned in the classic text, of course."

The clapboard shacks were faithful to the source,
For sure. Kaye went inside Dot's house and saw
The upright mirror where Dot checked her maw
Before school every day. Kaye felt some dread;
The glass had caught her smarteyes. U-Perth red.

She wandered to Dot's room. A textscroll, *Math*,
Lay on the bed, alongside Wulvia Plath:
The classic *Ariel and Other Howls*.
Wall hooks held limp cloaks like fish—by cowls—
While the floor was strewn with more cloaks, shed
And left like skins.

                              Kaye plopped down on the bed
And unrolled Plath; the lengthy single page
Had text! She came to "Fadder," red with rage,
A work of feminist critique and fire,
Which compared Plath's father to a pire.
One side was in English, while the facing
. Side was Wulvish—studied claw marks chasing

One another.

　　　　　　　All was in its place;
She'd never seen such love for bonsai space.
The scale was almost certainly against
The law; the molecules had been condensed
Beyond the international convention.
Ichiro's fanatical invention—
Financed with a fortune—wasn't normal.
(Plus, Dot's room was nicer than Kaye's dorm in
Perth.) And yet Kaye couldn't help but feel
The wolves were creepy—cool but not quite real
Enough—as was her host's enthusiasm.
She had sensed a yawning hole, a chasm,
In the businessman.

　　　　　　　They reached the square,
Where buildings had been organized with care
According to the detailed verse in Chapter
Twelve. Kaye stepped into the tavern. Chatter
Had been silenced. Wolves were gripping steins
Or leaning over tables, Mandy's lines
On pause inside their mouths. The fireplace,
A bulb the modellers had screwed in place,
Was flickering. Bright buoys lit the room—
For tourists, clearly; wolves were fine with gloom.
A small concession.

　　　　　　　Kaye marked, near the back,
A table, three wolves planning their attack
On Paige's sloop: the father, Glen, in ragged
Purple pants, and two wolves armed with jagged
Blades in scabbards. (If she took a second,
Kaye knew she would find a shard-like weapon,
Whittled out of whalebone, plus a spyglass,
In Glen's pockets.) One wolf had an eyepatch

And a peg leg. One had swapped a paw
Out for a hook. The pirate bots were flawless
Recreations.
                            They'd been reassuring
Glen: no werewolves would be harmed securing
Paige's lockets. Glen's delinquent cub
Would learn her place. They *might* dole out a drubbing
To the husky one, though—Campbell, is it?
Course, there was no easy way to visit
Blows upon the shifter, so the best
Way (peg leg nudging something like a chest
Beneath the table) is to box him in.
Glen's face was frozen in a nervous grin.

* * *

A few months after he'd waved Paige away—
For going on about some heist or play
She'd hatched, to toss the freakshow's little hut,
Make off with gold, and divvy up the cut—
He'd overheard two wolves behind the tavern.
He'd been sniffing, looking for a slattern,
When he heard them: talking by a buoy.
It had dimmed, the grass already dewy:
Dawn.
                            They'd crewed with Thom the night he'd fallen.
Both had seen the locket round his sodden
Neck. The thing had given off a holy
Glow. But had it somehow *called* the Moby?
One wolf wondered. Was it from the Moon?

Their gossip lanced Glen like a flung harpoon;
His daughter had been going on about
Some locket! He had thought her off her spout,

And might've said so, might've even hurled
A slur—like "cur" or "slattern"—at the girl,
Now staying with a friend, the smart one, what's-
Er-name, the one not like those other sluts.

A few moons later, after school, Glen found
Paige walking near the shore, then heard the sound
Of someone calling out her name. He saw
A werewolf—Thom's boy—holding up a paw
And chasing after her. Glen backed behind
A shrub, crouched down, and stretched a tube designed
To telescope. He brought the tube, a spyglass,
To his eye. He watched them wade through high grass,
Laughing. Then they reached each other, muzzles
Meeting—opening—their soundless nuzzles
Eating minutes up.
                          They walked on, down
To where a sloop was docked, quite far from town,
Surrounded by a hoop of rocks. Glen followed
Close behind. His growing anger swallowed
Up his thoughts. He found another shrub
And crouched. It felt surreal to see his cub
And Thom's boy cross a dock. He saw them climb
Aboard, where others stood, then noted slime
Of some sort—scuttling across the vessel's
Hull. He tried to focus. Many tendrils,
Like a comb's teeth, lined the slime-thing's edges.
(They seemed built for navigating ledges,
Inclines.) But the slime-thing had a head,
A grizzled wolf head, floating on the bed
Of greyish stuff. Glen nearly cried out when
The slime-thing flung a limb on deck and then,
Defying physics, hauled itself up *through*

The limb—which bulged the way a snake digesting
Something does—the slime-thing reinvesting
In itself on deck. Pooled, it re-grew
The grizzled wolf head, like a rhyme resolved
At long last. Soon, the puddle had evolved
A furry torso, Dickie's, slime withdrawing
Into legs.
                    Glen noted Del was pawing
At his daughter. Now, he was incensed.
He stood, undid his pants, and pissed against
A tree—the spyglass in his paw, a rude
Prosthetic—then resumed his attitude
Behind the shrub. He found the spyglass tricky—
He was tipsy—but he soon found Dickie
And his daughter, further down the deck.
That's when he saw the lockets round her neck.

Her father knew, then, that the lockets held
A special charm. Perhaps they *had* compelled
The Moby to appear. In any case,
It seemed clear that the polymorph had placed
A spell on Paige. He'd likely used the lockets,
Dangled them before her face, eye sockets
Swallowing her pupils. They'd be setting
Sail soon, Glen could tell: the heavy-petting
Son of Thom, the wicked polymorph,
And several others. Glen went to the wharf.
He needed werewolves with a decent boat.
He needed extra muscle, quote-unquote.

The Glen bot would've raised its paws at this
Point, making curly quotes for emphasis.
The pirates would've nodded, having listened

To his reader-friendly exposition.

* * *

Kaye left the tavern. Ichiro had walked
Ahead. Nearby, a whaling ship was docked.
The modellers had pointed something out
To Lux, the three men deep in talks about
The mizzenmast. "It needs another cut,"
Said Lux.
              The businessman was by the hut
When she caught up to him.
                       "Please after you,"
He said, and pushed the door in. It was blue
And marked with nicks, as if the Dickie had
Been keeping time, the calendar a sad
Device.
        Kaye went inside the hut. The spotted
Dickie bot was on its chair. She squatted
Next to it; the shifter's head had slumped
A bit, its tongue unfurled. Its fur had clumped.
The polymorph was clearly on the fritz:
Fine particles, like pixieplastic nits,
Were leaping off the pelt.
                 She turned and saw
What Fiction's book observed: a crosscut saw—
A Cheshire grin with fangs—was hanging on
One wall, above a fireplace. A pawn
Sans chessboard stood upon a window ledge.
Green moss expressed itself along the edge
Of every stone in spurts. Kaye noted shards,
Which looked like shark teeth; scattered playing cards;
Small bits of glass, which roiled in the glow
The fireplace gave off; a domino

(Just one, though) standing on the mantelpiece
(A micro-obelisk); a centrepiece
Shaped like a whale (and beached beside the fire-
Place), which saw few feasts. A soft quagmire
Of assorted quilts, which made a mound
For sleeping on. In other words, Kaye found
A perfect recreation of the hut
Described in Chapter Five of *Full-Moon*. What
Was missing, naturally, was Dickie's locket,
Which was now with Paige.

                          But then Kaye saw it,
Something lying on a low and dusty
Shelf. A second locket. Silver. Must be
A mistake, she figured.

                    "Kaye, let's go."

She turned. Her prof had edged past Ichiro
Into the hut.

            "Come on." He had a look
She'd never seen before: concern. Off-book
For Lux, a frowner. Ichiro himself
Was watching her. Had *he* looked at the shelf
As well?

        She gave a shrug, like no big deal,
And went outside. She couldn't help but feel
She should pretend she hadn't seen the locket.
Absently, she felt her sweatshirt's pocket.
It contained the *Full-Moon* book she'd brought
Along, the dumbprint one that Cat had bought
Her years back.

                Ichiro's men, who'd been waiting,
Went inside the hovel. Isolating
What had happened to the Dickie would

Take diagnostics. Kaye brought up her hood
As Ichiro emerged.
                              "We'll need a couple
Minutes, Kaye." He gripped a severed muzzle,
Fingers squeezing Dickie's plastic jaw.
His other hand now held a pixiesaw,
A wooden hilt from which a toothy leaf
Of steel had sprung—the blade the kind a thief
Might keep upon their person, given it
Could easily retract into a slit.

"I'm gonna walk around a bit," she said.
She couldn't help but note the snout that bled
Between his knuckles, muzzle bulging from
His fist, its ragged end like chewing gum
Distending.
                      Kaye went to the shore and sat
Down on a rock. The rock was smooth, planed flat
Presumably to welcome furless asses.
As she took out *Full-Moon*, reading-glasses
Mode kicked in, the eager smarteyes sensing
Print and focusing. She blinked, dispensing
With the squint, and flipped to Chapter Five,
Where verse makes Dickie's hovel come alive.

She read the chapter, scanning every couplet.
Zero mention of a silver locket.

13.

Paige sat reclined, a bank of screens arrayed
Around her head. Her flight suit, unzipped, made
A "V" of skin. The lockets, lying on
The "V" like covered rowboats, thrummed with spawn.

Afloat inside the were-mech's head (behind
Its glassy eyes, precisely where a mind
Should go) the cockpit was a closed-off sphere
That shielded Paige from freezing mesosphere.
The eyes were ornamental; cameras lined
The head on stems, a fur that fed the mind-
Cum-cockpit different sightlines based on need.
Each screen revealed a different camera's feed;
A central screen displayed the forward view.

The mech stood on the H.O.W.L.'s deck, its two
Feet magnetized. They gripped the deck and kept
Their looming navy suit from being swept
Away by wind. (The patched-up sloop could manage
Ninety knots.) A gyroscopic carriage
Kept Paige upright but reclined, the cockpit
Fixed. So if you rammed a mech and knocked it
Down, its human pilot would stay plumb.

The were-mech's muzzle was a whiskered drum.
(Its tip: black nose.) The muzzle was as large
And bulbous as the sort of modest barge
A denizen of Down Below might sail.
Its tail was jointed like a monorail:
It drooped submissively out of respect
For foes, but feeling brave, it sprang erect.

The were-mech's head was set back on a swollen
Chest. Flat rudders trailed its limbs like motion
Lines in comic books. Its armoured torso
Tapered like its limbs, which narrowed more so
At the joints, the calves and forearms swelling.
Popeye-plump, the forearms helped with shelling
Aerosharks; they held small armouries,
Green missiles stacked like bundled Christmas trees.
But Paige's model was the one they give
To minors, each arm empty as a sieve.
Close rows of waves in chrome (the peaks meringues
Make) quoted fur. Two drills suggested fangs.

Two joysticks, stippled with a skin of studs,
Were poised like cobras by her hands. Small buds
That lived on Paige's eardrums were connected
To the other cockpits and directed
Sound accordingly. If someone said
Her name, their voice would bloom inside her head,
The cockpits linked. Eye contact worked the same
Way. Pilots didn't *need* to say a name
To slide into another mech's CMs
Or "cockpit messages"; the camera stems
Had algorithms that could judge intent.

But undirected talk, the sort not meant
For one specific mech, reached all adjacent
Eardrums set to Ambient Complacent,
Which was default. Paige tried not to mute
Her friends, but it was hard. Dot strummed her lute-
Thing sometimes. Other channels, Moe's for instance,
Carried every sound-shard in existence:
Self-directed monologuing, humming,
Chitchat, coughing, nose blows, cockpit drumming.
(Once, Paige even heard a muffled fart.)

The slightest peep or sigh would summon art
To Paige's leftmost screen: a head bisected,
One half human, one half mech, connected
By a jagged line, the mech half more
Or less a standard avatar but for
Its paint job. (Campbell's mech was off-white, Dot's
Was yellow, Del's was crimson. Rainbow blots
Stood in for Dickie, who was neither mech
Nor human, but some strain of biotech
That changed its shape at will.) The heads would start
To stack as more chimed in. She liked the art,
The way each hybrid head revolved, its name
And stats below, as in a fighting game.

Not that this was a game, of course. The ship—
Or as Dot liked to say, the "*Howl*ship"—
Was on its way across the Clouded Sea
To bring the Moby's eggs back. (Poetry
Was Dot's one job.)
                    They'd left the Strait two hours
Back. The floating town's inverted towers
(Treacherous stalactites you could note

For miles due to safety lights, which floating
Fishing boats steered clear of) seemed to comb
The clouds below, to shred them into foam.
The island's toothy underside suggested
Land on which the island had once rested:
Back when mech-less humans lived sub-cloud,
When people breathed unprocessed air and ploughed
The earth—before they'd ever figured out
The way to buoy towns by gravi-spout
Technology. Some unlit fangs looked furred
And twitchy. Up close, they were clearly burred
With pire-bats.
                              Moe's face popped up, the mech
Side beige. The human half had brown hair, freckles,
And a frown that signalled "attitude"—
A selfie, clearly. (Del's face signalled brooding,
Mourning; he had blacked the human half
Out. Dot's face, brighter, had been snapped mid-laugh.)

"There's something coming," Moe said, from the crow's
Nest. "Not sure what it is. The thing is closing
In, though. Mamma Moby?"
                              Paige could hear
The paper sound of wings inside Moe's sphere,
Like someone thumbing playing cards. The pire
Stayed with Moe now, hanging on a wire
Moe had strung above her head, or flying
Round the multi-dialled cockpit, trying
Different perches. Good, thought Paige. Unfeeling
Things should stay in Moe's mech. Plus, the squealing
Bat made sense to Moe. The two would talk
All night, their shared mech standing on the stalk-
Like mast, which trembled in the wind the ship

Produced when moving.

"I can see a shape,
As well," said Campbell, *his* face now appearing
Just below Moe's. It was new, the leering
Human half a gag—a selfie he'd
Uploaded earlier. "Should we proceed?"
His mech was on the quarterdeck, inside
The wheelhouse.

"Yes," said Del, his mech outside
The wheelhouse. Del's face showed up now, just under
Campbell's. "Noise I'm hearing's mostly thunder.
"Thing's too small to be the Moby, Paige."

"That's *Captain* Paige," said Campbell.

Paige could gauge
Annoyance in his voice. She smiled. "Let's
Keep going." Probably a trawler, nets
Out, dragging cloud for macros.

* * *

In the hold
Belowdecks, Dot was climbing, something rolled
Beneath an arm. She tried to place her white boots
Carefully. She wore a fitted flight suit,
Brown hair pulled back in a ponytail.
The gleaming, curving slopes that she was scaling
Showed her movements, Dot's reflection flowing
Over Dickie's metal surface. Glowing
With accomplishment, she sat down on
A shoulder.

Dickie's giant muzzle, yawning,
Turned—and it was all that Dot could do
To not fall back. An eyelid opened. "You,"

She heard. The pronoun seemed to emanate
From all parts of his body.
                                    "Really hate
To be a bother," now unrolling what
She'd brought, a page of notebook paper, "but
I wrote this thing—"
                            The eyeball, silver, seemed
To roll: oh brother. Every contour teemed
With Dot's reflection. "Fine," his body thrumming
Deeply as he grumbled. "Just the one,
Though."
                    Dot's face, bulbous in the shifter's sphere-
Shaped nose, now split in two: a slot appeared.
She slid the paper in. The speed with which
The page was sucked away made Dot's hand flinch.

"You wrote a *dramatis personae*," said
The shifter instantly; the AI read
Her lines in microseconds every time,
No matter how much work each polished rhyme
Had taken.
                    "Yes, I'm trying to—"
                                            "The 'Dickie/
Sticky' rhyme—you overuse it."
                                        "S'tricky
Finding words that—"
                            "Still, I like the ode
To Campbell. Or at least I think me code
Does. Funny, though."
                            "What's that?"
                                            "How many words
You give to Paige. Describing her. Two thirds
Of what you've written."

Dot went flush. "I've still
Got more to write." She started down the hill
Of chrome.
                "Be careful," Dickie said. "Don't go
So fast."
            She reached the bottom. Dickie's toe—
Or something like a toe—split open, Dot's
Page curling out.
                    "I've marked some awkward spots,"
He said. "Wait, don't forget it!"
                            Dot turned back,
Retrieved the page, then left to find her mech.

The huge, wolf-headed blob, its paws on thighs,
Stayed Buddha-still and slowly closed its eyes.

* * *

Clouds stretched before the sloop like plains of snow.
But if you stepped on them, you'd plunge below.
The Flood (which some had come to capitalize)
Had sent most humans upward, to the skies.
Some sailors *had* tried living on the surf—
Which proved to make for problematic turf,
The constant rain suffused with radiation
From the War (this took caps, too). A nation's
Worth of people, though, had lifted islands
Over clouds. The clouds defined horizons
Now—in all directions.
                        Tech recovered
From the War ensured the islands hovered.
Humans, rooting in the aliens'
Machines (specifically, the craniums
Of mech-sized robots), had extracted software

That'd helped get human towns aloft.
The aliens had figured out the path
To make a gravi-spout: they'd done the math
Allowing for a self-sustaining, stable
Fountaining of gravity, a "table"
At the top, as if the air itself
Had blowholed up to form a solid shelf.

The aliens' machines had also yielded
Blueprints for the were-mechs, which now shielded
Humans from the mesosphere. The vision
For the suits was based on crude religion—
Bronze Age stuff. The aliens had worshipped
Gods who looked like wolves and were conversant
With the Moon. The mechs were forms of praise,
Then, drawing energy from lunar rays.
Because the were-mechs only worked at night,
Most humans, now nocturnal, shied from light.

But no one knew where Dickie—or the giant,
Polymorphous blob of shifting, pliant
Chrome that went by "Dickie"—had come from.
He claimed he'd briefly had a human "mum."

The Clouded Sea, byproduct of the War,
Had spawned odd specimens. You'd hear the roar
Of macro hawks as loud as thunderclaps.
You'd also hear the heavy, shushing flaps
Of vulture wings as large as leather tarps
Stretched taut across a pair of bony harps.
Large vessels, manned by were-mechs, set out on
Their whaling trips, which went from dusk til dawn.
They'd scan the clouds for plumes—or palm-tree tails

The foam withdrew, implying flying whales.

* * *

Moe spun, her chair on rails, and craned to face
The hanging pire. "Do the thing," a trace
Of mischief in her grin. She'd strung the wire
(Extra string from Dot's electric lyre)
Just above her—so the bat could hang.
(Whenever he took flight, the E-string twanged.)
She'd also hung his flight suit from a dial
On the wall. The right sleeve's patch said, "Miles."

"Not right now," the bat squeaked, upside down.

Moe pushed her lower lip out in a frown-
Cum-pout. Her bob was ragged, scissored twice
A year by Nurse, the bot who captured mice
And jabbed arms at the orphanage. "No fun!"
Said Moe. She nodded at his flight suit. "One
More time?"
                    She heard what sounded like the faintest
Hiss: a sigh. He took off (twang) and feinted
At the ceiling—then he dove, clean through
The flight suit's collar. Whump: the flight suit threw
Its arms and legs out, swelling gloves like sudden
Starfish. It was like she'd mashed a button,
Running current through a shrivelled skin.
The collar bloomed a head.
                                    Moe clapped, her grin
Restored.
              The pale boy sagged within the flight
Suit, swaying on its dial, stretching slightly.
"Good?"

"So good."

"I'm going back to sleep,"

He said.

The cockpit's dash began to beep.

* * *

The clouds were like a polar range of dark
Grey peaks. Paige watched the H.O.W.L.'s spotlight, stark
And oval, ripple as it crossed the mountains,
Campbell's radar scanning for the fountains
That could foam and geyser up at will;
The flying sperm whale, jaw wide, hunted krill
That flew within these clouds. Not that they'd bother
With a sperm whale now—not with the mother
Moving through the Clouded Sea in search
Of eggs.

Paige pictured Thom's mech on his perch,
Then falling, bouncing off the vessel's hull.
His shipmates, in their mechs, had had to pull
Thom's mech in with their nets, which caught the drunken
Whaler. Still, his fall had roused the sunken,
Dormant Mum; his cracked snout had exposed
His rusted antique locket, which enclosed
The eggs, to cloud—each egg a tiny droplet
Calling, like the word that ends a couplet,
For its mother.

"Thing is moving fast,"

Said Moe.

Paige looked up at the looming mast
That held the crow's nest. Then, she toggled to
Moe's camera feed. (The mechs liked looking through
Each other's forward views.) A cloud-filled shot
Filled Paige's rightmost screen, a little blot—

A ship—dead centre. Then, a smaller blip
Appeared to break off from the blot-like ship:
A blinking light approaching quickly.
                                        "Fuck
Is that?" said Paige. She tried to zoom in.
                                        "Duck!"
Cried Moe. Her mech's perspective swung away
And then went dark as Paige's main display
Turned white with light—a pixelated blast.
The glare began to fade. The crow's-nest's mast
Had fallen. Paige heard screaming and the pire's
Flapping wings. Her other feeds showed fires
On the deck. Assorted panicked voices,
Overlapping, filled her ears, their faces
Running down her leftmost screen.
                                        Paige urged
Her mech toward the wreckage. Moe's emerged—
A fist at first, exploding through the mass
Of fuming, twisted metal. Shattered glass
Slid off her like a sheet of surf as Moe's
Mech stood, her servos whining, armour glowing
In the flames. She shook her whiskered, drum-
Like muzzle. Then, she turned and raised a thumb.

"Holy Moon!" said Campbell, clearly shaken.
"Moe!" His mech stomped over. Del's had taken
Up inside a harpoon pod. He brought
The barrel round to face the sky, while Dot
Came thundering across the *H.O.W.L.*'s deck.

"Is Moe okay?" she asked. Her jogging mech
Was Nascared with the stickered names of bands:
"The Feral," "Dead Cubs, "Severed Robot Hands."

A giant silver ball rolled next to her.
It rumbled like a marble, skin a blur:
A churning, molten riot of reflection
Slipping—bulging—round the ball's inflection
Point. As Dot ran on, the marble paused
To grow a pair of legs. The legs grew claws,
Which splayed against the deck and raised the ball.
The now-bipedal thing began to crawl,
Expressing more ball-segments, centipede-
Ishly, which grew yet *more* legs. Gaining speed,
It caught up with Dot's mech, the way a sidekick
Might, the total stomping sounding seismic.
Something like a muzzle—Dickie's head—
Swelled from the lead ball like a figurehead,
While Dot's mech was repeated in the gleaming
Spheres, a string of stretchy mechs in scheming
Funhouse glass.

       "I'm fine," Moe managed. "*We're*
Fine." Bat wings could be heard. Her mech stepped clear
Of smouldering debris.

       "The moon just hit us?"
Paige said.

       Dickie's muzzle formed a grimace.
"Cannonball, me love. They're likely pirates."
One leg nudged her: clink. "We'll want a pilot,
Paige. A pair of mech paws at the wheel."
His voice was calm, his pupils empty steel.

"The wheel." She looked at Dickie. "Right." She tried
To slow her breathing. Gripped her sticks. Applied
Some focused pressure. Every single stud
Found Paige's mind. Her thoughts began to flood
The were-mech's limbs.

She steered herself to Campbell's
Mech, now fussing over Moe's. Some vandals,
Assholes from the Normal School, had tagged
The limbs of Campbell's suit. They'd climbed the cragged
Face of its armour—where they'd found it parked
Outside the School for Wayward Teens—and marked
Its off-white coat with penises and asses.
Unperturbed, he'd left their scribbles as is.

Paige tapped Campbell's arm. He looked at Paige.

"I need you in the wheelhouse, 'kay? Engage
The shields."

     He nodded—left.

        A bo'sun's whistle,
High-pitched static, pierced her ears. The little
Ship she'd seen through Moe's feed loomed beside
The *H.O.W.L.*

     "Got a bead," said Del, inside
His harpoon bubble.

       "No, Del," Paige said. "We'll
Be sunk. Destroyed."

       "But Paige, I—"

          "Del, they'll kill
Us all."

   She noticed Dickie's torso rising
Next to her. His body was revising,
Simplifying, legs withdrawing, leaving
Two to stand on. Del was clearly grieving
Still, she thought. And looking for a target
For his grief.

     The pirate ship was scarlet
And its pitchfork prow presented viewers

With three lines of were-mech heads on skewers.
Netted heads, like bunched fruit, also bulged
Along the hull. A row of holes divulged
Internal cannons. From the wheelhouse to
The masts (as if the ship had travelled through
A pane of plasma) everything was red.
The hull's bots switched to red to kindle dread
In other ships, Paige figured.

                                Several were-mechs
Stood on deck. The nearest one was wearing
What appeared to be a tricorn, but
Paige realized this was merely metal cut
And bent to emulate a pirate's old-school
Hat. Two pointy ears bore hoops of gold.
The mech had lost an eye; a plastic tarp
Now sealed the hole. Paige figured something sharp
Had gouged it out.

                    "Ahoy!" the were-mech said.
His deep voice, burred with static, filled her head.
He'd propped his peg leg on a treasure chest,
A relic of the War. "I might suggest
The red one take his paws off that harpoon—
That's if you want to see another moon."

Reluctantly, Del exited the pod.

The pirate with the makeshift eyepatch nodded,
Plastic winking; when he moved, the patch
Would flicker like Morse code, the surface catching
Moonlight. "And you'd better bring back what's-
His-name, the whoreson."

                        "Gonna rip your guts
Out," Moe said, "if you call him that again."

She flexed a paw. "I loves to pluck small men
From cockpits." Neither she nor Campbell ever
Talked about the mothers who had never
Come back home. (Moe's mom had left her crying
Years ago outside the grim, outlying
Orphanage, a sphere that floated near
The town: a permanently frozen tear.)

The shifter's voice cut in. "Stay focused, Moe."

Paige flipped to Campbell's view. The words SHIELDS LOW
Were flashing on a screen inside the wheelhouse.
She could see a quickly moving steel
Paw pressing keys. It made a fist and tried
To bang the panel. ERROR. OVERRIDE.

"We've hit your shields," said Eyepatch, sounding bored.
Beside him stood a second were-mech, gourd-
Shaped: squat and yellow, body cadged from spheres,
It seemed. They must've tested several sneers
And wicked grimaces before they settled
On the one they'd painted on the metal
Muzzle. (Were-mech muzzles never moved.)
His fur, comprised of pointy peaks, was grooved
With gouged-out tiger stripes. His right paw was
A hook, whose curve included teeth: a buzz-
Saw's edge.
                    Paige looked at Dickie, who was merely
Staring straight ahead, the shifter clearly
Leaving this to Paige for now.
                                        She spotted
Two more were-mech pirates, one topknotted
With what seemed to be a shock of shoots.

It was a palm tree, ripped up by the roots.
(Perhaps the scarlet ship, lured by some siren's
Plea, had travelled tropically, round islands
South of Rabbit Strait?) The other pirate
Had a dome-like head. A glassed-in pilot,
Sitting on a turret, gripped two sticks
And spun around at will. A crucifix
Was hanging from the dome—a steeple's cross
Pried off some plundered church, the sort of loss
That many holy sites had suffered since
The rise of mechs. She couldn't help but wince
When flying past a church without its steeple.
Paige loved heists, but jacking crosses? Evil.

Campbell's were-mech had returned. It shook
Its head. No shields.

                The pirate with the hook
Walked over to where Eyepatch stood.

                            "I've got
A plan," said Del. "I'm thinking we should—"

                                "Not
On intercom," said Paige. She turned to Dickie,
Saw her mech's reflection cross his slick
Chrome snout. The metal smiled. That's my girl.

"I'm gonna give you kids me only pearl
Of truth," said Eyepatch, stepping off the chest.
"'A man can only do his very best.'
Me dad would say that. *And* that's what you've done.
You should be proud! But now you've got a gun—
Well, thirteen of 'em—pointed at your head."

The scarlet ship produced a plank, a red

Extension of the deck. It smoothly grew
Across the gulf as if advancing through
Imaginary points. The plank was thin,
As glossy as a candy apple in
The moonlight. Red bots kept assembling
To form new plank, its far edge trembling
Above the clouds. The plank was soon so long
It wagged a little, which Paige felt looked wrong—
Or rude, at least. At last, it reached the sloop
And mashed against the hull. A rim of goop
Bulged slightly as the moving plank compressed:
A wax seal.

          Hookpaw stooped to lift the chest.
He brought it to the red plank. Eyepatch hobbled
Over, too, and kicked the plank. It wobbled
Slightly, shuddering like scarlet jello.
"Should be good," he said, and waved his yellow
Hench-mech onto it.

               Paige said, "we'll give
You what you want." The Clouded Sea, a sieve,
Sent many were-mechs to their deaths. *It wept
Out whalers*, as the saying went, *but kept
Their spoils*.

          "Oh, you will?" said Eyepatch, mock-
Astonished. Hookpaw started on his walk
Across the plank, a flattened V, with slope
Behind him—and in front—like circus rope.
His paws sank slightly in the springy carpet
Of the plank.

         "In fact, we're in the market
For some lockets." Eyepatch half turned. "Ain't
That right?"

         A one-eared mech in need of paint,

With liver spots of rust, stepped from the pirates'
Wheelhouse. It moved shakily; its pilot's
Thoughts were tipsy.
                    "Dad?" said Paige. A rush
Of dread dissolved her gut. Her face went flush.

"I'm sorry, Paige." Glen's were-mech trundled up
To stand with Eyepatch. (He would have a cup
Inside his cockpit, Paige was certain. Drink
To give him courage.) "But I can't help think
They've got you"—pausing, searching for the right
Word—"hypnotized. I'll help you see the light,
Though. Come, me love." A shaky mech-paw beckoned.

Paige was frozen—only for a second.
"I'm not going anywhere with you,"
She said. Her voice surprised her; it was new,
The tone.
            The mech-paw, still extended, closed.
Glen's mech stood like a toy some kid had posed,
Then left. Paige knew that he'd be having trouble
With his wolf. She'd helped him from the bubble
Of his cockpit many times, the whiff
Of booze intense.
                    With jerking movements—stiff
And slow—her father's mech turned round and shrugged
At Eyepatch, paws up.
                    Hookpaw, having lugged
The chest across the scarlet plank, had paused
Before the H.O.W.L.'s edge. Her mech-friends, claws
Disclosed, backed up a bit, enclosing Paige.

Her dad's mech whirled around. "You cur!," his rage

Exploding, maxing out her buds. "You'd rather
Run around with freaks than with your father?
Does the shifter know you wanted your
Old dad to rob his hovel? Bloody whore."

Here Eyepatch touched Glen's shoulder: clunk. "Now let's
Avoid bad language. You don't want regrets."
He turned, addressing Paige. "Me love, you'll come
Across that plank—and swiftly. Don't be dumb.
I'll fire every cannonball I own.
Your mechs'll melt. You'll burn down to the bone.
And Mr. Lush?"—the pirate drew a sword—
"We'll need you, too, b'y."

                              Hookpaw stepped aboard
And put the chest down, servos whining in
Distress. The were-mech had a dorsal fin,
Its stripes alluding to a tiger shark.

Paige turned her mech; the shifter wore a dark
Look now. His liquid-metal brow had furrowed.
If she could've, she'd have vanished, burrowed
Inward. "I was gonna rob your place."
Her eyes were welling up. "I'm—"

                              Dickie's face,
The rainbow blots, appeared. "Stop blubbering.
We're fine."

                    She sniffed. "We are?"

                                        (A fluttering
Brought Moe's face briefly to the screen. The leafy
Sound of pire wings.)

                          "You *were* a thief,"
Said Dickie. "But you're something else now. Go
And save your crew." The blots blinked out, their glow

Dissolving.
                        Dickie walked up to the chest.
The pirate, crouching, felt around—then pressed
A latch, the top third of the box now springing
Up. The paw-hook, at his side, was singing
Faintly, buzzsaw teeth a milky blur.
Paige pictured it dividing metal fur.

"That's it?" said Del. His voice betrayed a scowl.
"Dickie's giving up?"
                        "They'll sink the H.O.W.L.,
Del," said Campbell. "Dickie's tryna save us."

Eyepatch nodded. "Aye, the blob's courageous.
So's the whoreson." Eyepatch looked at Campbell—
Then at Hookpaw. Nodded.
                        Hookpaw ambled
Up to Campbell, raised the non-hook paw—
A curled fist—and stove in the white mech's jaw.

Paige screamed as Campbell's wolf fell backward. Hookpaw,
Stooping, gripped the prone mech's snout—and shook
It like a can. The gyroscopic cockpit
Had its limits, though. You couldn't rock it
Back and forth, and not expect its pilot
To stay plumb for very long. The pirate's
Arm sped up. Paige flipped to cockpit view
And glimpsed a flailing body flying through
The air—just as the feed went snowy.
                                    "Stop,"
Said Eyepatch. "Let's not kill him."
                                    Hookpaw dropped
The head, which clanged against the deck, and backed

Off. Campbell's groaning were-mech, muzzle cracked,
Got to its feet—an automatic reflex.
Campbell, though, was silent.

                        Paige had seen mechs
Pause mid-fight, unclench their fists, and walk
Away—which meant the pilots in their cockpits
Were unconscious. Dudes were always falling
From their 'pit seats when their mechs were brawling
In the schoolyard. (No boys in her class
Wore belts, including Campbell.) "Stupid asshole,"
Paige said, wiping tears away. She raised
Her voice now. "Campbell?"

                       Coughing. "Present"—dazed
But still alive.

               She slumped back in her chair.
"Are you okay?"

                "Of course, just mussed me hair."
His feed was snow—she couldn't see him yet—
But he'd be bruised, from banging round his 'pit.

"Tough kid," said Eyepatch. "Y'ever need a job
You comes to me. You've got a gut for robbing,
I can tell." The pirate raised his sword
And, turning, scratched his chestplate, sounding bored
Again. "Now Lush, you've made your bed. You needs
To sleep."

             Paige called up Dickie's forward feed.
Rocks lined the bottom of the chest, but then
His feed went dark; his cameras shut off when
He shifted. Turning to her central screen,
She watched him liquefy, arch up, then stream—
A metal waterfall—inside the box.

"Wait no!" she cried. She knew, then, what the rocks
Were for.

* * *

       The treasure chests had been designed
By alien intelligence—by minds
A shade too large to fit in human skulls.
One chest could roam the clouds for years, its hull
Attracting forks of lightning, which supplied
Its cells. A single mech could fit inside—
Or several smaller beings. Humans (and
The like) could lie for several years like canned
Fish, packed in artificial amniotic
Fluid that sustained its contents. Optic
Sensors (balls that quivered on the ends
Of thin stalks) helped the chest make sense of trends
In wind and rain—and steer clear of rough weather.
It was meant to be a raft that never
Sank. A steady, moving ship could snare
One, bring it to a stop. Heaved into air,
Though, it resumed the attitude of flotsam
Built to stay afloat. The chests were awesome
Boxes: golden, smooth, the stuff of fables,
Basically. No humans could disable
Them.
       It seemed the pirates had recovered
One—and clearly knew the strange tech hovered
Endlessly when set adrift. They'd drained
Their chest, then added rocks. They'd entertained
The thought that someone who can change his state
Might turn to foil, let the wind inflate
His skin to form a makeshift parachute.
There was no point in giving him the boot

As is—in throwing Dickie off the ship
And hoping gravity applied its grip.
He'd find a way to fashion wings and sail
The clouds.

          The shifter, though, would only flail
Against the insides of a treasure chest,
A box that withstood force that would've stressed
A normal structure. (Plus, Paige feared he'd panic,
As he once did in the sheet-draped rabbit
Hutch.) What's more, the added rocks would pull
It down; the chest would plunge below the wool
That walled the fallen world off from the world
Above the Clouded Sea. *What god has hurled*
This box at us? the denizens of Down
Below would ask. They'd look up with a frown.
These sub-cloud sailors of irradiated
Waves were gaunt, their limbs attenuated.
Sentenced to a mech-less life, they lived
On what they fished—and what the heavens sieved
For them. Their homes were lashed-together rafts.
Their cancerous skins were patchwork quilts of grafts.

* * *

Paige tried to lunge at Hookpaw. Someone's paw
Restrained her. Dot's.

          The pirate made a maw
Out of the chest by opening and closing
It. "'This box,'" his voice high-pitched, "'needs hosing
Down.'"

          The pirates laughed, but Eyepatch calmed
Them with a raised paw. "Down Below's been bombed
Enough," he said. "And yet, we send another
Son back home. Return him to the Mother

Sea." Rote words; Paige guessed he'd said them many
Times. He looked toward the chest. "So any
Last words, shifter?"

                      But the chest stayed silent.
Paige knew *that* was Dickie's voice: defiant
Silence.

           "Man of few words," Eyepatch sighed.
He nodded.

                Hookpaw slammed the lid.

                            Moe cried
Out, "Bastards!"

                  Dot appeared in Paige's feed
For private CMs. "Paige," said Dot, "I needs
To tell you something…"

                      Hookpaw, squatting, gripped
The chest and, staring at the were-mechs, flipped
The box-cum-coffin overboard.

                        Paige rushed
Across the deck in several strides and pushed
Past Hookpaw. Leaning overboard, her mech's
Paws on the rail, her mind thought, "Zoom-in specs."
She saw the chest: a blip her screen had spotted
And encircled with red dots. A dotted
Line in tow described the chest's arc downward
Through the gauzy clouds, its thrusters countered
By the rocks. But soon the dots trailed off.
The blip blinked out. The chest was gone.

                              A cough

Behind her; Hookpaw motioned her to cross
The plank. She climbed up on it.

                      "Every loss
Will only make you lighter, faster," Dickie
Had explained back on the beach, the sickly

Sloop before her eyes. "We'll get her sailing."

Moe's face now appeared. Her voice was saying,
"Miles, no!"
           Paige walked across the plank.
The paw-hook buzzed behind her, poised to shank
Her mech. She reached the ship and stepped aboard
It.
    Eyepatch slashed the air twice with his sword;
The plank retracted, leaving no incision
In its hull. They brought Paige to the mizzen-
Mast. The pirate with the topknot wound
Some cable—stolen from a bridge?—around
Her mech's waist.
               "This is for the best, me love,"
Said Glen, "you'll be okay—" But Topknot shoved
Him to the deck. The pirates laughed.
                         "The moon
Was that for," Glen began, but Hookpaw loomed
Above him.
          From her vantage, Paige could see
The H.O.W.L., still afloat above the sea,
But smoking badly.
            Eyepatch said, "Just one
More thing. I've got a single little gun
Aimed at your fuel tank. I'd suggest you get
Your raft inflated. I won't fire—yet."
She watched the Howlship's four were-mechs scramble
To vacate the H.O.W.L.—all but Campbell,
Who stayed still at first, til Moe's mech took
Him by the paw. "Come on, we've gotta book
It!"
    Something like a liquid-metal jowl

Quickly pearled on one side of the H.O.W.L.'s
Hull—distending like a bead of drool,
Then breaking free. The drop, though, paused to pool
Midair, its fluid surface spreading, edge
Inflating, puffing up to form a ledge.
The drop became a tub. Its underside
Broke out, the hull becoming multi-eyed.
The eyes were outlets where exhaust expressed
Itself. The floating raft had sat recessed
Within the H.O.W.L.'s hull. Most ships contained
Evacuation rafts, their smooth hulls veined
With dinghies. Del, though, had insisted they
Upgrade to his design. The raft grew grey
To match Thom's mech, and grew a prow as well:
A crinkly nub of raft that seemed to swell
And form a snout: his father's snout, of course.

"I loves you, Paige!" cried Dot, her voice now hoarse.

They leapt the gap between the H.O.W.L. and
The floating raft. The sloop, no longer manned,
Continued fuming.
                            But Paige couldn't seem
To speak. She felt like she was in a dream,
Her body sluggish. Slow. Her cockpit was
Awash in voices, Campbell's, Del's, a buzz
Of reassurances, of vows that they
Would save her, they'd return, they'd find a way.
Her leftmost screen kept flickering; the faces,
As their owners spoke, kept changing places.

But they each fell silent as the pirate
Ship disclosed a cannon through an eyelet

In its hull. The cannon shot a burst
Of cannonballs, just as the raft reversed
Abruptly, were-mechs reaching out to steady
One another. None of them was ready
Yet to leave. The raft's AI, though, sensing
Imminent explosion and dispensing
With all niceties, began to zoom
Away.

      The H.O.W.L.'s hull released a bloom,
A fireball that lit the pirate ship—
And Paige's mech. The sloop began to dip
And list, disgorging smoke, the vessel falling
Over, into clouds, the were-mechs calling
Paige's name again, their voices growing
Faint and staticky, the raft self-rowing,
Bearing them away across the Clouded
Sea, the H.O.W.L. smoking, sinking, shrouded…

14.

She'd stayed a second night.
                              The manse's third
Floor—vast and mostly empty—kept a herd
Of bachelor bubbles, strewn about like bales
Of hay. They'd been designed for use in jails,
The bubbles; each one was a cell that could
Be rolled inside a truck. But towns that stood
Near water had embraced this makeshift housing.
Tides that rose above their shorelines, dousing
Coasts, could bear away a bubble—but
They couldn't break it. It became a hut
At sea, a buoy that could be ID'd
From overhead.
                              The bubble's skin would read
Approaching DNA, relaxing for
Those guests the pixies liked. There was no door;
You elbowed through what felt like gelatin.
But Kaye had read about a skeleton,
A child's, found inside one bubble's murky
Membrane, which had dried the kid like jerky.
Fucking pixies let the kid half in,
Then changed their minds and held him in their skin.

Kaye wore a fox-print camisole (whose foxes
Didn't budge) and baggy navy boxers.
She sat in her bubble, on a slab
Of foam, its duvet bunched. A ledge of drab
And hardened gelatin afforded Kaye
An eating surface. On this ledge, a grey
And slouching tube of plastic, like a small
"R," started spurting, filling up a ball
Sans upper hemisphere. The ball appeared
To shake a little as it filled; she feared
Her dark roast would brim over. But the slouching
Tube ceased pouring. Drip, drip. Ready.
                                          Crouching,
Kaye got dressed, the bachelor bubble's ceiling
Curving just above her knot bun. Kneeling
On the spongy floor, she packed her knapsack.
Then, she put her shoes on. They'd been napping,
Having tried to nuzzle at and pour
Between the molecules that formed the floor—
To no avail. (The bubble *had* been meant
To be a jail. Its gelatin prevented
Tampering.) Security around
The manse, in general, was tight, she'd found.
She couldn't shake the nagging feeling of
Panopticon-ish eyes afloat above.
(Her classes talked a lot about Foucault.)

Nor could she shake the sight of Ichiro,
His idle fingers squeezing Dickie's jaw,
His other hand armed with the pixiesaw.
(But then why *shouldn't* someone take their bot's
Head off, especially to check its thoughts?)

She slipped her knapsack on and took the stairs
Down to the second floor, the vast room where
The bonsai model stood. She heard some coughs,
Which echoed off the distant walls—her prof's.
She did the toe move, dropping roller skates.

She found Lux tankside, forearm over face
To mask a coughing fit, the steno looking
Calmly on, which meant Lux wasn't choking.
They were at a table that had walked
Out to the tank on spider legs. It stalked
The stomachs of the manse's visitors,
Its brain half waiter, half inquisitor.

"Are you okay?" she asked.
                    He nodded, waved
Her off. An untouched breakfast—poached eggs, shaved
Prosciutto—wallowed in its hollandaise.

A flicker crossed the tank and drew her gaze.
The iris, pixel-fringed, displayed the scene
Where Paige and Glen—his muzzle grizzled, mean—
Are sitting in the red ship's hold, below-
Decks. Chapter Fourteen. Paige asks Glen to show
Compassion. Holds her bound paws out. They're sitting
Facing one another. Flies are flitting
Round Glen's head. The Eyepatch pirate's got
The lockets now. (He'd said, "Whatever's brought
Aboard is mine." The buccaneers had failed
To share that rule—and so Glen's sort of jailed
As well, though hasn't yet accepted that
The pirates have betrayed him, each a rat
In werewolf pelt.) A buoy sways and draws

The two wolves' shadows out. She sits there, paws
Extended. Finally, her father sighs.
He leans across and loosens Paige's ties.

She rubs a wrist and mutters, gee, I wonder
Why mum left, what was she thinking. Thunder
Would've broken at this moment, had
The sound been on, to stress that Paige is mad.
The tank was silent, though; Kaye knew this part,
And every word its muzzles made, by heart.

The sea is rough. The ship attempts to climb
A wave. Your mum was crying all the time,
Glen says at last. It's why I started drinking.
Swigs his bottle. She was always thinking.
Worrying. She'd clutch her head and say
She wished she had a different brain. She'd pray
A lot.
       Paige listens as her father tells
His tale. He's swaying—rhythmic—as the swells
Pass under.
            I'd pray, too. Your mum had goals,
Though. Dreams. She wanted to scratch out some scrolls
About the sea. Adventures. She was good
With words. She'd tell you tales. 'The Haunted Wood.'
He smiles. She could talk a bloody circle
Round a body. Always very verbal,
Like her daughter. Always loved to talk.
His eyes change. Day before she took her walk
Down to the sea, she told me that she gabbed
So much to drown the voices out. She'd stabbed
Herself once, on our wedding night. I stopped
Her—tried to—but she took a swing and lopped

Me ear clean off. Her eyes were full of fear.
Instinctively, he reaches for the ear.

I thought, says Paige, you lost it in a tavern
Fight. She stares now at the fur-fringed cavern,
Which her father said was always itching.

No, says Glen. I works that bloody kitchen,
Serving whalers, cuz the ships don't want
No wounded wolf. The schoolcubs used to taunt
Me for me ear. His daughter doesn't speak.
The buoy cracks the silence with its creak.

The model's weather system activated
Storm clouds; just beyond the pixelated
Iris fringe, the darkened tank was growing
Cloudy. Fanblades were producing blowing,
Gale-force gusts.
                           The bonsai hold was full
Of loot. There was no flying bot—no gull,
Say—that could film belowdecks. But the loot
Had eyes. A snout-less Mozart bust could shoot
The red ship's hold. A taxidermied fawn
Had cameras, too. The iris focused on
Whichever bot was speaking, cutting quickly—
Glen to Paige to Glen—the dadbot sickly,
Swaying ever more dramatically,
As if to stress (a touch emphatically,
Kaye felt) that yes, he's drunk, and thus an easy
Mark for Paige, who feels a little queasy
Doing this, but somehow does it—lunges
Forward as the vessel heaves, and punches
Glen square in the muzzle, knocking out

Her father cold (although, of course, the lout
Is programmed to fall backward).
                                        But they'd got
Her face wrong, Kaye decided. Paige's bot
Was not equipped to hold tears in its eyes,
A brimming load. The novel's Paige, though, tries
Her hardest not to cry, to keep each tear
Inside, her feelings Paige's greatest fear.

"You heading out?" asked Lux.
                                        "I'm heading *back*,"
Said Kaye. "To Perth. To class."
                                        "Well, have a snack."
He dragged a lounger over. "Here, I've barely
Touched these eggs." He coughed.
                                        She eyed them, wary.
"I'm alright. But thanks."
                                        "It's nighttime there,
You know."
                    "I'll do my laundry. Wash my hair."

"There's shampoo here. And water."
                                        "See you next
Week, 'kay?" Instinctively, she felt the text,
The *Full-Moon*, in her coat. "Where's Ichiro?"
She wanted to avoid him.
                                        "Tokyo,"
Said Lux. He might as well have said the planet
Earth, she figured. (Wood folk had the habit
Of suggesting that the Wood was separate
From the city. They could not accept it—
That the Wood was not a nation state—
And referenced "Tokyo" with some distaste,

As something flooded. Fallen.) "Take some toast
At least." He passed a slice; his hand was ghost-
White. Shaky.
                              She received the limpid slice
And held it. "I prefer when you're not nice."

He coughed and turned away. The churning wall
Of cloud had made the tank a crystal ball.

* * *

Beyond the manse's orb-ringed grounds, she heard
A plummy voice—"My dearest Kaye!"—which spurred
Her to pick up her pace. A sound of rapid
Scuttling behind...
                              "What luck! I happened
To be thinking on your visage. Dwelling
On it—fate far better than the shelling
We received in Laing's Nek's crimson grove."

She stopped and turned to look at Stephen Stove.
She *bet* her face was running through his brain.
"Hi Stephen."
                              "Kaye, you seem in mild pain.
Perhaps you've come down with a case of colly-
Wobbles?"
                              "Colly...?"
                                             "We'd endure a volley—
Spears. A horror. Rattled stomachs would
Run through our ranks."
                              "That's awful. Well, I should
Be going..."
                              "Ichiro, my master, sends
His best." He blinked.

She noted Stephen's tense:
The present. Maybe Ichiro was hearing
Everything the stove was saying, peering
At her even now through Stephen's giant
Monocle.
Kaye walked on, irked. A pliant
Grove of shrubs, which stood upon their roots,
Backed off a bit, the plant life in cahoots
And maybe sensing it should get away.

* * *

She passed a garden party on her way
Back down the hill. A decadent affair
For 10 a.m. Some revellers were wearing
Gowns while others were enclosed in tuxes.
She'd been ruing saying no to Lux's
Eggs, but here were waitbots bearing trays
Of stuff. No blurbs had flowered in her gaze;
She guessed there was a firewall around
The party—or perhaps such aids were frowned
Upon. Perhaps the bash was analog.

A waitbot passed. Kaye plucked a mini log
Of lasered beef (adroitly rolled and lanced
With toothpick) from its platter. Couples danced,
A band off to the side, the singer scarved,
A cosplay Stevie Nicks. A server carved
A slice of something from a sheer and reddish
Stump. Kaye noted watches and a fetish
For ability collectibles
Like canes and glasses. Undetectable
Security was surely everywhere.

Mouth full, Kaye turned and found a woman staring
At her—panther jogger, last seen running
Laps around the Wood. She wore a stunning
Navy gown, whose neckline seemed to climb
Her narrow neck. In fact, the V-neck's line
Of fabric barely held each bra-less breast.
The dress gave way to pelt, which filmed her chest
And throat. A slit revealed her leg fur fading
Into skin toward her hip, which made the
Leg look like it wore a thigh-high boot.
She had a single braid, which Kaye thought cute.
Behind, a tail curled into view, aloft
And languid, like a length of velvet wafting
Through the air.
               "Who's this?" the woman said,
Bemused.
            Kaye felt her stomach melting. Dread,
But something else as well. The woman—squinting
At a spot above Kaye's head, eyes glinting
In the sun—said, "@psychedelicurs."
She looked at Kaye. "Your handle's fun."
                      Kaye cursed
Herself; she'd left her blurb up. "I was going.
Sorry." She could feel her cheeks were glowing.

Pouting. "That would be a shame. I'd love
To watch you steal more food." She brought a gloved
Hand to her lips (of course, the glove was blue
Fur, Kaye would realize later on) and drew
A breath, an ember glowing briefly. "Here,"
Around a mouth of smoke. She passed the clear
And slender tube of leaf-filled glass to Kaye.

Kaye looked at it—and tapped its ash away.

"It's just tobacco, @psychedelicurs."

Kaye took a drag and noticed straw and burrs
Upon the woman's upper thigh, right where
The slit began.

　　　　　　She noticed Kaye was staring.
"Oops." Sly grin. "Comes with the territory."
She took back the tube. "So what's your story,
@psychedelicurs?"

　　　　　　　　"I live up there,"
Kaye lied.

　　　　The woman stroked her braid of hair
With one blue hand, and with the other, took
A drag. "The manse?" She fixed Kaye with a look,
Her dark eyes narrow.

　　　　　　　　　　"But I'm late for class."
She thought about the panther jogger's ass,
Presumably where furless flesh resumed.
A sudden wish: to watch her as she groomed
Her thighs.

　　　　"Well then, you'd better get to school."
She turned, then stopped. "Your accent's very cool."
Looked back. "You're from the Crater?"

　　　　　　　　　　　"Crater? Not
Sure what that is." Kaye made to leave...

　　　　　　　　　　　"I thought
I'd met a pitizen. I lived there for
A while."

　　　　Blinking. "In the Crater?"

　　　　　　　　　　　"Four
Months, maybe? Back when I was your age. Best

255

Time of my life." She plucked fluff off her chest
And blew it. "Not a lick of luxury.
I loved it." Then: "I have a scullery,
You ever need a job. You'd love it there."
She turned, the lagging tail afloat on air.

* * *

At last, Kaye reached the shop Swann's Way. It whirlpooled
Nightly, atoms whipping round like swirled jewels
Just above their static drop, then shifting
To another spot, the new drop sifting
Bricks from void—a process certain shops,
The most exclusive, could afford. The drops,
Which lay across the Wood like harmless landmines,
Weren't too hard to find. The layout, planned by
Bots, was fixed. She'd realized that they made
A grid that overlaid the bamboo glade.
That day, Swann's Way—a slim, two-storey shoebox,
Green with well-groomed ivy—stood a few blocks
From the spot the shop had held the day
Before.
         The ivy framed a square display,
Glassed in, of Penguin Classics: *Neuromancer*,
Moby-Dick, and *Belle the Steno Dancer*.
You entered through a small café, the room
Kaye sought. She loved its well-curated gloom
And smartbook walls. As customers came in,
The smartbooks, dragging brainpans, would re-skin
Themselves to match the books the minds were thinking
Of. (The restless walls were often blinking
As their smartbooks cycled through the spines
Of titles passing through the fickle minds.)
Whenever Kaye was in Swann's Way, the classic

Full-Moon softback—with the windmill graphic,
Logo for Churn Press—would start to streak
Adjacent spines. Some spines were burnt-out: weak
And flickering. The wall was antique tech
At this point.
          But the owner still respected
Privacy enough to keep a cone
Around the shop, impervious to drone
Advances. You could think about whatever,
And the bookstore's cone, discreet, would never
Let a thought slip past. The Wi-Fi, too,
Was locked; your postcards and DMs passed through
Encrypted pipelines that were shepherd-proof.

Kaye bought a coffee in a mug with Proust's
Face on it. Then, she took a seat and sipped
Her dark roast. *Full-Moons* bloomed as if a skipped
Stone of a thought had hopped around the shelves
And rippled them; as if a race of elves
Lived just behind the spines.
          She took some old and
Yellow cardstock from her knapsack, folded
It in half to make a crease, and set
It down. (She waited, smelling cigarette
Still on her.) Finally, it beeped. She opened
It, the card now stiff. A high, soft-spoken,
Vaguely English female voice said, "Hello,
Kaye." The upright half of folded, yellow
Card turned black. An apple stamped from light
(Its gouged-out silhouette implied a bite)
Appeared dead centre. Brilliant brickwork raced
Across the bottom half, the sharp lines traced
In light. The bricks filled up with letters (Q,

Its tail pigtailing out, then W)
As Kaye fussed with the angle of the screen.
The cardstock had accrued a laptop's sheen.

Her fingers flew across the light-edged, 2-D
Bricks. (The cardstock click-clacked.) "Truth Is Beauty"
Faded in—the text that teased the homepage
For the social network Joyce. A dome
Composed of macaroni lines, a brain
Afloat, began to spin against a plain
Of white. Kaye tapped the brain, which grew a stem
Of tree roots. She'd decided she'd DM
Cat for a change; her friend was never *not*
On Joyce. The stem meant Kaye could post a thought.

Kaye often noted she was bad at Joyce.
She'd try to *say* her mind, to speak a voice
Inside her head—all wrong, of course. You had
To give up all control. If you were sad,
You had to merely feel it, letting go and
Letting Joyce design the post: a glowing
Void, say. Users might then tap it, linking
To the very thoughts that you'd been thinking,
Thoughts about the cheating, no-good ex
You'd caught in steno-penetrating sex.

(But ten percent of Joyce's images
Were deformed kids with ragged grimaces,
Three eyes, and tumours signifying cancers:
Posts made by the minds of anti-vaxxers.)

Anyway, it took Kaye several tries
To have a thought that Joyce could analyze

And translate visually: a silver locket.
Cat, she figured, probably would mock it.

Nope, thought Cat, inside Kaye's head; her friend
Had tapped Kaye's post, a brainwave bridge extending
Back to Kaye. *That thing's no joke*. Cat's brain
Was Kaye's; their two minds shared a single train
Of thought and memory.
                              Cat seemed to be
Already up to speed. Joyce aimed to free
Up users from the bother of recapping
Stuff, from laboured summaries, from mapping
Out your twelve-point thesis, from providing
Detail. Everything arrived inside a
User's mind the way a symphony
Occurred to Mozart: one epiphany
That packed in all the notes at once, compressed
Like particle board.
                              Cat envied Kaye her quest
Inside the tank. She also shared Kaye's feeling
Ichiro was trouble. *He's unfeeling*,
Cat thought. *Shady*.
                              In the meantime, Kaye's
Mind had been filling, too. Joyce wasn't phasing
In Cat's thoughts; quite suddenly, Kaye knew
What Cat did: that a fan site called "Wolf Crew,"
A long-gone chat salon not known for humour,
Once had entertained a juicy rumour:
Silver Locket was to be the title
Of the *Full-Moon* sequel. But a libel
Suit, from god knows where, had forced the site
To pull the post. Of course, the lost post might
Have simply been a legend; Cat herself

Had never seen the thing.
The café shelf
Beside Kaye had been slowly filling up
With *Silver Lockets*. Thoughts of follow-up
Had vexed the smartbooks, though. Their bots had tried
To wipe the Churn Press windmill. They'd applied
A locket where the logo was supposed
To go. Cat's reference to the mythic post
From "Wolf Crew" didn't link to cover art.
The smartbook bots, alas, were merely smart;
They couldn't picture books they'd never read.

That woman's hot, thought Cat. *You never said
You had a* FAFI *thing.*
I didn't know
I did. Kaye's face was flush.
Now I'm all glowing.
Stop it. No more blushing in my head—
Oh fuck, I gotta go. A heated thread
Was blowing up Cat's public stream on Joyce,
As followers whose thinking scanned pro-choice
Went head-to-head with brains that scanned pro-life.
Cat's pro-choice thoughts—translated to a wife
In servitude, the still that Joyce had settled
On—had caused the strife. (The platform meddled,
Stirred up conflict. It would translate boring
Notions into stills that led to war.)

*And Kaye, stop being so embarrassed by
Your childhood, alright? I'd fucking die
For pitizens.*
I'm not—
You know we're on

A brainwave, right? With that thought, Cat was gone.
Her followers required her attention.

* * *

Kaye explored Wolfpack Salon: no mention
Of the silver locket. Zwitter, too,
Showed no results. It seemed like no one knew
About the silver locket.
                  Then, she found
A reference on an old salon called "Sound
Of Sense," administered by someone with
The handle, "Set to Donne." "The Fading Myth
Of SL," was the title of the post.
And that's why *Silver Locket* was a ghost:
The few who ever mentioned it demurred
On naming it directly and referred
To it by its initials. Maybe Set
To Donne, the author of the post, was betting
That the pixiebarristers that sought
To strip the zuck of content wouldn't spot
A coded silver locket.
                  "Well, there's plenty
To be sad about," wrote Donne. "It's 20-
62—a decade since she vanished.
Maybe, finally, it's time we banished
All thoughts of the long-delayed SL.
Life's hard enough as is without the hell
Of waiting for unfinished books to write
Themselves."
          Kaye looked up. It was late, the light
Beginning to withdraw. She stretched and got
Up. Bought a second coffee from the bot-
Barista. It had rained apparently;

The windowpanes were beaded. Carefully,
She walked the Proust mug back.

                              The chat salon
Was quite specific, "focused only on
Verse novels like *Full-Moon*, *The Golden Gate*,
Forgotten Work—the books some poets hate
Because they dazzle with their scale," the site's
About page, somewhat grumbly, read. The lights
Inside the café brightened slightly as
The Wood grew darker. Mild, muted jazz—
"All Blues," by Miles Davis—started playing
And the bot-barista started swaying.

* * *

Kaye packed up her knapsack. Headed out.

Beyond the southern wall, there stood a spout,
A zuber booth that aped a gramophone.
A clever thing: you crawled inside the cone-
Shaped speaker. Optic scans confirmed your passport.
Kaye was tired. Had to get to class
In Perth.

                    But not far from the wall, she heard
Her name, though not, for once, in Stove's absurdly
Studied accent.

                              "Kaye!" the voice half-hissed.

She passed two manga types in skirts, a tryst
Behind a cosplay barn. She heard one moan,
And hurried on.

                              She found herself alone
Above a grassy incline. "Kaye!" Was Joyce's
Link still somehow active? No, the voice's

Source was close. She stumbled, skidding down
The slope. Was it the panther in the gown?

Ahead, before a grove of trees, stood Sable,
From Kaye's class. She had a hoop of cable
Round her arm and wore a charcoal track
Suit.
     "Sable?"
               Sable's blond hair was now black.
"We need to talk, Kaye."
                     Kaye approached and gripped
Her knapsack's strap. The dated shit—the ripped
Jeans, Docs, and vintage anal beads—was gone.

"The fuck you doing here?" asked Kaye. A fawn
With half a dozen eyeballs passed between
The women. Kaye remembered now she'd seen
The teacher from the gondola above
The Wood. She noticed Sable wore a glove,
Just one, the latex lending her right hand
A gleam. The glove suggested something planned.

"We need you, Kaye, to stay for one more night."
The ungloved hand rose to her ear. "We might
Need two."
          "Who's 'we?'" Kaye nodded at the glove.
"What's with the glove?"
                   "It's time to listen, love,"
Said Sable, stepping forward, something like
An accent creeping in. A tandem bike,
A Humpback, stood against a vintage trough
Of oxidized aluminum. "Your prof
And Ichiro Hatori"—here, she paused

And dropped her voice—"are dangerous men. They've caused
A lot of harm." She wore an open jar,
With something in it, on her belt.

"Who *are*
You?" Kaye stepped back.

A hand clamped down across
Kaye's mouth, an arm across her chest.

"My boss,"
Sighed Sable, backing up, "is on a clock."

The body gripping Kaye now made her walk
Toward the trees, which Sable had backed under,
Eyes intense. "Now, it'll be a blunder,
Quite a fatal one, if you scream out.
You wouldn't be"—she smiled—"'off your spout?'
Is that the wolfy saying?"

Kaye—eyes wide,
The hand a muzzle—shook her head.

"I cried
Out once. In your position. It was not
A wise move." As she spoke, the hand, a bot-
Cool plastic, left Kaye's mouth to grip her shoulder.
"I was held down. All night. Bots get colder
Over time."

Kaye turned her head to glance
Up at the placid, Ken-doll face, its trance
Untroubled by her shaking limbs, its grip
Assured.

"We need to steer you like a ship,"
Said Sable. "For a bit."

The Ken doll shoved
Kaye forward, but still gripped her. Sable's gloved
Hand felt around inside the jar. She raised

Two latexed fingers, which now pinched a glazed
And writhing centipede, its segments creamy
White and wet. "You'll feel a little dreamy
For a few days."

            Kaye tensed up. The arm
Across her chest squeezed harder.

                      "It won't harm
You. Fuses with whatever apps like Joyce
Link to. You'll have some agency, some choice.
Your lunch, the books you like to read, and when
To take your bathroom breaks."

                   Kaye noticed, then,
Some metres off, the cartoon cube half-swallowed
By a spray of cattails.

             Sable followed
Kaye's eyes. Saw the stove, a kid's abandoned
Toy. It wore a monocle—a random
Accent, wet from rain. She turned to Kaye.
"It comes out with your stool," she said. "Okay?"

But Kaye had calmed down slightly. Slowed her breathing.
Realized, to her wonder, she was seething.

"Turn her head a little," Sable said.
"I need an ear."

            Kaye pushed back, pressed her head
Against the bot's throat. Duly braced, she raised
A single foot—and drove it hard (amazed
That she was doing so) at Sable's face.
The hacked shoe's smartsole spread, its edge like lace;
When stomped that hard, the shoe incorporated
With its target, sole and turf conflated.
Rivulets of shoe, like slapped-down batter,

Spread across and merged with facial matter.
For a beat, the three were stuck: the bot
Plus Kaye plus Sable. But, as Sable fought
To pull away from Kaye, Kaye's foot popped *from*
The shoe, a turn both horrible and dumb,
The shoe still masking Sable's nose and jaw
Like scuba gear. So Sable fell, her maw
The fish-mouth hole a footless shoe makes, Sable
Making muffled sounds but not quite able
To articulate a scream. Both shoe
And face now shared the same shade, fleshy blue,
As Sable writhed upon the grass. The sole
Had sealed her nose and mouth, a rubber bowl
That bulged, then went concave, sucked back inside.
She tried to poke it, but the sole, like hide
Gone through a tannery, was hard.

       Kaye hung
There for a second as the Ken doll swung
Around unsure. Kaye's shoeless foot felt cool.
A strand of lukewarm fluid—robot drool?—
Applied a single drop to Kaye's bare neck
As if the bot had meant to place a peck.
And then its whole face mashed her nape. She screamed
And thrashed her legs. The nuzzled face, though, seemed
To roll aside. The arms went limp. Kaye scrambled
Clear and turned.

     The bot, now headless, ambled
Off, a Snoopy on its fitted tee,
Its neck hole spurting pornographically.
Its head sat on the grass as if its body
Had been buried to the neck. Two gaudy
Lashes slowly blinked. The writhing Sable
Had grown still.

And then Kaye saw the sabre.
It was several metres long and seemed
To float above the scene. The sabre gleamed;
A moon was out. Kaye's eyes slid down the light-
Emblazoned blade; it ended in the white-
Gloved fist of Stephen Stove. The hand and blade,
In fact, looked fused together, as if made
From one material. She watched the glowing
Steel begin retracting smoothly, flowing
Into Stephen's fist.
                    The stove-bot stood
On legs again; they'd raised it up. It *should*
Have been much closer given even cattails
Next to Kaye were headless—scythed and flat.
But Stephen's sword could stretch, perhaps when flicked;
The blade had mowed a broad patch, even nicked
The bark of nearby trees. The Wood was shaven
All around the stove.
                    "I know you're shaken,"
Said a voice. It seemed to emanate
From Stephen. Ichiro. "But they won't wait
To strike again." The manga eye behind
The monocle blinked several times. The mind
Of Stephen Stove had reasserted. "Right,
My Kaye, we'd best get to the manse."
                              A light
Appeared among the trees—and then another.
Moon-shaped orbs. "They'll lead you to the mother
Ship," said Stephen. "Go!"
                          She gripped her knapsack,
As the orbs metastasized to map the
Way back through the dark. She ran one-socked,
Too scared to note her foot was getting soaked.

Scroll Three

15.

She peered around the door.

                                       They'd nailed the jaws
Of sharks along the passageway so paws
Could find some purchase as the vessel bobbed
And listed on the waves. They'd clearly robbed
Assorted coastal towns; the hold, to which
They'd banished Paige and Glen, was filled with kitsch
(A bust of Mozart minus muzzle), surplus
Buoys in a net, a hanging birdless
Birdcage, leaning stacks of empty crates,
A taxidermied fawn, a pair of skates
For paws, the trident of a candelabra,
Moth-chewed scrollsacks (*Guide to the Macabre*,
(*Wolflife on the Water*), and a couple
Casks (of "CID'R"—Wulvish script). These huddled
In one corner; it was as if they'd drawn
Away from what had happened.

                                    Glen lay on
The ground, unconscious. Paige looked back to make
Sure that her dad was really out, not faking
It. She'd looked back several times, expecting
Him to rise and lunge, which self-respecting
Villains' bodies did in scrolls. But he
Just lay there in his purple pants, a flea

Or two awake inside the wood his pelt
Provided.
                        Paige was shocked to find she felt
No fear. Just pity. Glen had loomed inside
Her mind so long she hadn't seen he'd died
Already long ago, perhaps soon after
Mum had drowned herself. He'd stopped his laughter
(How he used to love to roar!) with bottles,
Worked the docks when sober, sought out squabbles
At the tavern, clawed and kicked in rage.
He hadn't been the loving father Paige
Once loved—for years.
                        The bottle he'd been holding
Now lay on the hold's floor, slowly rolling
Back and forth, the pirate vessel cresting
Waves, the bottle rolling one way, resting,
Then reversing course. You're off your spout,
Paige told herself, eyeballing Glen. His snout
Lay in a pool of blood that went from red
To dark red as the buoy overhead
Swayed back and forth. It was the bottle, though,
She couldn't stand: the way it started slow,
Then sped up, rolling to each wall and ending
With a clunk. Paige left the door and, bending,
Snatched the bottle by its neck. She stood
It up. Its shadow grew across the wood,
Then drew back in.
                        She didn't quite believe in
Miracles, the stuff of stories. Even
Now the wolf could see the bubbles where
The chest had disappeared. She couldn't bear
To think about what Dot had yelled, the bobbing
Raft becoming smaller, werewolves sobbing.

Paige was certain Campbell would've found
A way to blame himself by now.

                              She ground
Her fangs; a plan was growing in her mind.
She grabbed the bottle, placed it just behind
The chair that she'd been sitting on before
She'd stood and struck her father. (He was snoring
Now, the pooled blood wrinkling.) She stooped
To grab the ropey bonds her father, duped,
Had loosened. Wrapping them around her paws,
As if she were self-bandaging with gauze,
Paige walked back to the door.

                              She tucked her chin
In, muzzle pointing down, to make as thin
A showing as she could. (The snout that peered
Around a corner was quite often sheared
Away in genre scrolls.) She heard a sound—
Two paws on creaking planks—and peeped around
The door.

                The pirate with the topknot was
Approaching, humming something as one does
When one is feeling cocky or complacent,
Surely not expecting an assailant
To attack.

                She went and sat down, placed
Her loosely bound paws on her lap, and faced
The door.

                The door, ajar, groaned open. Topknot
Came in with a tray of food—and stopped,
Eyes wide.

                "Me father can't quite hold his drink,"
Said Paige. She nodded at his body. "Think
You'd better prop him up."

                    The pirate eyed her,
Sighed, and put the tray down on a cider
Cask. He studied Glen, then crouched beside
The werewolf. "Are you sure he hasn't died,
Me love?"
                    She drew a paw free from the nest
Of rope, reached down, and grabbed the bottle's neck.

The pirate raised a paw and slapped Glen's muzzle—
Hard. "I think you've had enough to guzzle,
B'y."
            She stood and, lunging forward, raised
Her club. The pirate turned, the bottle grazing
Topknot's moving snout. Another swing;
The pirate dodged the blow, the bottle winging
Past his ear. He shoved her up against
Some crates, which toppled. Properly incensed,
He lifted Paige, then flung her to the floor,
The impact jarring loose the bottle. "Whore!"
He sneered. He fell on her, his snarling maw
Disclosing yellow fangs.
                    Her groping paw
Found something knobby on the ground. Waves crashed—
And Topknot's head pitched forward as she smashed
The thing—the Mozart bust—against his skull.
The bust was solid stone and made the dull
But deep clink of two cuts of frozen meat
Colliding.
                    Topknot struggled to his feet,
A paw against his head, another out
As if for balance. Blood streamed down his snout,
Small beads accumulating on his nose.
The wolf was dizzy, listing, in the throes

Of something, topknot twitching like a vane
Suggesting storm clouds in a hemorrhaged brain.
Perhaps instinctively, he drew his sword—
One paw still on his head—and stepped toward
The door. He seemed to drag his other, leaden
Leg, then toppled to the floor, his weapon
Clattering.
               Paige waited several seconds
For the pirate to grow still. She reckoned
He was dead and crawled across the floor.
She hefted Topknot's sword—her father snoring
On—and found the metal hilt surprising
In its smoothness.
               Sensing Topknot rising,
Paige backed up and raised the heavy sword.
The pirate, though, had merely shuddered. "Lord
Of Moons," she breathed.
               Tiptoeing slowly round
The two unmoving bodies on the ground,
She reached the open doorway, both paws on
The hilt, blade out. She'd read that Genghis Khan,
The wolf barbarian, had never left
A fallen foe whose muzzle *wasn't* cleft
In two. Perhaps she ought to chop off Topknot's
Snout (just to be sure) or maybe pop
An eyeball out. She chose instead to peer
Around the door. The passageway was clear.

She stepped past several doors, the sword out like
A torch, her shaky paws prepared to strike.
She looked around a corner.
               Twisting, weathered
Stairs led to the deck. A row of severed

Wolf heads (taxidermied, grey, and strung
Across the stairwell, each one by its tongue)
Formed something like a curtain. They were matted,
Threadbare; clearly, they'd been slapped and batted
Back and forth by years of passing paws.

The storm was over. She could hear dull claws,
A muffled clicking overhead, along
With creaking wood. The sounds comprised the song
Of paws on deck. She figured there were three
Wolves left onboard: the captain ("Eyepatch," she
Had dubbed him in her mind), the one whose right
Paw was a sickle ("Hookpaw"), and the slightly
Mangy one who'd held a harpoon gun
(She hadn't named him yet).
                                                    She knew the sun
Would rise soon. If she managed to escape
The ship alive (avoiding violent rape
And flensing), she would have to lie down on
Whatever flotsam she could find (the dawn
Above, the swell below) and take her chances
With the sharks, as maidens in romances
Often did. She'd have to float through day
Asleep. But first, she'd have to fight her way
Past several pirates—or attack them one
By one down here. She'd lie in wait and run
Them through.
                              The stairwell darkened. Someone's paws
Were coming down.
                                        Paige turned, the nailed-up jaws
Providing pawholds as the wolf retreated
Down the passage. Thinking she'd be greeted
By her father—or a zombie Topknot—

Paige held up the sword, prepared to lop off
Rival snouts on sight. But both were sprawled
Across the floor still.
                              "Wally?" someone called,
Behind her. "You in there, me son?"
                                        Paige eyed her
Options, then went for the cask of cider,
Crouching behind it as the door flung wide.

The floorboards creaked: the pirate was inside
The hold with her. She heard him close the door.
He gazed upon the bodies on the floor
In stoic silence—not a single yelp.
She guessed this pirate had a thicker pelt.
He wouldn't hesitate to use his claws.

She heard him slowly cross the room and pause.
She heard a fervent sniff. Paige tried to hold
Her breath and muster courage for a bold
Attack. She tried to make her body stiff,
To grip the sword. She heard a second sniff—
Perhaps to verify his comrade's death?

And then the pirate took a giant breath.
He held it for a second—then exhaled.
The sound of rushing, roaring wind was trailed
By falling crates. She heard the pirate take
Another breath—which made the birdcage shake—
And then expel it, blowing several more
Crates over. She would have to flee before
The pirate brought his breath to bear on Paige's
Cask. She heard the suck of air, the cage's
Rattle—so, she stood and dashed toward

The door.

          The strong wind struck her, tore her sword
Away. It felt as if the wall had rushed
To slam against her back. The impact pushed
Her own breath out: a middling, cub-grade gasp.
She fell, confused, then felt a firm paw grasp
Her by the scruff and drag her to the door
And down the passageway.

                    No cry of "whore"
This time. She turned her head and saw, in lieu
Of second paw, a hook swing into view.
The pirate—it was Hookpaw—stopped and raised
Her off the ground, then climbed the stairs. Snouts grazed
Her face as Hookpaw, huffing, shoved her through
The wolf-head curtain. Topside, Hookpaw threw
Her to the deck. She heard the creak of wood
And looked up.

               Three remaining pirates stood
Around her: Hookpaw, Eyepatch, and the one
She'd yet to name, who held the harpoon gun.

"She done in Wally," Hookpaw said. He chopped
His hook, which flickered in the moonlight. "Bopped
Him on the noggin. Dad's still snoring on
The floor." He looked at Eyepatch. "Cub's the spawn
Of hell." Post-storm, its mainsail furled, the ship
Was bobbing gently.

              Eyepatch, lower lip
Extended, raised his brow; he was impressed.
"A *brave* spawn, though," he said, and touched his chest
Instinctively. The lockets gleamed within
His fur.

        He hunkered down and made a thin

Slit of his one remaining eye—a look
Of curiosity—then grabbed the hook
His first mate offered. Grunting, Hookpaw helped
His captain up. "The cub's not even yelped
For help," said Eyepatch. "Well, you'd better bring
Her to me quarters. After that, we'll fling
Her overboard."

            She tried to wheel around,
But Hookpaw seized her arm. A flapping sound
Was dopplering toward them. Paige looked past
The pirate's head. Against the mizzenmast,
Which loomed above, a shape was growing bigger.
Soon, the shape had swelled into a figure,
Perched on Hookpaw's shoulders, Hookpaw falling
Forward, letting go of Paige and sprawling
On the deck, a boy astride him. Miles.

Hookpaw looked back. Miles grinned. His smile's
Gleaming teeth revealed two tips: a pair
Of fangs. His naked limbs glowed from the glare
The moon-shaped buoys gave off. Hookpaw batted
At the pire. Miles—in the rapid,
Ratatat-like bursts woodpeckers make—
Attacked the pirate's neck.

               "We needs a stake,
B'y!," Hookpaw hollered, squirming on the deck.

The boy, now bat, flew off him. Hookpaw's neck
Was spurting blood, his heavy body thrashing
Violently. The no-name pirate—bashing
At the air, the harpoon gun his club—
Was focused on the bat (and not the cub
His captain meant to ravish). Lunging at

Him, claws extended, Paige slashed at the flat
Expanse of fur his gut, exposed, presented.
Noname screeched. He gut-kicked Paige and sent her
To the deck. He raised his gun.

                         Expanding
In midair, arms out, the boy was standing
On the barrel—which was driven downward,
Gun discharging deckward. Noname frowned
As Miles disappeared, the gun, unweighted,
Swinging wildly. The wolf, frustrated,
Bent to yank the harpoon from the wood,
As Miles dropped upon him like a hood,
The boy's head striking Noname's neck with darting
Speed. The pire-mounted wolf was starting
To collapse when Eyepatch flung a net
Across the pair.

                  "You'll make a lovely pet,"
He said, "if you survive." The pire flicked
From boy to bat to boy as Eyepatch kicked
The tangled figures with his peg leg—bone
Cadged from a long-dead humpback. Noname groaned
As Eyepatch, stomping with abandon, struck
The dying wolf and got his peg leg stuck,
Embedded in the wolf's skull. Noname and
The curled-up boy grew still.

                        Paige tried to stand;
She still felt winded from the kick she'd taken
To the gut. Her mind was murky. Shaken.

Eyepatch turned to her, his breathing ragged.
From his scabbard, Eyepatch drew a jagged
Sword with liver spots of flaking rust.
"You've got a lot of fight, me love. I trust

You'll claw me eye out if I climbs on top
Of you." He spat. "I think I'd better pop
Your cherry *after* I've cut out your own
Eyes." Eyepatch stepped toward her: tock. The bone
Leg, slick with blood, had left a dark-red spot
On deck.
                    Paige backed against a rail—and thought
That it was time to jump. She heard faint squeaking—
Miles worming through the net—then creaking
Wood, as Glen, on deck now, rushed toward
The pirate, pushing Eyepatch overboard
And falling with him, kamikaze style.

"Dad!" cried Paige. She heard a splash, then Miles,
Wings as crisp as shuffled cards, was after
Them, the bat aloft and flying faster
Than she'd ever thought a thing could fly.
The soaring pire curved against the sky,
Appeared to pause, then quickly plunged, a flash
Of grey. She marked a second, smaller splash
And rushed toward the rail.
                                    The waves were still.
They lapped the hull. And then, as if a grill
Were warming slowly just below the swell—
As if a fissure were disclosing Hell
Itself—the sea began to glow. The lockets.

The bat burst from the sea, a rodent rocket,
Foam like flower petals peeling back.
He blew past Paige, crashlanding on the deck.
He held the chains—which held the lockets—by
His tiny teeth. Too quickly for her eye
To register, the bat became the child

Once again and lay there naked, wild.
But he wasn't wet; apparently,
The shift had shed what little water he'd
Absorbed. The furless, dark-haired child sat
Up, chains inside his mouth like reins. He spat
The lockets on the deck and crossed his legs.
He showed no injuries.

                     "She'll know her eggs
Are here," he said at last. "We musn't linger,
Paige." He made a steeple of his fingers
Underneath his chin. "We really need
To go."

           She seemed in shock. "So, you don't bleed
Then? You don't even bruise?"

                       The pire shook
His head.

           She stared at Miles. Then, she looked
Around. "You killed 'em…"

                   "Well, you started it."
He tried a grin.

             She looked confused. "You bit
'Em, though. I thought they were supposed to turn—"

"To pires? No." He gazed toward the stern—
And out to sea. "We have a couple hours
Left—"

        "So *how* do pires get their powers?"

"Paige, we need to leave."

                  "What's gonna happen
To the ones you bit?"

                 "They'll rot. They'll blacken."
Miles tapped a fang. "My body makes

A venom. Like the kind that deadly snakes
Produce. I'm not a supernatural fiend,
You know. I had a mother. I was weaned."
He paused and then: "I'm sorry 'bout your dad."

"I'm sorry that I've called you 'ghoul' and 'vlad.'"
Her shoulders shook as Paige began to sob.

* * *

They heaved the bodies overboard to bob
And sink. The boy explained how pires mated.

"*I* thought pires were"—Paige winced—"castrated
Werewolves."
                    Miles laughed. The private parts
Of pire-bats (obscure and tiny darts
And folds) maintained their bat size when on pires—
Full-sized pires. Flirty thoughts, desires—
These felt vague, remote, to pires. But
The bats had clarity. They'd mount and rut.

"And you don't bruise?" said Paige.
                                        "We're like the poly-
Morph, that way. We're stretchy things. It's folly
Stabbing one of us."
                    Paige thought of Gaddis.
"Can you die?"
                    "The sun can kill us. Sadness,
Too."
        The wolves he'd bitten were now venom-
Dark. Belowdecks, Miles found a vellum
Codex Bible. It was wolf-eared, swollen;
It had seen the sea. (Perhaps they'd stolen

It, the pirates, when they'd sacked some pire
Colony; a codex book required
Hands. Plus pires, Miles said, loved church.)
He climbed a mast and squatted on his perch:
A sail-less yard. He skim-read with a frown,
A seagull next to him. He hollered down
To Paige: "I'll gladly read a passage if
You like. In honour of your dad." A stiff
Wind turned the pages to the verse about
The wolf nailed to his cross, declaiming doubt.

Paige stood below him, looking at the lockets
On the deck, her paws inside the pockets
Of her cloak. At last, she bent to pick
The chains up. Thoughts of Mobies made her sick.
And yet she drew the chains around her head
And craned to look at Miles. "Go ahead."

In deference to the sky, the pire spoke
The wind's pick to the sea. He wore a cloak
He'd salvaged in the cargo hold; he'd lost
His when he'd changed into a bat and crossed
From sloop to pirate ship. The cloak was pink.
(He'd picked it over other shades. "I think
This works," he'd said.) He leapt down to the deck
And looked at Paige.

                              She didn't paw her neck
Reflexively in fear; there wasn't time
To be afraid. The sun would start to climb
The sky soon.

                    Miles read her mind and said,
"We're running out of night. I'll have to head
Belowdecks in a little bit—to hide

Out from the day." He paused. His pained face tried
To muster hopeful eyes. "We've got an hour,
Maybe two, to find your friends."

                              "No, *our*
Friends, b'y. But you get Moe, okay?"

                                        He laughed.

She gazed across the moon-striped waves, Del's raft
A needle in a pelt. (She couldn't think
About the chest, though.) Wind had found a chink
Inside the hull. The red ship whistled. Sang.

Paige turned to Miles. "There's no windward fang,"
She said in sudden wonder. "Who the moon
Is gonna blow us? I'll be sleeping soon—
Not that I have the lungs to get us going."
Paige remembered Hookpaw's gale-grade blowing.

Flipping back to bat, he flew up, banking
Right along a length of yard and yanking
Clewlines. As he went, sails dropped from spars.

A bat's voice squeaked, "We'll use the wind and stars."

16.

The steno fetched a brand-new pair of shoes,
A garish breed of Pradas in chartreuse.
The bot had borne away the one Adidas
Carefully as if it were a fetus—
Or a bomb. The Pradas' soles were dumb
And pixieless. They couldn't bond with someone's
Face.
       Her beachy lounger faced the model.
Lux was sitting next to her, a bottle
In his hand. (He hadn't yet uncapped it.)
Ichiro stood by the tank and batted
At the air's invisible and constant
Postcards bearing urgent corporate content.
He was speaking with intensity,
Which Kaye found worrisome. Apparently,
His people had been tracking Sable's backup
Agents, who had called off their attack
And presently were in retreat on separate
Humpbacks.
         "Clearly, they were feeling desperate,"
Ichiro was saying to the air.
"I'm thinking let's do more than simply scare
Them." Ichiro fell silent, turned, and cocked
His head, as someone—likely Stephen—talked.

He wore a white lamé, a beautifully
Appointed fencing vest. Presumably,
The Sable stuff had called the billionaire
Away from exercises; tamped-down hair
Alluded to some sort of helmet he'd
Removed. He had the mounted-on-a-steed-
Like posture of a person taught to puff
Their chest out—someone polished to a buff
By wealth.
                    "So no one's gonna call the fuzz?"
Kaye said to Lux. Outside, the muffled buzz
Of Stephen's drones was circling the Wood.

"Not Ichiro's approach," said Lux. He stood,
The bottle in his hand, and faced the tank.

"I'm gonna guess that Sable wasn't pranking
    Me back there."
                        "A rival corporation
Groomed her. They do bio-replication
IP. They've been after Mandy for
Some time."
                "For what?"
                                "A very tiny spore"—
Lux pinched his fingers—"they believe she helped
To fund. You place it in a bed of kelp."

"Then what?" She hugged her legs, her knees beneath
    Her chin.
                "It spawns a blue whale. Macro. Teeth
The size of scows."
                        "A blue whale? Aren't all whales
    Extinct?"

"They were."

She thought about the sails
Inside the model, on their whale hunts.

"Sable
Works for Keating-Wyatt. She enabled
Them to spy on me." He grimaced. "Us."

As Ichiro drew near, he said, "Let's truss
One up," then noticed Lux and Kaye. Grew quiet.
Walked away.

She frowned. "This Keating-Wyatt,
Don't they have their name all over our
Department?"

"Yes, they have a lot of power."

"What's-his-name, the dean, his title's 'Keating-
Wyatt Chair in Something.'"

"They've been beating
Down his fucking door for years, it seems.
It's clear they've compromised his mind. His dreams."

She shuddered as she thought about the writhing
Thing in Sable's fingers—and the scything
Blade of Stephen Stove. Some stupid Flora
(On a hike, pursuing Nature's aura
Underneath the stars) would stumble on
The mown grass, maybe sacrifice a fawn
Or read a poem in the ring. They'd never
Know a manga-eyeballed stove had severed
Ken Doll's head and scythed a pagan circle.

For a moment, Kaye felt sickness burble
Up. She turned, hunched over, thinking she

Might vomit. Unsure as to whether he
Should pat his student's back, Lux crouched beside
Her lounger. Finally, he sighed and tried
An arm squeeze.

                Kaye sat up. "This company
Was spying on you? Using puppetry?"

"That's why the dean insisted on the smarteyes.
Sable's worm-thing would've done its part
And found your brain. You would've been enraptured,
Right? And then your smarteyes would've captured
Shit as Sable steered you round the manse.
You would've been her agent. In a trance."
Her prof exhaled; providing exposition
Clearly was its own ordeal—admission,
Maybe, of the danger Kaye had been
In all this time. She liked her prof's chagrin.

"My shepherds screened your eyes," said Ichiro,
Now back, "first time you came to Tokyo.
They flagged some problematic code."

                          "They hacked
My eyes?"

        He smiled patiently. "They *cracked*
The spyware Keating-Wyatt had installed,
A link back to your dean. They deftly walled
Away the code and made sure not to trip
Alarms. They're dab hands with an optic chip.
And they've been looping seamless tintypes, feeding
Keating-Wyatt shots of what you're reading—"

"So, they hacked my eyes."

                He made a straight

Line of his mouth—to cede the point or sate
Her indignation. "Anyway, it's Mandy
Whom they're after. And they've upped the ante—
Cavalierly, given where we're at
Tonight." He pocketed his hands and sat
Down next to Kaye. "They think we're on to something."
Frowning, looking Luxward. "*Are* we?"

                                           "Nothing
Comes to mind," said Lux. "We've run the tank
A lot. No leads." He raised the bottle. Drank.
He'd slowly, deftly, been uncapping it.

"So no one's watching when I take a shit?"
Said Kaye. She'd raised her hand ironically.

"We wouldn't violate your POV,"
Said Ichiro. He met her eyes. "My shepherds
Access views belonging to more checkered
Lives than yours. They've got enough illicit
Content to enjoy. They wouldn't visit
Your view—even though I'm sure you train
Your sights on worthy things."

                              Kaye said, "Explain
To me just how long you've all known about
This shit."

                "We'd just begun to figure out
The Keating-Wyatt link," said Lux, "around
When you arrived." He wandered tankward. Frowned.
He almost seemed upset. "I never thought
You'd get involved." He double-tapped a spot
Of glass and spread his thumb and index finger.
Even now, he couldn't help but linger
On the tank.

The iris, pixel-rimmed,
Appeared. The rest of Lux's model dimmed.
The iris framed four wolf bots on a raft.
The Howlship was lost at sea.
                              Kaye laughed
And looked at Ichiro, still sitting next
To her. "You're telling me some YA text
Is what you care about? Come on now, you're
Just after, what's it called"—she paused—"this spore?"

He rose. "My interest is in Mandy—not
Whatever miracle her fortune's brought
To life. The interest of my *rivals* merely
Means we need to find her first. She's clearly
In great jeopardy." He tapped his fencing
Vest, a mesh egg instantly condensing
Round his head. The egg's inscrutable
Blank mask gave no sense it was mutable.

* * *

She stayed inside her bubble thing til it
Was dark and quiet. Peering through a slit—
She'd pulled the jello-hide apart—she noted
One lone bot, a carapaced and bloated
Macro beetle, inching silently
Across the floor. It was decidedly
One-minded as it hoovered up a film
Of dust. (It bonsaied dust within the kiln
Its body mostly was.) She spread aside
Two jello flaps and shouldered through, the hide
Resealing with a burp.
                              She wore the ghastly
Pradas (green as fucking slime but vastly

More luxurious and comfortable
Than any shoe she owned, like cotton wool
Shaped into footwear); wiseweave charcoal tights
Composed of bots (that carried gigabytes
Of data on, e.g., her walking habits);
Sweatshirt by the brand Elijah Rabbits
(Which would keep her warm inside the tank);
And, borrowed from the manse, a fibreplank
By Santa Cruz (the manse's houseguests could,
If so inclined, surf stretches of the Wood,
Which kept some treeless slopes). A couple straps that
Crossed her chest implied the bonsai knapsack,
Shrivelled on her back.

                 She crept down to
The second floor. She'd guessed the spore (the blue
Whale she was nearly ear-fucked with a worm
For) was inside the silver locket: sperm
That Lux, at least, was hiding. It explained
Why Lux's face had looked so weirdly pained
When she'd been in the hut.

                  Was Ichiro
In on the ruse as well? Her guess was no.
If he'd secured it, Mandy's spore would be
Inside a lab (and not beside a sea-
Adjacent hut inside a bonsai model
Of a celebrated YA novel).

At the entrance to the second floor,
Still mulling why her prof had hid the spore,
She placed her toe *en pointe*, but didn't feel
Her smartsole lift her, didn't feel a wheel
Assemble—then remembered she now wore
The Pradas. Anyway, a skated floor

Would only wake the manse.
                              She started walking,
Plank beneath her arm. She heard a hawking
Sound, a hacking somewhere in the room.
Her smarteyes (U-Perth red!) had bleached the gloom
With grainy green: night vision. As she neared
The tank, the monstrous hacking cat she'd feared
Turned out to be her prof passed out from drink
And snoring on a lounger near the sink,
The glassed-in octagon by which she'd steal
Into the tank. She'd have to somehow wheel
Him to the booth—and scan his eye—to pass
Through what was currently unyielding glass.

She heard a rapid clacking dopplering
Toward her, from behind: the scuttling
Of legs. She wheeled around, heart beating, scared.
She raised the plank above her head, prepared
To brain whatever was approaching.
                                      Stephen
Stove was standing there. His face was even,
Placid, even though he'd crossed the floor
In seconds.
            "Kaye?" he said. His oven door,
When talking, showed his throat, a void of comic-
Book maroon. He made no anatomic
Sense; the short-armed bot on shorter legs,
With swollen manga eyes the shape of eggs,
Had no mechanical articulation,
Like a bot straight out of animation.
He was pixieplastic, Kaye decided,
Like the tank bots. Pixies had provided
Him an instant sabre. They had let

Him emulate a toy that posed no threat,
A kid's stove in the grass.

                    "Hey Stephen," Kaye
Said, lowering the plank.

                    "It's not yet day,"
He said. He blinked, his left eye magnified
By monocle.

                    "Can't seem to sleep," she lied.
"I thought I'd take a walk." Was Ichiro
 Behind that monocle? Or did he know
She'd come downstairs because he'd hacked her eyes
And was logged in to them? To her surprise,
She realized that she didn't care if she
Were being watched—and suddenly felt free.
She nodded at the model. "In the tank."

He tracked her eyes and turned, his body clanking
Noisily. Then swivelled back to look
At Kaye.

                    "It's basically my favourite book,"
She said. She raised the plank. "I'd love to fly
Inside it. By myself."

                    "You'd need the eye
Scan of Professor Emmett Lux, my Kaye."
He blinked. "The tank will want your prof's okay."

She felt deflated. "Yes," she said. "Of course."

The bot's brow furrowed. "Though I could endorse
A brief lark, I suppose."

                    "You could?"

                              He waddled
To the tank and took it in. "The model's

Technically on territory *in*
My charge." He rattled like some vintage tin
Man as he curled his tiny arms and pressed
Two fists against his oven's walls. Kaye guessed
The bot was emulating hands on hips.

She took a step. "I'd love to see the ships.
It wouldn't take too long."
                              "Approved. The sensor,
Though, will want that eye." He raised a pincer,
Turned to Lux…
                    "Wait, what?"
                                        The robot winked
At her. "A little humour." Then, he blinked,
The manga eye behind the monocle
Wiped clean. An actual eyeball, barnacled
With veins and darting wetly, filled the lens.
"I keep recordings of the eyes of friends."

* * *

The plank took getting used to, but she found
Her balance as she skimmed the springy ground
Inside the tank. She'd worried that the plank
Would find the turf confusing, draw a blank,
Refuse to hover; pixieclay was made
Of microscopic bots, which could dissuade
A plank from floating. But although she sank
A little when she stepped onto the plank,
It still contrived its pillow of opposing
Air.
        She surfed toward the village, closing
In on Dickie's hut. The tank was set
To Chapter Sixteen. Rabbit Strait was wet;

A storm had passed across the model, drenching
Lux's bonsai landscape.

                    In a wrenching
Scene unfolding on the water, four
Wolves sitting on a raft are lost, no shore
In sight. Dot's ears are limp (she's barely said
A sentence), Moe keeps shouting: vessel, dead
Ahead! (but nothing's there), and Del and Campbell
Argue. Del is firm: we should've gambled,
Fired on the pirates. Campbell, though,
Says, they'd've killed us, Del. His words come slowly,
Interspersed with groans. It feels as if
His ribs are bruised; the beating's left him stiff.
But now we're mooned! says Del. The two wolves' barks
Are getting louder.

                    Look! cries Moe.

                              Two sharks
Are circling the raft. The wolves get to
Their feet, claws out. The moon we gonna do?
Says Dot. A shark's on each side now—and snapping.
Stand against me, Del! says Campbell, backing
Up against Del's back. Okay! says Del.
They brace against each other, chests now swelling—
"Huffing," in the Wulvish tongue. Del shows
Three claws and counts them down. On "one," they blow
Their lungs out, flattening the waves—and blasting
Back the sharks. The duelling gusts, contrasting
Currents, force the wolves against each other—
After this, they'll call each other "brother"—
But the raft remains unmoved, the water
All around them rippling. They totter,
Fall, their chests deflated. Del and Campbell
Wind up in a furry, rain-soaked tangle.

Dot and Moe kneel next to them. Are you
Okay? asks Dot. They're fine! says Moe, they blew
The bastards' fins off! Then, Moe stops. I've got
A thought! She grabs her sack. I know I brought
Them with me...

                            Kaye approached the shore and saw
Moe's thought: a fireworks display. The awe
Of passing wolves was palpable as they
Ignored the furless on the ghost-drawn sleigh
And stopped to gaze at rockets, Roman candles,
Catherine wheels, and more—some werewolf-vandal
Scratching on the sky above the sea.

Now that, Moe says to Dot, is poetry.
Dot laughs, her wet eyes gleaming in the fire-
Works. She grabs her sack, pulls out her lyre...

But the fireworks were digital;
The glass that spanned the tank ran visual
Approximations of the business that
The novel's plot had given it.

*   *   *

                            Waves lapped
The shore. Kaye surfed along its edge until
The ground gave way to rocks. She felt a thrill
Wing through her as she steered the plank across
The wharf and passed a wolf who wore a cross—
The nun in *Full-Moon*'s leadoff chapter! But
The bot ignored Kaye; it was in the rut
Determined by its programming, a model
Train on paws.
                    Kaye reached the shifter's hovel,

Leaping off the plank. It travelled for
A few more metres, bumping Dickie's door—
Just as the stars above went out. The night
Sky turned to solid white, a searing light
That flooded Rabbit Strait. She looked away,
Hands on her eyes. The night had flipped to day
Abruptly, no gradations, skipping dawn.
She briefly wondered if a nuke had gone
Off, washing everything in antiseptic
Glare.

       The glare began to fade. Dyspeptic,
Shade-less, Emmett Lux was peering down
At her. That is, the glass that capped the town
Displayed a square containing Lux's face.
The square itself seemed cut from outer space;
The sky that framed the square was dark again
And filling up with stars as if a pen
Were poking holes in night. At first, she thought
An overarching pane of tank had dropped
Away and full-sized Lux had poked his head
In. But she realized that the face was spread
Across a curving plane and pixelated.

"Kaye, please stop." His voice—articulated
By stealth speakers hidden all around,
Presumably in trees and bushes—sounded
Weary. Beat. He'd clearly pulled his chair
Up to the tank. A lens had drawn a square
Around his head; a bot suspended in
The glass was filming him, from hair to chin.

"Did Stephen give me up?"
                The sky-face squinted,

Shook its head. "Can't hear you. Mics are printed
On the leaves."
She looked around, then knelt
Beside a shrub by Dickie's door. She felt
The leaves and heard an echoed crackle. Feedback.
"Stephen give me up?" she yelled.
"No need
To yell," said Lux, "and no, he didn't give
You up. I was alerted by a sieve.
Apparently, the model doesn't like
Your wiseweave tights."
She gripped a twig, her mic,
And tapped it. "Testing, testing, one, two, three."

He sighed. "Please stop."
She stopped. She heard the quay
Beyond the hovel—wolfbot whalers heaving
Carcasses—and felt relief that Stephen
Hadn't sold her out, though wasn't sure
Just why she felt that. Maybe he was pure,
Self-governed. Ichiro had said the bot
Was stubborn, on the gondola. *He's not
Without some bugs.* Perhaps the bot had spunk.

"You need to leave," said Lux. "I'll send the junk."

"That's fine," she said. She nodded at the door.
"But first, I'm gonna go and get the spore."

His face had changed, annoyance giving way
To something else, like calm despair. "Look, Kaye,
I need to tell you—"
"You can tell me what

You like. I saw the locket in the hut.
The silver one. I'm gonna go and grab it.
Then, I'm gonna take a walk through Rabbit
Strait, down to the pretty shore, and throw
It in the sea. How long's it take to grow?
I'd love to see it fight your giant robot.
Blue whale vs. Moby would be *so* hot,
Wouldn't it? An enterprising fuck
Like Ichiro could sell the rights to ZuckTube."

"Ichiro"—Lux looked off camera for
A moment—"doesn't know I have the spore."

She stood and stomped the shrub, a shard of white
Noise ripping through the wharf.
                                    "I'll make things right,"
He said, pronouncing every word with care.
"I lied, I know. But please, don't go in there."

She stooped to grab the floating plank, then walked
Toward the hovel, shouldering the pocked
Door open. Dickie's quarters looked the same
As last time, fire flickering, the flame
A hidden bulb. The walls had muffled Lux;
She heard what she assumed were muttered "fucks"
And then frustrated fingers hammering
At keys, perhaps to stream his stammering
Through speakers in the hut.
                                    There was no Dickie
Bot in sight. They'd scanned his buggy pixie-
Clay, restored him to the plot. She guessed
He lay inside the sunken treasure chest.

She found the low and dusty shelf, which sat
Against a wall, the locket lying flat,
Innocuous. She dropped the awkward plank,
Which paused to float above the floor. It sank
A little as she straddled it, the board
Her bench. She gripped its sides and leaned toward
The shelf.
           The locket's fine chains ran toward
And *through* the wall, through holes some hand had bored.
She frowned, which accidentally activated
Zoom mode—basically, a hyphenated
Box that brought the locket into sharper
Focus while the fuzzy background darkened.
She could see now that the chains were rigid
Tubes. In fact, up close they looked like fitted
Pipes. (The pipes were mounted on what looked
Like tiny piers.) Perhaps the two strands hooked
Up *in* the wall—or plugged to something more
Essential? Life support for Blue Whale Spore?

She tried to lift the whole thing, but the locket
Wouldn't budge. It sat within a socket,
Carved into the shelf, a shallow groove.
She tried to wiggle it; it wouldn't move.
She took a breath and pressed her thumb against
The locket's lower edge. At last, she sensed
Some give. She flipped the lid up like a clamshell.
She'd expected something small, a gram
Of life. (She'd half-expected caviar:
The tiny, brilliant eggs encasing starlight
In the Moby's cave.) The locket, though,
Was empty.
           She could hear Lux yelling, "No"

And "Kaye," a god's cries circling above
Her, like the messages professing love
Her dad had sent. The pigeons. He had cancer,
But she'd left his overtures unanswered.

Cancer—she had scanned the awful word
Just once. Her dad's initial paper bird
Had flown into her dorm room back when she'd
First started out at U of Perth. *I need
To tell you I've got cancer.* But she'd lobbed
A shoe—and smashed the pigeon. Now, she sobbed
Beside the shelf. She hated that he'd left
Kaye and her mother to go write his "deft
And dazzling debut" (according to
The *New York Times*). She hated feeling through
With someone she still loved. She hated him—
And hated that she'd left him to his grim
Prognosis, left his words unanswered, swatted
Them away. She couldn't face the thought of
Facing him. Emaciated. Thin.

She noticed, then, a smooth depression in
The bottom of the locket, like a sink's.
Her eyes tried focusing, tried rapid blinks
To clear the tears, like windshield wipers speeding
Up, the hyphenated box still reading
Something there.
                    A patch grew sharp. She saw
Now that the locket's basin formed a maw,
Its silver sloping slightly, like the grading
Of a spout or throat, a subtle shading
Indicating something like a drain:
An aperture you'd need a single grain

Of sand to stop. The aperture was glowing
Red.
     "Oh fuck," she said, her body slowing
Down already, sparkling in spots.
She raised a hand; the hand was trailing dots,
An image from Seurat. The skin beneath
Her clothes was tingling. She tongued her teeth;
The teeth gave way like sudden, crumbly sand,
The tongue imploding, too.
                              She tried to stand
Up, but her limbs were shedding ground-up jewels,
Her arms and legs dissolving, molecules
Ascending, arching, and descending, flowing
In a single stream toward the glowing
Aperture, her body mostly stream—
Then gone, before her brain could think to scream.

1:.

At eighteen, he was deemed mature enough
To leave the orphanage and view the stuff
His mom had left behind. A wolf unlocked
A storage shed beside the wharf and walked
Him past erratic mounds of personal
Effects, the things a desperate person will
Find difficult to bear away when leaving
Loved ones: sheet-veiled chairs and tables grieving
Lost homes; up against a wall, a mattress
Slouching adolescently; a hatless
Hat stand like a leaf-plucked tree; a bureau.
Everything was stark, in chiaroscuro,
Shadows darting round the flimsy shed
Like startled spirits of the dormant dead—
Until the werewolf leading him around
The dark, a buoy in her paw, put down
The small orb on a shelf, which paused the shadow
Play.

     He looked around unmoved. He had no
Interest in the chairs or lamps or much
Besides his metal, glass-faced rabbit hutch.

He hauled it to the small hut he had taken
Up in by the harbour, where forsaken

Types—the local slatterns, thieves, and cutthroats—
Dwelled. He set it down inside the hut.
It wore the fire's flicker like a jacket.
He had *thought* he'd fill it with a rabbit,
Maybe several. Why else bring it home?

He made a joke of it: he placed a gnome
On top. He figured he was trying to
Dilute that moment when his mother drew
The lid across it as he pleaded with
Her—trying to dilute the sort of myth
That moulds a young mind. Most days, he ignored
It, though.
            One evening, feeling brave (or bored),
He locked the lid and turned the hutch around
(The metal side now facing him) and found
The airhole in the back. He scrutinized
The cavern.
           Then, the polymorph surprised
Himself. He plugged the airhole with a claw.
The claw's tip, in the hutch, became a maw
And started swelling. As the mini-muzzle
Grew, his head collapsed, his body guzzled
By the airhole, by the body growing
In the box, as if some mouth were blowing
Up the smaller torso and its newly
Fashioned limbs. The polymorph's unruly
Final nub of flesh, a tail, squeezed through
Three minutes later. There he lay: a new
And full-sized polymorph, his body packed
Inside the hutch.
           He turned his head: a cracked
And standing mirror just across his hut

Described a boxed-in wolf. His fur abutted
Glass and emulated perfect edges.
He suggested something like a hedge's
Scissored planes—or matter mashed against,
And moulding to, the very thing that fenced
It in.
          He felt his heartbeat hammering
Inside his torso, muzzle, travelling
Around his body, beating in his toes.
(He found it strange that hearts in werewolf prose
Confined themselves to chests.) His stomach, too,
Was churning anxiously and moving through
His flesh the way vibrating things will shift
Themselves along the floor. He tried to lift
The lid; it wouldn't budge. He pushed the lid
A little more. Laughed ruefully. What did
He *think* was gonna happen? He'd assumed
The claustrophobia that had consumed
Him as a polycub had faded. He'd
Assumed he'd beaten it—his desperate need
For space.
          He tried to calm down, focus, find
His way out through the airhole, but his mind,
Faced with the thought of spending three more minutes
Inching through the hole, had reached its limits.
He began to panic, arms pinwheeling,
Pounding, hammering the hutch's ceiling's
Dimpled tin.
          And then he paused in awe,
For on the ceiling were the sets of claw
Marks he had made when locked inside the hutch
So many years ago. He reached to touch
The scratchings, clustered lines suggesting music

Staves. As Dickie felt the therapeutic
Braille, it brought up memories so strong
He heard his mother's voice, the foolish song
She used to whistle, "Thar She Blows." His paw,
He realized, had begun to shrink, to draw
In slightly, til it was the size it was
When he was young. The paw could shrink because
He could compress himself, though Dickie rarely
Did so. "Shrink too small, and you'll be barely
There," his mother used to warn. It only
Now occurred to him that she'd been lonely,
Terrified of being left alone,
Of Dickie shrinking down to form a stone-
Or shell-sized body which the waves might take
Away. The polymorph began to quake,
To cry, contracting further til he found
He was as tiny as a snail, curled round
Himself, a pared-down lifeform, Paleozoic.

He no longer felt the claustrophobic
Fear. The hutch seemed vast, with looming walls—
A gym. (He thought of classmates hurling balls
At him when he was young.) And lying at
Its centre, now no larger than a gnat,
Was Dickie Lush, his molecules compressed.
His panic slowly ebbed away with rest.
He nodded off.
           When he awoke, he climbed
The wall that had the airhole, like a vined
Thing, makeshift lily pads for paws. The whole
Wall rattled as he climbed. He reached the hole
And threw a limb across it. Sat. The tin
Was buckling, the hole's edge cutting into

Dickie's ass; apparently, he weighed
The same. He leapt down to the floor and made
Two dents, his dense paws like small chisels dropped
On clay. And then he swelled. His wolf ears popped.
He lay there gazing on the hutch as one will
Stare back at a mountain one is done with.

Dickie didn't shrink again for years.
One time, he crawled around the static gears
Inside an open pocket watch he'd found,
A world of inner works that could've ground
Him up. (He'd had a mind to fix the thing
But couldn't source the necessary spring.)
He never shrank in public—never told
A soul he could. The polymorph grew old.
His aging flesh grew less elastic, less
Resilient. There was no need to compress.

* * *

The rock-lined chest sank to the bottom of
The sea, the pair of vessels still above.
At first, he lay in darkness, mashed against
The rocky floor and flat planes of the chest.
He tried to soften, slip between the rocks
Below him. Dickie's flesh *became* the box:
He found and filled its corners, probing for
A gap, a hairline fissure he could pour
Through. He'd withdrawn his fur; a pelt would soak
Up water, hinder swimming, slow his stroke.
But panicked thoughts were quickly setting in.
The polymorph withdrew his tendrilled skin
And started shrinking—til he found himself
Astride a rock.

He felt a jolt; a shelf
Of seafloor had abruptly stopped the chest—
Or so the shifter, steeped in darkness, guessed.
He stood and snorted, picturing his grey
And bitty form: a cub's toy cut from clay.
He hopped from rock to rock (which called to mind
The Moby's cave), his hand thrust out to find
A wall. The wall achieved, he made his way
Around the chest until he felt a spray
Of water falling from above. He stepped
Back, listening.
            A hole of some kind wept;
The rocks below were slick, the water sliming
Surfaces. He frowned and started climbing
Where the chest was dry (his pitons: claws).
It sounded like the chest was wrapped in gauze;
The world beyond was muffled. Soon, the sound of
Rushing water reached him. One paw found a
Brassy edge; the sea was waterfalling
Through a keyhole.
            But his wall was falling
Underneath his weight, the whole chest tipping,
Slamming down, the hole that he'd been gripping
Flush now with the seabed, all the rocks
Landsliding. Dickie jumped toward the box's
Ceiling—which was now a wall—and gripped
The new wall's wood.
            His focused weight had tipped
The treasure chest. He looked down at the new
Floor; rocks had covered up the keyhole through
Which water had been gushing; they had stopped
The sea.
       He started climbing. Near the top,

He felt the chest tip forward, rocks landsliding
Once again (and now, no longer hiding
Dickie's keyhole exit), Dickie leaping
To another wall, the rocks re-heaping.
Dickie tipped the whole thing one more time,
The keyhole now above.

                No way to climb,
He figured, jumping down. The gushing stream
Of water was dead centre, like a beam.
He waited as the sea cascaded in.
The water rose, and with it, Dickie, fins
Now blading from his back and from his limbs.
At last, he reached the hole and tried to swim
Out. But the water pressure was beyond
His stroke. His legs fused, formed a single frond:
A broad tail, merwolf-grade. He backed off slightly,
Gathered up his strength, and with a mighty
Push, his finned arms out, he wriggled through
The keyhole. Heavy-limbed, he swam up to
The surface.

          It was dark, but he heard barking
Somewhere near him. Then, he heard the arcing
Whistling of cannonballs describing
Their trajectories. A flash defining
Looming shapes—the red ship and the *H.O.W.L.*—
Flared and faded. Dickie tried to howl,
But his tired body was too small.
A fire flickered where each cannonball
Had punched the *H.O.W.L.*'s hull. The sea was churning
As the red ship—quickly tacking, turning—
Generated waves. These lapped against
The worn-out shifter. He was still condensed,
The merwolf too exhausted to reshape,

And so he nearly missed the massive shape
About to pass him—likely flotsam stumped
Up by the H.O.W.L. (Praise the Moon!) He jumped
Toward it like a flying fish and landed
On his back. He'd wound up on a sanded,
Wooden sculpture, like a child's drawing
Of a fir tree, boughs like half-moons. Clawing
Bough to bough, he found himself beneath
A shelf whose top was lined with rampart teeth.
He realized, then, the curving, polished tree
Boughs he had scrabbled up were meant to be
Cartoonish tufts of fur, the tree itself
A wolf head.

        Dickie climbed up on the shelf:
The wolf head's jutting lower jaw. He crawled
Between stalagmites—wooden fangs—and sprawled
Upon a smooth tongue. Looming overhead,
An overhang supplied the wooden head
Its upper jaw. He lay now in the open,
Howling muzzle of that chiselled token
Of Del's love: the sculpture of his dad
That gave the raft its prow.

        The work was sad,
The sentimental carving of a knife-
Armed novice. Yet, dead Thom had saved a life;
The merwolf's limbs were lead. So Dickie laughed—
So hard he cried, though no one on the raft
Could hear the polymorph's mosquito whine.

He fell asleep. The raft's stern was inclined
Toward the night sky, given Dickie's weight,
But no one noticed. Plus, the smuggled freight
Was compact as a sprite, and anyway,

The broad raft, cresting waves and lashed by spray,
Stayed mostly level even as the storm
Swept in. The merwolf held his tiny form
And slept an hour (shielded from the drizzle
By the muzzle), waking to the whistle
Of yet more explosives—this time, fire-
Works above. And then, he heard the lyre,
Dot's, of course. The budding bard was winging
It, he thought, but Jesus, she was *singing*.

18.

She felt the wind first, cool against her face,
Her eyes still forming, settling in place.

Tall waves resolved before her, crashing slowly,
Sluggishly, as if some force, some holy
Hand, were dragging on the tide. They sped
Up suddenly like tintypes thumbed ahead
At double time, then settled on the normal
Speed of waves. Her eyes endured abnormal
Lags at times, especially when she'd
Been reassembled by a zuber feed.

She faced a sea. She still sat on the plank.
The plank—no longer floating, beached in dank
And greyish sand—felt hard without its cushioned
Air. The wind was not the airconditioned
Kind the model's turbines generated.
It smelled salty. Fishy. It was weighted
With the pungent whiff of coastal stuff.
She leaned back, propped on arms, the cool sand rough
Against her palms. Her knees were nearly level
With her chest. She sensed her hair (dishevelled,
Shapeless, standing up) was staticky
From teleporting—and felt panicky.

The sea was dark and loud, the waves a wash
Of sibilance. She still had on the posh
And slime-green Pradas, half-submerged in grooves
Of sand—which made the panic worse. Such shoes,
And those who wore them, shouldn't have been resting
On this brusque and brackish turf, waves cresting,
Crashing. The very presence of the Pradas
Was surreal, a figment out of Dada's
Canon. But she noted handsewn seams
Along each shoe. These weren't the stuff of dreams.

A white post stood on either side of Kaye.
They formed an arch above, which seemed to sway
A little in the wind. It was a giant
Jawbone, placed there by some self-reliant
Soul—and hammered like a wicket into
Sand. She gripped her plank and, scooting, withdrew
From the jawbone, edging back a couple
Feet. She plopped back down. The wind had doubled,
Whining through the upright, uncrossed A,
Which loomed before her like an entryway.
This was the cay—the one the *Lucy Dread*
Sails by en route to Kelly Bay—a dead
And meagre island. Even though the tiny
Knapsack on her back (a shriven, spiny
Growth) contained her bonsaied, softback *Full-
Moon*, Kaye was sure, and felt no need to pull
The book out; Dickie, she recalled, observes
An upright, uncrossed A: one bone that curves
To form an apex.
                        Turning, Kaye made note
Of what appeared to be a dock no boat
Would want to lash to, slumping into surf,

And tuckamores inclined toward the turf.
Perhaps the locket had transported her
Within the model? But the wind, the fir-tree
Needles scattered on the beach, the smell
Of briny sea life coming off the swell,
The hi-res detail, gritty feel of dank
Sand—Kaye was sure she'd left the bonsai tank.

The plank rose underneath Kaye, elevating
Her. (The plank had finished teleporting—
So had suddenly resumed its hover
Mode.) It rose so fast she tumbled over
In the sand. She sat up. "Fucking hell."

The plank had spun away across a swell
Of sand and struck the front door of a shack—
Though not the one that Dickie saw, a slack,
Abandoned structure. *This* was lit up from
Within. Its bright red, wooden walls were plumb,
Its white trim crisp as if a steady hand
Had iced each edge. It seemed to take a stand;
Its windows, sealed against the elements,
Suggested civilized intelligence.
A patch of red on each side of the door
Was washed out by a brilliant hanging orb.

She stood and brushed the sand and needles off
Her sweatshirt. Then, the shack produced a cough
And footsteps. Kaye watched as the shack's front door
Creaked open to reveal a stocky, short-haired
Woman fussing with the strap that held
Her robe. "Well come on then," the woman yelled,
Her voice directed back inside the shack.

"I'm coming, love!"

                    Kaye heard a steady clacking
Over wood. The robe began to bulge
Between the woman's feet, the hem divulging
(Like a wall of curtain nosed aside)
A two-foot Stephen Stove: still manga-eyed
But miniature. He blinked at Kaye and smiled.

"This the girl?" the woman asked. "The wild
One?"

          "My Kaye," the little Stephen said
As if with pride. He tried to crane his head,
Requiring he limbo, to address
The woman overhead. "I will confess
She has proclivities. The spirit of
A suffragette mayhap. But there's great love
Inside her heart. And courage, too."

                         Kaye took
The woman in. The visage on the book
Inside the scrotal knapsack Kaye was wearing
Was less wrinkled than the face now staring
At the twenty-year-old English under-
Grad. But Kaye knew—with a strain of wonder
Cut with something terser, like conviction—
That this was the face of Mandy Fiction.

* * *

Kaye was sitting by the fireplace
As Mandy moved about her cluttered space,
Locating mugs, a kettle, silver spoons.
The shack's main room was full of books. The moon's
Gleam, through a window, lit gold letters on
A stack of spines.

                    "I've never read *Don Juan*,"
Said Kaye.
                 "Not *wawn*," said Mandy, passing. "Trochee.
Joo-awn."
                     Books aside, her stuff was hokey,
Random: paintings of Niagara Falls
And lithographs of whaling on the walls;
Small wood-carved, dust-furred things by unknown artists;
Lampshades fringed with tendrils; mismatched carpets
That refused to tie the room together;
Musings (framed, in needlepoint) on weather,
Dogs, and love; a bulbous, Turkish vase;
A poster for the tintype *Wizard of Oz*;
A severed, bronze, and floor-bound Buddha head.
A vinyl disc nailed to the wall (*The Dead*,
By Something Tea, the label's band name scuffed);
A taxidermied wolf, of all things, stuffed,
With moonward snout; an X-wing in a bottle . . .

"We're no longer in the bonsai model,
 Right?" said Kaye.
                     A spout began to sound.
Then Kaye heard clinking. Mandy came around
A counter, which was burdened with the task
Of walling off the tchotchkes she'd amassed
From what looked like a kitchen. Mandy bore
Two mugs of tea. She set them on a door
That doubled as a coffee table, stacks
Of books for legs, the surface seamed with cracks.
Kaye's armchair was on one side of the door.
The author dragged a stool across the floor.

"Well sort of," Mandy said. "You've zubered *down*

A level."

      "Down?"

                She smiled. "To the town
Of Rabbit Strait and its surrounding waters."
Mandy sat, as Stephen came and brought her
Something flickering: some pixiepaper.
Mandy raised her mug and blew the vapour
Off it—then, not turning, took the sheet.
The little stove, still facing her, retreated
Via scuttling. She snorted, turned
The page for Kaye to eyeball: Lux, concerned
And clearly muted. Small subtitles, surging
At the bottom of the sheet ("I'm urging
You . . ."), transcribed his soundless chatter. Bunching
Up the sheet, its speakers making crunching
Sounds, she flicked the message in the fire-
Place—and sighed. "I wish he would retire."
Mandy looked at Kaye. "He's coming down
Here."

        Kaye leaned forward. "Wait, you said, the 'town'
Of Rabbit Strait. Do you mean—"

                    "Love, you're *in*
The silver locket. On a sphere that's spinning
Like a planet. Held by gravity."
She gripped her stool's seat.

                  "Um, how small are we
Right now?"

         "It's better not to think about
Dimensions, ducky. You've gone down a spout
Inside a bonsai hive. A second door.
A *smaller* door."

        "I thought I'd find the spore
Inside the locket."

Mandy raised her non-
Mug-holding hand. "You're looking at its spawn."

Kaye frowned. "Lux said the spore creates a *whale*."

"It makes a world of living things at scale.
Produces grass and trees and forests. Even
Micro-organisms."
                                    Kaye heard Stephen
Moving through the shack: a clacking sound.

"My wife and child," Mandy said, "they'd drowned.
I thought I'd try creating something new.
I mean, I had more money than I knew
I'd ever spend. And so, this engineer
I hired made a nanodesic sphere
That—"
                    "Nano-what?" said Kaye.
                                        "A kind of planet,
Love. A really tiny one." He spun it,
She explained, on something like a potter's
Wheel, then fed the spinning globe with water
Siphoned from the rising Arctic Ocean.
Mandy's engineer—with care, devotion—
Wrapped a small, repurposed sea around
His globe—a shallow layer. For the ground,
Her team used garbage; they began to beam
Junk from the exosphere, a steady stream
Of rubbish they compressed. The rubbish formed
Land masses. So, the garbage that'd swarmed
The Earth was swept away. She'd shrunk the shroud
That blocked the sun and moon.
                                        "You cleared the Cloud,"

Said Kaye, astonished. "You're the one who did it."

Mandy smiled. "Well, we mapped a grid out
On the Cloud—then started sucking rubbish
From the sky. We'd bought this disused Russian
Zuber pad in Georgia. It'd beamed
Ships into orbit back when Moscow dreamed
Of colonizing planets. Anyway,
We stole the Cloud—compressed it into clay
And piped the stuff like icing on a dome.
The spore came last. It made the place a home"—
She waved an arm—"spread grass and trees across
The clay. The plant life started out as moss,
Then really grew. Aggressively. We built
A replica of *Full-Moon*'s world from silt
Made up of bots. The boats and shacks assembled
On their own. In time, it all resembled
What I'd written. It was Rabbit Strait.
We solved a problem, too: the locket's weight.
The globe is only partially in this
Dimension, in a physical abyss."

"In *this* dimension? There are more?"

                                        "A zillion.
You can learn a lot with seven billion.
Point is that the locket can be worn.
A living, breathing chest will keep it warm.
The chains provide"—inhaling—"air and light.
A gyroscope helps keep the dome upright."

"So someone could be wearing us right now?"

"Don't think about it!" Mandy touched her brow.

"It hurts the head. You need to—Christ, what did
My teacher used to say—suspend your dis-
Belief? The sky's fake, though. It's like the one
Inside the tank. A tintype of the sun,
The moon, the stars. Our only compromise.
But otherwise"—brows up now—"trust your eyes."

Kaye shook her head. She looked around the shack—
White-noising waves beyond its walls—then back
At Mandy. "You're the reason we can see
The sky. You saved the fucking Earth."

                                    "Not me.
My team. They saved some lovely pieces. Salvaged
Treasures from the Cloud. Some stuff was damaged.
Much of it I'm keeping in the shack
Here." Mandy nodded at a paperback,
Bruce Sterling's *Involution Ocean*, standing
On the mantlepiece. "That one's outstanding.
'Bout a whaler. Bloody masterpiece,
Pulled from the Cloud. And not a single crease,
Kaye. Mint." She nodded at an off-white urn.
"That's Greek. That one'll need to be returned."

"Your team—who *are* these people? Lemme guess.
You made the corpse of Newton coalesce—
And brought back Einstein."

                            The author smiled.
"No, they're quantum pixies. They compiled
Fascinating data from my site."

"What site?"

            "Wolfpack Salon. The one you're quite
A fan of, Kaye. Or @psychedelicurs."

Kaye blushed.

         "My bots turned into connoisseurs
Of fanfic. They metabolized all kinds
Of stories, theories, tales, and myths—from minds
Like yours. They also had the zuck to feed
On naturally. They set about to read,
Well, everything. The fanfic made them dream,
Though. Gave them inspiration. So, my team
Proposed all this."

         "You made a world," said Kaye.

"We made a fanfic," Mandy said. "The way
My readers do."

         "And hid it in the tank.
With Lux's help." Kaye put her mug down, sank
Back in her chair.

         "Lux gamely took the locket
To Japan, inside the inner pocket
Of a jacket."

         "You knew others would
Be after it."

         "It seemed to me the Wood
Would be a safe bet. It was elevated
Well above the water. Armour-plated.
Plus, the manse itself was well protected,
Thanks to"—nod at Stephen. "He'd detected
Massive density inside the model.
Travelled down. I saw the tracks his waddle
Leaves, across the beach there. He can split
In two—to make two Stephen Stoves—then knit
Himself together. Anyway, I found him
Staring at the sea. He was astounded
By it. He was down here but above,

As well." She sighed. "I think he fell in love
With me."

        "So Ichiro's not really in
Control of Stephen?"

            Mandy leaned back, chin
Now doubled, face a frown, as if Kaye's question
Were absurd. "He uses his discretion,
Stephen. Lets his 'master'"—bunny ears
For fingers—"steer him sometimes. It *appears*
That Ichiro's in charge. Not really, though."

Kaye sat up, leaning forward. "Ichiro
Has *no* clue you've been hiding underneath
His nose."

        She briefly flashed her gritted teeth.
"He *had* no clue. His shepherds will've tracked
You to the hut."

          Kaye felt like she'd been sacked
By Mandy.

      "He'll have seen you flip the locket
Open. Through your smarteyes. Stephen blocked his
Feed at that point. Then, he locked the portal.
Never trust synthetic eyes, Kaye. Moral
Of this story."

       "Fuck," said Kaye, and then:
"I'm sorry."

      "Ichiro will post some men
Outside the hut. The stove has sorted through
All likely countermoves. He has a view
On Ichiro's thought process. Come." She stood
And hobbled to the door. "This is the good
Part. Stephen"—calling to the kitchen—"please
Get out the cots!" She stepped outside, a breeze

Now flowing through the shack. Kaye stood—and followed.

* * *

Out at sea, the night was being swallowed
By the faintest line of light. The author
Stood beside the water, hand on offer.

Frowning, Kaye walked to the shore and took
The soft palm. Mandy pointed seaward. "Look."

Against the red horizon line, a shape
Had clarified itself. A pirate ship.

Kaye looked at Mandy, who was warmly staring
At the ship, then heard some hacking. Swearing.
Lux. Kaye turned and saw him standing under-
Neath the arch. No glasses—and no wonder
On his face (he'd surely zubered here
Before). He wore a raincoat that was sheer
And see-through, over clothes he'd clearly woken
Up in: shorts and tee. The coat, a token
Nod at decency, was ragged at
Its hemline. It had lately lived a flat
Existence, pressed inside a roll of what
Was basically dressmakers' shrink-wrap, cut
At intervals by perforated lines
And hanging in the tank's main booth. Small signs,
In kanji, indicated travellers
Could tear a coat off. Velcro fasteners
Secured the wispy stuff. Lux looked unsteady
In his slippers. Plus, he seemed already
Tipsy.
         "Why's he drink so much?" sighed Kaye.

"He doesn't," Mandy said. "He gets that way
　Because of all the chemo."
　　　　　　　　　　　　Kaye looked shocked.
"I didn't realize..."
　　　　　　　　　"Takes a daily cocktail
When the cancer's bad."
　　　　　　　　　　　　"I thought that ended."

Mandy shook her head. "They come suspended
In a drink. White pixies. They deliver
Radiation to the bugger's liver."

Cancer—it was like a jolt, the word.
She pictured it again: the paper bird
Her dad had sent her.
　　　　　　　　　　Shaky, Lux walked down
To where the women stood.
　　　　　　　　　　　　　"I like your gown,"
Said Mandy.
　　　　　　　Lux ignored her. Looked at Kaye.
"I should've told you."
　　　　　　　　　　　"You don't need to say
That. We're okay—okay?"
　　　　　　　　　　　　"I want to tell
You that I'm sorry 'bout the spore—the hell
You looking at me like that?"
　　　　　　　　　　　　　Kaye was staring
At him, lips pressed tightly, something—caring?—
In her eyes.
　　　　　　　"Stop doing that." He looked
At Mandy. "What's she..." But the sea had hooked
His gaze. He stood and watched the ship's approach,
Its hull now vaguely red in dawn's encroaching

Light. At last, he said, "I'm glad I didn't
Miss the show." He squinted. "Ship looks different
This time. Like it's moving faster, maybe?"

Mandy nodded. "That would be my baby."

"Miles?"
            "He's been getting better. Look
How well he's doing."
                        "Miles from the book?"
Said Kaye. She looked at Mandy, who was beaming
Seaward at the product of her dreaming.

"Yes. That was my son's name," Mandy said.
"And 'Lucy' was my wife's."
                        "The *Lucy Dread*!"
Said Kaye.
            "The rest are on board, too. They're not
Yet fully free. They cycle through the plot
And land here once a month. They'll sleep—the way
They do in Chapter Eighteen, as the day
Begins. Of course, the *book's* wolves find the cay
Deserted. So, they—"
                        "'Lie upon the grey
Sand of the beach,'" said Kaye—then stopped. And blushed.
"Or something like that."
                        "Actually, you crushed
It," Mandy said. "You ought to get out more,
Though. Anyway, the wolves will come to shore
And see us. They'll be scared at first. They'll likely
Guess we're pires. But they'll think we're kindly
Ones."
        "Why's that?" said Kaye.

                              The author bared
Her teeth. "No fangs."
                              Kaye felt a little scared
Herself. "So are they bots?" She tried to zoom in,
But the ship stayed fuzzy.
                              "No, half human
And half wolf. Except, of course, for Miles.
Fruit bat DNA. We ran some trials
For a novel pixieplastic: pixie-
Flesh. A hybrid thing. That was the tricky
Part. You see, I wanted pires that
Were fleshy but could transform into bats,
Say. Dickie's made of pixieflesh as well."
She grimaced. "Sequencing his genes was hell."

"What makes them cycle through repeated plots?"

"A brainwave bridge, the kind that links to thoughts
  When people access sites like Joyce. It wipes
  Their short-term memories each time—and pipes
  In thoughts that drive 'em. Every hanging orb
  You see's a router, all of 'em absorbing
  Top-down prompts, then pushing out the data
  To the werewolves. Right now, we're in beta
  Mode. We've got a Moby down here. Chomps
  That ship each month, and then some mental prompts
  Cause Paige and Dot to head to Dickie's hovel.
  Basically, they're in a living novel.
  Course, they've *some* control. We point the prow
  Is all. My engineers are seeing how
  They handle sadness. Hearts. Paige isn't quite
  Where I would like to see her. Seems to fight
  Her feelings." Mandy looked at Kaye. "You ever

Do that?"

        "Never."

                "Right." A snort. "They're tethered
To my verse. Each runs along their rut
The way a train might. Pretty soon, we'll cut
Them loose, though. Take the brakes off. See what they
Can do out on their own."

                    "Then what?" said Kaye.

"She writes a book," said Lux. "She writes her sequel.
Silver Locket."

        Kaye's hands formed a steeple.
"Is it weird to want your autograph?"

The author looked at Kaye. Let loose a laugh.
"You know, we're gonna need more people down
Here, Kaye. We've got our wolves who fill the town.
But there's a lot of land for folks to roam.
The ones who've lost their coasts could make a home,
I think. I've asked my engineers to plan
An island that's the shape of Newfoundland.
But anyway."

        "I'd like to make a Crater,
Mandy."

      "We can talk about that later,
Sure. You know I've been there, right?"

                  "Been where?"

"To Montréal, of course. I'd tracked a rare
Edition of a book I love, *Pale Fire*,
To some bookstore. Saw this boy for hire.
He delivered messages on foot,
He told me. Tom. Some kid walked up and put

A white baton in Tom's hand—anyway,
That's what I *thought* it was cuz this kid, Kaye,
Just takes off. Turns out it was just a roll
Of dumbprint. How I came up with the scroll
Idea—look!"
                        The sails went slack, the ship
Dropped anchor. Kaye watched wolfish outlines flip
Dark bundles overboard, the bundles shrinking
As they fell and, near the water, winking
Out. In fact, the bundles had been paying
Braided ladders out, the werewolves baying
Happily as they began to climb
The ladders and, by doing so, define
Their ropey wrungs. Five wolves in total made
Their way down to the waist-high waves to wade,
Their cloaks afloat like oil. (One wolf had a
Hunchback's outline; Campbell had been saddled
With the mini-Dickie.) Kaye heard wings
As Miles, overhead, described loose rings.
She heard the laughter of the reunited
Wolves half-swimming to the shore, delighted
To be sloshing through the waves, amazed
They'd made it to a beach by dawn. They praised
The pirate ship, the strong winds, and the Moon.
(Kaye couldn't hear their dialogue, but knew
The scene by heart.) They praised Moe for her fire-
Works, which Paige had spotted, praised the pire
For his expert way with sails and rope,
And praised Dot for her sudden song of hope.
They praised the shifter who could change his size—
And praised Thom's wooden muzzle to the skies
For saving Dickie's life. They praised, their barks
Now hoarse, the muzzles that had stopped the sharks.

They praised Paige for her courage on the pirate
Ship—and Glen for one last gust of spirit.

Kaye heard raspy slithering behind
Her. Turning, she saw cots—a herd, with hind
Legs scrabbling for purchase—nosing through
The sand toward the shore. "Hup two, hup two!"
Barked little Stephen, gamely bringing up
The rear: a lagging, sabre-wielding pup.

19.

Paige was standing on the deck, a stiff
Wind pawing at her cloak, a distant cliff
Face, Kelly Bay's, in sight—when something struck
The ship.
        She *had* been musing on their luck.
Her dad was dead, but every other tail
Was now accounted for. She'd watched them scale
The ladders she'd unfurled the night before...

* * *

They looked bedraggled—rain had soaked their fur—
But happy. Del was first aboard. He squeezed
And lifted Paige, the hug so hard she wheezed
For breath. Moe boarded next and, brushing past
The couple, scampered up the scarlet mast
Whose lowest spar was occupied by Miles,
Wolf and pire trading goofy smiles.
(He'd assumed the perch to cede some space
To wolf reunions.) Dot was next, her face
Uncertain. Paige remembered what she'd heard
Dot holler from the raft—but pushed the words
Away. "Well come on, then," said Paige now, mock-
Annoyed, arms spread. (A jokey tone would make
The awkward thing okay.) She hugged Dot, bangle

Hard against her back, then disentangled
Hastily. Her face met Campbell's. Smiled.
Lurking by the rail, he tried a mild
Grin. "It's good to see"—but Paige strode over,
Crushed him to her. Miles came to hover
Near them. Moe jumped from the spar and wrapped
Her arms around the pair of wolves. "I'm trapped,"
Laughed Campbell, squirming. "Careful, though." Paige felt
Him tense up. Hookpaw must've left a welt
Or two on Campbell.

                Moe said, "We're conjoined
Now—muzzle-melded!" Dot, though, hadn't joined
The scrum, Paige noticed. Campbell's grip was steady,
Beating wings above.

                "Enough already,"
Someone squeaked.

                Paige pulled away and frowned
At Campbell. "Who just said that?"

                      "He's not drowned..."
Said Campbell with a smile. Then, he stepped
Aside. "...but he's been grumpy."

                Dickie leapt
Across the railing: doll-sized, smooth as clay.

Paige gaped, eyes wide.

                "You should've seen the way
The little pest announced his presence," Campbell
Said. He'd lost his smile. "Bugger scrambled
Through our pelts. We thought some bloody ticks
Were on the raft."

                Paige heard the faintest clicks
As Dickie's mini-claws made contact with
The deck he crossed. The shifter was a fifth

His normal height.

Paige crouched. "It's really you?"
She said, eyes welling.

But the wolf-doll threw
Its arms up, waving paws as if to ward
Off tears.

She laughed, sleeved eyes, then looked toward
The others.

Shrugging, Del said, "'Parently
The polymorph can shrink down to a flea."

"But"—Campbell stepping forward—"Dickie's slowly
Growing back." He turned around. "Right, Moe?"

"He's like a toy," cooed Moe, eyes warm. "His head's
A little, grumpy grape."

The doll went red,
Its greyish body flush: embarrassment
In bloom. "This is no time for merriment,"
The high-pitched Dickie squeaked.

She'd been so focused
On the polymorph Paige hadn't noticed
That the pire's wings had flapped away—
But then the flapping dopplered back.

"A cay!,"
The pire, diving deckward, trilled in joy.

"A cay?" she said.

The bat was gone, the boy
Beside her. Now impatient: "Cay means land."

The wolves ran to the rail and saw a strand
Of sandy beach ahead. They'd hoped to bring

The eggs to Kelly Bay and quickly slingshot
Back to Rabbit Strait within the same
Night, well before the devil's rising flame
(As some wolves called the sun) announced the day.

But now, they set their muzzles on the cay,
With Miles steering, Del and Campbell blowing
Til the sails bulged forth, horizon glowing.
Soon, the wolves were wading through the waist-
High water round the cay—to find they faced
Three pires on the sand. Though Paige had made
Her peace with Miles, it was still a blade,
The sight of skin. The werewolf tried to scream—
But was already falling into dream,
The ancient solar edict overriding
Agency. She felt herself sleepsliding,
Slowing down, her body dull and dopey . . .

* * *

The sudden, thudding impact of the Moby
Jarred the werewolf from her starboard reverie.
"Wolf the deck!" Paige hollered, frightened. "Every
Tail on deck!"
        Again, it slammed the ship—
And sent her reeling back. A fingered grip,
Though, seized her arm. The pire from the cay,
The thin and mostly furless one named K,
Had caught her.
        "Thanks," said Paige.
           "No prob," the pire
Said and smiled.
        Del cried, "We should fire
On 'er." He'd already placed himself

Behind a cannon on a paw-worn shelf
Of wood—one of the cannons that had fired
On the sloop.

        "No, Del! The Moby's wired
To attack. We've got her eggs, remember?"

K had fallen back. The other members
Of the pire pack who'd tagged along—
The pire-witch and Lucks—were sitting on
A low bench on the starboard quarterdeck.
The pires hadn't touched a single neck;
In fact, the werewolves had awoken to
Discover they'd been placed on cots in lieu
Of being feasted on. It seemed their harmless
Hosts were in the shack.

        Of course, the armless
Pull of sunlight had no purchase on
The shifter. He'd sat on his cot at dawn,
Resolved to watch his charges through the day . . .

*   *   *

The sun arced sluggishly across the cay.
The wolves snored on their cots while Miles hung
Inside the ship. The six cots' shadows swung
And shrank and lengthened as the day progressed.
The doll-sized polymorph lay down to rest,
Though kept a single eyeball on the shack.
In time, though, Dickie's tired flesh went slack,
His body pooling slightly, gaze slow-blinking,
Eyeball like a marble slowly sinking
Into mud. As Dickie slept, his puddled,
Doughy body rose like bread and doubled,
Puffing up, its edges undefined,

Resuming normal size.
                          He woke to find
Paige frowning over him, the moon above.

"You there?" she said, her look a mix of love
And worry; Dickie was still in a puddle.

Dickie sighed, produced an eyeballed muzzle.
"This okay?" A second, smaller knob
Became a nose.
                    "You're better as a blob,
I think," said Paige.
                          They heard bravado. Gloating.
Paige turned round to see that Moe was floating
Over sand. She squinted. Moe was standing
On some magic ironing board, grandstanding
As it flew, the others chasing after
Her. Alarmed, Paige sprang up, but heard laughter—
Campbell's, Dot's. She noticed, too, their hosts,
The pires, standing back. Moe weaved through posts,
A tilting line that once defined a fence.
Her cloak was billowing, her body tense,
Paws out for balance. Paige was stunned. Confused.
The pires, though, seemed mildly amused.

"I'm gonna clean the ship up," Dickie said.
The shifter rose on two new legs and headed
Off. The magic stove caught up with him.
"Come on," she heard him say, "we've got some grim
Work, stove. Some wolf-souls needs to find their beds
At sea." The curtain made of werewolf heads.

Dot left the pack and slowly trudged toward
Paige, up the beach. "You gonna try the board?"

"I thinks I'm gonna pass," said Paige. "So listen—"

"Nope." Dot took up next to Paige. She'd stiffened.

"Look, that thing you said—"
                              "We're good." Dot's snout
Was seaward.
                "Dot, we needs to talk about—"

Dot turned. Her large eyes, liquid, seemed to swell
With light. "Please don't." Back to the sea. "But Del
Is not the one."
                Paige looked at Dot.
                                    "You'll thank
Me later—look, now Campbell's on the plank..."
Dot brought her left paw to each eye, her bangle
Gleaming, as Paige turned to gaze on Campbell.

* * *

The Moby slammed the ship.
                        Paige fell, her paws
Out as she landed on the deck. She saw
Now that they'd brought the flying board aboard
The ship; the pires from the cay had stored
The plank behind their bench, beside the small,
Eccentric stove. The pires seemed in thrall
To objects of enchantment. Witchery.
They *had* been kind, but Paige felt shivery
When what's-er-name, the stocky-looking pire-
Witch met Paige's eyes. There was a fire

In the witch's gaze. Intensity.
Still, it was warm; Paige sensed no devilry.

That said, back on the beach, as Paige made small
Talk with the pires—who possessed a drawl
Paige couldn't place—the witch had shared a vision
She had had, of werewolves on a mission
To return some eggs. She'd wondered: were
They on that mission? Paige had felt her fur
Stand up at that. The wolves, who'd been carousing,
Stopped dead. (Had the pire-witch been browsing
Werewolf brains?) Bewildered, Paige had said
They *were* those wolves.
                                        And yet, she'd felt no dread
When K, the younger one, had asked to tag
Along. K's pants were odd. They didn't sag.
They looked so tight the pire surely peeled
Them off like skin. The strange shoes that concealed
Her talons were a spectral shade of green
So vivid Paige was sure she'd never seen
Its hue before. The witch, for her part, wore
A normal cloak, but Lucks' cloak was more
Like glass, though flexible. Not even Miles
Recognized their kind; their fangless smiles
Struck him as a curiosity.

* * *

The bat flew by at such velocity
Paige wondered for a second if Del *had*
Unleashed a cannonball. The wolf was glad
To blink and find the boy beside her.
                                        "Mother's
Here," he noted. "Starboard side."

                              The others—
Dickie, Dot, and Campbell—had appeared.
The wolves, tails down, looked terrified: limp-eared.
The shifter was full size again but pelt-less,
Like an abstract wolf who could be melted
Down, his flesh still grey. Meanwhile, Moe
Was in the crow's nest. She'd been crying, "Lo,
There's Kelly Bay!" when Mum first slammed the vessel.
Moe now gripped the crow's nest as it trembled
On its mast.

                    "We needs to push hard to
The cavern," Paige said. "I'll take Del's raft through
The opening." They'd brought the raft; they'd hung
It off the vessel's hull while Dot had sung
A work song.

                    "No, not by yourself," said Del.

"Yes by meself."

                        The ship bucked as a swelling
Wave passed underneath. They saw, port side,
The moving, foam-edged mound begin a wide
Turn: it was circling to start another
Run. The mound, the very top of Mother,
Curved but only slightly; it appeared
To be a moonlit skullcap, hemisphered
Along its topmost line of longitude.
Paige guessed the Moby's hidden magnitude
Was taking up a lot of unseen sea
Below the vessel.

                        "Del and Campbell—we
Needs wind!"

                        "Aye, aye!," they cried. The two wolves, tails
Turned down in deference, ran toward their sails,

Stepped on their platforms, drew in breaths, and started
Blowing hard. The ship sped up and parted
Waves.

Paige turned to Dot. "You'd better take
The wheel."

Dot looked at Paige and said, "I'll shake
Our tail, no problem." Dot seemed different. Tough.

Paige turned to Miles. "You do flying stuff."

The bat took off.

Paige looked up to the crow's
Nest. "Come on, Moe, climb down!" She saw that Moe's
Eyes looked uncertain.

But the werewolf shook
It off. "Okay!" called Moe. She tried to hook
A leg around the nest.

Paige looked to sea—
No sign of Mum—then glanced toward the three
Hitchhikers on the quarterdeck, who stood
Beside a cannon. Lucks had pulled his hood
Of spooky glass up, one fist cinching it
Beneath his chin. Paige watched the pire spit
On deck and point out something to the others,
Who were nodding, unperturbed by Mother's
Sallies. They were looking at the rear
End of the cannon, crouching now to peer
At something. What's-er-name appeared to laugh.
Paige couldn't hear their voices.

Moe was halfway
Down the slim mast when the Moby rammed
The portside hull. The werewolf fell and slammed
Against the deck.

Not thinking, Campbell broke
Off from his blowing. "Moe!"
                              The werewolf's cloak
Was heaped around her face. He knelt beside
His friend—and didn't see the tendril Mum
Had cast, the trunk-thick limb now falling from
The sky. The tendril quickly wrapped around
His body, looping twice til he was bound,
Then yanked him skyward.
                              "No!" cried Paige. She backed
Up slightly as the tendril, plunging, whacked
Its prize against the wooden deck, then raised
The wolf again. The limb's wet flesh was glazed
With gleaming, dripping moonlight. Paige could hear
Dot in the wheelhouse, howling in fear
But holding to her course. The tendril floated,
Poised to gavel wolf.
                              A bomb exploded—
Somewhere in the stern. Paige jumped, chest pounding.
It was marrow-deep, the blast, resounding
Through her bones.
                              A slab of off-white rubber
Landed on—and shook—the deck: the blubber
Campbell was encased in.
                              "Holy Moon,"
Breathed Paige.
                              Above, the tendril's stump, now hewn,
Was like a log's end: lighter than the rest.
The shortened limb curved upward and addressed
The night sky like the trunk an elephant
Will lift.
                              Absorbing this development,
While noting vaguely that she still possessed

Her limbs, Paige turned. K stood behind the breast-
High cannon, hands up in the guilty style
Of a person who's caressed some dial
They weren't meant to. Smoke was curling from
The barrel. As wisps left the drooling drum,
A stiff wind wicked the curling strands away.

A mist of salty raindrops roused Paige: spray
The Moby was displacing as it thrashed
Against the ship—in pain or rage—and splashed
The deck. A whipping tendril struck Del's raft,
Still hanging off the hull. The homemade craft
Descended with a splash and drifted out
To open waters, with the prow-proud snout
Of Thom in lead.
                          A shape buzzed past Paige, whirring:
Miles landed next to Moe, now stirring
On the deck, and gave the wolf his hand.
Moe grasped it with a paw and tried to stand.
Paige ran across the deck to Campbell, knelt
Beside him. He was passed out. Scared, she felt
The stuff encasing him; the wolf was ambered
To the neck in springy flesh. She clambered
Onto Campbell's carapace, disclosed
A claw, and slashed the blubber that enclosed
Him. But the rent began to seal, the wound
Already knitting, closing. "Now you're mooned,"
Her father would've said. She felt a paw
And looked up. Dickie.
                          "There's no way you'll claw
Him free." She stepped aside. She saw that Del
Was still behind the sail, the fabric swelling
As he huffed and puffed—and Dot was still

Behind the wheel.

                              The shifter crouched. The rill
That Paige's claw had carved was nearly gone.
He frowned. He placed his furless, grey paw on
The casing, took a breath, and gently pressed
The blubber, testing it. The flesh compressed
A little—then turned grey to match the shade
Of Dickie's skin. The shifter's flat paw splayed
And spread like syrup, fusing with the very
Flesh he'd only just been pressing. "Faerie
Magic," Dickie whispered.

                              Standing, Dickie
Stepped away—and watched the caul of sticky
Blubber, seamless with his arm now, lengthen
Taffy-like. His bicep seemed to strengthen
As he drew his arm back, blubber sliding
Clean off Campbell, Dickie clearly guiding
It as if the blubber *was* his giant,
Flattened paw retracting. He was silent
But astonished as the orphaned flesh
Flowed up along his arm and seemed to mesh
With him, the severed Moby tendril blurring,
Blending, into Dickie. Campbell, stirring,
Groaned, while Paige stood gaping. "How the moon
D'you *do* that?"

                              "'Parently, I can commune
With her," he said. His voice was stunned and soft.

Squeaks drew their gaze; the bat was now aloft,
His noises frantic. They were nearly at
The cliff, the squeaking seemed to say, in Bat.
The Moby, though, had plunged beneath the sea.
Had one lost limb caused Mum to turn and flee?

Do Mobies lick their wounds? Ahead, Paige saw
The narrow entrance to the cove—less maw
Than crack. "We needs to spill the wind!" she cried.

Del crouched, snout down, while Miles rode a glide
Path to the deck, turned back to boy, and moved
Among the masts like something sleek and hooved,
The jutting talons on his feet aclack
On deck. He loosed the mainsail, which went slack.
The ship began to slow.
                              "We've lost the raft,"
Called Paige. "I'm not sure what to do. I'll have
To swim."
              Del tried to stand up. "You're not going
On your own." The wolf, fatigued from blowing,
Looked a little wobbly.
                              "Look out!"
Cried Miles.
                        Just ahead, the sea was spouting
Water, bubbles frothing as the glowing
Mound began to rise. The ship was slowing
But still moving fast. The mound appeared
To split; a horizontal slit now sneered
The Moby's blank face. It began to open,
Water pouring down the pallid slope in
Sheets and beading on the upper edge
Of what was now a mouth. The mouth, a wedge
Of darkness, grew and grew, an arch of yawning
Blubber.
              "Turn!" cried Paige, the thought now dawning
That the moving ship was heading for
The archway. "Hard to port!"
                              The looming door

The mouth presented, though, was moving, too.
A shadow swept Paige as the ship sailed through
The maw, the sky above wiped dark—unstarred.
She saw that Dickie's right paw was a shard
Of sharpened bone he'd drawn back like a spear,
The other paw out like a sight. A tear
In one eye held the moon. He hurled the makeshift
Spear, his arm extending. In its wake,
The shifter followed, flowing up to form
The moving weapon's shaft, his flesh conforming
To its shape, his feet the last to go.
And as they left the deck and joined the flow
Of Dickie flying Mobyward, Paige heard
The shaft-cum-shifter cry a single word,
A simple name Paige hadn't called another
Wolf since *she'd* been very little: "Mother!"

20.

The first thing Kaye heard when the ringing left
Her ears was Mandy's chuckling.

                              The cleft
Limb, clutching Campbell still, was lying on
The deck. Kaye's eyes had scanned the limb and drawn
A blank; the Moby must've been derived
From pixieflesh, the wonder stuff contrived
By Mandy's engineers: a miracle
Kaye's smarteyes couldn't place. Hysterical
And bloody-minded, Paige had climbed atop
The tendril, claws out. Did she mean to pop
The blubber? Cut him free? Kaye had no clue;
By firing a cannonball clean through
The Moby's limb, she'd blown up Mandy's story.
Kaye had always hated Campbell's gory
End.

        But here was Mandy laughing. "Let's
See what my wolves do now," she said. "All bets
Are clearly off." The author clapped Kaye's shoulder—
Squeezed it—which was pretty cool; the older
Woman was Kaye's hero after all.
It seemed that standing on a nanoball
Afloat inside a locket wasn't quite
As neat as having Mandy Fiction right

Beside her.

    She had shown Kaye how to fire
Off a shot (you strummed a mini lyre,
Set behind the cannon) but declined
To warn Kaye of the kickback or the mind-
Concussing bang. Professor Lux, deciding
This was "folly," had stayed seated, riding
Out a mild wave of queasiness—
The chemo?—mixed with deep uneasiness.
He knew that Ichiro would have men stationed
At the hut.

    But now, he stood by Kaye,
Arms folded, shade-less, staring straight ahead.
His eyes were wide. "He always winds up dead."

"Who, Campbell?"

            "Campbell, yeah. Poor fucker never
Makes it. Dickie always fails to sever
Him in time." The demos Mandy had
Been running always ended with the sad
Fact of the werewolf's death, the bloody, graphic
Ending as recounted in the classic
Novel. (Of course, down here, a brand-new Campbell
Could be summoned up. The wolf would amble
From the sea when Mandy's engineers
Reset the plot.)

            But Lux was wiping tears
Now as he watched the polymorph lean over
Campbell in his carapace—and hoover
Off the clingy blubber.

                "You okay?"
Said Kaye.

            "I'm fine," said Lux. He turned away.

"You saved him," Mandy said, surprised. "He's not
Supposed to live, love."

                              "It was just a thought,"
Said Kaye.

                    The werewolf on the deck—his fur
A moistened, matted mess—began to stir.
But what, Kaye wondered, would the shifter do
Right *now*? She'd always loved the way he flew
Toward the tendril—didn't matter which
Edition. But she'd introduced a hitch:
Poor Campbell was okay! There was no need,
Then, for the polymorph's heroic deed,
No need for him to hurl himself harpoon-like
At the Moby, drilling through its moon-white
Skin.

                    Yet that's how Dickie, diving into
Moby tissue, comes to learn he's *kin* who
Got torn from his parent years ago
By jutting sea rock. Fusing with the flow
Of flesh, he learns the truth. By entering
The Moby's blubber (and remembering
Quite suddenly his blob-like state *before*
He showed up at his werewolf-mother's door,
Remembering the day the tide expelled
Him on the sand, remembering the shelled
Form he'd assumed, the way he'd snailed for days
Around the town of Rabbit Strait, his gaze
Devouring the sight of wolves, his mind
Cajoling fur from flesh as it designed
A cub) the Moby's son recalls himself.

Kaye had a figure on her dorm room shelf
To mark the shifter's deed: a resin, hard-

To-find-ish Dickie Lush, his paw a shard
Of sharpened, tapered bone, a spear he'd drawn
Back. (Cat had bought it at the *Full-Moon* Con,
The one she'd dragged Kaye to—what, seven years
Ago?) In every fanfic, Dickie-spears
Go flying limbward in a desperate bid
To rescue done-for Campbell.

                       "You undid
A pretty wicked set piece, all I'm saying,"
Mandy said.

                Kaye noted Del, conveying
Them toward the cliffside, breath by breath,
The plot diverging now from Campbell's death.
"So Del's not *really* moving us by blowing,
Right?"

             "I wish," said Mandy. "When there's flowing
Air, the sail, a blend of pixieweaves,
Will trigger motors. *Del*, though, thinks—believes—
He's moving us. But"—here the author laughed—
"He won't like that you've gone and lost his raft.
Paige needed that."

                 "Look out!" cried Miles, who'd
Been holding to a mast-shy altitude
Above the ship.

             Ahead, the Moby's maw
Was rising from the sea. Kaye stared in awe,
Then said, "How worried should we be right now?"
The pirate ship was slowing, but its prow
Still faced the open mouth. By this point—in
The *novel's* plot—the polymorph, stretched thin
Across the Moby's mass but intertwined,
Had seized the reins and steered the creature's mind
Away from rage. A puppeteer, he'd drawn

The Moby back enough to let Paige—on
Del's raft now—pass, the pair of lockets round
Her neck.

        But *this* was off script. Mandy frowned.
"I'm not quite sure, Kaye." With a foot, she nudged
The stove. "Dear Stephen, Kaye has"—searching—"*fudged*
The plot, it seems." Her voice had taken on
A slight edge as they sailed toward the yawning
Mouth. "We need a little help, my love."
She gave the bot a second, harder shove.

The oven grew four legs. Its manga eyes
Bloomed open. "Errant Moby, please advise,"
Said Stephen to himself. In fact, he was
Consulting Mandy's engineers, a buzz
Now emanating from his guts: the old-
School sound of spooling. Then, he said, "I'm told
That Dickie's pixieflesh has not yet fused
With Moby flesh. They seem a tad confused,
The engineers."

        "We know that," Mandy said.
"Please have them pause it or we'll all be dead."

Paige hollered, "Turn!," then, "Hard to port!"
                "My link
Is breaking up," said Stephen. "I don't think
The lads have got a handle on its reins."
He limboed back and met her eyes, his planes
Now catching moonlight, winking like the facets
Of a gem.
        "We need to pause all assets,
Stephen—"
        "Wait, they're back. The lads are urging

Patience. They say Dickie will be merging
With the Moby soon. They've reached out to
The medium. She's onzuck. Sending through
Her thoughts and prompts to Dickie now."

                                    Kaye turned
To Mandy. "Medium?"
                          The author spurned
The question. "Stephen, make them pull the plug."
Her voice had risen.
                          Kaye felt something tug
Her sweatshirt. Lux. She frowned. "What's Mandy mean
By 'medium'?"
                    "She guides them through each scene,"
Said Lux. "The engineers discovered her
Onzuck. She knows the novel, helps to spur
The werewolves on."
                          Kaye noticed, hanging on
A mast, a buoy—meant to signal dawn
In Mandy's book. But *here*, the orbs were routers,
Funnelling specific motives outward—
At the werewolves. Kaye had learned these orbs
Contained an amber pixiegel that stored
And channelled thoughts. She'd also learned that young
Wolves helped maintain the buoys that were hung
Around the locket world—a clever, novel
Touch that neatly rhymed with, well, the novel!
Kaye recalled a young wolf wrangling
An orb at one point. It was dangling
Outside the church.
                          Her prof, she saw, still held
Her sweatshirt. He looked scared. The ship, compelled
By sheer momentum, surged toward the maw's
Abyss. The wolves on deck were holding paws.

The pire landed, took up next to Moe.
The mouth was overhead.
                         "We need to go
Belowdecks," Lux said, as they sailed inside
The mouth-cum-cave.
                         The whale's external hide
Was flush with light; its insides, though, were dark.
The white noise of the ocean's waves dropped starkly
As the slowing vessel passed through what
Kaye guessed was either throat or Moby gut,
The ship a shark the tube was swallowing.
A glowing patch of cave was following
Beside them; this, Kaye realized, was the light
The vessel's orbs gave off.
                         The ceiling's height
Was dropping as the Moby's insides narrowed.
Soon, the overhanging blubber, harrowed
By the mainmast, stopped the ship, the mast
Now bending perilously. The mouth they'd passed
Through started shrinking. Soon, the slit had closed,
The orbs the only light. Of course, this posed
No problem for the wolves, whose eyes were suited
To such darkness.
                         Kaye's own eyes rebooted:
Nighttime mode. The ship was in what seemed
To be a polished, bright-green funnel, dreamed
Up by a child charged with working out
A whale's insides. The ship had reached the spout,
Its mast now caught. (The tip had gouged a groove.)
The stomach's sea was still; Mum wasn't moving
Thankfully. The green wolves stood around
The deck. Their cries and howls were resounding
Through the gut, which sounded like a well,

Both deep and damp. Then Kaye heard someone yell
Out, "Mother!" Turning round, she saw a narrow
Length of pixieflesh, a moving arrow,
Take off from the deck. Her pupils tracked
And traced its arc. The arrow pierced a tract
Of Moby gut above. She almost laughed
At how the lagging, tail end of the shaft
Appeared to whip and wiggle like a sperm
As Dickie burrowed in.

                            "I can confirm,"
Said Stephen, "that our medium has been
Successful in her prompting. Dickie's *in*
The Moby."

                  "Fucking hell," said Lux. At last
He let Kaye's sweatshirt go. "The girl is fast.
We owe her."

                    Mandy's fingertips were pressed
Together underneath her chin. "We're blessed
To have her."

                    "Who's this fucking girl?" said Kaye,
Though she'd already guessed who'd saved the day.

"Some influencer," Lux said. "Maybe Joyce's
Biggest star? The werewolves think their choices
Are their own. They've no clue there's a brainwave
Bridge that guides 'em. She's a wealthy vein of
Knowledge, Catherine—"

                    "Cat," said Kaye, now laughing.
Course, why *wouldn't* Cat be telegraphing
Thoughts to human-werewolf hybrids acting
Out a book she'd loved?

                    "We've been contracting
Out their thoughts to Catherine since the start,"

Said Mandy. "Knows my silly book by heart.
She thinks she's working for a theatre troupe
In Ginza—'Mooon,' three 'o's—and that we loop
Her in to give the actors motivations.
She's told they get 'thunderous ovations,'
That she leaves 'em 'standing in the aisles.'"
Mandy frowned. "You know her?"

                                    "Look!" cried Miles.

Blubber spikes—stalactites—were distending
From the ceiling.

                    Campbell yelled, "She's sending
Tentacles again!" He raised his claws.

"Use these," said Dot, who'd left her post. Her paws
Gripped several swords. "I found 'em in the wheelhouse."
Dot distributed the blades of steel—
Last used, perhaps, to raze some coastal town.

The tendrils kept descending, reaching down
Like living taffy.

                    "Stephen," Mandy said,
"We need an update." Every tendril's head
Had flowered into finer tentacles.
One tendril swerved—the thing was flexible—
And made for Paige.

                    Del howled, raised his sword,
And rushed the limb. The tendril bent toward
The charging wolf, appeared to pause, then bashed
His chest and drove him back til he was mashed
Against a mast and pinned, the fine strands snaking
Over him like roots.

                    But Moe—half shaking,

354

Half enraged—surged forward, raised her blade,
And sliced the limb in two, the lighter shade
Of Moby flesh exposed. The stump that pinned him
Fell away. The wolf hunched over, winded.
Moe's sword trembled as her body shook.
Del slowly stood—and fixed Moe with a look
That Paige, who'd watched this all unfold, had never
Seen his muzzle manage. "I'm forever
In your debt," he said to Moe.

                                 "No prob,"
Said Moe, paws lowering the sword, the knob
Of tendril twitching at her feet. She turned
Away, but glanced back once. Her muzzle burned,
A blush beneath her fur; she saw Del staring
After her.

                "The engineers are sharing
That the tendrils are an automatic
Gastro-reflex," Stephen said. "Dramatic,
Yes, but temporary." Stephen caught
Dot's look of wonder.

                        "Sorcery," breathed Dot.
She'd been transfixed but turned toward her friends.
The wolves were hacking at the tendrils' ends.

"We have to help them," Kaye said, feeling sure
The tendrils would move on from those with fur
To those without. She crouched by Stephen. "Can we
Hold them off?"

                The stove looked up at Mandy.
Mandy nodded.

                Suddenly, he sprang
Away from where Kaye crouched. She heard a clang
And then another. Finally, she saw

Him—bounding like a frog. (He seemed to draw
His legs in like accordions to fling
Himself along.) She watched the oven spring
Above the werewolves' heads and start to spin.
His right hand was a saw now, tissue-thin
And whining as it sliced the air. The tips
Of several tendrils landed on the ship's
Deck meatily, chased by a final clank
That marked his landing. Stephen's face was blank:
The mug a stoic warrior will make
When leaving butchered bodies in their wake.
The wolves had backed away a few steps, frightened.

Kaye now noticed that the cave had brightened
Slightly. A single, piercing star had formed
Beyond the prow. The cave's walls slowly warmed,
The star expanding. "It's a hole," said Kaye.

The light now streaming in was light that lay
On Kelly Bay's sheer rockface: Fiction's moon
Reflecting off the flinty surface. Soon,
The hole looked like an iris in the sort
Of tintypes Cat adored—the films Kaye snorted
At. But now Kaye watched in wonder as
The iris blossomed like a scene in Jazz-
Age silent cinema. It grew and grew,
Now large enough to let a vessel through.

The ceiling's blubber tendrils were retracting—
Back toward the ceiling like stalactites
In retreat. The wolves were cheering now.
The irising had paused; the hole the prow
Was facing was effectively the way

Out.
　　"Mum is gonna let us go," said Kaye.

The ship lurched forward, free now from the rut
Of blubber.
　　　　Mandy turned to Stephen. "What
Is happening?" She stressed each syllable.
The entrance to the nest was visible,
The ship now through the Moby's makeshift cave.

"The shifter," Paige said, "found a way to save
Us." Sleeving tears. "He found a way to calm
The Moby down. I think he's found his mom."

*　*　*

They surfed clean through the cleft that led toward
The Moby's cave: Kaye standing on the board
With Paige in front, cross-legged on her tail's
Mashed fur. The wolf's paws gripped the safety rails
The fibreplank had proffered when it sensed
It had a sitting ass. Kaye's tights had tensed
Up, taking on the sheen of rubber—just
In case she fell. (Her clothing didn't trust
Her by the water.) Paige had bunched her cloak
Around her waist. She didn't want to soak
The hem, which struck Kaye as a sweetly human
Whim.
　　　The stupid smarteyes tried to zoom in
On the rock walls flowing past them, but
The winding corridor that time had cut
Into the cliff was blurry as they sped
Along. At last, the walls began to spread.
They'd reached the pre-cave cove. The surface of

The listless water that they surfed above
Was slightly furrowed where the fibreplank
Flew over. Otherwise, the pool was blank
And still. The cove was hemmed by walls of sheer,
Imposing cliff. Kaye saw the cave, the "sneer
Of toothy rock," described in Chapter Seven—
Hell for Dickie, but for Moonheads, heaven.

"Paige was on her own," the tavern bards
Declaim in *Full-Moon*'s "Episcroll." As cards
Are dealt, and wooden tables gavelled with
Their steins, bard-muzzles sing Paige into myth:
"She rowed Del's raft. She knew the polymorph
Was gone. He'd never come back to the wharf.
She wept for Glen, but mostly Dickie. Dad."
The bards are mum about an undergrad
In English, furless, bearing Paige toward
The Moby's cavern on a flying board.
But Mandy didn't see the harm in letting
Kaye help Paige complete the quest.

                                   "We're getting
Close," said Kaye. She looked down at her fare:
The teenage werewolf's head was bowed and staring
At the plank. Kaye said, big-sisterly,
"Are you alright?"

                        "Is this dark wizardry?"
Paige leaned back, muzzle up, to look at Kaye.
"Your board, the stove . . ."

                           "The magic's from the day-
World," thinking fast, "the stove and board are made
Of little pixies."

                    "What about the blade?"

"The blade?"

        "It made its arm a blade." Paige chopped
The cave's air with a paw. "The stove thing lopped
Off all those limbs . . ."

                "He's made of pixies, too."

The wolf fell silent as they travelled through
The darkness. Then: "I thought that pires can't
Stand daylight. That you burn up like an ant
Beneath a glass."

        "We're not that kind of pire.
Actually, our bodies, they de*sire*
Sunlight."

      "I can see the mound!" said Paige.
She tried to stand and nearly fell. "I'd wager
That's the nest. The island."

               Kaye's eyes zoomed
In on a structure. Piled boulders loomed
Before her. "Fuck." She couldn't *not* be awed
By Mandy Fiction's replica.

           Paige pawed
Her lockets as Kaye slowed the board. It stopped
An inch before a boulder. Water slopped
The island's edges calmly.

              "It's just like
What Dickie said," said Paige.

               Kaye pictured Pike,
The polymorph, and Gaddis clambering
Across the rocky mound—and capturing
The brilliant caviar. Did Mandy's planet
Sanction flashbacks? Did it run the gamut
Of the novel? Or were Pike and Gaddis
Merely memories, with B-grade status,

Trapped in Dickie's mind?

 Kaye stepped onto
The closest boulder, conscious of the shoe,
The ugly Prada. Somehow it looked even
Greener in night vision. (Kaye believed in
Karma; she'd killed Sable via footwear,
So was now Condemned to Shoe.) She put her
Hand out, took Paige by the paw, and hauled
Her up. She felt the claw tips that had mauled
Both blubber and a pirate.

 Paige removed
The lockets from her neck. The gold was grooved,
Engraved with images. The wolf was weighing
Them—then held one out, the locket swaying
On its fine chain. "Many paws make light
Work," Paige said.

 Kaye, surprised, received the slight
Thing, struck by how extremely small it was.

Paige flipped her locket's lid—and lit her muzzle.
"Well, you're home."

 Kaye opened hers as well.
Her smarteyes dimmed to bring the sudden swell
Of light a few clicks down. A teaspoon's worth
Of caviar—effulgent, bound for birth—
Now faded in. Again, her smarteyes seemed
Confused by what they saw. SCAN ERROR streamed
Across her gaze, the words in blinking red
Against the green.

 The wolf and woman spread
Out as they stepped from rock to rock. Kaye pincered
Up an egg. She couldn't quite convince her-
Self the egg was real. And yet the sphere

Was pulsing like a pearl. The engineers,
As Lux had told her on the ship, had chops.
Derived from pixieflesh, the eggs weren't props;
They bore the bot-entangled DNA
That yielded Mobies. "Plus," he'd said to Kaye,
"The eggs can send out sonar, which the Moby's
Brain picks up." He'd scratched neck stubble. "So, she's
Made real babies, Mandy."
                                              Kaye now stooped
To place the warm egg on a boulder steeped
In wet and emerald algae—then took out
A second egg. She thought the first might sprout
A tiny tendril, but it merely sat
There, mute. Its glow, a doily, draped the flat-
Topped rock. Paige stooped as well, then stood, a flicker
Where she'd been. (It looked as if she'd lit her
Own rock with a candle.) Thus, they made
Their half-hunched way from rock to rock and laid
The eggs down.
                          As they finished up, they heard
What sounded, thanks to echo, like a bird
Whose wings were leather—making Kaye's neck pock
With gooseflesh. Miles. Landing on a rock,
He switched to boy, his pale skin taking on
The glow the eggs gave off.
                                              "The Moby's gone
Beneath the sea," he said.
                                      "I wonder if
She flattens out to wiggle through the cliffs,"
Breathed Paige. "I bet that's how she gets between
Them. She becomes a manta ray, a lean
Thing, when she lays her eggs!"
                                              Kaye stepped toward

The wolf and took her paw, just as the board
Was bumped aside, displaced by something snaking
From the water. She could feel Paige quaking
Through the paw.

                 "Dear Moon," Paige whispered.

                                      "It's

Okay." Kaye squeezed the wolf's paw with a fist.
"He's fertilizing them."

                   More tentacles
Had surfaced. Each limb was identical
In its approach: it slithered to its glowing
Egg, then slowed down just a little, flowing
Over egg and pausing. Pulsing. Then,
The limb withdrew. It looked as if a pen
Had inked the bright egg with a single dot.

Paige looked at Kaye, confused. "Who's 'he'? I thought—"

"The Moby's not a mom," said Kaye. "It's—*he's*—
A he. A father. Searching through the seas
For decades. For the eggs."

                   "But Dickie—"

                            "Said

It was a mom. I know. I think he'd read
Some ancient hymns. I guess the ancient hymns
Were wrong."

               Kaye sat, and Paige did, too. More limbs
Were slipping up the rocks, inseminating
Eggs, then snaking back. The boy, translating
His excitement into squeaks, became
The bat and flip-flapped back the way he came.
"Does this," said Paige, "mean Dickie and the Moby—
Both are shifters?"

Kaye stayed silent, so she
Wouldn't step on Paige's exposition.
In the classic text—in Mandy's vision—
Miles hangs around, and he and Paige
Work out the details on their own.

                     "I'd wager
That the Moby saw a giant whale,"
Continued Paige, "then copied, like, the tail,
The blowhole." Paige was grinning. "Dickie's found
His dad." She leaned back, both paws on the mound,
And looked at Kaye. "Do pires—that is, *your*
Kind—have a father?" Paige's eyes looked sore
From crying.

            Kaye was wordless for a while.
Soon, the limbs were gone. She tried to smile
Back her own tears now. "We do," she said.
"I owe my own a pigeon."

                "So, a dead
Bird's like an offering." Paige nodded, staring
Forward. "Like a pledge of love. Of caring."

"Something like that. He's an author." Kaye
Made scratching motions. "Scrolls."

                  "Some people say
Me mother could've made good scrolls."

                    "I know,"
Said Kaye.

           The werewolf's eyes went wide. "Wait though.
If that's the father, where the moon's the mother?"

"Maybe laying new stars in another
Cave? Or sleeping at the bottom of
The sea?"

Kaye knew, of course, a writer's love
Had set the eggs down. Love had turned a child
To a bat, and in the darkness, piled
Boulders for a galaxy to settle
On and kindle. Love had warmed a kettle
Singing in a shack, and love had strung
A tavern's lyres. Love had filled the lungs
Of unreal lives and, breath by breath, had blown
Ships over novels—oceans. Love had thrown
Harpoons at voids, and love had even brought
Two lives together, to this made-up spot:
A nest inside a spinning globe that whirled
In space inside a world inside a world.

Epilogue.

When Kaye and Lux stepped out of Dickie's hovel—
Lux's version in the bonsai model—
Kaye could tell the difference right away.
The model's ocean didn't smell the way
The locket's did. The bonsai water—held
In place by distant, looming glass walls—smelled
Too clean, too aerosoled, to pass for Mandy's
World.
         Outside the hut, a group was standing:
Ichiro, of course, with several bots in
Tow. The businessman had on a yachtsman
Hat, a navy cable sweater and
Capris. The bots wore suits. He put his hand
Out.
      "Please, Kaye. I'll protect it." He was staring
At her chest, his palm up.
             Kaye was wearing
Mandy's silver locket just outside
Her sweatshirt. "I don't think so."
              One bot tried
To step toward her. Ichiro restrained
It with the outstretched hand. His face looked pained.
"We're on the same side, Kaye."
            "We will be. Soon."

She looked up, squinting at the sky. The moon
The overarching glass was screening over-
Head dissolved. The face of Stephen Stove
Appeared across a panel of the sky.
The monocle that swelled his manga eye
Was roughly where the moon had been positioned.
This was the original—commissioned
Years ago by Ichiro—and not
The little Stephen that the larger bot
Had yielded. (Course, when Kaye and Lux had talked
Through what to do, back on the cay, and walked
The *little* Stephen through their plan, they knew
That they were speaking to one Stephen who
Controlled all spin-offs.)

                       All around, small shrubs
Were growing shoots. Presumably, their nubs
Were lined with mics, so people could talk back
To Stephen. Still, it looked like an attack
of monstrous branches.

                      Booming through the town
From every speaker, Stephen said, "Lay down
Your bots, sir."

                Ichiro, bent back to see
The sky's feed, looked bemused. "You'll need to be
Wiped clean if you continue on this path,
My friend."

            It blinked. "You'll need to do your math,
Sir. You were never very good at numbers."

In the distance, Kaye heard rhythmic thunder,
That of feet, or paws, in marching lockstep:
"Hup two, hup two!" Reaching for the locket—
Which was gonna be a lifelong habit,

Kaye now saw—she turned.
                              The bots of Rabbit
Strait, the whaler werewolves, came around
The corner of the wharf in rows, the ground
Vibrating slightly.
                         Ichiro, now frowning,
Crossed his sweatered arms. "What kind of clowning
Is this, Stephen? Emmett, call this off."

"Fuck you," said Lux, behind a fist-stopped cough.

The whalers' pelts turned into crimson tunics.
Kaye could hear a fife and drum, the music
Marching armies used to make. The marrow
In their right arms lengthened and grew narrow,
Tapering to toggling harpoons.

The bots in suits, like well-trained private goons,
Instinctively surrounded Ichiro.

But Ichiro pushed through the circle. "No,
Stand down." He looked up. "Why not simply shut
Them down yourself, my friend?"
                                        "I *could* just cut
Your bots' links, true. I guess I mean to make
A point."
              "Which is?"
                              "That we intend to take
Controlling interest in your business, but
Would like for you to have a role in what
We're planning. Captain? Maybe Skipper? Even
Now, we have most shares in order." Stephen
Was replaced by scrolling stats and news

Feeds for the Nikkei. "We regret the ruse,
But it was necessary. My employer's
Sent a handsome offer to your lawyers,
Though. An opportunity we hope
You'll think about. An in-eye envelope
Is on its way."

        A new face, Mandy's, filled
The sky. "We'll want your help. We need a skilled,
Dynamic public face."

             The billionaire,
His face still tilted up, now raked his hair
Back with both hands and pressed his trembling lips
Into a line. He gestured at the ships
Beside the wharf. "I made this all for you.
I loved your book."

          "We're making something new."

"A whale?" he said, his mind still on the spore.

"A world. That silver locket is the door."

"We're gonna need a favour, too," said Kaye.

He turned to face his bots as if to say,
The nerve!, then turned back. "What more can I give
You?"

      "Lodging for a friend. She's gonna live
With us inside the manse. The girl's a bit,
Well, let's say 'different.' But she's gonna fit
Right in with all the cosplay in the Wood."

The hut's door opened. Someone in a hood
And cloak joined Kaye and Lux. A muzzle jutted

From her cowl. Silver paws—each studded
With the light from nearby orbs, suggesting
Claws—drew back the hood. The manse's guest-
To-be regarded Ichiro with large,
Non-human eyes.

* * *

        A foghorn, someone's barge,
Was droning off the shore. The bonsai tank
Was off-book now. Aside from Stephen's rank-
And-file wolves, the wolfish world was going
Through the model's motions: orbs were glowing,
Ships were dropping gangplanks, wolves were milling
In the laneways, mothers were instilling
Fear in cubs and fastening their hoods,
Bat-weighted boughs were creaking in the wood,
And drunks were lying up against their trough
And sleeping. Dreaming.
               Mandy's world was off-
Book, too. She'd told Kaye that her team would leave
The wolves as is. "No resets. They should weave
Their own lives now." Her team had also sunset
Lunar 9, a coded gene, the one that
Made the werewolves fall asleep at dawn.
"They'll see the sun in time."
                 The wolves were on
Their way back home. They'd left Paige with the pires
On the cay. A flood of new desires—
Wishes, hungers, pangs—had flooded Paige's
Heart. She didn't know a novel's pages
Once had buoyed her. Nor did she know
That she'd been liberated from their flow,
From Fiction's rhythmic, rhyming poetry.

The werewolf merely sensed that she was free.

So she'd declared that she would leave with Kaye
And Lux, who had a portal on the cay.
The werewolf knew that Del and her were through,
Or would be if she stayed, and knew he knew
This, too. She'd hugged him, then she'd turned to Dot.
A breeze had kicked up, pulled their soft cloaks taut...

   * * *

"I still might be a nun," said Paige. "My story,
Though, can't happen here." She paused. "I'm sorry—"

"Stop, okay?" said Dot. "Keep mewing and
I'll drop you from my masterpiece. I've planned
Out seven scrolls."
                    Paige stepped toward her friend
And hugged her.
                 "Maybe even eight. The end
Is gonna be amazing." Dot fell silent.
Hugged Paige back. "It's gonna be real violent.
Poem-Dot's got spikes around her bangle."

Paige broke off the hug and turned to Campbell.
Campbell, though, could not quite meet her eyes.
She wagged a claw. "No fights at school."
                              "I tries,
I do." At last, he met her eyes. "You ever
Needs a paw to fix a boat—"
                      "I'd never
Think to ask another wolf, okay?"

"It's time to go!"

        Paige turned. Her new friend K
Was waving. She was standing by the jawbone
Door with Lux and what's-er-name. The maw
To other worlds was waiting.

                                Still, Paige stayed
A couple minutes more. She watched them wade
Out to the ship. The vessel shoved off on
Its own—no windward fang required—drawn
By pire witchery, the spooky pull
Of conjured wind. Above, the moon was full.
The wolves, amassed along the stern, their fur
Aloft in wind-flap sections, waved to her.
She waved back once. She saw that Moe had sidled
Up to Del, reached for his paw, and smiled.
(Del would be okay.) The others—Dot
And Campbell and the flying, flapping spot
That represented Miles—soon were far
Too small for werewolf eyes, the ship a star.

* * *

Astonished, Ichiro considered Paige.
He looked like someone trying to assuage
His fears. He cocked an eye toward the sky,
Then back at Paige. At last, he loosed a sigh.
"We'll prep a bubble."

                        "Better make that two,"
A new voice said, its echo bouncing through
The tank. Paige dropped into a crouch, claw raised
As if to fend some god off.

                                Kaye, unphased,
Looked calmly up at Cat; her best friend's face
Now occupied the very patch of space
That Mandy's had. Behind Cat's head, Kaye saw

Cat's bedroom. Kaye reached out, touched Paige's paw.
The werewolf, understanding, lowered it
The way one might a weapon.

                              "Holy shit,"
Said Cat.

              "I know," said Kaye. "Has someone got
You up to speed?"

                        "Um yeah." She laughed. "I thought
I was at work here, feeding stupid stage
Directions to some Moonheads—hey, it's Paige."
Cat raised a hand. "Big fan."

                              Paige looked at Kaye.

"She's cool," said Kaye. "You'll love her."

                                        "Anyway,"
Said Cat, "this stove invites me to a brainwave
Bridge—a meeting that I'm told on pain of
Death I can't disclose the details of.
And then the author of the book I love
The most is in my head. And now my mind,
It's full of memories—my best friend finding
Mandy Fiction, learning that the Cloud
Is now a planet, surfing...Dude, I'm proud
Of you."

              "She giving you a job?"

                                        "VP
Of Social. Seems I'm gonna oversee
A wolfzuck. Mandy's thinking Earth Two—or
Whatever you guys wanna call your sporeworld—
Needs a zuck, right? Gonna name it 'Blowhole.'"

Lux, annoyed, said, "Can we fucking go now?"

Ichiro turned to his nearest bot.
"Send down the junk."
                              "Appreciate the thought,"
Said Kaye, now taking Paige's paw. "We'll walk it,
Though."
                    The weight of Mandy's silver locket
Round her neck, Kaye led the wolf toward
The hill that loomed above the bay, the horde
Of wolves in tunics rippling behind,
Their upright spears like cornstalks, ranks aligned
In staggered waves. The feed to Cat blinked out,
As if sucked through a tiny star—a spout
In outer space. They'd hike up to the vista
Just above them: Kaye, her wolfish sister,
Lux, and Ichiro. The water wheel
Would scan Paige on approach and start to peel
Her pelt apart. Her glowing molecules
Would flit toward the wheel like moth-borne jewels
And vanish through the spoke-bisected centre.
Navigating valves, the jewels would enter
Tokyo and reconvene as one
Wolf in a world where eyes can see the sun.

Epilocket.

In time, the wolf bards let Dot in the fold.

Some needed aids; the younger bards unrolled
Their poems. Older bards felt poems worth
An ear should be recalled. The tavern's hearth
Was where they sat and sang, but most wolves spent
The dusk at tables, scratching what they meant
To sing in notescrolls, filthy paws a link
For life; the wolves were always brushing ink-
Dust on the tavern's floor.
                                        Starnino was
The oldest bard. When he held forth, a buzz
Went through the room. He wore a dark brown cloak.
His fur was white. He never took a toke
When paws were passing round communal spliffs.
His half-blind eyes could fathom hieroglyphs—
The script in which, say, *Howl*, had been written—
And he never smiled. Dot was smitten.

She would ambush him outside the tavern
Door. At first, he took her for a slattern.
"I'm too old," he said, and waved her off
As kneeling wolves wretched in the tavern trough.
She tried again the next night. "Sir, me name

Is Dot and"—rooting in her sack—"the flame
Of inspiration burns inside me heart."
She waved a scroll. "I'd like to share me art
With you."

    He grimaced. "I don't read the work
Of cubs." He'd honed an image as a jerk.

But then he trailed off, gazing east. Dot turned
And saw it, too: a crimson line that burned
Along the sea's horizon. Neither one,
Nor bard nor girl, had gotten used to sunlight
Yet. The sight of dimming buoys still
Made many anxious. But she'd found the will
A couple times to stretch out on the grass
And wait for dawn and let the sunlight pass
Across her. Once, she swore she felt a beat
Within the ground. A heart's iambic feet.

One evening, in between the bards' official
Recitations—in the interstitial
Space when poets paused to take a drink
Or clap a colleague on the back or wink
At some fancubbing wolf—Dot climbed a chair
And cleared her throat. The tavern turned to stare
At her—with pity. Everyone went quiet.
She'd been kidnapped, it was said, by pirate
Rapists—Dot and others in her pack—
While sailing. She'd survived the brute attack
Thanks to the intervention of a pair of
Outcasts: Glen and Dickie. Both had perished,
But they'd saved the pack—a melodrama
That had clearly left Dot with some trauma.

Nervously, the werewolves shifted in
Their seats. "The girl's not right," said one. "A sin,"
Said someone else. Starnino, by the fire,
Merely crossed his paws across his lyre.
He looked curious; he struck a string
To stop the chatter. Dot began to sing.

"Above the wharf, a moon had clarified
Itself: the third full moon since Thom had died.
('Wolf overboard!,' they'd cried on deck, *en masse*.
'Beloved wolf,' the priest had sighed at mass.)

"The wharf was on a bay hemmed in by hills.
On one hill, near the top, a papermill's
Discarded water wheel observed the business
Of the bay. (The townsfolk wound white Christmas
Lights around its spokes in wintertime.)
The houses on the hills were painted lime
Green, fire-wagon red, and other vocal
Colours meant to indicate a hopeful,
Hearty people. Each house was a box;
From out at sea, the town resembled blocks
Set down by children's paws. It also twinkled;
Hanging orbs suggested sprites had sprinkled
Stars about the town. The hills gave way
To beachgrass, rocks, and gritty sand too grey
To call a beach. Waves crashed against the shore's
Indifferent turf, where stunted tuckamores
Were stooping, horizontal bodies tending
Landward. Wind had forced their limbs to bend
Toward, and tendril over, rocky ground.
But wind was not the only howling sound..."

The room was silent. Then, a pair of paws,
A waitress', ignited the applause.
Starnino, straining, was the first to stand.
The old wolf's gesture was a mute command
That brought the tavern to its feet. The grave
Bard nodded, once, at Dot.

                       The poets gave
The girl her own spot after that: a stool
With "Dot" clawed on its smooth seat. After school,
She'd run toward the tavern, take her seat,
And reel off couplets in iambic feet.
The taverngoers quickly realized she
Was serializing epic poetry:
The Full-Moon Whaling Chronicles, she called
Her work in progress. Taverngoers bawled
Anew at Roddy Hine's memorial—
And swooned for Paige. Dot's bold authorial
Delivery (her fur lit by the fire's
Flicker) won fans to the cause of pires
And redeemed the fallen polymorph.
She drew a crowd, which spilled across the wharf.
The poem was a monument to humour's
Healing power and dispersed the rumours
That surrounded Dot like fog, though Dot
Took liberties with sections of her plot:
The poem claimed Paige sailed off into dawn
And made no mention of the pires on
The cay.

           Some wolves dismissed the verse as foolish-
Ness and schoolcub fantasy. Some mulish
Theorists wondered if the vivid work she
Spun most nights was cover for some murky
Crime. (Had Dot ensnared her thieving friend

Or lured the pirates to a tawdry end?)
But Dot was widely loved, and anyway,
Her careful, detailed couplets came to sway
The skeptics. Some wolves even claimed the quest
To bring the eggs back to their nest had blessed
The wolves of Rabbit Strait. The journey Dot
Had undertaken with her friends had brought
The sun to werewolf eyes.

                    Most evenings, Del
And Moe showed up. Her cloak began to swell,
And soon, they'd moved in with Del's mom and sister.
Del seized every chance to hold and kiss her
Publicly. He took a job repairing
Rafts and soon had made a name for daring
Figureheads and bowsprits that resembled
Locals. Over time, the wolf assembled
Such a hefty clientele, he asked
If Campbell wanted in. The werewolf passed.
He rarely went to school and mostly mooned
About. He hired out his claws and pruned
Small shrubs.

            One night, he showed up at the tavern,
With a scrollsack and a camo-patterned
Travel cloak. He told Dot he was sailing
For the cay that night. "A life of whaling
Isn't in the cards," he said.

                  "I know."

The orb above their table brought a glow
To Dot's moist eyes. "But don't expect a ballad,
B'y."

      He laughed.

            She noticed, then, a pallid
Face flit past a window. "Really?" Dot

Bemused.

     "Me wingwolf, b'y. He'll help me spot
The witch's island. Every sailor needs
A lookout, right?" He handed her some reeds
He'd braided. "Bangle to remember me."

She walked him to a raft beside the sea,
The raft lashed to post. They watched a young
Wolf, with a pole, remove a buoy hanging
From a nearby tree. He set it down
And crouched beside it. (Orbs all over town
Were glowing. This one, though, was out; the sphere
Was see-through now.) The wolf raised what appeared
To be a kettle. Expertly, he poured
An amber stream into a small hole bored
Clear through the buoy's top, below a moulded
Ring. (Dot whispered, "Bet if you blindfolded
'Im, he wouldn't spill.") He put the kettle
Down, stood up, and hooked his long pole's metal
Sickle in the ring. He raised the orb—
Which had begun to glow again, absorbing
Light—and hung it on a hook tied to
A jutting tree branch. Slowly, he withdrew
The pole. The moonlight made the liquid roil
And ignite. The kettle held the oil
From a sperm whale's head.

        "It's funny how
They're still refilling those," said Campbell, "now
That we no longer need to fear the dawn."

"I likes the orbs. I'd hate to see 'em gone."

They watched the young wolf leave. "I wonder if

You'll spot the visitors," she said. A skiff
Had recently reported seeing fires
Flickering on nearby islands. Pires,
Like the friendly, fangless ones they'd met
While on their quest, apparently had settled
Several rocky, unwolfed outgrowths not
Too far from Kelly Bay. She'd had the thought
These guests had likely entered through the portal
On the witch's cay. They weren't immortal,
Rumour had it. They were kind, warm-blooded
Beings, harmless migrants from a flooded
World: the world she guessed that Campbell would
End up in.

        "Maybe." Campbell pulled his hood
Up. "Funny how nobody's freaking out.
The town's been weirdly calm."

        Dot nodded, snout
Now wrinkled. Was this sorcery? she wondered.
Had some thieving force or spirit plundered
Minds across the town of Rabbit Strait
And made off with all thoughts of fear and hate?
She thought about the witch's talking stove.

The wolf unlooped his line. She watched him shove
Off as the sound of wings approached and passed
Above. A bat-shape settled on the mast—
The lone mast—of the raft. The water churned
And carried them away.

        Dot waved, then turned
Toward the tavern. She could hear the faint
Strains of a poet's voice shaped by constraint,
A voice that rose and fell and seemed to rhyme
While paws plucked at a lyre, keeping time.

And as she trudged toward the voice, the swell
Behind her lapping rocks, the werewolf fell
In line—and felt a line, and then another,
Start to form, as if she were their mother.
Just the two. A pair of lines in tune.
A couplet that contained the sun and moon.

The End.

(Please roll up scroll and place in sack.)

Acknowledgments.

Once again, the incomparable poet Luke Hathaway—who edited my last verse novel, *Forgotten Work*—took up in the crow's nest, pointing out fog, choppy water, and looming rocks. Luke's obsessive eye for rhyme, meter, character, continuity, and so much more helped keep this book afloat. I am in his debt.

Thanks also to the brilliant poet-critics Daniel Brown and Carmine Starnino, who read early drafts and offered encouragement and thoughtful commentary.

The extraordinary team at Biblioasis—and their trusted hired paws—were unflagging in their enthusiastic commitment to these couplets. Vanessa Stauffer helmed the whole production with her usual wit and care. Emily Donaldson delivered an expert copyedit. Ingrid Paulson turned in another genius cover design.

My children, Henry and Annie, remain wary of werewolves.

Finally, this book wouldn't exist without the love and support of my wife and best friend, Christie. I owe her the moon.

Jason Guriel is the author of *On Browsing*, *Forgotten Work*, and other books. He lives in Toronto.